THE READER'S COMPANION

To

THE DEATH OF SHAKESPEARE

Part One

By Jon Benson

ISBN-10: 0-9970899-0-3
ISBN-13: 978-0-9970899-0-5

Published by Nedward, LLC, Annapolis, Maryland

Second Edition

Typeset in Garamond 11

Readers interested in further information about
The Death of Shakespeare–Part One
can visit

to purchase the ebook and paperback versions of

The Death of Shakespeare–Part One

and the ebook version of

The Reader's Companion to the Death of Shakespeare.

The Death of Shakespeare–Part Two will be forthcoming.

Table of Contents

Part One

Sources 3
The Earl of Oxford 3
William Shakespeare 8
The Plays, Sonnets and Poems 11
Christopher Marlowe 12
The Earl of Southampton 13
Recommended 13
Not Recommended 19
Front Matter 23
The Maps 26

Prologue: Stratford-upon-Avon – April 23, 1616 27

1588

1. Fisher's Folly – September 27, 1588 49
2. Greenwich Palace 55
3. The Boar's Head 69
4. Cecil House 80
5. St. Paul's Cathedral 87
6. Oxford Court 90
7. Lyly, Falstaff, and Robin 93
8. *The Poacher of Arden Forest* 94
9. *Procne's Revenge* 95
10. Billesley Hall – Christmas Eve, 1588 104

1589

11. Shackspear Pays an Unwelcome Visit 107
12. Westminster Palace 109
13. Billesley Hall 121
14. The Return to Oxford Court 124
15. Oxford's "Hand" in *Titus Andronicus* 124
16. *Titus Andronicus* at the Rose 124

17. Gray's Inn – *The Comedy of Errors* 129
18. A Summons from the Queen 129
19. The Boar's Head 144
20. Oxford Court – The Next Morning 144
21. The Trunk of Plays 149
22. Oxford Court – Late September, 1589 159
23. *Two Gentlemen of Verona* 167
24. Lord Willoughby's 178
25. Sonnets for Aemilia Bassano 198
26. Blackfriars – The Next Night 201
27. Newgate Prison – A Week Later 201
28. Christopher Marlowe 202
29. *Two Gentlemen* Finished 208
30. More Sonnets for Aemilia Bassano 209
31. *Two Gentlemen* before the Queen 209
32. Christmas at the Boar's Head 212
33. William the Conqueror 224
34. *Pericles, Prince of Tyre*
230Chapter 35

1590

35. Billesley Hall 237
36. Robin Is Gone 243
37. John Shackspear 244
38. The Earl of Surrey 246
39. Thomas Digby 248
40. Oxford Court 251
41. The Bastard 253
42. *King John* before the Queen 253
43. The Queen & Lady Elspeth Trentham 256
44. A Poem for Lady Elspeth 257
45. Miss Trentham 262
46. *Henry VI* and a Sonnet for the Earl of Southampton 263
47. Cecil House 267
48. The War of the Roses 268
49. John Marston and the Nature of Sin 267

1591

50. Aemilia Bassano (Again) 271
51. Signore Baldini's Love Philtre 274
52. The Boar's Head 274
53. A Sonnet for Aemilia Bassano 280
54. The Geneva Bible 280
55. Robin Returns 281
56. Ankerwycke 282
57. Windsor 285
58. *Henry VI, Part 2* 287
59. The Dinner in the Grotto 288
60. A Marriage Contract 289
61. Oxford Court – A Month Later 290
62. Castle Hedingham 292
63. That Night 304
64. Oxford Court – *Henry VI, Part 3* 305
65. A Wedding at Whitehall 305

1592

66. Oxford & Lady Elspeth Return 311
67. *Henry VI, Part 3* 311
68. *Love's Labour's Won* 313
69. *Much Ado About Nothing* 313
70. *Henry VI, Part 3*, at the Rose 317
71. The Tabard Inn 318
72. The Heat of a Luxurious Bed 318
73. Ditchley House 320
74. *Edward II* 326
75. Rosencrantz and Guildenstern 327
76. An Heir for His Lordship 332
77. The Taming of the Shrew 335
78. The Death of Robert Greene 337
79. Whitehall Palace 343

1593

80. Henry Is Christened in the Boar's Head 345
81. "If Thy Body Had Been As Deformed As Thy Mind Is Dishonorable" 348
82. López and the Ghost of Thomas Brincknell 352
83. "*Abandon'd & Despised*" 353
84. The Death of Christopher Marlowe 354
85. *Matrimonium Clandestinum* 355
86. Yorick 368
87. "*Graze on my lips; Feed where thou wilt*" 370
88. Richard Field and *Venus and Adonis* 377
89. The Sign of the Ship 378
90. A Conference with Venus 378
91. Sir Robert Gibed at Christmas 381

1594

92. A Play for Lady Mary 383
93. *A Double Maske* 388
94. A Nidicock for Lady Lizbeth 394
95. The Lord Chamberlain's Men 399
96. The Execution of Dr. López 400
97. The Wedding of Sir Thomas Heneage and the Countess of Southampton 401

Lineage Tables 407

THE READER'S COMPANION

to

THE DEATH OF SHAKESPEARE

PART ONE

Introduction

The Death of Shakespeare imagines how the plays and poetry attributed to William Shakespeare were written. Unlike the outpourings of new biographies about Shakespeare, much of this novel is based on fact. Since it is not customary to add footnotes or endnotes to works of fiction, *The Reader's Companion to The Death of Shakespeare* tracks the chapters in the novel and explains what is supported in the historical record and what is not.

The author could say, as Moses Hadas wrote in the Preface to his *Ancilla to Classical Reading*: "I have not written [this] merely to salvage what had to be left in the inkwell and what could be swept up from unemptied filing drawers. Long preoccupation with a subject begets curiosity about matters essentially peripheral or even irrelevant to its main issues, and I have thought that others … might enjoy such partial satisfaction of similar curiosity as I am able to offer."

The *Reader's Companion* is divided into two parts: the first part is an annotated bibliography of principal sources used by the author in writing *The Death of Shakespeare*; the second part is a treasure trove of little-known details that may be of interest those who love history.

Sources

The following sources, among many others, were used in the writing of *The Death of Shakespeare.*

The Earl of Oxford

Allen, Percy, *The Life Story of Edward de Vere as "William Shakespeare,"* William Farquahar Payson, New York, 1932. Dated, but contains many interesting insights. The discussion of the ancestry of the de Veres at the beginning and the ancestry chart at the end are fascinating, even though it may be a stretch to say Oxford was descended from Charlemagne as well as "Alfonsus De Vere of the town of Veer on the island of Walcheren in Zealand." There is a town called "Veere" on the island of "Zealand" in Holland and the ancestry chart at p. 368 has Alfonsus marrying a daughter of one of the Counts of Flanders. Allen says that this doesn't upset the theory that the Veres were of Danish descent since the Normans considered themselves descendants of Danes, Swedes, or Norwegians. Alfonsus' ancestors, therefore, must have come to Veere from further north.[1]

Anderson, Mark, *Shakespeare By Another Name,* New York, Gotham Press, 2005. Excellent work that connects the plays and Oxford. The end notes are worth the price of the book alone.

Beauclerk, Charles, *Shakespeare's Lost Kingdom*, Grove Press, 2010. Beauclerk claims that Oxford not only wrote the plays but that he was the son of Elizabeth by Thomas Seymour. Elizabeth later slept with Oxford (her son) and gave birth to Southampton (their son). There are facts that support a conclusion that Seymour was hot for the young Elizabeth, but Elizabeth, only 15 at the time, survived a week's intense examination by unfriendly inquisitors to successfully deny Seymour was intimate with her. There are no facts to show that she gave birth

---

[1] Nelson, p. 10, believes that the first earl (Aubrey III) came over with William. Ward, however, p. 3, claims that the Veres settled in England before William arrived and that Aubrey I provided such service to William that he was rewarded with many estates. William's son, Henry I, created Aubrey's grandson, also named Aubrey (Aubrey III), Lord Great Chamberlain but "[i]t was probably the religious Aubrey's son, the fourth successive Aubrey, who was created first Earl of Oxford in the reign of King Richard I." At p. 4-5. Ward cites the *Register of Colne Priory*, which is preserved in the Colchester Public Library.

to a child at the time. Therefore, the conclusion that she had sex with Seymour is unsupported, as is the claim that she gave birth to a child who was placed with the Sixteenth Earl of Oxford who conveniently died at the age of twelve so that Burghley could raise the 'changeling' (Oxford). Beyond all this, however, it is very difficult to imagine Elizabeth sleeping with her son and having a child by him (although the movie *Anonymous* has Sir Robert Cecil suggesting to Oxford that the Queen didn't know he was her son when she slept with him). Beauclerk fails to mention many facts that are contrary to his conclusions and makes connections others find fiction at best. See, for example, Christopher Paul's review of *Shakespeare's Lost Kingdom* in *Brief Chronicles: An Interdisciplinary Journal of Authorship Studies*, 2010. However, there is the riddle at the beginning of *Pericles,* which quite clearly shows that the king was having sex with his daughter, a curious way to begin a play attributed to Shakespeare. Beauclerk's book is worth the price just to see the superb reproductions in the center. Among others are the tilt list from 1571, Titian's *Venus and Adonis* (although not the version with the hat which Oxford obviously saw in Venice), the Ashbourne Portrait, showing the boar's head ring, and, best of all, the Pregnancy Portrait. The latter is 7' by 4' 6" and must be seen close up to appreciate its impact.

Brazil, Robert Sean, *Edward de Vere and the Shakespeare Printers,* Corticle Output, LLC, Seattle, Washington, 2010. Useful information about the printers in Shakespeare's time by a non-scholar, including reproductions of covers of many of the plays, accompanied by interesting commentary.

Bullough, Geoffrey, *Narrative and Dramatic Sources of Shakespeare,* in four volumes, London and New York, 1962.

Clark, Eva Lee Turner, *Hidden Allusions in Shakespeare's Plays – A Study of the Early Court Revels and Personalities of the Times,* Miller, Ruth Lloyd, ed., New York, Kennikat Press, 1974 3rd rev. ed. An extraordinary work linking the plays to actual events and other works, such as by Spenser, that, if you follow the connections, shed light on Oxford. Clark argues cogently from events that the bulk of the plays were composed in the 1570s and 1580s and buffed up over the succeeding 20 years.

Clark, Eva Lee Turner, *The Man Who Was Shakespeare*, Richard R. Smith, New York, 1937. Difficult to find because it is far surpassed by Looney, Anderson, and the Ogburns.

Farina, William, *De Vere as Shakespeare – An Oxfordian Reading of the Canon*, McFarland & Co., Jefferson, North Carolina, and London 2006. Each chapter considers an individual play. The format makes it difficult to dig out a narrative but the excellent footnoting (better than many 'scholarly' works) gives the reader the sources for the author's comments and is an excellent reference for that reason alone.

Feldman, Bronson, *Hamlet Himself*, iUniverse, 2010 (although Professor Bronson died in 1982). An examination of the play from the point of view that it was written by the Earl of Oxford. Some interesting comments.

Golding, Louis Thorn, *An Elizabethan Puritan – Arthur Golding the Translator of Ovid's Metamorphoses and also of John Calvin's Sermons*, Richard R. Smith, New York, 1937. A descendant of Arthur Golding tries his hand at a biography of his illustrious ancestor, which touches on the Seventeenth Earl of Oxford at many points. Arthur was brother to Marjory Golding, the Sixteenth earl's second wife, and was one of the Seventeenth earl's tutors. Arthur is famous for his translation of Ovid's *Metamorphoses*, the text Oxford relied upon the most in writing the plays attributed to the man from Stratford-upon-Avon. Arthur translated Ovid while living at Burghley House and tutoring the earl at the same time. An interesting discussion about Ezra Pound's view of Arthur's translation, which begins at p. 207, ends with "And I hold that the real poet is sufficiently absorbed in his content to care more for the content than the rumble; and also that Chaucer and Golding are more likely to find the mot juste … than were for some centuries their successors, saving the author of Hamlet." Unless, of course, Golding was really Oxford as well as the author of Hamlet. The only poem that can be attributed to Golding is printed on pp. 199-201. Did Golding really translate Ovid? The reader can reach his or her own decision by comparing a representative passage from the *Metamorphoses* with the poem Golding's descendant reproduces on pp. 199-201.

Looney, John Thomas. *"Shakespeare" Identified In Edward de Vere, Seventeenth Earl of Oxford, and the Poems of Edward de Vere*, 2 vols., Ruth Lloyd Miller, ed. Jennings, La.: Minos Pub. Co. (1920, reprinted 1975), now available online at the Shakespeare Fellowship website: *http://www.shakespearefellowship.org/*. Pronounced "Loney," this is the seminal work and may still be the best. Looney spent his career teaching the plays attributed to Shakespeare and became convinced the man from Stratford could not have been the author. He assembled a list of characteristics from examining the plays that the true author must have possessed and went searching for who wrote them. Anyone who loves a detective story will love reading how Looney put the pieces together.

Nelson, Alan H., *Monstrous Adversary,* Liverpool, Liverpool University Press, 2003. More anti-Oxford than Ward is pro-Oxford. For example, in discussing Oxford's parentage, Professor Nelson writes how Oxford's father was previously married to a lady of good ancestry but that his second wife, Oxford's mother, was decidedly of a lower rank: "Katherine [Oxford's older half-sister] was an uncharacteristic product of the Oxford line, for her mother was an earl's daughter. After [Katherine's mother died] in 1548, Earl John [Oxford's father] took a commoner as his next wife. The difference in lineage between the pure-bred Katherine and her mongrel half-brother would have serious repercussions following [Earl John's] death in 1562." p. 14. (Emphasis added.) Doubtless, the Earl of Oxford, who believed all grace and intelligence came from good breeding, would agree with Professor Nelson were he alive to read this passage. Professor Nelson seems to have adopted many of the claims against Oxford made by Charles Arundel and Henry Howard. Indeed, the title to his book is based on Charles Arundel's characterization of Oxford as his 'monstrous adversary' in a letter that Arundel wrote to Sir Christopher Hatton in December, 1581. Nelson, p. 275. However, the information Oxford provided to the Queen about what Arundel and Howard were up to appears to have been correct: Arundel and Howard *were* Catholic sympathizers and working for Spain. See the discussion in Ward beginning at p. 206. Arundel fled England and died in Spain. Spanish records show he was on the Spanish payroll. Spain even paid for his funeral. Ward, p. 222. Howard fared better. He was released from the Tower but not given any favor until 1599. After Elizabeth died. James gave him titles and awards, probably because James had suggested Howard as an intermediary between James and Robert Cecil. Howard's favor obviously arose from his known Catholic leanings, just as Oxford had pointed out. Professor Nelson may be biased, but he took the time to seek out primary sources and has contributed greatly to the documented information about Oxford's life, for which those who are interested in "the mongrel half-brother" give thanks. The transcripts of the depositions and interrogatories of Arundel and others (which have been posted on the internet by Professor Nelson) contain fascinating material:

http://socrates.berkeley.edu/~ahnelson/LIBELS/libelndx.html.

Ogburn, Charlton, Sr., and Dorothy Ogburn, *This Star of England,* New York, Coward-McCann, 1952. Cited as *This Star of England* or "Ogburns" to distinguish it from *The Mysterious William Shakespeare* penned by their son, Charlton Ogburn. The parent's book contains more scholarship than any other book, despite Alan notwithstanding Professor Nelson's dismissal. Nelson, p. 5. The connections and quotations are exhaustive. It is nearly 1,000 pages long and has an excellent index, something that modern publishers can no longer afford. The text covers Oxford's life in detail. The Ogburns not only believe Oxford wrote the plays but that Southampton was his son by Elizabeth (The Prince Tudor Theory). To most Oxfordians, this is the third rail of the authorship question. The more recent claim by Charles Beauclerk, discussed above, that Elizabeth was Oxford's mother and the two of them produced Southampton, may likely replace the unfortunate spelling of Looney's name as the Stratfordians' greatest defense to the claim that Oxford wrote the plays.

Ogburn, Charlton, *The Mysterious William Shakespeare – The Myth & The Reality,* EPM Publications, Inc., 1984. The Ogburns' son, who thought he could write nearly 800 pages on the subject that had been so ably handled by his parents. A poor table of contents makes it difficult to find the many nuggets in this book. His parents' book was longer and contained more interesting original material. Still, the son's book is worth reading. Ogburn could not bring himself to accept his parent's conclusion that Oxford was the father of Southampton, but he is said to have adopted their view late in life.

Pearson, Daphne, *Edward de Vere (1550-1604) The Crisis and Consequences of Wardship*, Ashgate Publishing Company, Hants, England, and Burlington, Vermont (2005. This is primarily a study of the finances involved in the Seventeenth Earl of Oxford's life, but there is much well-documented information in this book. No mention is made of the authorship question.

Solly-Flood, F., *Transactions of the Royal Historical Society*, Vol. III, London, Longmans, Green & Co. 1886, a 100-page paper read to the Royal Historical Society in 1885 in which the author examines the sources for the antics attributed to Prince Hal in the *Henriad* plays. The author examined historical accounts as well as the court rolls to argue that history and Shakespeare have done Prince Hal wrong.

Stritmatter, Roger A., and Kositsky, Lynne, *On the Date, Sources and Design of Shakespeare's The Tempest,* MacFarland & Co., Inc., Jefferson,

North Carolina, and London (2013), challenges the belief that *The Tempest* could not have been written before 1611.

Ward, B. M., *Seventeenth Earl of Oxford 1550-1604,* London, 1928. Ward is pro-Oxford, but the information contained here is invaluable because he went to the original manuscript records and refutes many of the slanders that earlier historians have made about Oxford. However, as with any source, errors creep in. For example, Ward thought Ann married Sir Henry Lee when they could not marry because they were both married to others.) P. 229. See Nelson, p. 280. The relationship between Ann Vavasor and Sir Henry Lee is very important because Oxford's son by Ann, later knighted by Sir Francis Vere, was raised in Sir Henry's household.

Ward, B. M., *The Famous Victories of Henry V: Its Place In Elizabethan Dramatic Literature*, Review of English Studies, 1928, p. 270, *et seq*., downloadable from http://res.oxfordjournals.org/ for a modest fee. Ward focuses on the *Victories* and its relationship to the Henriad trilogy.

Oxford was praised in many Elizabeth publications as a poet and playwright. Francis Meres said he was "the best for comedy." None of his plays and few of his poems have survived. Some of his poems were signed by him and are accepted as his. Others that some scholars attribute to him were signed "Ignoto" or with similar names. Those that are attributed to him are listed in Looney, in *Miscellanies of the Fuller Worthies' Library*, Vol. IV (1872), and can be found on the internet at *Elizabethan Authors: www.elizabethan authors.com/oxfordpoems.htm.* Also, there are chapters in Nelson devoted to Oxford's poetry.

William Shakespeare

Chute, Marchette, *Shakespeare of London,* New York, E.P. Dutton and Company, Inc., 1949. Well-written, fun to read, and full of facts about Shakespeare and London, but nothing on the authorship question.

Ellis, David, *The Truth About William Shakespeare: Fact, Fiction, and Modern Biographies*, Edinburgh University Press (2012). From a review of the book by Dr. Richard M. Waugaman: "Ellis closely examines the lack of evidence underlying recent biographies by Peter Ackroyd, Jonathan Bate, Katherine Duncan-Jones, Stephen Greenblatt, James Shapiro, and René Weis. Ellis points to 'the trend whereby biography [of Shakespeare] becomes a prize for those Shakespeareans from the

Academy who had become eminent in their profession. Given the limitations of data with which they then had to deal, this was if highly trained athletes were required to qualify at [an] international level so that they could then participate in an annual British sack race.'" (p. 11).

Munro, John James, The Shakspere [sic] allusion-book; a collection of allusions to Shakspere from 1591 to 1700, London , *Chatto & Windus; 1909.* Available online at:

http://catalog.hathitrust.org/Record/001365768.

Two volumes of references to works which have allusions in them to Shakespeare. Interestingly, Volume II has an appendix beginning at p. 461 that lists "exclusions," i.e., allusions that a reader might think referred to Shakespeare but don't make the cut. A table of the quartos of the poems and plays from 1593 begins at p. 419.

Northrup Frye on Shakespeare, ed. by Robert Sandler, Yale University Press, New Haven & London 1986. Frye wrote many books on Shakespeare. This one appears to be based on his teaching notes. Frye, like Schoenbaum, was a consummate scholar whose ability to communicate is surpassed by few. He does not touch on the authorship question except to say "I'm not going into the so-called controversies about whether the plays were written by someone else or not—they're not serious issues." He thinks Shakespeare "had the best education anyone in his job could possibly have … the theatre." With all due respect, one does not learn about power politics within the noble class by writing plays. (35 of the 36 plays in the First Folio are about the upper class.). Frye, however, like Schoenbaum, is well worth reading.

Hamilton, Charles, *In Search of Shakespeare - A Reconnaissance into the Poet's Life and Handwriting,* New York, Harcourt Brace Jovanovich 1985. A fascinating examination of Shakespeare's handwriting, with excellent reproductions of other handwriting documents. Compare Sam's chapter on handwriting, p. 193.

Matus, Irvin Leigh, *Shakespeare, In Fact,* New York, The Continuum Publishing Company, 1999. It would be interesting to go through this thorough work and highlight those facts that identify William as the author of the plays as opposed to facts that only tell us something about Shakespeare the landowner and businessman.

Nicholl, Charles, *The Lodger Shakespeare,* New York, Penguin Books, 2007. Excellent research on Shakespeare and his lodgings on Silver Street and the people around him.

Sams, Eric, *The Real Shakespeare: Retrieving the Early Years, 1564-1594,* New Haven, Yale Univ. Press 1995. Excellent exposition of the facts known about William, at least up to 1594. The chronological listing of documents that connect with Shakespeare's life, beginning at page 197, is worth the price of the book. Of course, few of these documents are evidence that Shakespeare wrote the plays. See, footnote 4 below.

Schoenbaum, Samuel, *William Shakespeare: A Compact Documentary Life*, Oxford University Press, 1987, Revised ed. The best biography about Shakespeare, with many interesting facts, as opposed to later works about Shakespeare. Referred to herein as *A Compact Documentary Life.*

Schoenbaum, Samuel, 'The Life: A Survey.' *In William Shakespeare: His Worth, His Work, His Influence.* Ed. John F. Andrews. 3 vols. New York: Charles Scribner's Sons, 1985. Three volumes! And other authors thought the lemon had been squeezed dry! Referred to herein as *The Life in Three Volumes.*

Schoenbaum, Samuel, *A Documentary Life,* New York, Oxford University Press, 1975, Revised ed. A large format book with excellent reproductions of many documents, not just those related to Shakespeare. Referred to herein as *A Documentary Life In Large Format.*

Schoenbaum was an honest biographer and there is much to be gained from reading his works. His credo was best expressed in the following: "The task of the responsible biographer is to clear away the cobwebs, and sift, as disinterestedly as he may, the facts that chance and industry have brought to light. Those facts are admittedly sometimes perplexing." *A Compact Documentary Life*, pp. 75-76. Yes, if you devote your life to studying the wrong man.

The Plays, Sonnets, and Poems

The Arden Shakespeare, London, Thomas Nelson & Sons, Ltd., 2001. First published in 1899, this is the 3rd revised edition. Easy to read. Minimal commentary. Line numbers help find a quotation. References to lines from the plays and poems will be given from the Arden Shakespeare.

The Applause First Folio of Shakespeare, Folio Scripts, Vancouver, Canada, 2001. Page-by page reproduction of the First Folio of 1623 printed in modern type with introductions, endnotes, annotations, etc.

Brooke, D. F. Tucker, and Paradise, Nathaniel Burton, *English Drama 1580-1642*, D.C. Heath & Co. (1933). Thirty plays plus introductions, some quarto covers,

Gilvary, Kevin, ed., *Dating Shakespeare's Plays – A Critical Review of the Evidence*, Parapress, Tunbridge Wells, 2010. A valuable condensation of all the evidence about the dating of each of the plays.

The Globe Illustrated Shakespeare, Gramercy Books, New York, 1979, with illustrations, an introduction to each play followed by Illustrative Comments and Critical Opinions by scholars such as Samuel Taylor Coleridge (1772-1834), Samuel Johnson (1709-1784), James Orchard Halliwell (1820-1889), Edmund Malone (1741-1812), and George Steevens (1736-1800). The Preface contains an excellent overview of the publications of Shakespeare's plays over the years. The first edition was published in three volumes in 1860. Not a whiff of the authorship question is present. The comments of earlier scholars, even where wrong, are worth reading.

Hunter, G. K., *English Drama 1586-1642: The Age of Shakespeare,* Clarendon Press, Oxford, 1997. See, Wilson, below, for the period 1485 to 1585.

Hunter, G. K., *John Lyly – The Humanist as Courtier,* Harvard Univ. Press, 1962.

Kiernan, Pauline, *Filthy Shakespeare – Shakespeare's Most Outrageous Sexual Puns,* Gotham Books, New York, 2007. The puns are more frequent and filthier than modern tastes might allow, a reflection more of the prudishness of modern tastes than what was acceptable in Elizabethan times.

Narrative and Dramatic Sources of Shakespeare, ed. by Geoffrey Bullough, Geoffrey, Routledge and Kegan Paul, London, and

Columbia Univ. Press, New York 1962 (in four volumes). Compare with Clark and Satin.

Quennel, Peter and Johnson, Hamish, *Who's Who in Shakespeare*, Routledge, London, 2002. Useful reference to what's in the plays and poems but not as to who lived in England at the time Oxford wrote the plays.

Satin, Joseph, *Shakespeare and His Sources*, Boston, Houghton Mifflin Company, 1966. Excellent resource as to where the author got his plots from. Compare with Bullough and Clark.

Variorum Editions: William Shakespeare, A New Variorum Edition of Shakespeare: The Poems (Hyder Edward Rollins ed., 1938).

Whittemore, Hank, *The Monument*, Meadow Geese Press, Marshfield Hills, Massachusetts, 2005. Scholars have concluded that the Earl of Southampton is the object of many of the sonnets. Whittemore makes the claim that the sonnets are the Earl of Oxford's concern for his son, the Earl of Southampton, many of which were written after Southampton was imprisoned by the Queen in 1601 for his participation in Essex's rebellion.

William Shakespeare & Others, Collaborative Plays, Jonathan Bate and Eric Rasmussen, eds., Palgrave Macmillan (2013). Ten plays not in the First Folio, but leaving out five plays (*Famous Victories, True Traj Rich III, Troublesome Reign of John, The Taming of a Shrew,* and *Leir,* as well as *Edmund Ironside* and *Thomas of Woodstock (1 Richard II*).

Wilson, F. P., and Hunter, G. K., *The English Drama 1485-1585*, Oxford University Press, 1969. See, Hunter, above, for 1586-1642.

Christopher Marlowe

Bolt, Rodney, *History Play – The Lives and Afterlife of Christopher Marlowe,* Bloomsbury, New York, New York (2004), argues that Marlowe wrote the plays attributed to Shakespeare.

Nicholl, Charles, *The Reckoning – The Murder of Christopher Marlowe*, Chicago, Univ. of Chicago Press, 1992. This book on Marlowe contains excellent scholarship.

Riggs, David, *Christopher Marlowe,* New York, Henry Holt & Co., 2004. Another excellent study of Marlowe. It has been said that Philip of Macedon would have been great if he had not been succeeded by Alexander the Great. The same applies to Marlowe and Shakespeare

(Oxford). Both Philip and Marlowe were murdered, and both were succeeded by geniuses. Although Lyly also influenced Oxford, Shakespeare cannot be understood without spending time to understand where Marlowe was as a poet and playwright when he died in 1593. *The Cambridge Companion to Christopher Marlowe,* Patrick Cheney, ed., Cambridge Univ. Press, 2004, is a useful source.

The Earl of Southampton

Akrigg, G.P.V., *Shakespeare & the Earl of Southampton,* Cambridge, Massachusetts, Harvard Univ. Press, 1968. The author is eager to associate the Sonnets and his subject but has nothing about the authorship question or the Prince Tudor theory.

Stopes, Charlotte Carmichael, *The Life of Henry, Third Earl of Southampton, Shakespeare's Patron,* Cambridge, The University Press 1922. Despite years of searching, Ms. Stopes was unable to find any connection between the Third Earl and Shakespeare. She did uncover rumors that the Third Earl had been a second son, although no one could identify the first. The absence of a record that the Third Earl was baptized has opened the door to thoughts that he was the child of the Queen and Oxford.

Recommended

Bloom, Harold, *Shakespeare – The Invention of the Human,* Riverhead Books, New York, 1998. Yale professor and Shakespeare scholar argues that "Shakespeare created human nature as we know it today." (Inside flyleaf.) Bloom has the best mind examining the plays and poems.

Chamberlin, Frederick Carleton, *The Private Character of Queen Elizabeth,* Dodd Mead & Co., New York, 1922. Thorough research into Elizabeth's earlier history, her illnesses, and the effect upon her of her father's treatment of his wives, the beheading of her mother, and the Seymour affair, where she had to defend herself at a very young age against claims that she had slept with Sir Thomas Seymour, brother of the Protector, and made pregnant by him.

Chambers, E. K., *Sir Henry Lee – An Elizabethan Portrait,* The Clarendon Press, 1936. Sir Henry Lee was Elizabeth's champion and master of the armory. He was in charge of the Tower when the Queen sent the Earl of Oxford and his lover, Anne Vavasor, and their baby, after Anne gave birth to Oxford's son in the palace. Sir Henry apparently fell in love with her (he had a suit of armor made with her initials engraved all over it) and she "drove a whole bevy of youthful lovers to despair … by accepting this ancient relic of the age of chivalry." P. 161. But she was married to another, as was he. Despite never being able to marry, Sir Henry and Anne remained true to each other throughout a long relationship during which they lived at his estate, Ditchley. This was where the Queen forgave them in 1592, causing Sir Henry to have the larger-than-life "Forgiveness Portrait" painted by Marcus Gheeraerts which now hangs in the British Portrait Gallery in London.

Chambers, E. K., *The Elizabethan Stage*, Volume 1, Oxford University, the Clarendon Press, 1923. The court and the control of the stage. Volume II – the Companies. Volume III – Staging, Plays, and Playwrights. From the Revels Office to the Actor's Economics, from each company of players (35 different ones) to each playhouse (18 public and private, not counting the court).

Crystal, David, and Crystal, Ben, *Shakespeare's Words— A Glossary & Language Companion*, London, Penguin Books, 2002. If you see a word in Shakespeare you don't understand, you can look it up here. Or, go to *www.rhymezone.com*, where you can search any word in the plays and poetry.

Donaldson, Ian, *Ben Jonson A Life,* Oxford Univ. Press 2011.

The English Drama – An Anthology 900-1642, W.W. Norton & Co., Inc., New York 1935.

English Drama 1580-1642, ed. By B.F. Tucker Brooke and Nathaniel Burton Paradise, D.C. Heath and Company, Lexington, Massachusetts, 1933. Non-Shakespearean plays edited by two Yale professors, from George Peele's *The Arraignment of Paris* to James Shirley's *the Cardinal*, including plays by Marlowe, Jonson, Dekker, Chapman, and Webster.

Erickson, Carolly, *The First Elizabeth,* St. Martin's Griffin, New York, 1991. A well-written easy-to-read overview of Elizabeth's reign.

Gurr, Andrew, *The Shakespearean Stage 1574 – 1642*, 3rd Ed., Cambridge, 1991. A scholarly work that sorts out the theatres, the companies that played in them, and the history of the period that ran to the closing of the plays in 1642. A very complicated subject, made more difficult by the lack of records and the continually changing alignments (except for Henslowe/Alleyn and Burbage/Burbage) that plague anyone trying to ferret out who was working with whom and on what.

Haynes, Alan, *Invisible Power – The Elizabethan Secret Services – 1570-1603*, Alan Sutton Publishing, 1992.

Hunter, G. K., *English Drama 1586-1642*, Volume VI of the Oxford History of English Literature, Clarendon Press, Oxford, 1995.

Kermode, Frank, *The Age of Shakespeare*, The Modern Library, New York, 2004. A noted scholar turns his attention to the environment in which the plays were written. Much interesting information, somewhat like Chute.

Law, Earnest, *The Royal Gallery of Hampton Court*, London, George Bell & Sons, 1898, is a compendium of the portraits at Hampton Court as of 1898. Many portraits are reproduced, although the reproductions are in black and white and of very poor quality. However, many of the notes to the portraits contain valuable information. See, *The Reader's Companion*, Chapter 2 – Greenwich Palace, and Chapter 43 – The Queen and Elizabeth Trentham.

Lewis, C. S., *English Literature in the Sixteenth Century excluding Drama,* part of the *Oxford History of English Literature,* Clarendon Press, Oxford, 1953, from the Clark Lectures, Trinity College, Cambridge, 1944. Excellent review of the writers of the 16th century. There is a very useful chronological table beginning at p. 559 and a bibliography beginning at p. 594 that includes in Part VI a listing of individual Elizabethan authors and their works. For drama, See, Hunter, above.

Life in Elizabethan England – A Compendium of Common Knowledge 1558-1603. http://renaissance.dueling modems.com/ compendium/ home.html. A well-organized overview of life in Elizabeth's time from money to religion to food to domestic servants and more. "Elizabethan Commonplaces for Writers, Actors, and Re-enactors." A goldmine of information.

Loades, David, *Elizabeth I – The Golden Reign of Gloriana*, The National Archives (2003). Excellent color reproductions of documents and art from Elizabeth's reign.

Hunter, G. K., *John Lyly – The Humanist as Courier*, Harvard Univ. Press, 1962. Lyly was Oxford's secretary at one point. He was involved with Oxford and others in writing and directing plays at the Blackfriars beginning in 1576 that were acted by the children of St. George's Chapel, Windsor, and of the Chapel Royal.

Mikhaila, Ninya, and Malcolm-Davies, *The Tudor Tailor – Reconstructing 16th Century Dress*, Costume and Fashion Press, Hollywood, 2006. Large format color reproductions and patterns of Tudor clothing.

Norris, Herbert, *Tudor Costume and Fashion*, Dover Publications, Inc., 1997, originally published in 1938 in two volumes as part of *Costume and Fashion, Volume Three: The Tudors, Book 1 and 2.* 800+ pages of costumes and other information.

Ovid (Publius Ovidius Naso), *Metamorphoses*, the Arthur Golding translation, edited by John Frederick Nims, Paul Dry Books, Philadelphia, 2000. *Metamorphoses* (from the Greek μεταμορφώσεις, "transformations") is a Latin narrative poem in fifteen books by the Roman poet Ovid, describing the history of the world from its creation to the deification of Julius Caesar. Completed in AD 8, it is recognized as a masterpiece of Golden Age Latin literature. Oxford relied heavily on Golding's translation, completed in 1567, in writing the plays attributed to Shakespeare. Golding was Oxford's uncle and wrote his translation while both of them (Oxford being 17 at the time) were living at Burghley's house on the Strand. Useful notes and an overview of the *Metamorphoses* can be read in *Ovid's Metamorphoses*, Elaine Fantham, Oxford University Press, 2004. The line references are not to the Golding translation, which is much longer than Ovid's original text.

The Oxford Companion to Shakespeare, Oxford Univ. Press, ed. by Michael Dobson and Stanley Wells, 2001. An easily accessed source about the people and the times.

Read, Conyers, *Lord Burghley and Queen Elizabeth*, Alfred A. Knopf, New York, 1960. A reasoned, well-written although dry account of Burghley and the Queen.

Read, Conyers, *Mr. Secretary Walsingham and the policy of Queen Elizabeth*, 3 vols., The Clarendon Press, 1925, 1967.

Roe, Richard Paul, *The Shakespeare Guide to Italy: Retracing the Bard's Unknown Travels*, HarperCollins Publishing, New York, New York, 2011. The author decided to see if he could link geographic locations in the plays to actual locations in Italy. Verona for the locale of *Romeo and Juliet* was easy; figuring out what part of Italy Oxford was thinking about when he wrote *The Tempest* was a little more difficult, but discovering the location for *Midsummer Night's Dream* was a stroke of brilliance (and luck).

Rosenthal, Margaret F., *The Honest Courtesan*, Univ. of Chicago Press, 1992. A book about Veronica Franco, "Citizen and Writer in 16th Century Venice." Although Oxford is not even in the index, fascinating information about what was going on in Venice in the year Oxford was there, including the 10-day visit of Henri III on his way from Poland to France to become Henri III of France.

Rowse, A. L., *The Elizabethan Renaissance – The Life of the Society*, Ivan R. Dee, Chicago, 1971. Tightly packed with fascinating facts and fresh material on Elizabethan England.

Rowse, A. L., *The Casebook of Simon Forman,* London, 1974. For a more readable narrative about the famous Simon Forman, see Cook, Judith, *Dr. Simon Forman – A Most Notorious Physician*, London, 1991. Simon Forman's notes have survived and show he treated a number of prominent and not-so-prominent Elizabethans, including Bridget Vere, Oxford's second daughter, and Aemilia Bassano, believed by many (including Professor Rowse) to be the dark lady of the sonnets. Forman was apparently present with the Queen when news came in 1601 that Essex had been beheaded. Cook, p. 150. The book makes no mention of Oxford also being present, but it was on the same occasion that he made his famous quip that when jacks go up, heads go down. *Cameos from English History, (Fifth Edition) England and Spain*, London, Charlotte Mary Yonge, London 1895, p. 393. According to Ms. Yonge, Sir Walter Raleigh was there as well.

Schmidt, Alexander, *Shakespeare Lexicon and Quotation Dictionary – Every Word Defined and Located, More than 50,000 Quotations Identified,* 2 vols., New York, Dover Publications, 1st ed. 1874, 3rd rev. ed., 1971. If it's in Shakespeare, it's in here. A good example of the difference between these two volumes and *Shakespeare's Word* is "hay." *Shakespeare's Word* does not list it because the word is taken to mean provender, food for animals. It isn't a "Shakespeare" word so it doesn't make the smaller lexicon. It is, of course, in the two-volume lexicon. Unfortunately, the Dover publication does not explain what Bottom is talking about when he says he has a great desire "for a bottle of hay." One cannot drink hay so Shakespeare is obviously having some fun here, although we're not quite sure about what.

Secara, Maggie, *A Compendium of Common Knowledge 1558-1603 – Elizabethan Commonplaces for Writers, Actors & Re-enactors*, Popinjay Press, Los Angeles, 1990-2008. Useful information for those interested in Elizabethan times and how to re-enact them (without having to go there).

Shakespeare's England - Life in Elizabethan & Jacobean Times, ed by R.E. Pritchard, Sutton Publishing , 2003. Eleven chapters (Women and Men, House and Home, etc.) filled with nothing but quotations from writers of the Elizabeth and Jacobean period on the various subjects in the book. See, Winter, below, for an older book with the same title.

Shakespeare's England - An Account of the Life and Manners of His Age, Oxford University, the Clarendon Press, 1916, 1966. Two volumes, different authors for each chapter. A great deal of interesting information, for example, The Fine Arts, Heraldry, Costume, The Home, London, Authors and Patrons, Booksellers, Printers, and the Stationers' Trade, Sports (from hunting to falconry, etc.).

Singman, Jeffrey L., *Daily Life In Elizabethan England*, Greenwood Press "Daily life through history" series, 1995. Good facts on what it was like to live in Elizabethan England.

Smith, Alan G. R., *Servant of the Cecils – The Life of Sir Michael Hickes, 1543-1612*, Jonathan Cape, London, 1977. (Hereinafter "Hickes".) The life of a man who served both Lord Burghley and his son, Sir Robert Cecil, held numerous government posts, became a very wealthy man, primarily by being a money lender, and established a line that is still titled in England to this day. He was the son of Juliana Penn, she who couldn't get the Earl of Oxford to pay a debt he owed her and threatened to lock up the poet, Thomas Churchyard for it. (Oxford was apparently exempt from arrest for debt.) Ms. Penn wrote a third party that she was going to seek relief from Oxford's wife, Elizabeth Trentham.

Tames, Richard, *Shakespeare's London On 5 Groats A Day*, Thames & Hudson. Based on the popular $5 a day travel books. Must-see sights? What are the holidays? They're all here.

Tanner, Tony, *Prefaces to Shakespeare*, Cambridge, Massachusetts, Harvard Univ. Press, 2010. The comments on the plays are culled from the prefaces Professor Tanner wrote to the Everyman's Library edition of the Shakespeare plays. The book is long – 825 pages – and has no index, a sign of a book published in 2010. With the coming of electronic versions of books, no index will be necessary because a computer can search an entire book in a second. And indexers cost money. The subject matter is meaty. Professor Tanner's comments are among the best about the plays, which he divides into three categories – comedies, histories, and tragedies – and addresses each play in turn.

Vendler, Helen, *The Art of Shakespeare's Sonnets*, Harvard Univ. Press, Cambridge, 1997. An examination of the art of the sonnets that reveals a mind (Oxford's) far beyond the capabilities of the rest of us. Vendler says she found a key word in every sonnet except one. The key word (or a variant of it) is repeated in each stanza and the couplet. Try writing a sonnet that conveys heartfelt feelings in beautiful words written in iambic pentameter and follows a rhyme scheme of aabb, ccdd, eeff, and gg, and make sure you recycle one word through all four parts of the poem. Trying to understand the structure of the sonnets gives you a peep into Oxford's mind, much like Salieri in *Amadeus* reading Mozart's music and seeing God between the carefully written notes.

Wagner, John A., *The Historical Dictionary of the Elizabethan World*, New York, The Oryx Press, 2002. Useful maps and information about the people and the times.

Warton, Thomas, *The History of English Poetry from the Close of the Eleventh Century to the Commencement of the Eighteenth Century*, London.

Wells, Stanley, *Shakespeare & Co.*, Vintage Books, New York, 2006. Excellent review of the players who acted the plays. This should be read with Gurr, above.

Winter, William, *Shakespeare's England*, McMillan & Co., London & New York, 1898. An excellent source of information in printed form similar to the information contained online in *Life in Elizabethan England*, although more directed toward scholars than writers, actors, or re-enactors.

Not Recommended

(See, Ellis, above, for a scholar's comments on the work of the following writers.)

Greenblatt, Stephen, *Will in the World – How Shakespeare Became Shakespeare*, New York, W.W. Norton & Co., 2004. Another apology for Shakespeare. If Thomas Nashe could accuse playwrights (Thomas Kyd, not Shakespeare) of "bodging up a verse with ifs and ands" in his

Preface to Greene's *Menaphon*, a lot of current university professors are mining the market for books on Shakespeare by "bodging" up Shakespeare's life with "he must have ..." or "undoubtedly he ..." One example from Greenblatt will suffice: "Let us imagine that Shakespeare found himself from boyhood fascinated by language, obsessed with the magic of words. There is overwhelming evidence for this obsession from his earliest writings, so it is a very safe assumption that it began early, perhaps from the first moment his mother whispered a nursery rhyme in his ear:" Opening line, p. 1. Yes, if William was the author. Greenblatt, by the way, goes on to give the rhyme that, according to him, Shakespeare's mother whispered into her son's ear. Most scholars think Shakespeare's mom was illiterate. Of course, she could have heard the rhyme and then repeated it into her son's ear.

Shapiro, James, *A Year In The Life of William Shakespeare – 1599*, New York, Harper Collins, 2005. The author makes the following confession in his preface: "Conventional biographies of Shakespeare are necessary fictions that will always be with us – less for what they tell us about Shakespeare's life than for what they reveal about our fantasies of who we want Shakespeare to be." p. xv. Having acknowledged this, Shapiro gives us 333 pages of his fantasies before he gets to a "Bibliography Essay" that runs another 43 pages.

Shapiro, James, *Contested Will: Who Wrote Shakespeare?*, New York, Simon & Schuster, 2010. Shapiro returns with another rehash of the arguments that Shakespeare wrote the plays. The pattern of these works that defend William is to throw every name that has been suggested as the author of the plays into the mix (and thereby avoid the need to examine the claims for Oxford head-on) and then dismiss those whose qualifications might raise eyebrows by hinting that they suffer from some kind of delusion for believing Oxford was the author (Freud, for example). It is always important, of course, to mention that the first serious work examining Oxford's claim was written by someone named Looney. Looney pronounced his name "Loney." His editor tried to get him to change it, knowing that scholars like Shapiro and Wells would use Looney's name to dismiss his arguments that Oxford wrote the plays. Almost a hundred years have passed and the critics are still thrilled that what may be the best book on Oxford was written by a man named Looney. Stanley Wells, no impartial scholar himself, assured readers in his review of Shapiro's book that if Looney had known "what we know about Oxford's repulsive character and vicious behavior as chronicled in Professor Nelson's biography *Monstrous Adversary* (2003), he might have been less keen to support the earl's case." The bias in Professor Nelson's book has been noted above, and it is doubtful that Mr. Looney would change the conclusions he reached if he could come back and read it. Even if Professor Nelson's tomahawk attack on Oxford's life shows that Oxford was guilty of "repulsive … and vicious behavior," the idea that a man cannot be a genius if he fails in his relationships with others would eliminate many of the world's most famous authors, historians, generals, politicians, and painters. Oxford may or may not have been a nice man; his failure to behave acceptably does not lessen his claim as author of the plays, no more than Shakespeare's abandonment of his family to pursue a career in London makes him incapable of being the author.

Front Matter

The cover is the portrait of the Earl of Oxford, circa 1575. The quotations are from *Troilus and Cressida,* Sonnet 76, and a poem by John Marston that speaks for itself (try to think of an Elizabethan poet other than Edward de Vere whose name begins and ends with the same letter).

The first stanza and the last couplet of the poem *To The Gentle Reader* are a parody of the loopy poem Ben Jonson wrote that is printed opposite the engraving of Shakespeare in The First Folio:

> *This Figure, that thou here seest put,*
> *It was for gentle Shakespeare cut;*
> *Wherein the Graver had a strife*
> *With Nature, to out-doo the life:*
> *O, could he but have drawne his wit*
> *As well in brasse as he hath hit*
> *His face; the print would then surpasse*
> *All, that was ever writ in brasse,*
> *But, since he cannot, Reader, looke*
> *Not on his Picture, but his Book. — B.J.*

The second stanza is based on a second poem Ben Jonson added to the First Folio entitled *To the memory of my beloved, the Author, Mr. William Shakespeare, and what he hath left us*, which reads, in part:

> *I will not lodge thee by*
> *Chaucer or Spenser, or bid Beaumont lye*
> *A little further, to make thee a roome:*
> *Thou art a Moniment, without a tomb.*

It may come as no surprise that Ben stole these lines (and more) from a poem entitled *On Mr. Wm. Shakespeare, he died in April 1616* by William Basse:

> *Renowned Spenser, lie a thought more nigh*
> *To learned Chaucer, and rare Beaumont lie*
> *A little nearer Spenser to make room*
> *For Shakespeare in your threefold, fourfold tomb.*
> *To lodge all four in one bed make a shift*
> *Until Doomsday, for hardly will a fifth*
> *Betwixt this day and that by fate be slain*
> *For whom your curtains may be drawn again.*
> *If your precedency in death doth bar*

A fourth place in your sacred sepulcher,
Under this carved marble of thine own
Sleep rare tragedian Shakespeare, sleep alone,
Thy unmolested peace, unshared cave,
Possess as lord not tenant of thy grave,
That unto us and others it may be
Honor hereafter to be laid by thee.

Both poets were suggesting that Spenser, Chaucer, and Beaumont in Westminster Abby's Poet's Corner be shifted to make room for Shakespeare.

The third stanza and couplet are based on the comment in the Preface to *The Arte of English Poesy* (1589):

> *'I know very many notable gentlemen in the Court that have written commendably, and suppressed it again, or else suffered it to be published without their own names. There are sprung up a crew of Courtly makers, Noblemen and Gentlemen of Her Majesty's servants, who have written excellently well as it would appear if their doings could be found out and made public with the rest, of which number is first that noble gentleman Edward Earl of Oxford.'"*

The following is a comparison of the front matter to the First Folio and the front matter to *The Death of Shakespeare*:

To The Gentle Reader

This Booke, that thou here seest put,
It was for gentle Oxford cut;
Wherein the Author had a strife
With History to show Lord Oxford's life.

O, if only those who knew his wit
Had said the plays by him were writ,
There'd be no need to here reclaim
The name purloined by Shakespeare's fame.
Grave Spenser need not shift more nigh
Great Chaucer, nor Beaumont nearer Spenser lye;
Let them sleep, Westminster lords.
The world now knows the plays are Oxenford's.
Their every word sings he wrote the plays,
And in his Moniment Shakespeare slays.

Elizabeth knew of noble lords
Who wrote well but suppressed their words,
Or had them published in another's name,
Thereby losing deservèd fame.

Therefore, Gentle Reader, looke
Not on his Name but his Book.—J.B.

To The Gentle Reader

This Figure, that thou here seest put,
It was for gentle Shakespeare cut;
Wherein the Graver had a strife
With Nature, to out-doo the life:

O, could he but have drawne his wit
As well in brasse as he hath hit
His face; the print would then surpasse
All, that was ever writ in brasse,

I will not lodge thee by
Chaucer or Spenser, or bid Beaumont lye
A little further, to make thee a roome:

Thou art a Moniment, without a tomb.

But, since he cannot, Reader, looke
Not on his Picture, but his Book.—B.J.

Ward quotes the poem written by Henry Lok, a long-time servant of Oxford's (printed by Richard Field in 1597), which concludes, after the usual fulsome praise: *Whereof your own experience much might say, / Would you vouchsafe your knowledge to bewray.* P. 298. Why Oxford would not 'bewray' his knowledge is not explained in the poem.

Ben Jonson's poem has been parodied before. There is a drawing in a copy of the Third Folio of 1664 in the Colgate University Library some people believe may be a portrait of Anne Hathaway. The verse reads:

This figure, that thou there seest put
It was for Shakespear's Consort cut
Wherein the Graver had a strife
With Nature to outdo the Life
O had he Her Complexion shewn
As plain as He's the outline Drawn
The plate, believe me, would surpass
All that was ever made in brass.[2]

Since the assumption of *The Death of Shakespeare* is that Oxford wrote the plays but his work appeared under Shakespeare's name, the author of *The Death of Shakespeare* must also 'feign' his name lest his reputation in academia be 'slain.'

The ⸬ is the crown in Oxford's signature.

The Maps

The maps of England and London were hand drawn for *The Death of Shakespeare* by Joan B. Machinchick of Annapolis, Maryland.

---

[2] Schoenbaum, pp. 92-93. The drawing is dated 1708. If accurate, Anne looks like she was someone to be reckoned with. The quality of the verse gives meaning to John Clarke's dismal view of teaching students how to write poetry: "[T]he best you can make of it is a Diversion, a Degree above Fiddling. … The Scribbling of paultry, wretched Verse is no Way for them to improve their Parts in." Quoted by Schoenbaum in a footnote at p. 70.

Prologue
April 23, 1616 - The Death of Shakespeare

There is little evidence about the life of the man we know as William Shakespeare.[3] His most prominent biographer, William

---

[3] As was common in Elizabethan times, Shakespeare's name was spelled different ways. The six signatures that have come down to us are all different. See Hamilton, pp 70-72 for the three pages of his will and p. 39 for a table showing all six signatures. The six signatures are:

William Shackper (Belot-Mountjoy deposition);
William Shakspear (conveyance for a gatehouse in London);
Wm. Shakspea (on a mortgage to the gatehouse);
William Shackspere (page one of his will);
Willm. Shakspere (page two of his will); and
William Shakspeare (page three of his will).

Thus, the sly allusion in the movie, *Shakespeare In Love,* when Shakespeare sits down to write and the camera, coming over his shoulder, shows him practicing his signature. It appears that the six signatures the actor writes are all different, each a reproduction of the six signatures that have been found; three on the will, two on a deed, and the sixth on a deposition taken in a case in London in 1612.

Notice that none of the six signatures has an 'e' between the 'k' and the consonant that follows it, which indicates that William's last name was pronounced "*Shack-spear*" in his day and not "*Shake-spear*" as we pronounce it today. In *The Death of Shakespeare*, William is referred to as "William Shackspear" and not "William Shakespeare." Justice John Paul Stevens opined in his article, "The Shakespeare Canon of Statutory Construction," *University of Pennsylvania Law Review,* vol. 140, no. 4, April 1992, after examining the six signatures, that Shakespeare's "name was Shaksper rather than Shakespeare." Spelling William's name 'Shackspear' instead of 'Shaksper' makes it clear that Shakespeare's name was spoken with a short 'a', and is the name adopted in *The Death of Shakespeare* for the character who acts as the mask for the Earl of Oxford. References to William Shakespeare in *The Reader's Companion* are to the historical man and not the fictional character in *The Death of Shakespeare.* The first publication to spell the name "Shakespeare" was the 1593 *Venus and Adonis* poem. In Chapter 88, Richard Field will suggest that Shackspear have his name spelled "Shakespeare" on the poem.

Schoenbaum, once remarked that everything that is known about Shakespeare could be written on a post card with room left for the address.[4] His birth date is assumed from the record of his baptism -

---

Shackspear agrees, and decides he will henceforth pronounce his name "Shakes-pare."

[4] "We are told that that all the facts [about Shakespeare's life] can be written on a postcard – with plenty of room for an address." Schoenbaum, Samuel, *'The Life: A Survey.'* In William Shakespeare: His Worth His Work, His Influence. Ed. John F. Andrews. 3 vols., New York: Charles Scribner's Sons, 1985. Vol 2, pp 281- 90. Schoenbaum, of course, went on to disagree with his own statement. Otherwise, he could not have written so much on the man from Stratford. A well-organized treatment of the facts known about Shakespeare up to 1594 is found in Sams, Eric, *The Real Shakespeare: Retrieving the Early Years, 1564-1594,* Yale Univ. Press 1994, particularly p. 197-226 - *The Documents 1500-1594*. But few scholars, including Schoenbaum, distinguish facts about the *life* of the man from Stratford (his wife, marriage, children, birthplace, involvement in the Lord Chamberlain's Men, etc.) and facts that identify Shakespeare as the *author* of the plays. This is because the *authorship* facts are so few they could be placed in the area for the stamp on Schoenbaum's postcard. There is room enough in this footnote to list them:

(1) the First Folio;

(2) some of the quartos published before the First Folio that identify Shakespeare as the author;

(3) the major poems - *Venus and Adonis* and *The Rape of Lucrece;*

(4) the Sonnets;

(5) the references to Shakespeare as an author in Frances Meres, *Palladis Tamia, Wits Treasury* (1598), in John Davies, *Scourge of Folly* (1610);

(6) the references to Shakespeare in the *Parnassus* plays (1599, 1601); and

(7) the references to Shakespeare in the writings of Ben Jonson.

A careful reader will immediately notice that, if Shakespeare was a front man for someone else, all of the title pages that identify the author as Shakespeare (##1-4) are no proof at all that the man from Stratford wrote the plays. Similarly, references to Shakespeare in contemporary writings (##5 and 6) are also no proof because the writers of those publications may have been duped as well. Ben Jonson's comments about Shakespeare, particularly in his later life, are more difficult. However, Ben may have been in on the conspiracy. If so, his testimony disappears as well. The reader need not be

April 26, 1564 - and backdated to the commonly accepted date of April 23, 1564.[5] Likewise, his date of death is backdated to April 23, 1616 from the record of his burial on April 25, 1616.[6]

The congruity between the date of his birth and the date of his death has excited lesser minds. Edmund, in *King Lear*, expressed his opinion of those who found their fortunes in the stars (or in congruent birth and death dates):

> *This is the excellent foppery of the world, that, when we are sick in fortune,--often the surfeit of our own behavior,--we make guilty of our disasters the sun, the moon, and the stars: as if we were villains by necessity; fools by heavenly compulsion; knaves, thieves, and treachers, by spherical predominance;*[7]

Another interesting fact is that Miguel de Cervantes and Shakespeare both died on the same *date*, April 23, 1616, but not on the same *day*. How can that be? Europe had abandoned the Julian calendar by the time the two literary giants died in 1616. The papal bull of February 1582 decreed that 10 days should be dropped from October 1582 so that 15 October should follow immediately after 4 October, and from then on the reformed calendar was to be used.[8] This papal

---

reminded that records of William Shakespeare as an actor and a member of the Lord Chamberlain's Men provide no evidence that he wrote anything. Evidence from a third source, such as meeting Shakespeare or corresponding with him *as an author*, would be very helpful, but none exists. No one reported in any diary or letter that they had met him, talked to him, or even talked *about* him, much less referred to him as the *author* of any plays.

[5] Schoenbaum has an excellent discussion of the dating of Shakespeare's birth at p. 24, *et seq*. April 23, 1564 appears to have been a Saturday. Shakespeare's christening (the only hard fact known) was on Wednesday, April 26. The monument to Shakespeare in Holy Trinity Church states that Shakespeare was born on April 23, 1564. The burial register says he was buried on April 25, 1616. There is no record of when he actually died.

[6] Schoenbaum, p. 296.

[7] Act 1, Scene 2.

[8] "Give us back our days," people demanded. They obviously believed in horoscopes and would have rejected Edmund's criticism. However, historians can find no evidence of riots, and have concluded that a painting by Hogarth

decree was followed in Italy, Poland, Portugal, and Spain. Other Catholic countries followed shortly thereafter, but Protestant countries were reluctant to change, and the Greek orthodox countries didn't update their calendars until the start of the 1900s.[9] England adopted the Gregorian calendar on September 2, 1752, meaning that there was no September 3 that year. The next day was September 14.[10]

England was, accordingly, still on the Julian calendar when Shakespeare died. Therefore, Cervantes and Shakespeare did not die on the same day. Under the Gregorian calendar, Cervantes died ten days before Shakespeare. Under the modern calendar, Shakespeare died on May 3, 1616.[11]

This doesn't answer the related question of what day of the week Shakespeare died because that is determined by what the people in Stratford believed at the time of Shakespeare's death. We can move numbers around, and they will affect the day of the week associated with them, but the day of the week cannot be changed; people in Christian countries, for example, always go to church on Sunday.

Under the calendar in existence at the time of Shakespeare's death, April 23, 1616 appears to have been a Saturday.[12] As noted in footnote 4 above, Schoenbaum concluded it was a Sunday. Whatever the day actually was, the opening scene in *the Death of Shakespeare* is Saturday, April 23, 1616.

---

in which the slogan is on a sign being held by one of the people in the painting was the source of the story. Poole, Robert, "'Give us our eleven days!': calendar reform in eighteenth-century England", *Past & Present* 149(1) (November 1995) 95–139, section I.

[9] An excellent discussion of the adoption/rejection of the Gregorian calendar can be read in a paper prepared by Dr. Robert Poole, St. Martin's College, titled *John Dee and the English Calendar: Science, Religion and Empire*, 1996, which can be read at *http://www.hermetic.ch/cal_stud/jdee.html.*

[10] *http://www.tondering.dk/claus/cal/christian.php*. Internet websites are unreliable sources of information. Furthermore, they tend to disappear (although the data they contain seems to live on forever). However, in calculating dates and days of the week, they are useful.

[11] *A Compact Documentary Life*, xv; Durant, Will, and Durant, Aerial, *The Age of Reason Begins,* Simon and Schuster, New York (1961), footnote, p. 304.

[12] *http://www.fourmilab.ch/documents/calendar/*

There is no evidence that Shakespeare ever met Cervantes, the author of the great novel that took Europe by storm when it was published in Spain in 1605, but the two men might have met in Palermo or Naples.[13] Cervantes fought at the Battle of Lepanto in 1570 where he suffered two gunshot wounds to the chest and the loss of his left arm. He remained in hospital for six months and then spent the next few years in the military in Naples.

The records of the Earl of Oxford's sojourn in Italy in 1575/6 do not show that he journeyed farther south than Siena, but a book published 14 years later in 1590 by an English officer claimed that Oxford was in Palermo, Sicily, where he issued a challenge to fight anyone for the honor of his queen. No one accepted the challenge. The officer's report on Oxford's presence in Palermo is as follows.

> Many things I have omitted to speak of, which I have seen and noted in the time of my troublesome travel. One

---

[13] Mark Anderson, in, *Shakespeare By Another Name,* wonders at p. 91 whether the meeting could have happened. If it did, and if Cervantes had already come up with the idea of Pancho Sanza, Falstaff may have been born in Sicily. Or was it the other way around? Vladimir Nabokov also thought Shakespeare and Cervantes may have met. In a poem he wrote in 1924 in Russian, translated into English by his son, Dimitri, Nabokov imagined such a meeting:

> My inclination
> is to imagine, possibly, the droll
> and kind creator of Don Quixote
> exchanging with you a few casual words
> while waiting for fresh horses - and the evening
> was surely blue. The well behind the tavern
> contained a pail's pure tinkling sound... Reply
> whom did you love? Reveal yourself - whose memoirs
> refer to you in passing? Look what numbers
> of lowly, worthless souls have left their trace,
> what countless names Brantome has for the asking!
> Reveal yourself, god of iambic thunder,
> you hundred-mouthed, unthinkably great bard!

http://www.wjray.net/shakespeare_papers/nabokovs-premonition.htm. Copyright 1979 Vladimir Nabokov Estate; English version copyright 1988 Dmitri Nabokov.

> thing did greatly comfort me which I saw long since in Sicilia, in the city of Palermo, a thing worthy of memory, where the Right Honourable the Earl of Oxford, a famous man of Chivalry, at what time he travelled into foreign countries, being then personally present, made there a challenge against all manner of persons whatsoever, and at all manner of weapons … to fight a combat with any whatsoever in the defence of his Prince and Country. For which he was very highly commended, and yet no man durst be so hardy to encounter with him, so that all Italy over he is acknowledged the only Chevalier and Nobleman of England. This title they give unto him as worthily deserved.

Webbe, Edward, *The Travels of Edward Webbe,* 1590, quoted in Ward, p. 112; Ogburn, p. 551; Anderson, p. 90; Nelson, p. 131; and Gilvary, p. 99. If Webbe's account is true, it is significant evidence that Oxford traveled south through Italy into Sicily. This is important because there are so many moments and characters in the plays that reflect the author's personal knowledge of people and customs he would have encountered in southern Italy and Sicily. There is the reference to a nasal accent known to be the way the Neapolitans spoke. *Othello,* Act III, Scene 1. *Much Ado About Nothing* takes place in Messina, Sicily. Don John of Austria was the illegitimate son of Emperor Charles V and the "glass" of Europe, having just defeated the Turks at the Battle of Lepanto in 1574. He was based in Naples and seems to be the model for the Don John in *Much Ado.* Of course, Oxford could have based Don John on the historical Don John who showed up on the Spanish side in the Lowlands a few years later. Anderson's end note to page 90, at p. 464, gives his customary thorough examination of the subject and lays out the efforts to acquire more information about Webbe's presence in Sicily and the English and Italian sources.

Oxford will refer to his meeting with Cervantes when he hears, as he is dying, that *Don Quixote* is finally going to print. See *The Death of Shakespeare, Part Two.*

Since *The Winter's Tale* is based in Palermo, it is pleasant to think of Oxford and Cervantes enjoying a glass of cool wine on the Palermo waterfront while they discussed the prototypes for Falstaff and Sancho Panza, the two greatest philosophizing sidekicks in the history of literature. But Webbe's book is too thin a reed to support such a wonderful thought since he says nothing about whether Oxford met Cervantes. Still, it is an intriguing idea, and undoubtedly grist for someone else's literary mill.

The house the priest enters to give last rites to Shakespeare no longer exists. The townspeople knew it as New Place. It was, at the time, the second-largest house in Stratford. It was a massive brick and half-timbered structure with five bays of windows and 60 feet of frontage on Church Lane. Ten chimneys rose out of its gabled roofs, which ran back 70 feet in places and looked out over a garden 180 feet deep that contained a barn and a private well.

New Place had been built *circa* 1475 by Sir Hugh Clopton, famous in Stratford for being mayor of London and for having built the stone bridge that crosses the Avon and still stands to this day. Despite its amenities, New Place did not enjoy a favored existence. It acquired a history of death when William Bott bought it in 1560 and soon thereafter poisoned his daughter with ratsbane.[14] Because of this, the townspeople thought the house was cursed. No one lived in it for years, and it fell derelict.

William Shakespeare, a practical man, obviously put little store in these tales. He bought New Place in 1597 from a man who had never lived there but whose son confirmed the curse by poisoning his father two months later to get his hands on the proceeds of the sale.[15] The son was hung. In 1602, when the murderer's brother came of age, Shakespeare had to pay the brother additional money to clear the title because a murderer cannot inherit property from his victim or give good title to a third person. If the brother had successfully claimed that the murderer had conveyed the house, Shakespeare's deed might have been worthless. Shakespeare paid a quarter of the yearly value of the property and got rid of the threatened "nuisance" lawsuit. He did not wait for the claim to be resolved, however. He moved into New

---

[14] Schoenbaum, p. 232-238. Bott was apparently not prosecuted for poisoning his daughter although Schoenbaum sets out a deposition by a witness to the poisoning.

[15] Schoenbaum, p. 232-238; Hamilton, p. 98, footnote 85. The poison used by Botts was ratsbane, *vide* Schoenbaum, not arsenic. The second poisoning of the man who sold New Place to Shakespeare was brought about by arsenic.

Place with his wife, Anne, and his two daughters, Susanna and Judith, sometime after he had concluded the purchase in 1597.

Oxford's life was littered with Annes and Elizabeths. Historic verisimilitude does not always lead to clarity in novels, particularly when so many principal characters have the same name.

First, there are the vagaries of Elizabethan spelling. People were not consistent in how they wrote words, much less first and last names. The spelling of Shakespeare's name will serve as an adequate example. Six of Shakespeare's signatures have been set out above. Each is spelled differently. See, footnote 2 above. A survey of how other people in Warwickshire at the time wrote their signature shows scores of different ways of spelling a name.

Second, there are many "Annes." Some are spelled "Ann." Conyers Read spells Anne Cecil's name "Ann." Read, p. 17. The Ogburns in *This Star of England* refers to her as "Anne." So does Professor Nelson. Which was it? The record of her birth in the Calendar of State Papers is in Latin and provides no help: "1566 December 5 inter horas 11a et 12a noctis nata est Anna Cecill." Nelson, footnote 10, p. 448. (Notice the aberrant spelling of "Cecil.") Burghley reported his daughter's birth in Latin as well: "v Decembris die Dominica Anna filia mea nata, postea uxor Edwardi Comitis Oxon." *Ibid.* So the information about her birth date resolves nothing about the correct spelling of her name.

Anne Vavasor is referred to as "Anne" by Professor Nelson (p. 5), by Ward (p. 228), by the Ogburns (*This Star of England*, p. 143), and by Anderson (p xvii). However, buried in Charles Arundel's libels against Oxford is a statement that refers to her as 'Nan': "His device to carry away Nan Vaviser at Easter was a 12 month [sic] when he thought her first to have been with child and one the other side [i.e. in Spain] to have married her disposing his bank of money to the purpose." [Spelling modernized except for 'Vaviser.'] There is a letter in Ward at p. 227 that refers to her as "Bessie Vavisar."

But there is also Anne Hathaway, referred to as "Anne" by the *Oxford Companion to Shakespeare* and by Schoenbaum (p. 3), not to mention "Anna Whatley," the name given as the woman Shakespeare was to marry in a license issued the day *before* Shakespeare married Anne Hathaway. The Stratfordians are content to think that the clerk was mistaken and meant Anne Hathaway despite the fact that Anna Whatley was listed as being from a different village.

And then there are the Elizabeths: Elizabeth Tudor, the Queen; Elizabeth Trentham, Oxford's second wife; and Elizabeth Vere,[16] Oxford's oldest daughter, along with a host of other Elizabeths scattered through the court.

In order to bring some kind of order out of this, Anne Cecil will be referred to as 'Nan' instead of Anne Vavasor, despite Arundel's statement. Queen Elizabeth will be called 'Elizabeth' and Elizabeth Trentham will be called "Elspeth." Anne Hathaway and Anna Whatley will keep their respective names.

'Nan' fits Anne Cecil better than Anne Vavasor. Even though 'Nan' is dead when the book begins and 'Anne Vavasor' will make two appearances in *The Death of Shakespeare*, Nan Cecil is referred to more often because she is the mother of five of Oxford's children (three girls who survived; two boys who did not) and because she is the most likely candidate for Ophelia in *Hamlet.*

Elizabeth Vere, Oxford's older daughter, who will claim in Chapter 4 that her mother took her life by throwing herself into a pond behind Burghley's estate at Hatfield, will be referred to as 'Lisbeth.' This despite the notation by Burghley that Oxford had only four servants "at any time" and not fifteen as was reported by others: "One of them waiteth upon his wife my daughter, *another is in my house upon his daughter Bess*, a third is a kind of tumbling boy [!?], and the fourth is the son of a broth of Sir John Cutts." *This Star of England,* p. 378. 'Bess' is too much associated with Queen Elizabeth to be used as the name for another character.

In the Prologue, Anne Shakespeare makes mention of the recent marriage of her second daughter, Judith. This occurred on February 10, 1616, only two months before Shakespeare dies, and 'besmutched' the family. The changes to Shakespeare's will suggest that he was not pleased with his new son-in-law, Thomas Quiney. He cut Judith and

---

[16] Not 'Elizabeth de Vere.' John Hamill explains that the 'de' was only added to the name of the male who inherited the title of the Earl of Oxford. Thus, Horatio Vere and Francis Vere, Oxford's cousins, and oxford's illegitimate son, Edward Vere, did not use 'de' in their names. *The Shakespeare Oxford Newsletter,* Spring 2003, page 1, available at: http://shakespeare-oxford.com/wp-content/Oxfordian/ SOSNL_2003_2.pdf. Henry de Vere, Oxford's son by Elizabeth Trentham, who became the 18th Earl of Oxford, included the 'de' in his name.

her new husband out of his will. Thomas had gotten Margaret Wheeler pregnant shortly before his marriage to Judith. Thomas was fined 5 shillings by the Court of Peculiars in March and ordered to do penance by the Consistory Court in Worcester. Margaret and her baby died in March, 1616, thus removing two people who would have, had they lived, been an embarrassment to the Shakespeare family, but Shakespeare, concerned about his reputation in the community, may not have felt as good about Judith as he did about Susanna. He left the bulk of his estate to Susanna and her husband, Dr. John Hall.[17]

Some scholars have speculated that Quiney poisoned Shakespeare. Quiney had access to drugs as the keeper of a tavern. The suspicion that Quiney had a hand in Shakespeare's death finds support in the erratic handling of the will, the interlineations, and the execrable signatures. Some have suggested Shakespeare's grave should be opened and his bones tested for arsenic. Arsenic was known as "inheritance powder"[18] in Elizabethan times and would still be detectible. The gentle folk who guard Shakespeare's grave have so far refused requests to open Shakespeare's grave and see what's in there.[19]

Shackspear's statement that "They crowd the bar," waving a bony finger over the priest's head as if a gallery of wraiths was hooting 'Guilty! Guilty!'" is based on Richard III's lamentation the night before his death when he saw a parade of ghosts of those he had slain:[20]

> *I rather hate myself*
> *For hateful deeds committed by myself!*

---

[17] Schoenbaum, p. 297. "During the winter of 1616 Shakespeare summoned his lawyer Francis Collins [...]. [...] Revisions were necessitated by the marriage of Judith, with its aftermath of the Margaret Wheeler affair. The lawyer came on 25 March. [...] Shakespeare was dying that March, although he would linger for another month." In the will, Susanna is called by her married name; Judith is not. Quiney is not even mentioned.

[18] Hamilton, footnote 85, page 98.

[19] The best discussion of these events is found in Hamilton. Chapter VIII is devoted to the question of whether Shakespeare was murdered by Quiney. Hamilton's book contains many excellent reproductions of handwriting and images from Shakespeare's time. Hamilton makes the claim that he has examined documents that were written by Shakespeare but his evidence that they were indeed by Shakespeare is thin.

[20] See a discussion about Richard's speech in Tanner, pp. 356-7.

I am a villain: yet I lie. I am not.
Fool, of thyself speak well: fool, do not flatter.
My conscience hath a thousand several tongues,
And every tongue brings in a several tale,
And every tale condemns me for a villain.
Perjury, perjury, in the high'st degree
Murder, stem murder, in the direst degree;
All several sins, all used in each degree,
Throng to the bar, crying all, Guilty! Guilty!

Scholars have spent lifetimes sifting through the life of William Shakespeare and puzzling over his will and the changes he made to it.[21] The will shows a number of changes in handwriting, many of which have been the subject of much discussion (the gift "to my fellowes John Hemynges, Richard Burbage, and Henry Cundell" to make them rings). Hemynges and Cundell, known to us as John Heminges and Henry Condell (Burbage having died in the meantime), assisted in the publication of the First Folio in 1623.

The second most examined change was the addition that gave Shakespeare's widow the second-best bed.[22] Since no one knows what Shakespeare's handwriting looks like, the additions and strikeouts may have been done by others.

The will is signed on each page. Each signature is different from the others, and different from the three other known signatures research has uncovered. The will is also witnessed and not sealed. The will called for a seal:" In witnes [sic] whereof I have hereunto put my ~~Seale~~ hand the Daie and Yeare first above Written." The word "seal" was struck through and the word "hand" was added.

In 1810, a seal ring with the initials "WS" on it was found outside of Stratford near Holy Trinity Church. There is no evidence that Shakespeare owned a seal ring, although it would not be surprising if he had. Michael Woods, in his documentary for BBC on Shakespeare,

---

[21] A copy of the actual will is presented in Hamilton, pages 70-72, and in Schoenbaum, *A Documentary Life*. A transcription of the will, with all the changes underlined, is presented in Hamilton, pages 81-83. A description of who got what can be read at *http://en.wikipedia.org/wiki/Thomas_Quiney*.

[22] "The second-best bed" remains one of the most discussed provisions of Shakespeare's will.

thought the ring was Shakespeare's.[23] Being starved for information about the Bard, Mr. Woods, like all the other Shakespearean scholars searching for clues to explain how a man from Stratford-upon-Avon could have written the plays, was more than pleased to think of Shakespeare having lost it while traveling near Stratford, and, fumbling to finish the will, scratching out "seal" and substituting "hand."

The man who takes the ring in *The Death of Shakespeare*, Nicholas Skerres, was one of three men present when Christopher Marlowe was killed in a fight with Ingram Frizer in May, 1593.[24] The three men who survived the fight were also the only witnesses to Marlowe's death. They testified that Marlowe attacked Frizer with Frizer's knife, which Frizer managed to turn back toward Marlowe where it entered Marlowe's eye and killed him instantly. Nicholas Skerres and Robert Poley testified that they were jammed either side of Frizer at a table when Marlowe attacked Frizer from behind and were thus unable to prevent the incident or help Frizer.

Considerable information is known about these three men, all of whom led checkered lives before and after Marlowe's death. They all worked for various spymasters like Sir Thomas Walsingham and Lord Burghley. Nicholl thinks Robert Cecil was involved. P. 316. Skerres' age at the time of Marlowe's death is unknown, but if he was a young man in 1593, he would have been in his forties or early fifties when he suffocates Shakespeare in *The Death of Shakespeare.*

Robert Poley was a secret messenger throughout the 1590s and disappears in 1601, although not before being one of two planted spies in Newgate Prison who tried to entrap Ben Jonson when Ben was a guest of the prison in 1597. (Jonson wrote an anagram that praised good company without spies and included the line "we shall have no Poley or Parrott.")

Nicholas Skerres got caught up in the Earl of Essex's uprising in 1601 and was first lodged in Newgate Prison before being transferred to Bridewell Prison where he disappeared.

Ingram Frizer, the man who killed Christopher Marlowe, was pardoned by the Queen on June 29, 1593, and returned to work for

---

[23] Wood, p.337.

[24] The coroner's report, which cleared Frizer the next day, can be read at *http://www.marlowe-society.org/*.

Thomas Walsingham. When James came to the throne in 1603, Frizer became a favorite of Robert Cecil and Lady Walsingham who, given a lease of crown lands by James, farmed them out to Frizer. Frizer lived on his estate in Kent until his death in 1627. Riggs, pp. 339-342. Skerres, therefore, *could* have strangled Shakespeare in 1616. Poley and Frizer also might have been alive in 1616. Robert Cecil ("A monster sent by cruel Fate to plague the country and the State" according to an anonymous poet in the year of his death) died in 1612.[25] In *The Death of Shakespeare,* Cecil will still be alive in 1623. In September, he will board the *Jupiter* anchored downstream from Greenwich Palace to join King James, Sir Horace Vere, and Ben Jonson in a meeting that decides that the plays written by the Earl of Oxford would be published under Shakespeare's name.

Shakespeare's marriage and the birth of his three children are recorded in the church records in Stratford. Little else is known about him or his children.[26] However, some interesting assumptions can be made from the fact that Anne Hathaway was pregnant when

---

[25] Handover, P. M., *The Second Cecil – The Rise to Power 1563-1604 of Sir Robert Cecil later first Earl of Salisbury,* London, Eyre & Spottiswoode, 1959, p. xi.

[26] The record tends to support a conclusion that Shakespeare's parents, wife, and children were illiterate. This conclusion is hard to swallow, given the fact that the author of the plays had one of the greatest vocabularies of any writer (estimated by Durant, p.97, at 15,000 words) and invented countless phrases we unknowingly use all the time. But even Durant, a skilled historian with a gift for seeing into people and events, dismisses any thought that the provincial Shakespeare could not have acquired his knowledge without attending college or going overseas. "How did a man of so little education come to write plays of such varied erudition?" At p. 96. A good question, answered in three long paragraphs in which he repeats the 19th century observation that "he gave Bohemia a seacoast [but acknowledges in a footnote that Bohemia did, for a short while in the 1200s, have a seacoast], and he sent Valentine by sea from Verona to Milan, and Prospero from Milan in an ocean-going vessel," and other evidence that "Shakespeare had the incidental learning of a man of affairs too busy with acting, managing, and living to sink his head into books." At p. 97. More current research displaces many of Durant's conclusions, and these three paragraphs are more evidence of how much shoe-horning one has to engage in to defend Shakespeare as the author. A detailed analysis of each claim might be a useful exercise for an Oxfordian supporter to undertake.

Shakespeare married her (Susanna was born six months later). Also, William was eight years younger than Anne. He was, therefore, a minor of eighteen at the time of his marriage to Anne, a woman of twenty-six. Needless to say, this difference in age was unusual. Consent for his marriage would normally have been required. There is no record of whether any such consent was given.

Church records that have survived show that the Bishop of Worcester issued a marriage license for Shakespeare to marry a woman named Anna Whatley from the village of Temple Grafton, which lay a half-dozen miles from Stratford.[27] However, the day *after* the license to marry Anna Whatley was issued, a bond was posted by two friends of Anne Hathaway's recently deceased father to exempt the Bishop of Worcester from any liability that might arise from the forthcoming marriage of Anne Hathaway to William Shakespeare.[28] No marriage license has ever been found for William's marriage to Anne, who lived in the village of Shottery, a mile from Stratford.[29]

These facts are brushed away by Shakespearean scholars as if they were an annoying piece of lint. Researchers have pored over the marriage records and claim that the clerk made numerous mistakes. According to them, the reference to Anna Whatley of Temple Grafton should have been to Anne Hathaway of Shottery. See,, for example, Sams, at page 50: "Perhaps this was a mere mistake; a dispute involving William Whatley, before the same court on the same day." This is a good example of how Shakespearean scholars have a hard time dealing with facts that smudge or diminish Shakespeare's reputation. By looking the other way and constructing theories of mistake-prone clerks, they ignore a very interesting fact, i.e., that William may have intended to marry Anna Whatley from Temple

---

[27] Sams, 205.

[28] Ibid.

[29] It is a curious parallel that Oxford's father, Earl John, the Seventeenth Earl, was to marry a woman named Dorothy Fosser when, on the day before the wedding, he married Margery Golding, Oxford's mother, instead. See Chapter 9, where Oxford's lawyer reveals these details about Oxford's father, and Chapters 85 and 86 where Oxford is almost stripped of his titles because of a claim that his father had been married to another woman when he married Oxford's mother.

Grafton. Instead, it seems likely that he was forced to marry the woman he had made pregnant and not the woman he loved. Anthony Burgess wrote a novel about this lost love called *Shakespeare*, published in London in 1970 by Jonathan Cape, as did Frank Harris, *The Man Shakespeare*, BiblioBazaar, LLC, 2007, (reprint).

The effort to find information about William Shakespeare has been the most intensive investigation ever conducted. No stone has been left unturned. Unfortunately, the scholars have been looking under the wrong stones. William did not write the plays. In fact, it is surprising how much more information has come down to us about Shakespeare's father than about Shakespeare himself. From these fuller facts, the imagery of Shakespearean scholars has taken flight, using the mundane information about John Shakespeare to try to fill in the blanks about the life of his more famous son.

For example, in 1757, a Catholic Confession was found in the rafters of the house previously owned by John Shakespeare.[30] It had apparently been smuggled into Protestant England by a priest known as Father Campion who was captured by Elizabeth's agents and executed. Obviously, the Confession was never used. But maybe Shakespeare had it, or had seen it. Scholars have tried to ferret out whether the author of the plays was a closet-Catholic. Of course, if William didn't write the plays, what John or William believed is irrelevant to the question of whether the plays were written by a Catholic.

We have no idea who added the interlineations between the lines in Shakespeare's will to give rings to his three fellow-partners in the Globe, nor who wrote that his widow should get the 'second-best' bed. Skerres is just as good a candidate as anyone else. What is interesting, and ignored by most Shakespearean scholars, is the absence of any mention of books, plays, or other writing materials in Shakespeare's will. To dismiss this by stating that the plays were owned by the theater companies does not explain why the man who was the author of the greatest works of literary endeavor in any language made no mention of books or other written materials in his will.

---

[30] *A Documentary Life*, p. 41, *et seq.*; Schoenbaum, 45, *et seq.*, for a discussion of the document; Sams, 32, for a discussion of the document and the times.

Shackspear's recall of how the patrons at the Mermaid Inn called out to him as "Roscius" and "Soul of our Age" is taken from a reference to Shakespeare as "our Roscius" in an annotation written by Richard Hunt to his 1590 edition of William Camden's *Brittania*, "*et Gulielmo Shakespear Roscio planè nostro*" (which can be translated as "*and to William Shakespeare, manifestly our Roscius*"),[31] and to Ben Jonson's calling him Shakespeare "the soul of our age" in one of his poems that preface the First Folio.

The evidence that Shakespeare was an actor is thin. Professor Schoenbaum gives a measured account of the sources which, aside from Jonson's listing of Shakespeare as an actor in two of his plays, begin about 100 years after Shakespeare's death.[32] The sources of our knowledge of Shakespeare and the events of the years he lived comes from documents that existed before the closing of the theaters in 1642 and from investigations into his life after the restoration of the monarchy in 1660. Charles I was beheaded in 1649 and the theaters remained closed until the monarchy was restored. It was not until the early 1700s that people began to be interested in learning more about the author of the plays attributed to Shakespeare. Thus, any statements made 100 years after the plays were written must be taken with a grain of salt. Any statements were not only hearsay but double-hearsay. This gap is one of the main reasons so little is known about the plays and

---

[31] Hunt may have felt the need to add Shakespeare's name to Camden's list of famous Stratfordians which, for some reason, did not include the Bard. Oxfordians believe Camden knew who the true author was and left Shakespeare out intentionally.

[32] P. 200, *et seq.* Professor Schoenbaum sifts through each anecdote hoping that *something* will pass muster as evidence of Will's acting career, but, as he reviews each piece of information, his integrity prevents his imagination from displacing his scholarship and he sadly ends up discarding each of them into a mental trash can labeled "unfortunately not credible." As an aside, it is indeed sad to see scholars such as Professor Schoenbaum and other honorable men digging through the refuse from the life of a man who was not the author, hoping to find *something* to support their belief that William Shakespeare wrote the plays. It's as if Samuel Clemens had done a better job of hiding himself and scholars in search of Mark Twain had settled on someone else, devoting their lives to the pursuit of the wrong man. The lack of evidence connecting Clemens' work and the life of the person they had mistakenly selected would be excruciatingly frustrating.

who wrote them, and why it was not until the 1800s that astute readers began to wonder whether Shakespeare was the author.

Francis Langley lived in London and was, among other things, a goldsmith and a member of the Draper's Guild,[33] but he is better known as the owner of the Swan theater, which opened near the Rose in 1596, and for being named, along with "William Shakspere" (and two women no one has been able to identify), in a writ filed by William Wayte in November, 1596, for sureties of the peace "for fear of death and mutilation of limbs."[34] (The Wayte Writ.) Schoenbaum, a gentle scholar in love with his subject, admits that the writ is "a puzzling episode." He does not explain why this is so, but goes on to say that its discoverer (Leslie Hotson, who found the writ in the Public Record Office in 1931) connected the document with *The Merry Wives of Windsor.* This is probably so, but the most interesting aspect of this piece of evidence is the window it opens into Shakespeare's world. Schoenbaum calls it a "minor legal drama." It is not minor; it is a major insight into a man who made money as a successful businessman in the theater world, the land speculating/grain hoarding world of Stratford, and in the underworld of London.

Schoenbaum does not shy away from reciting the sordid facts known about Langely; he simply glides away after he's done with the observation that "[s]omehow Shakespeare was drawn into this feud" to focus on whether Justice Shallow is based on the other participant in this feud, Justice Gardner, or on Sir Thomas Lucy of William Shakespeare's alleged deer-stealing youth. If the Wayte writ is a test, the professor gets a failing grade for not exploring further what this tells us about the Bard. The writ is significant because it gives us a snippet of information about Shakespeare the man, not more fodder for scholarly musings over whether Justice Gardner is the model for Justice Shallow. There is no evidence that Shakespeare was "drawn into" this feud. The only conclusion that can be drawn from the writ is that Shakespeare was a participant in whatever had set Wayte against Shakespeare and Langley. Scholars who believe Shakespeare wrote the plays will never be able to see their subject until they view the facts without putting on 'gentle Shakespeare' glasses that distort their vision.

---

[33] Chute, p. 42.

[34] Schoenbaum, p. 198, *et seq.*; Wood, p. 169; and Michell, John, *Who Wrote Shakespeare?*, London, Thames & Hudson, 1996, p. 248.

Skerres' accusation that Shakespeare made money with Langley in the prostitution business is not based on fact but is a logical extrapolation of William Wayte's writ and what we know about Francis Langley's involvement (and Shakespeare's) in the London underworld.

In 1786, an anonymous pamphlet titled *The Story of the Learned Pig, By an officer of the Royal Navy* was published. It purported to be the personal reminiscences of a pig as told to the author. The pig goes through many transmigrations (Brutus, an insect, a shark, a mouse, etc.). In the middle of this wandering phantasmagoria, Shakespeare makes his appearance:

> I am now come to a period in which, to my great joy, I once more got possession of a human body. My parents, indeed, were of low extraction; my mother sold fish about the streets of this metropolis, and my father was a water-carrier celebrated by Ben Jonson in his comedy of ' Every Man in his Humour.' I was early in life initiated in the profession of horse-holder to those who came to visit the playhouse, where I was well-known by the name of 'Pimping Billy.' My sprightly genius soon distinguished me here from the common herd of that calling, insomuch that I added considerably to my income by standing 'pander,' as it is politely called, to country ladies and gentlemen who were unacquainted with the ways of the town. But this employment getting me frequently engaged in lewd quarrels, I was content to give it up at the expense of many a well-tanned hide. I soon after contracted a friendship with that great man and first of geniuses, the ' Immortal Shakspeare,' and am happy in now having it in my power to refuse the prevailing opinion of his having run his country for deer-stealing, which is as false as it is disgracing. The fact is, Sir, that he had contracted an intimacy with the wife of a country Justice near Stratford, from his having extolled her beauty in a common ballad; and was unfortunately, by his worship himself, detected in a very aukward situation with her. Shakspeare, to avoid the consequences of this discovery, thought it most prudent to decamp. This I had from his own mouth.
>
> With equal falsehood has he been father'd with many spurious dramatic pieces. 'Hamlet, Othello, As you like it, the Tempest, and Midsummer's Night Dream,' for five; of all which I confess myself to be the author. And that I should turn poet is not to be wondered at, since nothing is more natural than to contract the

ways and manners of those with whom we live in habits of strict intimacy.

You will of course expect me to say something of the comments that have been made by various hands on these works of mine and his: but the fact is, they all run so wide of the real sense, sense, that it would be hard to say who has erred most. "In this condition I for some time enjoyed an uninterrupted happiness, living at my ease on the profits of my stage-pieces, and what I got by horse-holding. But, alas! How transient is all human felicity! The preference given to Shakspeare over me, and the great countenance shewn him by the *first* crowned head in the world, and all people of taste and quality, threw me into so violent a fit of the spleen, that it soon put a period to my existence.

[The pig next becomes a bear which is baited by dogs and dies a horrible death.]

Being a work that first appears in 1786, *The Story of the Learned Pig* is no evidence of anything about Shakespeare but does encourage speculation as to what Shakespeare was doing with Langley in 1596. Calling Shakespeare "Pimping Billy" was too wonderful to leave out of *The Death of Shakespeare.* And now you can decipher another hidden joke in the movie *Shakespeare In Love* where Lord Wessex rides up in hot pursuit of his new bride and hands the reins to his horse to an actor reciting his lines outside the theater. The story that Shakespeare started out as a horse-parking valet in the theater district in London is one of the more colorful additions to his sparse résumé by the 18th century citizens who fell in love with the man and sought to put more meat on his thin bones.

The poem Skerres reads after he murders Shakespeare ("*Good friend for Jesus sake forbeare*") is on Shakespeare's grave. Stratfordians have difficulty admitting that this piece of doggerel came from the greatest writer who ever lived.[35]

---

[35] "The little learning these verses contain, would be a very strong argument for the want of it in the author." William Hall in a letter dated 1694, quoted in Ogburn, p. 39. The scholars attribute it to Shakespeare: "[R]ude doggerl though it be, there is no serious bar to our accepting the attribution." Giles E. Dawson, former curator of the Folger Library, quoted in Ogburn, p. 39.

The portrait of Shakespeare, hanging on the wall of his bedroom in *The Death of Shakespeare,* is the portrait that appears on the title page to the 1623 First Folio, and is reproduced in a modified, washed-out version in the front matter to *The Death of Shakespeare.* Many have marveled at the unusual arrangement of arms, head, and torso used to depict Shakespeare.[36] Skerres repeats their disbelief, and notes that the face is a mask (the skin is smooth; only the eyes are alive; the line that runs up the right-hand side of the head reinforces the conclusion that the face is a mask) and that is seems float over what appears to be a trencher. Readers can examine the portrait and reach their own conclusions. "Ben Jonson Made Me Laugh" in the Winter 2011 edition of *Shakespeare Matters,* Vol. 10:1, by Ted Story, connects the portrait with the Ben Jonson description in *Every Man Out of His Humour* of Sogliardo, who even non-Oxfordian scholars believe is a send-up of Shakespeare ("Not Without Mustard," etc.). Sogliardo is describing how he has bought a coat of arms for £30 which he is showing to a character named Puntarvarlo (whom many believe is Oxford). Sogliardo says that "it is your boar without a head, rampant [standing on its hind legs with its forefeet in the air]. A boar without a head, that's very rare." Another character remarks: "I commend the herald's wit, he has deciphered him well; a swine without a head, without brain, wit, anything indeed, ramping to gentility."

The Droeshout portrait looks like a masked head floating on a trencher, and some have thought it was a boar's trencher at that. Ted Story concludes that Jonson's poem, "Reader, looke not on his picture, but his book," was slyly telling readers that the portrait was not of the true author of the plays in the First Folio. It might not even be of Shakespeare, since the bust in the church in Stratford is equally unusual and different from the portrait.[37] Whatever the answers are to

---

[36] "The picture has never been greatly liked. Lord Brain, the scientist, says that it has two right eyes. *The Tailor and Cutter*[?] observed that the coat has two left sides. The face is the face of a commercial traveler growing bald in the service of an ungrateful firm." Anthony Burgess, *Shakespeare*, an avowed Stratfordian, at p. 258. The doublet is immaculately dissected in "Shakespeare's Impossible Doublet – Drousheout's Engraving Anatomized," by John M. Rollett in *Brief Chronicles: An Interdisciplinary Journal of Authorship Studies*, 2010, Vol. II, beginning at p. 9.

[37] Mark Twain described the bust as a "bladder-face." Of course, he didn't think Shakespeare wrote the plays, so he may have been prejudiced

these questions, neither does anything to bring us closer to identifying who wrote the plays.

Like all of the little alleyways that permeate the Shakespeare question, the bust of Shakespeare on the wall of the Holy Trinity Church has led many scholars down ever more fictional byways. It was first depicted by William Dugdale in the early 18th century. Dugdale was wending his way through Warwickshire recording antiquities. He pictured Shakespeare without pen and paper.[38] The bust was refurbished in 1748-9 and the quill and paper were probably added then. If the restoration added the quill and paper, the restorers were as embarrassed as modern Stratfordians who have to explain why the bust had been put together without any reference to writing materials.

Stratfordians have gone to considerable efforts to discredit Dugdale, taking the time to compare many of his other renderings of church monuments and finding mistakes. They get their logic from the claim that the clerk who issued a marriage license for Will Shakespeare to marry Anna Whatley must have made a mistake. They claim that Dugdale must have made another mistake in leaving out the quill and paper when he drew the bust of Shakespeare. Poor Shakespeare; the recipient of an incredible series of blunders by clerks and artists. Logic and common sense, however, drives one to believe that something so prominent and noticeable and so easy to reproduce in a drawing as a pen and paper would not have gone unnoticed by Dugdale.

But Shakespeare was a grain dealer. If the restoration added the quill and paper, the restorers were probably trying to get rid of the need to constantly explain why their hero's bust contained no writing materials. Empty hands resting on a sack of grain would have raised

---

when he made the comment. Also, there is no reason the greatest writer who ever lived could not have had a bladder-face.

[38] Even without the quill, some have wondered what he was doing resting his hands on a cushion. With the quill, of course, the question then becomes why anyone would choose a grain bag as a writing surface. The answer, according to some, is that Shakespeare was better known as a grain merchant, and the cushion is really a grain bag. Anderson suggests Ben Jonson moved the bust from the Guild Hall and added the pen and the inscriptions. See p. 369-370. Germaine Greer, in her fact-laden (but not about William) book, *Shakespeare's Wife,* HarperCollins, 2007, imagines that the bust was refurbished later. See p. 342. It was.

difficult questions, questions that might have started unraveling the mystery of who wrote the plays hundreds of years earlier. Putting a quill and paper into Shakespeare's hands was a brilliant solution to an embarrassing problem.

In *The Death of Shakespeare,* Skerres is searching for the plays as well as silencing Shakespeare, but the plays, scholars will say, were never lost. They were assembled by Heminges and Condell with the assistance of Ben Jonson. But, assuming this to be true, no one knows who had the plays prior to 1623. In *The Death of Shakespeare, Part Two,* the plays will be hidden away but, because exposing the true author would bring shame on the family of Lord Burghley, Oxford's guardian and father-in-law, and on Sir Robert Cecil, Burghley's son, the guardians of the plays are forced to allow them to be printed in 1623 in The First Folio. Cecil, who succeeded Burghley in ruling England, will be the driving force behind the arrangement.

The First Folio was dedicated to two brothers, the Earl of Pembroke and the Earl of Montgomery. The former was engaged at one time to Oxford's older daughter who ended up marrying William Stanley, the Earl of Derby (who was the patron of Derby's Men). The Earl of Montgomery married Oxford's third daughter, Susan. He and his brother are the two 'incomparable brethren' to whom the First Folio was dedicated.

Were the two brothers the "Grand Possessors" of the plays? In 1609, a few of the plays were published in quarto format and the preface stated they were obtained from the "Grand Possessors". Who these Grand Possessors were and what they possessed is a sub-category of Shakespeare studies. However, the Earl of Montgomery and his brother, the Earl of Pembroke, are prime candidates. Both earls were not only "the most noble and incomparable pair of brethren" but patrons of Pembroke's Men, who, like the Earl of Derby's Men, performed many of the plays attributed to Shakespeare. Also, the Earl of Pembroke, the elder brother, was Lord Chamberlain and in charge of the plays from 1615 to 1625, the time the First Folio was printed. He was succeeded as Lord Chamberlain by his brother, who was married to Oxford's youngest daughter, Susan.

Chapter 1
Fisher's Folly - London – September 27, 1588

Oxford was known for spending money on clothes, swords, books, gifts, and everything else. Ward, p. 32.

Fisher's Folly was built by Jasper Fisher, one of the six clerks of the Court of Chancery. It afterwards belonged to the Earl of Oxford and in Stow's time to Sir Roger Manners. (S. 167). References to it can be found in *'Finsbury Pavement - Fisher's Folly', A Dictionary of London* (1918), viewable at *http://www.british-history.ac.uk/no-series/dictionary-of-london/finsbury-pavement-fishers-folly#h2-0020*: "Mockingly called Fisher's folly, he being a man of no great possessions and indebted to many." "Capital messuage, buildings, yards, etc., at Bishopsgate, formerly the six gardens late purchased of Martin Bowes, etc., belonging to Jasper Fisher," 22 Eliz. 1580 (Lond. I. p.m. III. p. 19). Anderson quotes a description from Chapman at p. 158, and Dorothy Ogburn discusses who lived there and in the neighborhood. P. 784.

Stephanie Hughes has a colored rendition of the Bishopsgate area taken from the Agas Map that can be seen at *https://politicworm.files.wordpress.com/2009/09/bishopsgate-birdseye6.jpg*.

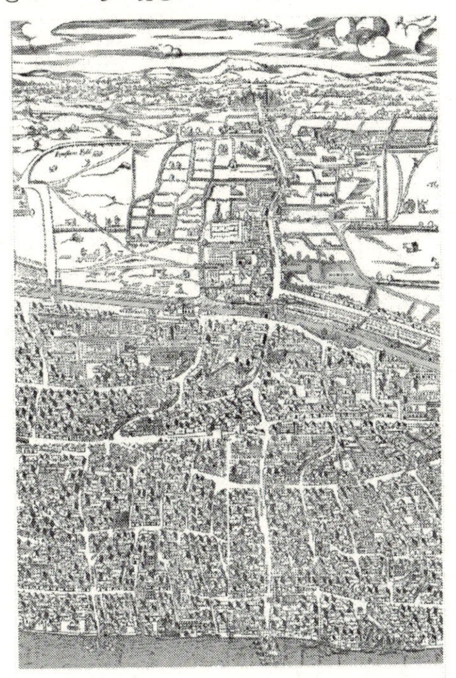

Fisher's Folly is shown in green on the above map. For more detail on the other buildings identified in color, visit Ms. Hughes' site. Further descriptions are found in Anderson, p. 229, and *This Star of England*, p. 711.

Anthony Munday was born in 1553 and died at the age of 80 in 1633. Oxford was his patron in the early years, and he was a member of Oxford's Players. Munday wrote *The Mirror of Mutability* in 1579 and dedicated it to Oxford, who had hired him as secretary.[39] He was a prolific author and wrote, among other plays, *Fidele and Fortunatus*, also known as *Two Italian Gentlemen,* which is considered the precursor to or contemporary with *The Two Gentlemen of Verona.* He translated *Palmerin of England* in 1588.[40] He also collaborated with many other writers, including possibly with Shakespeare on the play *Sir Thomas More.* He was also a draper, and made money in that trade as well. It is reported that he also worked for the Queen and was a pursuivant from 1588 to 1596.

John Lyly lived from 1553 to 1606 and is best known for his books *Euphues, The Anatomy of Wit* and *Euphues and His England.* His biographer quotes Thomas Nashe's description of him—"He is but a little fellow, but he hath one of the best wits in England"—and goes on to write that "almost inevitably the image builds up of Lyly as a small, dapper, essentially frivolous and affected figure, his clothes to be presumed as elegant as his style was neat, forever blowing his epigrams through clouds of smoke." *John Lyly – The Humanist as Courtier,* G. K. Hunter, Harvard Univ. Press, 1962, p. 42.

Lyly's linguistic style is known as *Euphuism* and greatly influenced the authors of his time, including Shakespeare. The word "euphuism" lives on in our language to mean "artificial elegance of language." One example will suffice: "This noble man," he writes of Burghley in the *Glasse for Europe* in the second part of *Euphues* (1580), "I found so ready being but a straunger to do me good, that neyther I ought to forget him, neyther cease to pray for him, that as he hath the wisdom

---

[39] Anderson, p. 140, p. 159.

[40] Introduction to *Don Quixote de la Mancha* by Miguel de Cervantes Saavedra, translated by Peter Mooeux, Random House, New York (1941). Cervantes refers to *Palmerin of England* on p. 27 of his great novel. *Don Quixote* was published in 1605, a year after Oxford died, and translated into English in 1610. *Palmerin* was a figure in a series of romances that were famous in Spain.

of Nestor, so he may have the age, that having the policies of Ulysses he may have his honor, worthy to lyve long, by whom so many lyve in quiet, and not unworthy to be advaunced by whose care so many have been preferred." Lyly is also credited with "all is fair in love and war." *Civilization's Quotations; Life's Ideal,* Krieger, Richard Alan, 2002, p. 42.

Lyly attended Oxford for a while but was unable to stay because of financial reasons or because he could not bring himself to study. He went into the service with Lord Burghley early on but was accused of some dereliction of duty, thus ending his hopes for preferment in that direction. He became the secretary of the Earl of Oxford and wrote many plays for performance by the boys' theaters.

"The lively lark stretched forth her wing' appeared in *Paradyse of Dainty Devices,* 1576 as "Judgement of Desire by EO." Looney, #11, Fuller, #21. Dorothy Ogburn, p. 50.

The Cambridge History of English and American Literature in 18 Volumes (1907–21). Volume V. The Drama to 1642, Part One; VI. The Plays of the University Wits; § 6. Authorship of the songs in Lyly's plays (available at *http://www.bartleby.com/ 215/0606.html*) makes the following comment:

> "Whoever knows his Shakespeare and his Lyly well can hardly miss the many evidences that Shakespeare had read Lyly's plays almost as closely as Lyly had read Pliny's *Natural History.* It is not merely that certain words of the song of the birds' notes in *Campaspe* gave Shakespeare, subconsciously, probably, his hint for "Hark, hark, the lark"; or that, in the talk of Viola and the duke [footnote omitted] he was thinking of Phillida and Galathea; [footnote omitted] but that we could hardly imagine *Love's Labour's Lost* as existent in the period from 1590 to 1600, had not Lyly's work just preceded it. Setting aside the element of interesting story skillfully developed, which Shakespeare, after years of careful observation of his audiences, knew was his surest appeal, do we not find *Much Ado About Nothing* and *As You Like It,* in their essentials, only developments, through the intermediate experiments in *Love's Labour's Lost* and *Two Gentlemen of Verona,* from Lyly's comedies?"

Oxford was always in debt and looking for money, even after he received the £1,000 a year stipend from Queen Elizabeth in 1586 (1589 in *The Death of Shakespeare).* Lords and ladies were supposed to be nonchalant about money because it was considered beneath their concern. However, they did have large legitimate expenses in addition to paying for parties and fripperies. For example, Oxford was the Master of the Ewrie, which granted Oxford the right to wash the hands of the King or Queen at dinner, but he also had to keep ten people on duty to carry out this daily function in his absence. Looney, pp. 106-107. A "Sergeant," three "Yeomen," two "Groomes," two "Pages" and two "Clarks" were needed for this office, according to Dr. J. Horace Round, *Report on the Lord Great Chamberlainship*; MS. in the Library of the House of Lords, London, cited by Charles Wisner Barrell. Looney, p. 196. It appears that Oxford served King James in this capacity at James' coronation. Ward: *Seventeenth Earl of Oxford*, p. 346.

The actual ewer (a bottle with an insignia of a boar) may be in the Rosenbach Museum in Philadelphia. The Museum denies this claim, stating that the boar's head stopper is firmly dateable to the 19th century, and has no connection with the 1594 stoneware vessel. E-mail message of 14 April 1999 from John Foelster after personal communication with Elizabeth E. Fuller, Librarian at the Rosenbach Museum, Philadelphia. Nina Green;

http://www.oxford-Shakespeare.com/Oxmyths/OxmythsOxford.pdf.

Ms. Green also argues that Oxford did not hold the Office of the Ewrie. However, there is a letter dated January 29, 1973 from a Craig Huston, whose letterhead indicates he was an attorney, in which he writes that the ewer had the seal of England on three sides and the date "1594."

http://shakespeareoxfordfellowship.org/wp-content/uploads/SOSNL-1973.compressed.pdf.

Oxford lived large, and beyond his means. See, *The Reader's Companion* to Chapter 32 - Christmas at the Boar's Head. Numerous other lords and ladies also ended up bankrupt. Sir Thomas Heneage died in 1595 in more debt than Oxford. A letter to the Lord Treasurer is preserved among the records of the Office of the Revels, reproduced at page 65 in *Notes on the History of the Revels Office Under the Tudors* by E. K. Chambers, London (1906), from "Peeter Wrighte wyer Drawer, James Clark Chandler, Tayour, Richard Page Collyer, Thomas Jhones woodbroker, and Jhon Griffeth Porter of St. Johns gate, Creditors and Servitors of her Maiestes Office of the Revelles," who claim that that "whereas wee be now V years behinde unpayed for warres Delivered and service Done within that office."

Some have thought that *Timon of Athens* reflected Oxford's attitude toward money and efforts to collect debts he owed. Of course, a feudal system that required a wardship in which the Queen got a third of the income from a ward's lands (Oxford, for example), and management of the ward's lands (the Earl of Leicester, in this case), reduced any income could have derived from his lands. Combine this with a hefty price to buy back his rights and one can see how Oxford fell heavily into debt. See, the excellent discussion of what happened to Oxford's lands after his father died in Nina Green's article in *Brief Chronicles*, Vol. 1, 2009, "The Fall of the House of Oxford."

Nigel's description of his efforts to fend off Burghley and Leicester in their efforts to siphon off Oxford's assets while Oxford was a minor is not far off the truth. In 1577, Burghley had to publicly deny that he had used Oxford's funds improperly. Ogburns, p. 783. Burghley grew to be one of the richest men in England and some of his wealth probably came from Oxford, who, being the functional equivalent of illiterate when it came to money, never knew what was being taken from him.

Sprezzatura is an Italian word originating from Baldassare Castiglione's *The Book of the Courtier*, where it is defined by the author as "a certain nonchalance, so as to conceal all art and make whatever one does or says appear to be without effort and almost without any thought about it." It is the ability of the courtier to display "an easy facility in accomplishing difficult actions which hides the conscious effort that went into them." *Sprezzatura* has also been described "as a form of defensive irony: the ability to disguise what one really desires, feels, thinks, and means or intends behind a mask of apparent reticence and nonchalance." The word has entered the English language; the Oxford English Dictionary defines it as "studied carelessness".

Tobias is based on records in Hackney (to which Oxford moved in 1597) that indicate an African man died there at the age of 105 in 1630. It was easy to make him one of the slaves Sir Walter Raleigh brought back to England. Africans were not unknown in England, and some lords and ladies had African servants. Of the two Raleigh brought back to England, one ended up a domestic in London while the other waited on Raleigh while he was imprisoned in the Tower.

A "whiffler" was an attendant who clears the way for a procession. See, *Shakespeare's England*, p. 169. In *Henry* V, Act IV, Scene 8, the chorus says:

> *the deep mouth'd sea,*
> *Which like a mighty whiffler 'fore the king*
> *Seems to prepare his way:*

Servants of noblemen wore 'livry,' which identified who they were affiliated with. See, Roger Stritmatter's *"A Law Case In Verse: Venus and Adonis and the Authorship Question*, Tennessee Law Review, Vol. 27, 307, 340.

Richard Roe in *The Shakespeare Guide to Italy* notes that Oxford only took four servants with him when he left for the continent on his way to Italy but a 'harbinger,' or 'whiffler' was one of them. P. 214, footnote 8. Dorothy Ogburn agrees that a 'harbinger' was one of Oxford's servants as he traveled to Paris in 1575 but says there were a total of eight servants (two gentlemen; two grooms; one payend; one harbinger; one housekeeper; and one trenchman).

Bethlehem Hospital was across Bishopsgate Street from Fisher's Folly. The name "Bethlehem" was shortened to "Bedlam." The names of the taverns on Bishopsgate are accurate.

Senor Baldini is a fictional character. Perfumed gloves were introduced to England by Oxford when he returned from Italy and presented a pair to Queen Elizabeth, who loved them.

Agnes the tart-seller is fiction.

The Thames was the highway for London, and wherries were the large rowboats used by everyone to get around, ranging far up and down the river. The men who rowed them were organized into a guild and could, at times, exercise considerable effect upon politics and the economy. The fish pulled out of the waters far exceeded modern harvests, including salmon that migrated up the Thames in springtime. See, William Harrison, *A Description of England*, London (1587), quoted in *Shakespeare's England – Life in Elizabethan & Jacobean Times*, 2003, p. 166.

The man who rows Oxford to Greenwich Palace is John Taylor, the Water Poet. He will row Oxford and Robin to Oxford's wedding at Westminster in December 1591.

Greenwich was one of Elizabeth's many palaces, located down the Thames on the south side of the River. (Deptford, where Christopher Marlowe would be murdered in 1593, is just upstream from Greenwich.) Elizabeth was born at Greenwich. She and Oxford spent a lot of time there in the 1570s as well as at Hampton Court, which is further up the Thames past Westminster. Windsor Castle is even further up the Thames. Oxford spent time at Windsor Castle when he was very ill in 1570. He thus had intimate knowledge of the Castle and the town, where *The Merry Wives of Windsor* takes place.

Chapter 2
Greenwich Palace – The Same Day

Greenwich Palace has been extensively rebuilt and does not look now like it did in 1588.

Stephanie Hughes has an illustration of the palace but gives no citation for its source:

https://politicworm.files.wordpress.com/2009/05/thames-ank-birdseye-12.jpg

A slightly different version from 1544 is given at page 3 of *Elizabeth I: The Golden Reign of Gloriana* by David Loades, The National Archives (2003).

Robin, the page, is fiction. He is not Falstaff's page in *The Merry Wives of Windsor.* (There is no meat on that character.) His statement of what he will bring if he is allowed to become a servant to Oxford is based on the Kent's explanation to Lear in Act I, Scene 4 of *King Lear* as to why he wants to serve Lear:

> *I do profess to be no less than I seem; to serve him truly that will put me in trust: to love him that is honest; to converse with him that is wise, and says little; to fear judgment; to fight when I cannot choose; and to eat no fish.*

The claim that he eats 'no fish' means he is not Catholic.

Robin refers to "Mr. Kyd." "Mr." as a substitute for "Master" began to appear in use in 1545. Oxford English Dictionary. While not widely used by 1588, it will be used throughout *The Death of Shakespeare* because of its familiarity to modern readers who may associate the word "Master" with a young boy not yet old enough to be called "Mister."

Malfis, Oxford's lawyer, a fictional character, advises Oxford in Chapter 9 that the daughter of the man purchasing Fisher's Folly in 1589 has found a book of Oxford's poems. The poems found by Anne Cornwallis are the only contemporary Elizabethan poetry found to date. The rest of the poems in the book may well be Oxford's since they were found in Fisher's Folly which Oxford sold to Anne Cornwallis' father. Her book was found by J. O. Halliwell-Phillips in 1852 (Folger MS V.a.89). Anne had copied them out in her own hand. The book contains 33 poems. One of them had been published in 1599 in *The Passioniate Pilgrim*, which was published with the name "W. Shakespeare" on the title page. In fact, *The Passionate Pilgrim* contains two sonnets attributed to Shakespeare. They were the only ones published before the entire set of sonnets was published in 1609. Ogburn, p. 711 discusses the poems and compares them to other printed versions of the two sonnets.

Sir Thomas Heneage was one of Elizabeth's ministers. He will marry the Earl of Southampton's mother, the Countess of Southampton, in 1593 and die two years later. Heneage was the Lord Treasurer during this period, and had control over the court's expenditures for entertainment. After he died, the Queen demanded an accounting from the Countess of what Heneage had spent. The Countess supplied it with, among other things, a reference to a payment to Will Shakespeare, Richard Burbage, and Henry Condell for a performance on December 28, 1594. Stratfordians grasp at this mention of Shakespeare, his first appearance in any official record outside Stratford, but other records show that the performance was elsewhere, leading to the possibility that the Countess, like many who have had to reconstruct financial records, padded the record to reduce what she owed the Queen. In any event, the record says nothing about the man Shakespeare being the author of the plays, only that he was connected with the Lord Chamberlain's Men.

Heneage was not known for his poetry. A stanza from a poem written on the flyleaf of a book found in 1901 is ostensibly by Heneage and, if by him, is a good example of how poor a poet he was:

Most welcome love, thou mortall foe to lies,
thou roote of life and miner of debate,
an impe of heaven that troth to vertue ties,
a stone of choise that bastard lustes doth hate
a waye to fasten fancy most to reason
in all effects, and enemy most to treason.

Sir Walter Raleigh allegedly supplied a reply to Heneage's poem just below it that would seem to have the creativity Sir Thomas lacked:

Farewell falce love, thou oracle of lies,
a mortall foe and enemy to rest,
an envious boye from whome all cares arise
a bastard vile, a beast with rage possest, b
a way of error, a temple full of treason,
in all effectes contrary unto reason.
A poysened serpent, covered all with flowers,
mother of sighes and murderer of repose,
a sea of sorrowe from whence are drawen such showers
as moysture lendes to every griefe that growes,
a schoole of gyle, a nest of deep deceit,
a gylded hook that holdes a poysened bait.

Stopes, Charlotte Carmichael, *The Life of Henry, Third Earl of Southampton, Shakespeare's Patron*, Cambridge, The University Press 1922, p. 76.

Heneage's gossip that the Earl of Leicester may have poisoned himself when he intended the poison for his current wife was considered true by many people at the time. Whether true or not, Elizabeth was stricken by his loss, and kept Leicester's last letter close to her throughout the rest of her life.

Was Leicester's demise the seed from which Oxford developed the idea of the poisoned cup in *Hamlet*, which Claudius intended Hamlet to drink but which Gertrude drank instead?

"Her eyes are grey as glass, and so are mine" is from *Two Gentlemen of Verona*, Act IV, Scene 4. Julia is comparing herself to Silvia, who many people think is Elizabeth. Elizabeth is described in a comment to a portrait of her at Hampton Court (*The Royal Gallery of Hampton Court*, Portrait 616, p. 226-227). The author recalls the description given by Mary, Queen of Scots' ambassador: "[Elizabeth] delighted to show her golden-coloured hair, which was more reddish than yellow, and curled in appearance naturally. She desired to know of me what colour hair was reputed best; and whether my Queen's hair or hers was best; and which of them two was fairest? I answered the fairness of them both was not their worst fault. But she was earnest with me to declare which of them I judged fairest. I said she was the fairest Queen in England, and mine the fairest in Scotland. Yet she appeared earnest. I answered they were both the fairest ladies in their countries—that her Majesty was whiter, but my Queen was very lovely. She enquired which of them was of highest stature. I said my Queen. Then saith she, she is too high, for I myself am neither too high nor too low."

The note goes on to describe that she was no less vain about her hands, which "we are told were small, and the fingers long: this is no doubt the reason her hand is so prominent in this portrait (No. 616] and No. 619 … In audiences she would pull off her glove, above a hundred times, to show her hands, which were very fine and white."

Sir Christopher Hatton was another rival of Oxford's in the 1570s and 1580s. See, Ward, p. 74, *et seq*. In the 1571 tournament, Oxford bested Hatton, Charles Howard, and Sir Henry Lee (who would fall in love with Anne Vavasor and begin to live with her ten years later, raising Oxford's son, Edward). In a letter Hatton wrote to the Queen in 1572 (Ward, p. 74) he told her that she should prefer him over Oxford: "Reserve it to the Sheep, he hath no tooth to bite, where the Boar's tusk may raze and tear." Ward, p. 75. He was indeed a sheep and no match for Oxford's wit. In *Two Gentlemen of Verona*, there is the following dialogue between Speed and his master, Proteus:

Speed:	*Sir Proteus, save you! Saw you my master?*
Proteus:	*But now he parted hence, to embark for Milan.*
Speed: T	*Twenty to one then he is shipp'd already,* *And I have play'd the sheep in losing him.*
Proteus:	*Indeed, a sheep doth very often stray,* *An if the shepherd be a while away.*
Speed:	*You conclude that my master is a shepherd, then,* *and I a sheep?*

Proteus: *I do.*

Speed: *Why then, my horns are his horns, whether I wake or sleep.*

Proteus: *A silly answer and fitting well a sheep.*

This goes on for twenty or more lines and is typical of Shakespeare's early work. However, the allusions to the sheep-biter return in Act II, Scene 1, when Speed and Launce discuss a list of the virtues of a woman Launce has met.

Speed: *Item: She hath no teeth.*

Launce: *I care not for that neither, because I love crusts.*

Speed: *Item: She is curst.*

Launce: *Well, the best is, she hath no teeth to bite.*

These may be references to Hatton's letter to the Queen. Why Shakespeare would be writing in the 1590s about something that everyone would know referred to Hatton, a powerful minister, and which had occurred years earlier, has not been explained. There is no record of Shakespeare being punished for this effrontery. Hatton, however, appears to have acquired the right to sue Oxford for what Oxford owed the Court of Wards. See, below. His desire to bankrupt Oxford may have stemmed from Oxford's treatment of him in *Two Gentlemen*.[41]

Pauline Kiernan in *Filthy Shakespeare* thinks these references to teeth that cannot bite and a woman who "can milk" are allusions to sexual acts. The Elizabethan world was much bawdier than our world

---

[41] Scholars agonize over the order and dating of the plays. *Two Gentlemen* is a good example. If Shakespeare wrote *Two Gentlemen*, and if the sheep-biter references are to a letter Christopher Hatton wrote in the 1570s, why would Shakespeare throw these comments into a play written nearly twenty years later? *Two Gentlemen* seems to be a lightly-veiled dramatization of Elizabeth's on-again off-again marriage to the Duc d'Alençon. The subject would seem stale in the 1590s. However, if the play was written much earlier but reworked later, the references make sense. And if this is what happened, it is unlikely that Shakespeare could be the author. How would he have gotten permission to rework a drama that was apparently written by Oxford? Even more importantly, how would he have avoided retribution from Hatton or the Queen?

but sometimes Ms. Kiernan may stretch things too far. (No pun intended.)

Oxford's debts have been the subject of much investigation. He seems to have been profligate in his use of money, but so did many other lords and ladies. See, *The Reader's Companion* to Chapter 32 - Christmas at the Boar's Head for a more detailed discussion of Oxford's debts.

Oxford and Elizabeth apparently had a love affair when he was in his early twenties. The evidence comes partly from a letter written by Mary Stuart, Queen of Scots, in 1584, to Elizabeth reporting scandalous allegations about Elizabeth that Mary learned from the Countess of Shrewsbury. A translation of the letter is set out in full in Ogburns, Appendix 1, p. 1249, and referred to at p. 282. The letter is a gold mine of gossip, whether the allegations are true or not. Mary wrote that the Countess accused Elizabeth of "making love and gratifying yourself with master haton and another of this Kingdom," among many others, including the Frenchman she was being urged to marry and his go-between. Mary wrote that "even the count of Oxford dared not reconcile [some translators say 'cohabit'] with his wife for fear of losing the favour which he hoped to receive by becoming your lover."

Oxford's pun on 'regina' and 'vagina' is fiction. Although the Latin pronunciation of 'regina' is 're-JEE-na,' the Oxford English Dictionary gives the pronunciation as 're-JEYE-na,' thereby rhyming it with 'vagina.' Colin Firth in *Shakespeare in Love* tells Gwyneth Paltrow to hurry up lest they keep 'Re-JEYE-na Gloriana' waiting. The Elizabethan court was fluent in Latin and used it to communicate verbally and in writing. Letters in English from the period are full of Latin phrases. Elizabeth, near the end of her reign, was about to give a speech at Cambridge when she was told the Polish ambassador did not understand English. She gave the speech in Latin.

Oxford's description of Sidney as "a facile poet … imitative at best, and sentimental and silly at worst," is from *This Star of England*, p. 184.

"He could hiss like a serpent—*Sweet swelling lips well maist thou swell* —, gobble like a turkey—*Moddels such be wood globes*—and quack like a duck—*But God wot, wot not what they mean*" is from C.S. Lewis, *English Literature in the Sixteenth Century excluding Drama*, p. 329.

"The essence of civilized behavior," Burghley began magisterially, "is the ability to enact gracefully and convincing upon a public stage the role that fortune has selected for you. For her majesty, it is to be Queen of England. For me, it is to be Lord Treasurer. For you, it is to be . . . ." Based on *Advice to a Son, Precepts of Lord Burghley, Sir Walter Raleigh, and Francis Osborne*, edited by Louis B. Wright, published for the Folger Library by Cornell University Press, 1962, which can be viewed at *https://archive.org/stream/advicetoasonprec013268mbp/advicetoasonprec013268mbp_djvu.txt.*

The sonnet Oxford recites while he and Elizabeth sit at the base of the tree behind Greenwich Palace is Sonnet 57.

A marriage was valid if the proper words were spoken "per verba de praesenti" followed by consummation, even if the agreement was kept secret. Thus, in *The Duchess of Malfi,* by John Webster, the Duchess, to the surprise of Antonio, pulls her maid out from behind an arras as a witness to her claim that she and Antonio have agreed to be married. "I have heard lawyers say, a contract in a chamber *per verba [de] praesenti* is absolute marriage." Act I, Scene 3. An agreement "in futuro," however, was not, although suit could be filed for breach of promise. *Bouvier's Law Dictionary,* Rawle's 3rd Revision, 1914. There is an excellent discussion of this in relation to Shakespeare's marriage to Anne Hathaway in Schoenbaum beginning at page 89.

Elizabeth was seventeen years older and in her forties when her affair with Oxford began. Oxford turned twenty-one in April, 1571. He married Anne Cecil in December. Anne at the time was the daughter of Elizabeth's longest-standing minister, William Cecil, whom Elizabeth had created Baron Burghley earlier in the year. His elevation prevented his daughter's marriage to Oxford from being morganatic because Oxford was of superior status, being a lord, and Anne's father, before his elevation to the barony, was of inferior status. In a morganatic marriage, "a wife and her children have no claims to the husband's title or possessions." *Black's Law Dictionary,* 8th Ed., 1999. To prevent this from happening to Burghley's daughter and grandchildren, Burghley induced Queen Elizabeth to elevate him to the peerage. (The title of 'knight' confers nothing on a knight's heirs or children.)

Il Cortegiano was written by Baldassare Castiglione and published in Italy in the early 1500s. Bartholomew Clerke published an English translation in the 1560s; Oxford probably paid for the book's translation into Latin in 1572 and wrote the preface quoted by the Queen.[42] Why Latin? "[Oxford] ... achieved two important objections that would further the case for his cousin (the Earl of Norfolk, Oxford's cousin, who would eventually be executed). First, it would flatter Her Majesty's intellect—always useful for winning her heart. Second, it would recount for her in the tongue of learned society the crucial role of the aristocracy in the queen's world." Anderson, p. 52. *The Courtier*, as it was titled in its English translation, "seep[ed] into the very fiber of de Vere's writings [i.e., the works attributed to Shakespeare]." Anderson believes that the three great intellectual forbears to the man who wrote the plays are Plato, Ovid, and Castiglione." P. 53. Few scholars would disagree with including Castiglione in the list since the plays reflect the medieval world found in *The Courtier*.[43]

The Queen's reprimand of Sir Philip Sidney can be read in Ogburns at p. 188. The speech by Ulysses in *Troilus and Cressida,* Act I, Scene 3, sounds suspiciously like it. Oxford's comment on Sidney's poetry – 'Tis like the forced gait of a shuffling nag!" is from Act III, Scene 1, of *Henry IV, Part 2.*

That the Queen held Oxford back in his quest for military is true. In 1570, Oxford got himself attached to the Earl of Sussex and sent north where he acted so recklessly that he had to be rescued by other

---

[42] Oxford was twenty-two at the time. Ward has translated the 'Letter to the Reader' that Oxford wrote as a preface to the translation. It is remarkably well-written, and was recognized as such when *The Courtier* was published in 1572. In 1578 the Queen visited Cambridge, accompanied by the whole Court. Gabriel Harvey presented verses, in Latin, in honor of the event, one of which was addressed to Oxford, and which included the following lines (see *This Star of England*, p. 146; Anderson, p. 52):

> *Let that Courtly Epistle* [Oxford's 'Letter to the Reader' that prefaced the Latin translation of *The Courtier*]*—more polished even than the writings of Castiglione himself— witness how greatly thou dost excel in letters.*

[43] The heart of Castiglione's message was that the courtier had to affect a certain nonchalance—*sprezzatura*—(a word he coined, which has been absorbed into the English language) "to conceal all art and make whatever is done or said appear to be without effort and almost without any thought about it." Castiglione, Baldassare, *The Book of the Courtier: The Singleton Translation*, W. W. Norton, New York 2002, p.32.

men. Benedict (the son of a recently-deceased nobleman ordered by his king to marry a woman beneath him, hint, hint) makes Oxford's frustration clear in *All's Well That Ends Well* at being denied opportunity to acquire glory in battle:

> *I am commanded here, and kept a coil with*
> *'Too young' and 'the next year' and ''tis too early.'*
>
> ...
>
> *I shall stay here the forehorse to a smock,*
> *Creaking my shoes on the plain masonry,*
> *Till honour be bought up and no sword worn*
> *But one to dance with! By heaven, I'll steal away.*

Act II, Scene 1. And Oxford did steal away, running to the continent in the summer of 1574. The Queen yanked him back. Some think he may have been on a mission for Burghley or Walsingham to smoke out Catholic sympathizers. Clark, p. 116. The Queen did not punish him for leaving without her permission.

Elizabeth's comments about what she read to Sir Philip Sidney, that "a gentleman' neglect of nobility ... will result in the peasantry insulting us both," is derived from Fulke Greville's description of what he thinks is the Queen's attitude to Oxford and Sidney (Oxford being a lord and Sidney merely a knight): "[t]he Queen ... lays before him [Sidney] the difference in degree between Earls and Gentlemen; the respect inferiors [owed] to their superiors; and the necessity and Princes to maintain their own creations, has degrees descending between the people's licentiousness, and the anointed Sovereignty of Crowns: how the Gentleman's Neglect of the Nobility taught the Peasant to insult upon both." Nelson, p. 197. This exchange arose out of the "tennis court quarrel" between Oxford and Sidney in 1579 (Ogburns, pp. 186-189), which has been the subject of much scholarly noodling in trying to figure out who was the guilty party in this dispute and what it was about. *Shakespeare Matters* has had some interesting articles on this subject.

The Queen's comment that "[t]he heavens themselves ... observe degree, priority and place, proportion, season, form, office and custom, in all line of order," will reappear in *Troilus and Cressida*, Act I, Scene 3.

Oxford discovering Burghley behind the arras is a precursor (at least in fiction) to Hamlet stabbing Polonius hiding behind a similar hanging in *Hamlet.* As for Burghley's spying, see *The Reader's Companion* to Chapter 35.

"I am that I am, and I will serve myself first" is a paraphrase of a quote from a letter Oxford wrote Burghley from Italy, and is itself a paraphrase of 1st Corinthians 15.10 where Paul is explaining to the Corinthians that he is "the least of the apostles" but can tell them about Jesus and Jesus' resurrection because he, Paul, is filled with the grace of God :

> But by the grace of God *I am that I am*, and his grace which is in me, was not in vain; but I laboured more abundantly than they all, yet not I, but the grace of God which is with me.

The above quote comes from the Geneva Bible.[44] Oxford's copy of the Geneva Bible is in the Folger Library (of all places). They know it is Oxford's because of a receipt for it in Burghley's papers and Oxford's seal on the cover. 1st Corinthians 15:10 is underlined in Oxford's copy. Roger Stritmatter has written a doctoral thesis on the connections between the Geneva Bible and Oxford. The founder of the Folger Library bought the copy in 1925, which may indicate that he was aware that Shakespeare's claim to be the author of the plays was in doubt.

Paul was apparently remembering Exodus 3:14. In 3.13, Moses asks God what he should say when the Israelites ask him the name of

---

[44] The Geneva Bible was first published in 1560 by people who had fled England during Queen Mary's attempts to return England to the Catholic Church. Work on the King James Bible was not begun until 1604, the year of Oxford's death, and not issued until 1611, the year scholars believe Shakespeare retired to Stratford-upon-Avon. The King James Bible was based on the Bishops' Bible and the Great Bible ordered by Henry VIII. Both Bibles were large and difficult to read. Therefore, the Geneva Bible was the Bible everyone used during Elizabeth's reign. It was reprinted many times up to 1599 and was the favorite Bible of the English people for long after that. The Pilgrims took it with them to the new world in 1620. James had to ban it to get people to read his version, which was designed to reinforce the idea of the divine right of kings and eliminate the comments the editors of the Geneva Bible had added to the scriptures for the purpose of helping lay people understand them. The Geneva Bible did not "conform to the ecclesiology and reflect the episcopal structure of the Church of England and its beliefs about an ordained clergy." Daniell, David, *The Bible in English: its history and influence.* New Haven, Conn: Yale University Press (2003), p. 344.

God. In 3.14. God answers him: "And God said unto Moses, I AM THAT I AM [sic] …" [45]

Oxford used the phrase in a letter dated October 30, 1584 to Lord Burghley:

> "I mean not to be yowre ward nor yowre chyld, I server her magestie, and *I am that I am*, and by allyance neare to yowre lordship, but fre, and scorne to be offered that iniurie, to thinke I am so weake of gouernment as to be ruled by servants, or not able to gouerve my self." (Emphasis added.)

This is quoted more fully in Nelson, p. 294. Professor Nelson interprets this language to mean that Oxford is objecting to "Burghley's practice of treating Oxford's servants as if they were his [Burghley's] own." However, the operative words are "to be ruled by servants, or not able to govern myself." It seems that Oxford was objecting to being a servant of Burghley's, not to Burghley borrowing Oxford's servants without getting permission.

The more interesting question that Professor Nelson misses is what Oxford was intending when he used the phrase 'I am that I am.' The phrase brings with it considerable freight, based on its use in Corinthians and Exodus, particularly because Oxford omits the qualifying phrase used by Paul: "*But by the grace of God* I am that I am." Paul knew who he was because God allowed him to be God's spokesperson; it could be taken that Oxford was implying that he was above God.

It does not seem that Oxford wanted to impress upon Burghley that Oxford was filled with the grace of God and was, therefore, like Paul, someone special. Was Oxford referring to Exodus and claiming that he *was* God? Or was Oxford playing with Burghley, trying to rankle his religious father-in-law? There is no answer to this question, as with so many of Oxford's puns and allusions. But, given the context of the letter, it appears that Oxford was doing no more than reminding Burghley that he, Oxford, was a personage of significant importance who outranked Burghley.

---

[45] The King James version makes this "*I am what I am.*" Doubtless, scholars who understand "I am that I am" will understand the significance of the change to "I am what I am," whatever that might be.

The phrase 'I am that I am,' or a variation of it, appears in many places in the body of works attributed to William Shakespeare. Oxford (or Shakespeare?[46]) used the phrase in Sonnet 121:

'Tis better to be vile than vile esteem'd,
When not to be receives reproach of being,
And the just pleasure lost which is so deem'd
Not by our feeling but by others' seeing:
For why should others false adulterate eyes
Give salutation to my sportive blood?
Or on my frailties why are frailer spies,
Which in their wills count bad what I think good?
No, I am that I am, and they that level
At my abuses reckon up their own:
I may be straight, though they themselves be bevel;
By their rank thoughts my deeds must not be shown;
Unless this general evil they maintain,
All men are bad, and in their badness reign.

In *Lear.* Edmund says: "*I should have been that I am*, had the maidenliest star in the firmament twinked on my bastardizing." Act I, Scene 2.

In *King John,* Act I, Scene 1, the Bastard tells Queen Elinore "*I am I.*"

Madam, by chance but not by truth; what though?
Something about, a little from the right,
In at the window, or else o'er the hatch:
Who dares not stir by day must walk by night,
And have is have, however men do catch:
Near or far off, well won is still well shot,
And I am I, howe'er I was begot.

In Act V, Scene 3 of *Richard II*, Richard says "I am I," but his use of this phrase is an introduction into his great speech as he awakes from a dream in which he says: "Richard loves Richard; that is, I am I. Is there a murderer here? No. Yes, I am." This is similar to Antipholus

---

[46] This is one of those 'funny coincidences' Orson Welles was referring to when he said: "I think Oxford wrote Shakespeare. If you don't agree, there are some awfully funny coincidences to explain away."

of Syracuse's statement in *Comedy of Errors* that "But if I am I, then well I know your weeping sister is no wife of mine." Act III, Scene 2.

An interesting negative version shows up in *Twelfth Night,* where Viola says "*I am not what I am,*" Act III, Scene 1, and in *Othello,* where Iago says to Rodrigo: "*I am not what I am.*" Act I, Scene 1. In each play, the character speaking was *not* what he or she was: Viola was masquerading as a man; Iago was masquerading as a loyal servant to Othello while he plotted his master's downfall.

Oxford used the negative form of the phrase in one of his extant poems: "*I am not as I seem to be, nor when I smile I am not glad.*" Looney #14; Fuller #2 [*Not Attaining to his Desire he complaineth*] first printed in *Paradyse of Dainty Devices*, 1576 & updated in 1596 edition.

The use of the phrase *I am that I am*, without the qualifier Paul used, may be a significant insight into Oxford's mind. In *The Death of Shakespeare*, there is no implication that God is anywhere around when he speaks it to Burghley in front of the Queen. She could have chided him for leaving God out of his statement and misquoting the Bible but she has more important concerns at the time.

In *Venus & Adonis,* Venus tells Adonis that he doesn't have to worry about anyone finding out what they're up to because "these blue-vein'd violets whereon we lean/Never can blab, nor know not what we mean."

Elizabeth's comment that if had she married Oxford he would have been a sun and that, when the sun comes out, stars disappear, is based on a remark Toscanini allegedly made to a diva during the rehearsal of an opera. It was rumored that Toscanini was having an affair with the diva who objected to his direction during a rehearsal. She reportedly walked to the edge of the stage to inform him that she was a star. Toscanini replied that she was, but went on to say that, when the sun comes out, the stars cannot be seen.

Being your slave is the beginning of Sonnet 57.

Oxford's comment that the stage "is a universe away from poetry" may show he was aware of Giordano Bruno's ideas about multiple worlds. It is difficult to believe that Oxford would not have met with Bruno while Bruno was in England in the 1580s.

In 1564, Elizabeth was presented with a play by students at Hinchinbrook, on her way back from Cambridge, in which some of the students dressed as bishops. The Spanish ambassador reported: "*First came the Bishop of London, who was carrying a lamb in his hands as if he were eating it as he walked along, and then others with devices, one being the figure of a dog with [a] host in his mouth.*" Elizabeth was so angry that she "at once entered her chamber using strong language and the men who held the torches, it being night, left them [the players] in the dark, …" Hunter, at p. 148; also in *The Progresses, Pageants, and Entertainments of Queen Elizabeth I,* edited by Jayne Elisabeth Archer, Elizabeth Goldring, Sarah Knight, Oxford Univ. Press, 2007, p. vi. Another source for this quotation that can be read online: *The Great Lord Burghley (William Cecil): A Study in Elizabethan Statecraft*, by Martin Andrew Sharp Hume (1898), p. 147, accessed at:

> *https://books.google.com/books?id=GQDm3WqGk1oC&pg=PA148&lpg=PA148&dq=london+%22cecil+house%22&source=bl&ots=IJXBOD3cJ1&sig=VvWqSJhT9Dr82pA8BFl2Ruqxmvg&hl=en&sa=X&ei=E1I0VbSnEYGJgwST_4LACQ&ved=0CEkQ6AEwCQ#v=onepage&q=london%20%22cecil%20house%22&f=false.*

The Hitchinbrook incident reported by the Spanish ambassador may be the seed from which Oxford had Claudius cry out in *Hamlet,* '*Give me some light: away!*' Hunter sees a connection: "One is driven to wonder if any memory of the Hinchinbrook exit informed Claudius' angry exist from Hamlet's *Mousetrap.*" At p. 149. Oxford was one of a number who received degrees from Cambridge on Elizabeth's trip there and may have witnessed her exit with the torch bearers. Was this the seed for Claudius' call for light in *Hamlet*?.

Oxford's comment '*My name be buried where my body is*' is from Sonnet 72, which he may have penned the night the Queen told him he could write no more. (And why would Shakespeare write a sonnet that said his name would be buried where his body was?)

That Oxford was considered one of Elizabeth's foremost earls is not disputed. At the time Oxford went to Europe in 1575, the French ambassador, La Mothe de Fénelon, wrote the following: "…he is as it were the premier earl and Great Chamberlain of England, and thus the chief nobleman of the realm …" Nelson, p. 120.

Chapter 3
The Boar's Head Tavern – The Same Day

Henry VII formed the Yeomen of the Guard in 1485. They numbered 130 by 1578. Dovey, Zillah, *An Elizabethan Progress: The Queen's Journey into East Anglia, 1578,* Farleigh Dickinson Univ. Press (date of publication not given), p. 21. Sir Christopher Hatton was made Captain of the Yeomen of the Guard in 1578 and held the post until 1587 when the Queen made him Lord Chancellor. Gentlemen Pensioners also guarded the Queen. They were a mounted bodyguard created by Henry VIII and used mainly on ceremonial occasions. They carried a ceremonial gilt halberd. Dovey, *supra.* Dovey includes a charming sketch at page 11 made in 1575 of the royal barge being towed up the Thames by a pulling boat full of oarsmen with the royal barge surrounded by the halberds of the Gentlemen Pensioners.

The poem, *Fram'd in the front of forlorn hope,* is the beginning of an early poem of Oxford's. *Fuller's* #5 [*His good name being blemished he bewaileth*]; *JTL* #10. 1t was printed in *Paradyse of Dainty Devices*, 1576 and updated in the 1596 edition. It was probably written *circa* 1576 when Oxford came back to England after being absent for fourteen months and found out that he had become "the fable of the world" because word was out that his first wife had cuckolded him and he was not the father of his first child, Elizabeth.

There was more than one tavern named the Boar's Head in London at the end of the 16th century. The actual name is not mentioned in the plays. A stage direction added in 1733 introduced the name of the tavern, but all the early playgoers thought the tavern was the Boar's Head. The source for the name is not found in *The Famous Victories of Henry the Fift* either, although Prince Hal, when asked where they should go with the money they have stolen from the King's receivers, says:

Henry 5th:

> *Our hostes at Feuersham, blood what shal we do there?*
> *We haue a thousand pound about vs,*
> *And we shall go to a pettie Ale-house.*
> *No, no: you know the olde Tauerne in <u>Eastcheape</u>,*
> *There is good wine: besides, there is a pretie wench*
> *That can talke well, for I delight as much in their toongs,*
> *As any part about them. ...*

The "olde Tauerne in Eastcheape" was not a "pettie Ale-house," and it was noted for its "pretie wench that can talk well" and their "toongs." By 1654 a writer alluded to "Sir John of the Boar's Head in Eastcheap", and Decker refers to the "Bores-head" if not to Sir John in *The Shoemaker's Holiday*. Norman, Philip, *London Signs and Inscriptions*, London (1897), p. 52, *et seq*.

Given the fame the inn acquired in the plays, the location of the Boar's Head has been the subject of a great deal of research. (The fact that the boar was Oxford's emblem has been noted with quiet satisfaction by Oxfordians and quietly ignored by Stratfordians.) The inn that Shakespeare seems to be referring to in the Henry plays was on Eastcheap, a street that ran east-west paralleling the Thames River, and which became Candlewick Street further west. London streets, unlike streets in many other cities, often changed names as they crossed another street, even a minor one. The Boar's Head in Eastcheap was first mentioned in 1537. It burned in the Great Fire of 1666. Winter, *Shakespeare's England,* p. 173, thinks that the "statue of William IV in King Williams Street nearly marks the site of the old inn," but this is conjectural.

Modern maps of Elizabethan London are not reliable. While there is no doubt that there was a street named Eastcheap, and that it ran east to west parallel to the Thames, it is not known whether it was only to the east of the main north-south road from London Bridge to Bishopsgate or extended across the main road and became Candlewick Street.

Nashe's *Newes from Bartholomew Fayre* reports that there was a "Bore's Head, near London Stone." "*There hath been a great sale and utterance of wine / Besides beere, and ale, and ipocrass fine / But chiefly in Billingsgate at the Salutation / And the Bore's Head, near London Stone*." Quoted in *The Mirror of Literature, etc.*, Vol. XIX, J. Limbird, London (1832), p. 196.

Nashe places the Boar's Head "near London Stone." Stow, *A Survey of London,* reprinted from the text of 1603 in 1908 has the following comment at 1.24:

> *London stone*, Camden first suggested that it was 'a miliary like that in the Forum of Rome'. Wren (*Parentalia*, 265) at the time of the Great Fire formed the opinion, based on the discovery of extensive Roman remains, that 'by reason of the large foundation, it was rather some more considerable monument

in the Forum'. The position 'neare unto the channel' described by Stow would have been in the middle of the street. In 1742 it was removed to the kerb against the buildings on the north, and in 1798, being then reduced to a mere stump, was built into a niche in the wall of St. Swithin's Church. For the history of London Stone and theories as to its origin and significance see Lethaby *u. s.* pp. 179–84; J. E. Price, *Roman Pavement in Bucklersbury*, 55–65; and Gomme, *Governance of London.* In Stow's time London Stone was one of the countryman's sights in the capital; See, p. 310.

Nashe would seem to be a reliable source and the maps seem to indicate that the Boar's Head was near London Stone but Stow, at p. 217, says "there was no tauerne then in Eastcheape (at the time of Prince Hal's escapades).; In west cheap linnen cloth sold but no silkes spoken of.; Fripparia. Vpholders vpon Cornhill, sellers of olde apparell and household stuff, Eastcheape.; Candlewright or Candlewike street: wike is a working place.; Weauers in Candlewike streete. Weauers brought out of Flanders and Brabant.; S. Clements lane; parish church of S. Clement in Eastcheape.; Abchurch lane. Parish church of S. Marie Abchurch."

Some think the Boar's Head Inn referred to in the plays may have been outside Aldgate to the east of the City of London and north of the Tower area. Sisson, C. J., *The Boar's Head Theatre – An Inn-yard Theatre of the Elizabethan Age*, edited by Stanley Wells, (1972), argues that this was where the famous inn was located. The Privy Council referred to it in a letter in 1602 granting permission for the combined Oxford and Worcester companies to play there. p. 20. (This document is evidence that Oxford was still involved in the playhouses two years before his death in 1604.) There were other Boar's Head inns in the city, and it seems likely that the inn mentioned in 1604 as being outside Aldgate, which was to the east of Eastcheap and north of the Tower, was not the inn the author was referring to in *Famous Victories.* Nothing of importance seems to have occurred in the area outside Aldgate, as opposed to the events and buildings erected to the north such as the theaters outside Bishopsgate on the route north out of the City, fancy residences outside Cripplegate, and the traffic heading west out of London to Westminster through Newgate and Ludgate.

The Boar's Head in *The Death of Shakespeare* is near Oxford Court where most people in the 17th century believed the Boar's Head of the plays was located. When inns were used as playhouses, which was not uncommon even after the purpose-built theaters began to be built in 1576, the courtyard was used for performances, but there are no performances of plays at the fictional Boar's Head in *The Death of Shakespeare* and no mention of a courtyard. The floor paved with sheep knuckle bones is an idea taken from excavation of the Curtain Theater in 2012 where such a floor was found.

An interesting book on the subject is *The English Inn Past & Present A Review Of Its History and Social Life*, by A. E. Richardson & H. D. Eberlein, Benjamin Blom, New York/London, 1968, first published 1925. This slim volume is worth the copious photographs and drawings alone, and is a good example of how books were written, edited and printed when the publishing industry took pride in its work. Unfortunately, there is nothing in this book on the performance of plays, although Shakespeare and the Boar's Head are mentioned but only in relation to what innkeepers provided their patrons in the way of lodging, food, and drink.

Curiously, there are interesting comments in *The English Inn* about the Boar's Head that may confirm its existence inside the City. On page 11, the author states that the Boar's Head was located "by London Stone," a remark that may have been taken from Stow or a poem written in the reign of Charles I listing all the inns between Charing Cross and the Tower of London. The "Boreshead near London Stone," is listed as one such inn, but there is also the "Boreshead in Old Fish Street." The name was obviously popular (for obvious reasons, there is one in the Gad's Hill area of Kent and one over London Bridge in Southward, as noted below), but the location "near London Stone" may be an incorrect one even though London Stone was where Oxford Court was located. Old Fish Street, closer to the river, could also have been the location of the inn the author was thinking of. The description of the Boar's Head being near London Stone may be an example of how Oxford, Shakespeare, the plays, and the Boar's Head have been commingled in the collective subconscious of educated Britons. In any event, the Boar's Head in *The Death of Shakespeare* is located on Candlewick Street near London Stone (which still exists).

Sir Walter Raleigh (spelled, like Shakespeare's name, various ways, "Ralegh" apparently being the spelling preferred by the man himself) not only introduced the potato to Ireland (see *The Reader's Companion* 2) but tobacco to England. *The Story of Walter Ralegh: And a Day in a Tobacco Factory,* Hatton, Joseph, 1893, p. 275.

Sir John Falstaff is believed to be a fictional character in Shakespeare's plays. He may have been based on Captain Nicholas Dawtrey who fought for the Queen in Ireland. Ogburns, p. 706. Bullough has an extensive discussion of where Falstaff may have come from beginning at p. 76. Falstaff is a fictional character in *The Death of Shakespeare.* However, there was at least one Sir John Falstaff living in London at the time. Spelling his name "Falstoffe," he ran an inn in Southwark across the Thames called "The Boar's Head." Sadly, the sites of both taverns (the one on Eastcheape and the one in Southwark) now lie under the approaches to London Bridge. Norman, p. 59-60. Was Falstaff real, and did he retire when he got older to run a Boar's Head in Southwark? Not in Part One of *The Death of Shakespeare.*

There is a John Falstoffe in *The Famous Victories of Henry V* and a John Falstoffe in *Henry VI, Part 1.*

The description of the color of Sir John's face as the satin brown of a bruised medlar comes from the text and comments made on page 374 and in footnote 31, page 425, in Jean Anthelme Brillat-Savarin's *Physioligie de gout,* published in 1826 which was translated in 1949 as *The Physiology of Taste* by M.F.K. Fisher. Brillat-Savarin was discussing the interesting fact that "*[e]very substance has its peak of deliciousness: some of them have already reached it before their full development, like capers, asparagus, young grey partridges, and squab pigeons; others reach it at that precise moment when they are all that it is possible for them to be in perfection, like melons and almost all fruits, mutton, beef, venison, and red partridges; and finally still others at that point when they begin to decompose, like medlars, woodcock, and above all pheasant.*"

Brillat Savarin was referring to the process of decay as accentuating or improving the taste of fruit or game, as any hunter knows when it comes to venison. In footnote 31, page 425, Ms. Fisher fastens on the mention of medlars and notes that "this apple-like fruit was another name for a loquat, which I doubt, and that it is now very rare, which I do not doubt." She claims that they were the only thing she ever stole as a child because she was so in love with the taste of this "beautiful bruised fruit" which was best eaten when it began to smell. Ms. Fisher quotes Shakespeare's use of the word in *As You Like It.* Touchstone sees Rosalind reading a letter from Orlando which she has found on a tree (Act I, Scene 2):

Rosalind:

From the east to western Ind, No jewel is like Rosalind.
Her worth, being mounted on the wind,
Through all the world bears Rosalind.
All the pictures fairest lined
Are but black to Rosalind.
Let no fair be kept in mind
But the fair of Rosalind.

Touchstone objects to this as bad poetry (Shakespeare was obviously having it on with another poet here) and mimics her:

Touchstone:

Sweetest nut hath sourest rind,
Such a nut is Rosalind.
He that sweetest rose will find
Must find love's prick and Rosalind.
This is the very false gallop of verses: why do you infect yourself with them?

Rosalind:

Peace, you dull fool! I found them on a tree.

Touchstone:

Truly, the tree yields bad fruit.

Rosalind:

I'll graff it with you, and then I shall graff it with a medlar: then it will be the earliest fruit i' the country; for you'll be rotten ere you be half ripe, and that's the right virtue of the medlar.

The word 'medlar' appears in *Timon of Athens* and *Romeo and Juliet* as well so they were well-known in the 16th century and probably a favorite of the author.

Peaches Bottomsup is a fictional character in *The Death of Shakespeare,* just as Doll Tearsheet is in the plays.

The *Lucy is lousie* poem about Sir Thomas Lucy can be read at Sams, p. 206-207; Globe, p. 2332, fn. 32. Sir Thomas lived at Charlecote Hall, still in existence a few miles north of Stratford. The poetry recited by Shackspear is from a poem allegedly made by

Shakespeare and based on the anecdote that Shakespeare went to London to get away from Sir Thomas because Shakespeare had been poaching Sir Thomas' deer. Even Schoenbaum has difficulty accepting the story, not the least because there were no deer kept at Sir Thomas' estate at Charlecote at the time. Schoenbaum, *A Compact Documentary Life* p. 97-109.

The Poacher of Arden Forest that Shackspear will write in *The Death of Shakespeare* is fiction, and will be based on the claim (reluctantly recognized by even Stratfordian scholars as apocryphal) that Shakespeare was driven out of Stratford because he had to poach Sir Thomas' deer in order to feed his family. Sams, p. 206-210.

Oxford's troupe of actors visited Stratford in the 1583-1584 season. Schoenbaum, p. 115. Professor Nelson lists that they played at Coventry but not at Stratford, although the absence of a record is not proof they did not play at Stratford. Hamnet was born in 1585. The Queen's Men visited Stratford in 1587 and received the highest amount ever paid to a traveling company of actors performing in Stratford (20 shillings). Sams, p. 58. Four other acting troupes visited Stratford that year in addition to the Queen's Men: Essex's Men, Leicester's Men, Lord Stafford's Men, and another unnamed group (Oxford's?). Schoenbaum, p. 115.

William Knell had been killed earlier in the year. Schoenbaum asks: "Before leaving Stratford, had they enlisted Shakespeare, then aged twenty-three, as their latest recruit [to replace Knell]?" P. 90. You can almost hear the pleading in the good professor's voice: the theater bus to London went right through Stratford in 1587; Shakespeare *had* to be on it. Whether he was will never be known. On the other hand, Knell's widow did marry John Heminges, he of First Folio fame. See, *The Reader's Companion* to Chapter 32, Christmas at the Boar's Head.

Stratfordians have had to admit that many of the facts and stories about Shakespeare were fabrications that the 18th century produced when Shakespeare was rediscovered.[47] Even Marchette Chute, author of *Shakespeare of London*, had to reluctantly admit that most of the stories that came out of 18th century England about Shakespeare were fiction. "Edmund Malone, …one of the first, and one of the greatest, of the real Shakespearean scholars, … bitterly [had to admit that] that

---

[47] Sams, p. 206.

Nicholas Rowe had made eleven statements about Shakespeare's life and eight of them could be proven to be false." One of these stories he rejected was the deer-poaching tale. Sir Thomas had no deer. Sic transit one Shakespearean fable. Another was the horse-holding story that Will was some kind of Avis "I'll park your horse, sir" young man when he came to London. (Now you know where the idea came from in *Shakespeare in Love* for the Earl of Wessex to hand the reins to his horse to Mr. Fenniman, the 'money' and the apothecary in the play, as the Earl jumped off his horse and ran into the theater looking for Viola, his new wife.) *See,* Schoenbaum's discussion of many of these stories beginning at p. 196.

Why did Ms. Chute use the adjective "bitterly" in describing how hard it was for Malone to admit most of the information about Shakespeare was false? Because those who believe William wrote the plays are desperate for anything that will put flesh on Will Shakespeare's bones. They will never succeed, however, because William did not write the plays.

There is no support in the historical record that Shakespeare's son was named Hamnet because Shakespeare mistakenly believed that *Hamlet* was spelled *Hamnet.* (Although even Anthony Burgess, an avowed Stratfordian who dismisses any claim that Shakespeare did not write the plays attributed to him, comments that "Hamlet and Hamnet were interchangeable [in Elizabethan times as names for boys]." *Shakespeare*, Alfred A. Knopf, New York 1970. Burgess gives no citation to support this claim.)

In fact, it appears that Shakespeare's son was named after his good friend, Hamnet Sadler.[48] However, Oxford's players visited Stratford

---

[48] William Corbett, in an email on August 16, 2013, said that, "William Shakespeare's twins were named after his next-door neighbors Hamlette and Judith Sadler. Hamlet Sadler was christened at Solihull on 23rd March 1560 as 'Hamlette Sadler'. Not one single person has ever got this correct because nobody bothered to check the birth records for Solihull where it is clearly stated that he was christened 'Hamlette Sadler'. This myth that his son was called Hamnet is all because a clerk looped the bottom of his L and it looks like an N." Mr. Corbett appears to be right. 'Hamlet' was a fairly common name, as is shown by the fact that, in 1573, Oxford was paying an annuity to a Hamlet Fryer (Pearson, p. 222) and that Michael Hicks, secretary to Lord Burghley and facilitator to Sir Robert Cecil, was dealing with a Hamlet Clark in 1612. Hicks, p. 130.

in 1584,[49] and Shakespeare may have been bitten by the bug when he saw a play there. Shakespeare would have been 22 at the time and about to become the father of a son and daughter. Most scholars think Shakespeare left Stratford shortly after his twin children were born in 1585 (February 2).[50]

Others have noticed the similarity between "Shake-Spear" and "Fall-Staff." Akrigg, p. 246. "Many critics have pointed to the wordplay that is parallel: Fall/staff; Shake/spear." Bloom, p. 273. Thus, Oxford's comment to Falstaff as they are leaving the Boar's Head after having just met Shackspear. Falstaff rightly objects to the comparison.

As far as anyone knows, the name Sir John Falstaff was created by the author of *Henry IV*. However, the character in the play was originally named Sir John Oldcastle and was apparently changed to Sir John Falstaff at the request of the Brooke family when William Brooke, 7th Lord Cobham, succeeded Lord Hunsdon as Lord Chamberlain in charge of the plays. Oldcastle was an ancestor of Lord Cobham and was much revered by the Protestants because he had been executed for his beliefs. Cobham's daughter, Elizabeth Brooke, had married Sir Robert Cecil on August 31, 1589. In *Part Two*, Falstaff will suggest to Oxford that his name replace Oldcastle's to avoid any future complaints that the fat knight was defaming someone's ancestor.

The relationship between the Earl of Oxford and the *Edward Bonaventure* is a long one. Although Dorothy Ogburn claims at page 229 that Oxford bought a ship in 1581, the written record only shows that there was an offer made to purchase it, not documentation of a sale. Nelson, p. 188-189. Matus flatly states that the ship was purchased by others. Furthermore, it appears that the *Edward Bonaventure* was not involved in a shipwreck on Bermuda; it was lost off the southern coast of the Dominican Republic after it had been hijacked by some of its crewmembers while revictualizing nearby. One of the sailors left behind was Henry May, who was shipwrecked on

---

[49] Sams, p. 210. Oxford's Men were performing in Stratford in 1583-4. Schoenbaum, p. 95. Hamnet was born the following year. No one has [yet] claimed that Oxford was his father.

[50] February 2, 1585. Hamnet died in 1596; Judith died in 1662. Sams, p. 211.

Bermuda after he had gotten passage on a French ship in an attempt to get back to England. Nelson, p. 158-160, citing Julian S. Corbett, *Papers Relating to eh Navy During the Spanish War, 1585-1587,* ([London]: Navy Records Society, 1898), xx; and Kenneth R. Andrews, *English Privateering: English Privateering During the Spanish War, 1585-1603* (Cambridge: University Press, 1964), 210, 214-215.

Everyone seems to agree that the *Edward Bonaventure* participated in the defeat of the Spanish Armada, and was apparently under the command of a James Lancaster, who may have been in command when the ship was lost off the Dominican Republic in 1593. Matus, p. 159. Ogburn says that the indexes of ships in the National Maritime Museum of London disclose the following references to the *Edward Bonaventure*: a merchant vessel sailing with the Turkey Company; engaging the Spanish in November, 1585, and against the Armada in 1588; and participating in the first successful British voyage to India and back in 1591-93. At p. 741, fn. 2.

The reference to the Turkey Company is interesting because the Queen called Oxford her "Turk," among other nicknames.

A letter from Leicester to Walsingham from Tilbury on August 1, 1588, has Oxford at Tilbury and refusing to take command of Harwich, a seaport on the English Channel that was in Essex, Oxford's part of England. Whether he was on board any of the ships is unclear. Professor Nelson lays out interesting facts that show Lord Burghley took the time to pen drafts of a pamphlet to add Oxford as participating in the fight against the Armada. P. 315. The purpose was to convince the Spanish that there were no earls of Catholic persuasion who had failed to support the Queen against the Armada. This does not mean, however, that Oxford was not part of the fleet. In fact, a long ballad, which seems to have been written by John Lyly, put Oxford on a ship:

> *De Vere, whose fame and the loyalty hath pearst*
> *The Tuscan clime, and through the Belgike lands*
> *By winged fame for valour is rehearst,*
> *Like warlike Mars upon the hatches stands,*
> *His tusked Boar 'gan foam for inward ire,*
> *When Pallas filled his breast with warlike fire.*

In conclusion, there is no hard evidence that Oxford did or did not take part in the battle against the Spanish Armada. The letter from Leicester implies that Oxford was in the fleet: He "... was with me as he went [sic], and returnyd ageyn yesterday by me with Captain Huntley in his company he seemed only his voyag was to have gonn, to my lord Admyrall, & at his retourn seemed also to retorn agayn hether to me this day from London whether [=wither] he went yesternight for his armour & furnyture." (Emphasis added.) As with most Elizabeth letters, this one is difficult to understand, but it seems that he went to the "lord Admyrall" and returned. Unless the Lord Admiral was on land at the time, it seems Oxford was out in the fleet. July 28 was the date the fire ships were sent into the Spanish ships at Calais, so it appears that Oxford was not present to take part in that action.

Leicester's letter, however, does support a view that Oxford was not afraid to risk his life. He had shown this part of his character in his earlier forays in the earlier Northern Rebellion. Leicester concludes his July 28 letter with a back-handed compliment, almost with a tone admiration, when he writes: "I trust he be fre to goe to the enymy for he semes most wylling to hazard his life in this quarrell." Nelson, p. 316; Dorothy Ogburn, p. 774.

In a second letter, Leicester reports that Oxford first accepted command of Harwich, and then rejected it, vowing to go off to see the Queen and get something better. Professor Nelson, unable to accept the arrogance of an earl who was both gifted in many areas (Oxford won the tournament in front of the Queen against all comers on two separate occasions ten years apart, for example, so he was not just a poet who languished at second-story windows as life went by) and the seventeenth in a long line of distinguished forbears, concludes: "Thus Oxford positively refused a post in the Armada campaign …" P. 318. Oxford refused Harwich, but there is no proof he refused other commands. Professor Nelson has to admit, teeth grinding, that Oxford "was not only excused his dereliction, but lionized as revealed in a ballad celebrating a service of Thanksgiving at St. Paul's Cathedral [on November 24, 1588]." To Nelson's dismay and obvious disappointment, "[a] contemporary plan confirms the seating arrangements at St. Paul's." P. 319. Bad-boy Edward was apparently not as bad as Professor Nelson thinks he was, and these facts do not fit in with his thesis, announced clearly on page 14 of his book, that Oxford was a trouble-maker.

Lady Mary Sidney, Countess of Pembroke, was Philip Sidney's sister and an author in her own right. She was also the mother of the two learned brethren to whom the 1623 First Folio was dedicated. Her youngest son, the Earl of Montgomery, married Susan de Vere, Oxford's youngest daughter. See, the Pembroke Lineage chart in the appendix to *the Death of Shakespeare.*

Lady Mary was a poet and translator in her own right and considered the most prominent women of letters in England. In the fall of 1603, Lady Mary wrote to her son, the Earl of Pembroke (one of the two dedicatees of the First Folio) that she had "the man Shakespeare" at Wilton, her country estate. Her son was with King James and she urged him to bring the king to Wilton. Schoenbaum, p. 167. It is thought that *As You Like It* was put on there for James. The king did visit Wilton for a few days at the end of August. No one knows where Shakespeare was at the time.

A "kickshaw" was an appetizer. The word is believed to be a corruption of the French "quelquechose." Segan, Francine, *Shakespeare's Kitchen – Renaissance Recipes for the Contemporary Cook,* Random House, New York, 2003, p. 4. Thus: "Gentlemen, the world is so nice in these our times … for diet none but the French kickshaws that are delicate …." Introduction to *The Knight of the Burning Pestle,* Francis Beaumont and John Fletcher, circ 1607-1610, p. 1.

Chapter 4
Cecil House – The Next Day

Oxford arrived in London in 1562 at the age of twelve to take up residence at Cecil House as a ward of William Cecil.[51] Cecil House was described as "verie fayre … raysed with brickes, proportionable adorned with four turrets placed at the four corners of the howse." *Harl. MS. 570*, quoted in H. B. Wheatley, *London Past and Present*, London 1891, which is quoted in Akrigg at p. 23. In 1999, a colored site plan of Cecil House on the

---

[51] Actually, Oxford was a ward of the Queen, not Burghley. She handed Oxford over to Burghley, who would control his personal life, including who he would marry. The Queen gave the property Oxford had inherited from his father to the Earl of Leicester, the Queen's lover at the time, to "guard" it until Oxford came of age. Leicester was virtually penniless at the time, his father having been attainted and executed. It seems obvious that the Queen did this to bolster the finances of her new lover at the expense of Oxford's, who was only twelve at the time and not yet the focus of the Queen's attention.

Strand was discovered at Burghley House (Burghley's grand estate at Stamford north of London), which has been dated to the mid-1560s when Oxford was living there (1562-1571). An article explaining the valuable information provided by this discovery and a colored copy of the site plan can be read at *http://www.deveresociety.co.uk/articles/NL-2013june-cole-CecilHouse.pdf.* The site plan follows:

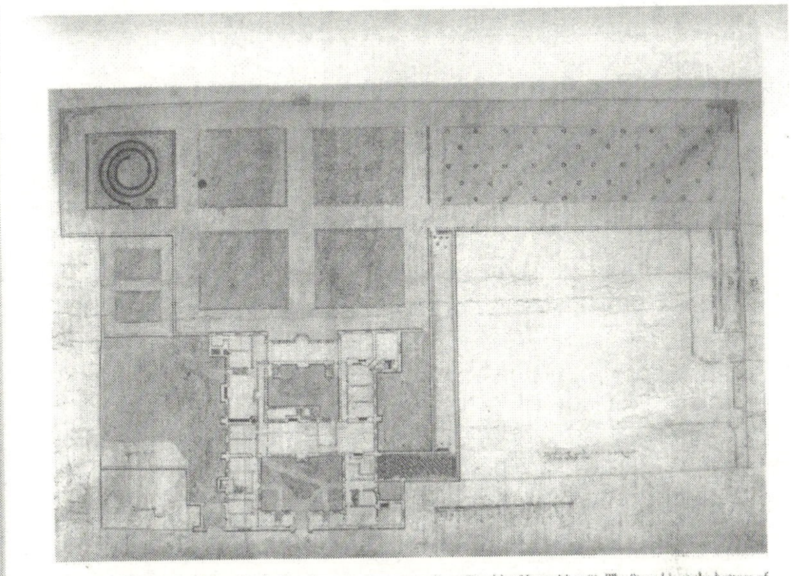

9 Plan of William Cecil's house in the Strand, executed between 1562–5 (Burghley House M 358). The Strand is at the bottom of the plan. To the left is a service court with a track for carts and a path leading to the kitchen and gardens. To the right of the house is the sports' complex with a tennis court and bowling alley. To the far right is Cecil's stable. At the top are the gardens with a spiral mount enclosed by a wall, a quadripartite central garden and an orchard planted in quincunxes. The garden buildings, which would be replaced in 1567, overlooked the open fields of 'Convent garden'. The parts of the plan that are left plain represent property that Cecil did not own. Burghley House

Oxford arrived at the head of four-score (80) men on horseback. He was also escorted by 100 yeomen dressed in reading tawney with a blue boar on their left shoulders who were wearing gold chains. (Stow says 180 men; Machyn says 140. Nelson, p. 34.) 80 servants staffed the house. The Ogburns, p. 26; p. 575. It was claimed that Cecil House cost Burghley £2,000 a year to staff and operate. Ward, p. 258

William Cecil was knighted by the Earl of Northumberland in 1551 and made Baron Burghley in 1571 by Queen Elizabeth. Thus, after 1571, William Cecil was no longer referred to as Sir

William Cecil but Lord Burghley. It seems that people continued to refer to Burghley's house on the Strand as 'Cecil House,' and will be referred to as 'Cecil House' in *the Death of Shakespeare.*

Southampton complains about the rigorous schedule wards had to put up with when they entered Cecil House. The activities started at 7 a.m. They included two sessions each of Latin and French plus writing, drawing, cosmography, and exercises with pen and paper. Nelson, p. 37. Other scholars love to quote the "Orders for the Earl of Oxfords Exercises" that Burghley drew up in his own hand as an example of how rigorous an education Burghley gave his wards. There were private tutors, and the education was better than any school in England. Oxford took advantage of this opportunity. What he learned at Cecil House became the bedrock on which he built everything he produced during his life. Southampton, however, did not take advantage of the opportunities Burghley placed in front of him. The evidence seems to support the same conclusion as to the other young men who were swept into Burghley's home.

Lady Mary was Mary Herbert, neé Mary Sidney, Philip Sidney's sister and the Countess of Pembroke. She was the doyenne of the literary world. She usually lived on her estate at Wilton where she patronized poets and writers, including Ben Jonson, and translated works from French. Her two sons, William Herbert, the Earl of Pembroke (after his father's death in 1601) and Philip Herbert, Earl of Montgomery, were the "Most Noble and Incomparable Brethren" to whom the First Folio would be dedicated in 1623. Lady Mary usually stayed at Pembroke House along the Thames when she was in London; placing her in Cecil House as if she had no London residence of her own does her a disservice in order that she may speak with Oxford early on in *The Death of Shakespeare.*

Dover Wilson speculates that Lady Mary commissioned Shakespeare's first seventeen sonnets, most of which are directed at a young man and urge him to procreate. *The Oxford Companion to Shakespeare,* p. 229. At Burghley's urging in *The Death of Shakespeare,* Oxford writes these sonnets to the Earl of Southampton urging him to marry Oxford's daughter, Lisbeth.

Oxford's mother was Margery Golding. Her hasty remarriage is thought to be reflected in Gertrude's hasty marriage after Hamlet's father dies. The effect of being abandoned by his mother must have had an effect upon Oxford. For comparison, consider how the author of *The Private Character of Queen Elizabeth* sums up the affect upon Elizabeth of finding out that her father had disowned her and murdered her mother (p.28):

> *[W]hat must have been the impressions of the daughter of this man [Henry VIII] who had murdered her mother?—a daughter, as somebody has said, not only motherless but worse than fatherless. … The effect must indeed have been tremendous. The shock of it must for ever have altered the whole outlook of the child [Elizabeth]. It must have sobered and saddened Elizabeth all through her youth, and could not have been long absent from her mind at any time in her after-life. These sad truths undoubtedly played a prominent part among the forces which now assailed and beat her down into what is most formative of character, protracted ill-health—with its introspection, its demand on patients, its melancholy, its disillusionment, its discovery of forces beyond human control; to which we may add in the case of Elizabeth, a deep sense of shame, of wrong, and of mortification. We may be certain that a child who had such a history could not have been like an average child of average parentage. We are compelled to expect something extraordinary.*

Hamlet seems like it was Oxford's way of dealing with his abandonment by his mother.

Margery Golding's brother was Arthur Golding, who left a large body of work behind him. He did many translations, including those of John Calvin's sermons, and was apparently a Puritan sympathizer. His translation of Ovid's *Metamorphoses* contained many racy passages that have puzzled scholars since they seem to be out of character for the man, and the text he was translating. Golding was Oxford's tutor at the time he was translating Ovid in Cecil House. As Burghley suggests in Chapter 4, Oxford may have done more than just hang over Golding's shoulder while his uncle translated Ovid.

A biography of Golding was published in 1937 by Louis Thorn Golding[52] which contains valuable information about Golding the translator and his times. Golding (the translator) was highly praised by his contemporaries (*See*, *An Elizabethan Puritan*, p. 202, *et seq.*) and by Ezra Pound, among others, in modern times. See, the discussion beginning at p. 207 in *An Elizabethan Puritan*.

Golding's translation of Ovid is the source used more than any other in the plays attributed to William Shakespeare. *The Cambridge History of English and American Literature*, Volume IV. Prose and Poetry, I, § 11, at page 24, has the following to say of Golding's *Ovid*:

> The chief characteristic of the translation is its evenness. It never falls below or rises above a certain level.[53] The craftsmanship is neither slovenly nor distinguished. The narrative flows through its easy channel without the smallest shock of interruption. In other words, the style is rapid, fluent and monotonous. The author is never a poet and never a shirk. You may read his mellifluous lines with something of the same simple pleasure which the original gives you. Strength and energy are beyond Golding's compass, and he wisely chose a poet to translate who made no demand upon the qualities he did

---

[52] *An Elizabeth Puritan*. Richard R. Smith, New York (1937). The author is sometimes referred to by other scholars as L. T. Golding.

[53] It may be of interest to compare the description of Golding's translation with Roger Ascham's description of Queen Elizabeth at age sixteen: "She very much admires metaphors when they are not too strained, and the use of antithesis when it is warranted and may be employed with good effect. Her attention is practiced in the discrimination of all these things, and her judgment is so sound, that in all Greek, Latin, or English prose or verse there is nothing loose on the one hand or concise upon the other that she does not at once notice it and condemn it strongly or praise it earnestly, as the case may be.".

not possess. He chose a metre, too, very apt for continuous narrative—the long line of fourteen syllables—and it is not strange that his contemporaries bestowed upon him their high approval.

http://www.bartleby.com/214/0111.html

Golding's only known original work is presented at p. 199 in *An Elizabethan Puritan*, a commendatory introduction to *Barrets Alvearie* (1580). A brief glimpse of one of the stanzas suggests that Golding must have been helped by a more creative mind when he translated the *Metamorphoses* into English:

> *And Barret here (good Reader) doth present*
> *A Hyve of honie to they gentle hand,*
> *By tract of time in painefull labor spent:*
> *Well wrought, and brought to such perfection and*
> *Good Purpose, as (if truth be rightly scand)*
> *Thou art to blame, but if you be his deter*
> *Of earned thankes, and fare by him the better.*

Professor Nelson has no problem with Golding's translation: "Margery's half-brother Arthur, born in 1536, would achieve lasting fame as an Elizabethan man of letters, his professed Puritanism well disguised in his sensuous translation of Ovid's *Metamorphoses.*" Nelson, p. 10

Scholars agree that Shakespeare borrowed more from Golding's translation than from any other book. An interesting Ph.D. thesis would be an analysis of the slippages between the formal Latin in the original *Metamorphoses* and the flamboyant phrasing of Golding's translation. Perhaps the author of the plays was not borrowing from Ovid but from himself!

The book Burghley offers Oxford is the *Essais* by Michel de Montaigne. They consist of three books published in 1580, 1588, and 1595. (Montaigne died in 1593.)

Oxford's daughter, Lisbeth, ended up marrying the Earl of Derby, William Stanley. Oxford's second daughter, Bridget married Francis Norris, Baron of Rycote, who shows up in Dr. Simon Forman's notebooks in 1601. Cook, p. 151. Oxford's third daughter, Susan, married William's brother Philip in 1604 and was still alive when the First Folio was published in 1623. See, Oxford Lineage Chart in *The Death of Shakespeare, Part One.*

Oxford's description of his daughter Lisbeth's eyes and protruding nether lip is based on his portraits (see two portraits of Oxford following p. 134 in Anderson, one of which is the cover of *The Death of Shakespeare*) and Falstaff's description of Prince Hal (Oxford) in Act II, Scene 4, of *Henry IV – Part One*:

> *That thou art my son, I have*
> *partly thy mother's word, partly my own opinion,*
> *but chiefly a villanous trick of thine eye and a*
> *foolish-hanging of thy nether lip, that doth warrant me.*

Colin Sanderson is fiction. In real life, Burghley's father, Richard Cecil, had so against William marrying Mary Cheke that he removed William from Cambridge and started making plans to disinherit him. However, Mary, who gave birth to Thomas, Burghley's oldest son, died shortly after Thomas' birth. (Did Burghley marry Mary because he had gotten her pregnant?) Burghley soon married Mildred Cooke, who was a well-educated woman. She gave Burghley Nan, Oxford's wife, and Robert, who would succeed his father in running England.

Anne de Vere, neé Cecil, died of a 'debilitating fever' at Greenwich Palace on June 5, 1588. She did not die at Hatfield House, as her daughter, Lisbeth, claims in *The Death of Shakespeare.* Anne was thirty-two, having married Oxford at fifteen. She had given birth to five children; two sons, both of whom died soon after birth, and three daughters who survived. Professor Nelson has the inscription on her tomb at Westminster Abbey at p. 309. She is credited by some with having written poems on the loss of her sons that are quite touching. Moody, Ellen, *English Literary Renaissance*, 19 (1989) as "Six Elegiac Poems, Possibly by Anne Cecil de Vere, Countess of Oxford" (with texts), pp. 152-70. See, Ms. Moody's reply to comments by other scholars on whether Anne Cecil wrote the plays attributed to her at *http://digilib.gmu.edu/xmlui/bitstream/handle/1920/1005/anne.cecil.poems.html?sequence=1.*

Chapter 5
November 24, 1588 – St. Paul's Cathedral

The Queen's celebratory march into London and the service at St. Paul's occurred on November 24, 1588. Anderson, p. 228, 229; Ogburn, p. 709, 810; Dorothy Ogburn, p. 777, 778. Sonnet 125 begins: *Were 't aught to me I bore the canopy.* There were few occasions that Oxford could have borne the canopy over the Queen. He was only eight when she was crowned in 1558, and he participated in only one coronation in his lifetime, that of King James in 1603. Unless Sonnet 125 was written after 1603, he probably bore the canopy in 1588 on the way to St. Paul's.

Stratfordians have difficulty explaining this reference to bearing the canopy in Sonnet 125, much less references in other sonnets, such as this part of # 76:

> *Why write I still all one, ever the same,*[54]
> *And keep invention in a noted weed,*[55]

---

[54] The Earl of Southampton's motto was 'un par tout, tout par un' (one for all, all for one). Queen Elizabeth's motto was "semper eadem," which is usually translated as "always the same" (not "ever the same"). The Earl of Oxford's motto was "vero nihil verius" which means "nothing but the truth" or "the truth, nothing but the truth." The Ogburns in *Star of England*, argue at p. 893, that Oxford 'brings the august trio together: himself, the Queen, and their son.' As with so much in the plays and sonnets, words carry multiple meanings. 'I still all one' not only brings in Elizabeth's motto but says *sotto voce* that the three of them are all 'one.' Or, to put it another way, "ever the same" is Elizabeth's motto "always the same" tweaked to sneak Oxford into the middle between Southampton ("one for all, all for one" or "all one") and Elizabeth. Some Oxfordians think Sonnet 76 was written after the Earl found out he was the father of Southampton.

[55] 'Weed' is a word used for clothes in Elizabethan times: 'Let us hence, and put on other weeds.' *Much Ado About Nothing*, Act V, Scene 3. The author may have used the word 'noted' to modify 'weed' to mean 'recognizable or well-known,' as Salisbury uses it in *King John,* Act Iv, Scene 2, '*the antique and well noted face.*' Shakespeare appears to be the "weed" who has become

That every word doth almost tell my name,[56]
Showing their birth[57] *and where they did proceed?*

or this part of Sonnet 110:

Alas, 'tis true I have gone here and there
And made myself a motley[58] *to the view,*
Gored mine own thoughts, sold cheap what is most dear.

or this part of Sonnet # 72:

My name be buried where my body is.[59]

It is doubtful that Oxford carried the Sword of State in the 1588 procession. He had that duty during coronations. Given his age and 'lameness,' it is doubtful he carried the sword in James' coronation, the only coronation that took place during his life. It appears that the Lord Marquis carried the sword in 1588. Ward, at p. 295, has a diagram of the role played by each participant. Oxford is said to have been mounted on a spirited horse in front of the Queen in the procession. He did carry the Sword of State at the opening of Parliament in February, 1589. See, the ballad quoted by Ward at p. 294 in which Oxford is described as '*The noble Earl of Oxford then High Chamberlain of England / Rode right before Her Majesty his bonnet in his hand.*'

'recognizable or well-known' in which the author keeps his 'invention,' i.e., the plays.

[56] Why would Shakespeare need to write that his '*every word doth almost tells my name*' or that he hides his '*invention*' (imagination, creative faculty — '*O for a Muse of fire, that would ascend the brightest heaven of invention,' As You Like It,* Act II, Scene *5*) '*in a noted weed?*' Why does the man from Stratford need to hide anything? He was the author, wasn't he? Wasn't he?

[57] And '*showing* [the] *birth* [of his words],' i.e., where his words came from?

[58] 'Motley' is a fool: '*Will you be married, motley*?" Jacques to Touchstone. *All's Well That Ends Well,* Act II, Scene 7.

[59] Why does Shakespeare lament that his name would be buried where his body lay?

Sir Robert Cecil, Burghley's son, succeeded his father as Lord Treasurer and was elevated by King James to the peerage as the Earl of Somerset, and died in 1612, fourteen years after his father. Cecil was physically unattractive, if not deformed, but very intelligent, even, some of his enemies would admit, brilliant. He was born in 1563, the year after Oxford moved into Cecil House as a ward. Cecil was only eight when Oxford left Cecil House but they must have interacted. Their letters later in life show Oxford expressing good feelings toward Cecil and Cecil sometimes helping Oxford but it is more probable than not that Cecil couldn't stand Oxford for the way Oxford treated Cecil's sister and Oxford's three daughters. Burghley had taken in the three girls after Nan had died in 1588. The oldest, Elizabeth, had been married off before Burghley died in 1598, but the two others were still minors. Burghley's will gave guardianship of them to Robert Cecil and had bequeathed them all the goods, money, plate, and valuables remaining in his bed-chamber in Cecil House. In a letter to Michael Hickes shortly after Burghley died, Cecil wrote the following:

> "Tell Mr. Bellot [who, with the dean of Westminster, were to determine what goods were included in the bequest], if the earl of Oxford should desire the custody [of his daughters], <u>he can not have them of anybody ... Whether he that never gave them [a] groat, [and] hath a second wife and another child, be a fit guardian, consider you</u> ... I wish Mr. Bellot to have good care they be not stolen away by his means When you are there I pray you take order with my wardrober, that any stuff they want or anything else may be given them." (Emphasis added.) Hickes, p. 135.

This makes clear what Cecil thought of Oxford. In *The Death of Shakespeare*, Burghley's machinations to trick Cecil into believing Oxford had prevented Cecil from marrying the woman he loved is fiction.

Chapter 6
Oxford Court - The Same Day

The London home of the earls of Oxford was located near London Stone,[60] which lay in the middle of Candlewick Street.[61] London Stone had been the center of London since it was placed there by the Romans, the starting point for measuring distances to other places in the Roman province of Britannia. It is famous for being the stone Jack Cade strikes in *Henry VI - Part 2* (with his sword in the 1594 Quarto, with his staff in the 1623 First Folio) when he and his rebels take London. Act IV, Scene 6. After the great fire of 1666, London Stone was moved to St. Swithin's church across the street, at the corner of Candlewick and St. Swithin's Lane. St. Swithin's was destroyed in 1941 in the blitz. The Stone was moved back across the street and is now embedded in a display box in the front of a bank near where Oxford Court once stood.

Ward quotes Stow at p. 49 that Oxford Court was sold to Sir John Hart but Stow does not specify when. Stow was published in 1598, so Oxford Court had been sold by then. Nelson, p. 97. Ward claims Oxford Court "was Lord Oxford's principal London dwelling until 1589, when Sir John Hart [an alderman] bought it," but does not identify his source. Ward, p. 49. Professor Nelson claims that Ward's reference "incorrectly identifies [Oxford Court by London Stone] as 'Lord Oxford's

---

[60] Nelson identifies Oxford Court as 'Vere House,' as does Ogburn, p. 712. Ogburn's parents in *This Star of England* identify Oxford Court as Vere House at p. 30, but seem to confuse Oxford Court with Fisher's Folly at p. 783. Ward refers to Stow in calling Oxford's London Stone house Vere House at p. 5 and p. 49, but refers to "Oxford Court, London Stone" in an appendix at p. 384. To prevent confusion in *The Death of Shakespeare*, Oxford's residence in London will be referred to as "Oxford Court." There is no evidence as to what Oxford called Oxford Court.

[61] A good description of the street and London Stone is found at the notes to the Agas Map, Section C6, for London Stone and for Candlewick Street. The Agas Map is held by the Guildhall Library, Corporation of the City of London, and can be viewed at *www.british-history.ac.uk/no-series/london-map-agas/1561*.

principal London dwelling until 1589,'" but does not make clear whether he's referring to the location or the date (1589).

Oxford may have moved to Plaistow House in Essex near Earls Colne by 1589. Anderson, P. 233. He hired workers to rebuild the house (they sued him for nonpayment) and may have spent time in Bilton or Billesley in Warwickshire as well. He may also have moved back into the Savoy in London across the Strand from Cecil House.

For the purposes of *The Death of Shakespeare,* Oxford keeps Oxford Court and sells Fisher's Folly, returning to Oxford Court from Billesley, not Bilton, as his interests become more focused on writing plays. In the book he moves to Hackney in 1597, although in real life he seems to have moved to Norton Folgate at some earlier point before moving to Hackney.

Oxford's title to Oxford House was confirmed in a patent dated June 11, 1573, which describes its location and what it comprised:

> "[A] great messuage in the parish of St. Swithin by London Stone and Candlewick Street in London, a great garden and a small garden adjoining the said messuage, with access thereto by two great gates (whereof one extends toward Candlewick Street by St. Swithin's church towards the south, and the other lower down towards the north), the land between the said Gates and all cottages and hereditaments adjoining and the longing to the messuages, the advowson of the rectory [and] vicarage of St. Swithin and all lands in the said Parish once of Tortington priory, County of Sussex ...."
> Nelson, p. 97.

Stow also describes it as a "faire and large builded house ... which house hath a faire garden ...." At l. 12., he writes:

> In Feb., 1286, Sir Robert Aguylon bequeathed his mansion, with courtyard and garden, in the parish of St. Swithin, to the prior of Tortington (*Cal. Wills*, i. 75). Robert had inherited it from his mother Joan, grand-

daughter of Henry Fitz-Alwin, the first mayor, who lived here, and is in consequence called 'Henricus filius Eylwini de Londene-stane' (*Lib. de Ant. Legg.* 1, and Preface, pp. ix–xi, lxxiv-vi). In 1490 Henry Eburton, draper, left some adjoining tenements called 'Draper's Halle', formerly belonging to Robert Auguylem, to his company (*Cal. Wills*, ii. 601). The Aguylons had land at Edburton in Sussex.

The prior of Tortington's house in Candlewick Street was granted to john de Vere (d. 1540), fifteenth Earl of Oxford, on June 8, 1539 (*Letters and Papers*, xiv. 1192 (8)). John (*d.* 1562), sixteenth earl, kept great state here (See, i. 89 above). Edward, seventeenth earl, moved to Fisher's Folly.

The property is described in a tax document after Oxford sold it as including "a longe garden." Nelson, p. 396. Nothing is known about its interior.

The Agas Map shows St. Swithin's Church located at the northwest corner of Candlewick Street, which runs east-west, and St. Swithin's Lane, which runs north-south. The Map locates London Stone in front of St. Swithin's Church. A row of houses extends along the north side of Candlewick Street from St. Swithin's to the intersection with Wallbrok Street to the west. Therefore, the most likely location for Oxford House is west of St. Swithin's Church on the north side of Candlewick Street.

The Agas Map shows gardens filling the land behind the row of houses on the north side of Candlewick Street. There are no gates allowing access from the gardens to Candlewick Street, a failure corrected in *The Death of Shakespeare.*

Stow says that a grammar school founded by the Merchant Taylors' Company in 1561 was located close to St. Swithin's. (Stow 1:74). However, the school is referenced as being originally in the Manor of the Rose (*The History and Antiquities of London*, Chapter XIX, Vol. 3.) The Agas Map, Section C6, shows the Manor of the Rose on St. Laurence Poultrey Hill, which ran from Candlewick Street to Fleet Street. Whatever its exact location, the school was within a half-block of Oxford Court. "Old Merchant Taylors," as alumni of the school were called, included Edmund Spenser, Thomas Kyd, John Webster, and Ben Jonson. The school is still one of the finest private schools in England, although it has been moved to a location outside of London.

Mistress Dinghen Vanderplasse had come from Holland in 1564 and taught English chambermaids (and Nigel, of course) how to make starch that allowed the ruffs they so carefully made to stay stiff (as long as they didn't get rained on). Erickson, Carolly, *The First Elizabeth,* p. 229.

The poem Oxford is reciting at the end of this chapter is *Grief of Mind,* was published in *England's Parnassus,* 1600, and in Sidney's *Astrophel and Stella.* Fuller (#15) and Looney (# 23) attribute the poem to Oxford, although not all scholars agree. The date *Grief of Mind* was written is unknown. It is an example of anadiplosus, where the end of a line is repeated in the succeeding line. Oxford used it in *The Comedy of Errors,* (Act I, Scene.2):

> *She is so hot because the meat is cold;*
> *The meat is cold because you come not home;*
> *You come not home because you have no stomach;*
> *You have no stomach, having broke your fast;*
> *But we that know what 'tis to fast and pray,*
> *Are penitent for your default today.*

Chapter 7
Lyly, Falstaff, and Robin

The style of Lyly's verbose complaint about the closing of the Folly is based on his writings.

Oxford's quote of Lyly that "hills and valleys, and mountains crowned with castles whose locks can be picked with a tongue!' is twisted from his verbose style of writing in *Eupheus* and other early works. He became famous in the late 1570s and 1580s but had little success after that. Some think Oxford was feeding him plots and verse.

Lyly was Oxford's secretary in the 1570s and possibly the early 1580s.

Ben Jonson is quoted as having said of Shakespeare that *sufflaminandus erat—it is sometimes necessary that he should be stopped!'* Oxford applies it to Falstaff in *The Death of Shakespeare.*

Chapter 8
The Poacher of Arden Forest

The Poacher of Arden Forest is fiction, loosely based on the apocryphal poem about Shakespeare poaching Sir Thomas Lucy's deer. See, *The Reader's Companion* to the Prologue, above.

Oxford may have landed at the stairs for Paris Garden but the Falcon Stairs were closer to the Rose. Agas Map held by the Guildhall Library, Corporation of the City of London.

When Shackspear assures Oxford that he learned Greek at the Stratford Grammar School, Oxford immediately says, "Μία γλώσσα δεν είναι ποτέ αρκετή," which means "one language is never enough."

The exchange between Oxford and Shackspear about how Shackspear shall swear that he will keep Oxford's assistance secret is based on the exchange between Leir and the Messenger in *King Leir*, Act IV, Scene 7:

Leir.	*Yet, gentle friend, grant one thing ere I die.*
Messenger.	*I will grant you anything, except your lives.*
Leir.	*Oh, but assure me by some certain token,* *That my two daughters hired thee to this deed:* *If I were once resolved of that, then I* *Would wish no longer life, but crave to die.*
Messenger.	*That to be true, in sight of heaven I swear.*
Leir.	*Swear not by heaven, for fear of punishment:* *The heavens are guiltless of such heinous acts.*
Messenger.	*I swear by earth, the mother of us all.*

Leir.	*Swear not by earth; for she abhors to bear* *Such bastards, as are murderers of her sons.*
Messenger.	*Why then, by hell, and all the devils I swear.*
Leir.	*Swear not by hell; for that stands gaping wide,* *To swallow thee, and if thou do this deed.* {*Thunder and lightning*}

And on Romeo's response to Juliet's question: "*Dost thou Love? I know thou wilt say aye. / And I will take th word, yet if thou swear'st, Thou maist prove false.*" Romeo answers, "*Lady, by yonder Moone I vow, / That tips with silver all these Fruite tree tops,*" but Juliet is more grounded than Romeo is: "*O sweare not by the Moone, th'inconstant Moone, / That monthly changes in her circled Orbe, / Lest that they Love prove likewise variab*le."

Oxford's thought—*He was but one hour mine*—will reappear as part of Sonnet 33:

> *Even so my sun one early morn did shine,*
> *With all triumphant splendour on my brow;*
> *But out, alack, he was but one hour mine.*

which he will compose upon hearing that his second wife, Elspeth Trentham, is pregnant. See, Chapter 76. He will rewrite Sonnet 33 when he finds out in *Part Two* that his son by the Queen did *not* die shortly after birth.

The arrow that nearly kills a member of the audience is based on a November, 1587 incident in which, during a performance by the Admiral's Men, a gun misfired and killed a pregnant woman and child. *Compact Documentary*, p. 146.

Chapter 9
Procne's Revenge

Procne's Revenge is fiction. It is true that Robert Greene accused someone of stealing his plays (which is another minor industry in Shakespearean studies) but it does not seem that he was thinking about Shakespeare. In *The Death of Shakespeare*, Shackspear presents Oxford with a play he says Greene threw away, which could have happened. One of the sources for *Titus*

Andronicus is the story in Ovid's *Metamorphoses* about Procne being raped by her sister's husband. The rapist then ripped out her tongue to keep her silent and imprisoned her, telling his wife that Procne was dead. Procne smuggled out a message to her sister who helped Procne escape. The sister then fed her son to her husband baked in a pie. The husband went mad and they all become birds.

Shackspear comes up with the idea of Procne/Lavinia using a stick to write in the sand, which is another bow by Oxford to Ovid's *Metamorphoses*, where Io, in Book I, having been turned into a cow, communicates with human beings by scratching her hoof in the sand.

It took two whacks to cut off Mary's head. Whether it was because the blade was dull or because Mary didn't tip the executioner enough is not known.

Bilton Hall is no longer in existence. It was located on the Avon River above Stratford and Warwick. 'Parishes: Bilton', *A History of the County of Warwick*: Volume 6: Knightlow hundred (1951), pp. 30-35, has the following quote: "In 1574 Edward, Earl of Oxford, leased it to John, Lord Darcy, in 1580 he sold it to John Shuckburgh."

http://www.british-history.ac.uk/report.aspx?compid=57089

The relationship between Shakespeare and the Trussells of Billesley Hall has been the subject of much conjecture. As with most things involving the search for information about William Shakespeare, it would be nice to know the two families were friendly, or even related. However, the evidence does not support a relationship. See, *Shakespeare and the Trussells of Billesley*, Gwynneth Bowen, The Shakespeare Fellowship Newsletter, 1958, which can be viewed online at

http://www.sourcetext.com/sourcebook/ library/bowen/05trussells.htm.

Such lack of historical connection will not stop Shackspear from claiming he is a relative of Oxford's in *Part Two* of *The Death of Shakespeare.*

The above quotation from *A History of Warwick* includes the following:

In 1481 Sir William Trussell died seised of the manor [Bilton], which was valued at £14 and was stated to be held of the Prior and Convent of Barnwell, Cambridgeshire. (fn. 36) At this time his son Edward was only 2 years old, and the manor came into the king's hands. (fn. 37) He died in 1499 when his daughter and ultimate heiress Elizabeth was still a minor, and his son John died, holding the manor of the Prior of Barnwell, in 1500. (fn. 38) Elizabeth was granted in wardship to John Vere, afterwards 15th Earl of Oxford, in 1507, (fn. 39) whose second wife she became, and to whose family the manor of Bilton passed for some 70 years.

Therefore, Oxford's grandfather had married Thomas's grandmother and Thomas Trussell was Oxford's cousin. Billesley was owned by the Trussells and Bowen thinks Oxford may have owned Billesley at one point. *Id.*

The "lyttle deske" Oxford used when traveling was described in a letter he wrote that survives. Nelson, p. 360.

There is a tradition in Warwickshire that Shakespeare wrote *As You Like It* at Billesley. Since many connections between the plays and Oxford have been shifted to Shakespeare (*vide* the Ashbourne Portrait, for example), it is likely that the tradition arose from memories of Oxford's stay at Billesley. Thus, Oxford's moves to Billesley in *The Death of Shakespeare.*

Billesley is now a destination resort for weddings and business meetings and can be visited in person or on the web at

https://www.thehotelcollection.co.uk/hotels/billesley-manor-hotel-stratford-upon-avon

The Hall was purchased by a major hotel chain and has been refurbished and sold on. The prior owners had a website that claimed they would show you the room in which *All's Well That Ends Well* was written. The new owners have removed that reference.

This is the original floor plan for the Hall:

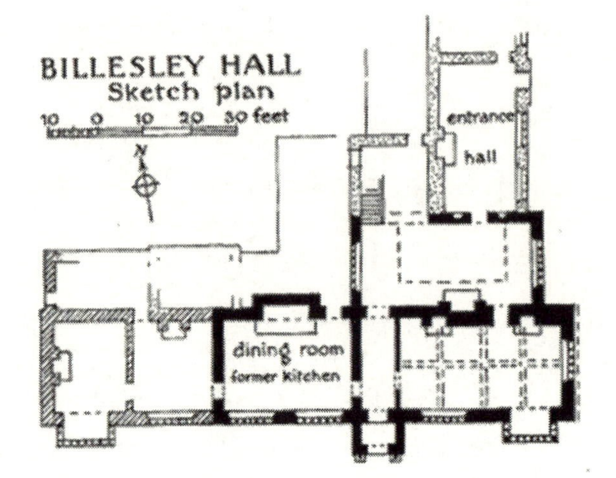

From: 'Parishes: Billesley', A History of the County of Warwick: Volume 3: Barlichway hundred (1945), pp. 58-61.

http://www.british-history.ac.uk/report.aspx? compid=56981.

There are further connections between the Trussells and Oxford. In 1585, Thomas Trussell committed robbery on the highway in Kent. He was convicted and sentenced to death. This is exactly what Oxford did twelve years earlier in the same county:[62] 'Parishes: Billesley', *A History of the County of Warwick*: Volume 3: Barlichway hundred (1945), pp. 58-61 has the following quote:

> On 6 August of [1585] Thomas committed robbery and felony on the highway at Bromley, Kent, and was in 1588 attainted and sentenced to death. Billesley manor passed to the Crown and was granted in 1590 to John Willes and others, being then held on lease by Richard Ognell.

Thomas was apparently not executed, for he seems to be identical with the 'Thomas Trussell of Billesley souldier', given in the 1619 Visitation, who wrote a treatise on military training,

---

[62] See the discussion of Oxford's caper in *The Reader's Companion,* Chapter 22.

'The Souldier Pleading his Own Cause', and was alive in 1610 (Dict. Nat. Biog. lvii, 269).

Oxford, of course, was not charged with robbery in 1573. Burghley was not going to press charges against his new son-in-law who was the central part of Burghley's design to insert his family line into the succession question that hovered over Elizabeth's reign. Thomas Trussell was not so fortunate.

But Trussell's conviction may have had an effect on Oxford. Some scholars think Oxford wrote *The Famous Victories of Henry Fifth* shortly after the Gad's Hill robbery of 1573. Ward, *The Famous Victories.* However, the similarity between Oxford's caper in 1573 and the predicament Trussell found himself in the 1580s may have spurred Oxford to pen *Famous Victories* in the late 1580s.[63] It would make for a good laugh;[64] and it may have been intended to influence the Queen to pardon Thomas. Ward thinks he wrote it in 1574 as an apology for his flight to the continent and for setting upon Lord Burghley's servants on Gad's Hill.

Famous Victories was not published until 1598. No record exists of its performance before the 1590s. The relationship between it and the far superior *Henry IV* (I & II) and *Henry V* (collectively referred to as the *Henriad*) has absorbed scholars for years. There are two principal theories as to how *Famous Victories* came about. It is either a play by another author that Shakespeare borrowed from, or a memorialized version of the *Henriad*, dumbed down for a dumber audience. Most scholars reject the latter claim: why would anyone throw out Falstaff if someone wanted a memorialized version of *The Henriad*?

---

63 The story of Prince Hal robbing his father's receivers on Gad's Hill is in all the sources. Did Oxford carry out the same acts in robbing Lord Burghley's receivers in 1573 as emulation of his favorite English hero? He must have known the story.

64 Prince Hal thought so in *Henry IV-I:* "*Now could thou [Falstaff] and I rob the thieves and go merrily to London, it would be argument for a week, laughter for a month <u>and a good jest for ever</u>.*" "For E-ver?"

Stratfordians conclude Shakespeare must have borrowed from it because he was too young to be writing plays in the 1580s. But there is a third possibility: *Famous Victories* and the *Henriad* were written by the same man, and that man was Oxford.

The title page to *Famous Victories* published in 1598 states that it was performed "by the Queen's Majestie's Players." Although many claims on the title pages of books and plays published during the Elizabethan era were not true, a reference to the Queen's Players pushes the performance back into the 1580s. This conclusion is reinforced by references in other documents that Jockey (the Falstaff predecessor) in *Famous Victories* was performed by Dick Tarlton who died in 1588. If these facts are true, William Shakespeare could not have written *Famous Victories.* If the same man who wrote *Famous Victories* wrote the *Henriad*, then Shakespeare did not write the plays. The implications of this argument are the reverse of the argument put forward by the Stratfordians that Oxford could not have written the plays because *The Tempest* was written after Oxford died (the "Silver Bullet" theory). That theory has been disputed. *On the Date, Sources and Design of Shakespeare's the Tempest*, Roger A Stritmatter, McFarland & Co., 2013.

If Shakespeare didn't write *Famous Victories,* he borrowed wholesale. This is the conclusion of conventional scholarship because, no matter what careful analysis says, Shakespeare couldn't have been writing plays in the 1570s or 1580s. Therefore, someone else wrote the early plays and Shakespeare borrowed from them. The congruity between *Famous Victories* and the *Henriad* (same scenes; same scenes in *same* order) will be visited in *Part Two.*

Oxford's older half-sister, Katherine, married to Lord Windsor, sued Oxford, her brother, in 1563, claiming Oxford's father's marriage to Marjory Golding was illegal because Earl John was married another woman at the time. See, *The Reader's Companion,* Chapter 83.

Malfis opinion that the marriage was neither *per verba de praesenti* or *in futuro* reflects the view of the time that there were two different types of marriages. Also, a valid marriage could be contracted simply by exchanging rings and promises, either alone or in front of witnesses. Dorothy Ogburn, p. 835. *A Documentary Life*, p. 73. Also, the discussion beginning above at the bottom of page 67.

Some believe that Oxford and the Queen contracted to marry each other based on his relationship with her in 1573 and 1574 and their visits together to the Archbishop of Canterbury. There are many references to an exchange of rings in the plays (*Two Gentlemen of Verona* - Act I, 2 - and *Romeo & Juliet* - Act III, 1, to mention two). The best exposition of this is in *Twelfth Night*, Act V, 1:

> *A contract of eternal bond of love,*
> *Confirm'd by mutual joinder of your hands,*
> *Attested by the holy close of lips,*
> *Strengthen'd by interchangement of your rings;*
> *And all the ceremony of this compact*
> *Seal'd in my function, by my testimony:*
> *Since when, my watch hath told me, toward my grave*
> *I have travell'd but two hours.*

Scholars suspect that Oxford's half-sister, Katherine, may have been the model for Katharina in *The Taming of the Shrew*, although others prefer Peregrine Bertie's wife, Oxford's full sister.

Oxford's mother, Marjory, abandoned him to Burghley. There are no letters from her to Oxford after he moved to Cecil House and the few letters from her to Burghley barely mention her son. She never asks Burghley to remember her to Oxford. It seems likely that he never saw her again in the six years between his father's death and her death when he would have been 17 years old. *Hamlet* may be evidence of how angry Oxford was with his mother's remarriage, which must have included anger over his abandonment as well. And he might have been unable to carry her coffin because of his young age and the emotions he felt when she died.

The only hand-written poems from the Elizabeth era are poems by Oxford that were found by Anne Cornwallis at Fisher's Folly, which her father had purchased at the end of 1588. Her book was found by J. O. Halliwell-Phillips in 1852. (Folger MS V.a.89. An excellent overview of the book and its circumstances can be found in *The Shakespeare Fellowship Quarterly*, April 1945, in an article by Charles Wisner Barrell, which can be read at

www.sourcetext.com/sourcebook/library/barrell/21-40/26earliest.htm

This is the book of poems Malfis refers to in his conversation with Oxford about closing down the Folly.

At the point this occurs in *The Death of Shakespeare*, title to the Folly has not changed hands, and it is likely that the poems were discovered later, but the information serves to show Oxford, in his typical dramatic fashion, washing his hands of poetry and plays and not caring about what Anne Cornwallis found at Fisher's Folly, even a poem by Anne Vavasor.

The Anne Vavasor poem in the Cornwallis book is entitled *Though I be strange* and dated 1581:

Though I be strange, sweet friend, be thou not so;
Do not annoy thyself with sullen will.
My heart hath vowed, although my tongue say no,
To rest thine own, in friendly liking still.

Thou seest we live amongst the lynx's eyes,
That pries and spies each privy thought of mind;
Thou knowest right well what sorrows may arise
If once they chance my settled looks to find.

Content thyself that once I made an oath
To shield myself in shroud of honest shame;
And when thou list, make trial of my troth,
So that thou save the honor of my name.

And let me seem, although I be not coy,
To cloak my sad conceits with smiling cheer;

Let not my gestures show wherein I joy,
Nor by my looks let not my love appear.

We silly dames, that false suspect do fear,
And live within the mouth of envy's lake,
Must in our hearts a secret meaning bear,
Far from the show that outwardly we make.

So where I like, I list not vaunt my love;
Where I desire, there must I feign debate.
One hath my hand, another hath my glove,
But he my heart whom most I seem to hate.

Thus farewell, friend: I will continue strange;
Thou shalt not hear by word or writing aught,
Let it suffice, my vow shall never change;
As for the rest, I leave it to thy thought.

The Cornwallis book contains thirty-three poems written in two different hands by some very interesting authors, among them the Earl of Oxford. The above poem, found on page 8, was attributed to "Ann Vavaser" while the poem on the opposite page, attributed to Oxford, is the so-called Echo poem acknowledged by Stephen May as Oxford's: "Oh heavens, who was the first that bred in me this fever? Vere."

An argument might be made that the lines:

One hath my hand, another hath my glove,
But he my heart whom most I seem to hate.

were answered by Oxford in Sonnet 145:

Those lips that Love's own hand did make
Breathed forth the sound that said 'I hate'
To me that languish'd for her sake;
But when she saw my woeful state,
Straight in her heart did mercy come,
Chiding that tongue that ever sweet
Was used in giving gentle doom,
And taught it thus anew to greet:
'I hate' she alter'd with an end,

That follow'd it as gentle day
Doth follow night, who like a fiend
From heaven to hell is flown away;
'I hate' from hate away she threw,
And saved my life, saying 'not you.'

Stratfordians like to see Sonnet 145 as Shakespeare's sonnet to his wife, since they see the word 'Hathaway' in 'hate away.' However, it is an odd way for the man from Stratford to praise his wife. Did she 'hate' him because he was never home? It seems more likely that Anne Vavasor was the object of this poem. In any event, this odd poem, when compared with the other 153 sonnets (eight beats per line rather than the ten of all the other sonnets), will be written by Oxford for Shackspear to take to his wife in *Part Two* to convince her and others he is a poet and has praised her for forgiving him for leaving her in Stratford with the children while he was having a good time in London.

The Cornwallis poems contain a line that reads "*Whenas thine eye hath chose the dame.*" The same line appears in *The Passionate Pilgrim*, which was published in 1599 under William Shakespeare's name. William Jaggard published twenty poems that were attributed to "W. Shakespeare" on the title page but only five are considered to be by William. Two were lifted from *Love's Labour's Lost*, and two sonnets later appeared in the sonnet collection under William's name in 1609. If the poems in the Cornwallis book were Oxford's, it seems unlikely that William would have had access to them. The connection, if anything, drives a possible conclusion that the poems in *The Passionate Pilgrim* are all by Oxford and none by William.

Chapter 10
Billesley – Christmas Eve 1588

For a description of Billesley Hall, see page 106 above.

Billesley is only a half-dozen miles from Stratford. Wincot ("Marian Hackett, the fat ale-wife of Wincot" – *The Taming of the Shrew*) is probably Wilmcote, a village a mile to the northeast of

Billesley. Temple Grafton (the home of the girl Shakespeare may have intended to marry, if he had not impregnated Anne Hathaway, is two miles to the southeast of Billesley. See, *The Reader's Companion*, the Prologue, for a discussion of the marriage records relating to Shakespeare and "Anna Whatley of Temple Grafton."

The recipe for roast olives of veal is from *Cindy Renfro - Elizabethan Food*, *www.thousandeggs.com/elizabethan.html#recipe*. "You shall take a leg of veal and cut the flesh from the bones, and cut it out into thin long slices; then take sweet herbs and the white parts of scallions, and chop them well together with the yolks of eggs, then roll it up within the slices of veal, and so spit them and roast them; then boil verjuice, butter, sugar, cinnamon, currants, and sweet herbs together, and, being seasoned with a little salt, serve the olives up upon that sauce with salt cast over them. (*The English Hus-wife*, by Gervase Markham, 1615.)"

There is no evidence Oxford ever had a cat. Or a dog named Crab. Oxford's comment that the cat was sucking forth his soul is from Marlowe's *The Tragical History of Doctor Faustus* when Mephistopheles brings Helen of Troy before Faust who says: *Sweet Helen, Make me immortal with a kiss.* [He kisses her.] / *Her lips suck forth my soul:* / See, *where it flies!*

Socrates will become Oxford's companion. In 1601, Oxford will gift Socrates to the Earl of Southampton to give the earl comfort during his imprisonment in the Tower of London. Akrigg, p. 132 and facing plate.

1589

Chapters 11-34

Chapter 11
Shakespeare Pays an Unwelcome Visit

Scholars agree that William Shakespeare married Anne Hathaway and had three children: Susanna (christened May 26, 1583); and Judith and Hamnet, fraternal twins (February 2, 1585). William and Anne were married in late 1582. There were no marriage certificates at the time; licenses were usually issued. There is none for Shakespeare's wedding to Anne.

There is, however, a bond dated November 28, 1582, in which two relatives of Anne pledged £40 to secure permission for the marriage without waiting for the saying of the customary banns in a church. The reason for the rush was made apparent when Susanna was born the following May. Anne was apparently three months pregnant when she married William. She was also 26 years old at the time of her marriage; William was 18, and a minor. There is no evidence as to whether John Shakespeare gave William permission to marry Anne.

The day before the bond was issued a notation was made in the clerk's records that a license had been issued for William to marry Anna Whateley of Temple Grafton (Anne Hathaway was from the village of Shottery.) The implication is clear: Shakespeare was in love with Anna Whatley of Temple Grafton and had intended to marry her, but he had apparently gotten Anne Hathaway pregnant the previous summer. When the Hathaways found out that William was going to marry Anna Whateley, they quickly dragged him to the altar and made him marry the woman he had impregnated.

The scholars, after carefully sifting all the extant records, have concluded that the "Worcester clerk appears to have been fairly careless, for he got a number of names wrong in the Register." Whateley is not even close to Hathaway, they acknowledge, but they found a Whateley in the records who was a party in other matters and conclude the clerk simply made a mistake.[65] Schoenbaum, beginning at page 83, gives a reasoned view of the evidence. He cites extensively from Anthony Burgess' novel, *Shakespeare*, to show how lurid one can get discussing the idea of a third woman "in a triangular drama—romantic, melodramatic, and moral—in which the passionate Will must choose between Love and Duty." Schoenbaum concludes: "Colourful, if a trifle tawdry, this 'persuasive reading' certainly is; but it is not so much biography as imaginative invention, and hence more appropriate to a novel …" P. 85. Shakespeare, if he could come back, would no doubt be amused to find so much energy expended on whether he loved another woman and had to abandon her to marry Anne Hathaway. What the scholars ignore is that Anne was pregnant when Shakespeare married her. The 19th century may have found this fault more significant than we do today but Shakespeare's dalliance with Anne is consistent with his dealings with Francis Langley and his quest for property and money. His monument shows his hands resting on a grain bag and, no matter how many quills are put in his hand, he was still a businessman. Infidelity is a central theme of the plays attributed to William yet there is no evidence of infidelity on Anne's part. Oxford's life, on the other hand, provides all the fodder needed to write plays about cheating women (or men).

Regardless of who William really wanted to marry, in *The Death of Shakespeare*, Anne Whateley will make her appearance, to Shackspear's annoyance and embarrassment in *Part Two.*

The beginning of the sonnet Oxford begins to quote as he bounds up the stairs at the end of this chapter is from Sonnet 93.

---

[65] The clerk made a further mistake, writing Temple Grafton for Shottery. The scholars pass over how much more this makes the 'mistake' theory untenable.

Chapter 12
Westminster Palace – February 4, 1589

Lady Mildred, Burghley's second wife and mother of Nan and Robert, died on April 4, 1589. Burghley erected an enormous Corinthian tomb twenty-four feet high in Westminster Abbey where he buried Lady Burghley and his daughter, Nan, who had died the previous year. An effigy of Lady Burghley on top of her sarcophagus is surrounded by figures of her three granddaughters Elizabeth, Bridget, and Susan. Lord Burghley is seen kneeling in his robes above them (although he was buried at Stamford). The epitaphs are from his pen and tell how his eyes were dim with tears for those who were dear to him beyond the whole race of womankind. He added a long Latin inscription on the tomb.

There is a drawing of the Parliament held in February, 1589, which shows Oxford holding the Sword of State in front of him, with Burghley to the right of the Queen, and various other identifiable noblemen and officials standing or sitting around the Queen. "Elizabeth Opening Parliament Following the Defeat of the Invincible Armada" from *Dewes Journals of the Parliaments of Elizabeth. http://www.sourcetext.com/sourcebook/library/barrell/21-40/22pictoral.htm.* The Sword of State disappeared after the beheading of Charles I. It had to be replaced for the coronation of Charles II in 1661.

Interestingly, a man can be seen peeping out from behind a hanging curtain in the upper corner. This may be Sir Robert Cecil, foreshadowing by twelve years his peering out from behind a curtain at the trial of Essex and Southampton in 1601. (Was the artists aware, from an early version of *Hamlet*, that Robert's father, Lord Burghley, was Polonius? If so, was the artist having fun sketching Robert peeking out from behind a similar wall hanging?)

Falstaff's comment that he was 'paddling in their packets' will surface in a more acceptable form in *Hamlet,* Act III, Scene 4, where Hamlet tells his mother to stay away from Claudius:

Not this, by no means, that I bid you do:
Let the bloat king tempt you again to bed;
Pinch wanton on your cheek; call you his mouse;
And let him, for a pair of reechy kisses,
Or paddling in your neck with his damn'd fingers
Make you ravel all this matter out,
That I essentially am not in madness,
But mad in craft.

As to Edmund Spenser's heavy eye-lids, see the painting of him in Looney at p. 57. He was considered, in his time, and even today by many literary scholars, to be England's best poet, but not many read his works then and fewer read him now. He spent many years of his creative life in Ireland.

Sir Walter Raleigh has left a larger footprint in the minds of modern people than he deserves because, among other things, he is credited with introducing the potato to Ireland and tobacco to England. Neither attribution is probably correct. The story of how he laid down his cloak to help the Queen cross a wet area is also probably apocryphal.

Anne Vavasor was a lady in waiting to the Queen who was twice impregnated by Oxford. Nelson, p. 232. The second pregnancy resulted in the birth of a male child and she, the baby, and Oxford were all sent to the Tower. The child was named Edward Vere, and raised by Anne and Sir Henry Lee, the man she later lived with but could not marry. (They were both already married to other people.) Sir Henry had been in charge of the Tower at the time Oxford and Anne were put in the Tower were arrested for their affair. Sir Henry was so smitten with Anne that he had a suit of armor made with her initials inscribed all over it. Anne married a ship captain after she was freed, whom she mentions in this chapter, but left him for Sir Henry in the late 1580s. She lived happily thereafter with Sir Henry. Some scholars have thought Anne was the Dark Lady of the Sonnets. Others have thought she was the model for Beatrice in *Much Ado About Nothing*, as well as other Shakespeare comedies.

When Elizabeth visited Ditchley in 1592, Sir Henry was so grateful to be forgiven for his ongoing illicit relationship with Anne that he had Marcus Gheeraerts the Younger paint a full-length portrait of Elizabeth that is known as the "Ditchley Portrait." It now hangs in the British Portrait Gallery in London. A link to the painting is:

http://en.wikipedia.org/wiki/File:Queen_Elizabeth_I_(%27The_Ditchley_portrait%27)_by_Marcus_Gheeraerts_the_Younger.jpg

A sonnet, possibly by Sir Henry, is inscribed on the canvas. It is difficult to read because of damage and reframing. The first line reads: *The prince of light / The Sonn by whom ...*" Beauclerk, p. 106.

The "Forgiveness Portrait" may have been the model for another portrait recovered in the 1600s after the monarchy fell. This portrait was originally known as the "Pregnancy Portrait." The Pregnancy Portrait is now part of the Royal Collection Trust. It hangs in Hampton Palace. A link to this painting with comments from the brochure for the 2013 exhibition at Buckingham Palace can be seen at:

https://www.royalcollection.org.uk/collection/406024/portrait-of-an-unknown-woman

An excellent reproduction is in Beauclerk. For 250 years, the portrait was believed to be of Elizabeth I. Upon the accession of Elizabeth II in 1952, however, the portrait was relabeled as "unknown lady in a Persian dress." It is now listed as "Portrait of an Unknown Lady." The reason is clear. The subject is obviously pregnant, something that is difficult to square with the unmarried, perpetually virgin, Elizabeth I. The "Unknown Lady" has a hand on the head of a stag standing next to her, who is weeping. There are three couplets in the tree. They read as follows:

Iniusti Justa querela [A just complaint of injustice]

Mea sic mihi [Thus to me my...tree was the only hope?]

Dolor est medicina [e] d[o]lori [Grief is medicine for grief]

The sonnet reads:

The restless swallow fits my restless minde,
In still revivinge still renewinge wronges;
her Just complaintes of cruelty unkinde,
are all the Musique, that of my life prolongs.

With pensive thoughtes my weeping Stagg I crowne
whose Melancholy teares my cares Expresse;
her Teares in silence, and my sighes unknowne
are all the physicke that my harmes redresse.

My onely hope was in this goodly tree,
which I did plant in love bringe up in care:
but all in vanie [sic], for now to late I see
the shales be mine, the kernels others are.

My Musique may be plaints, my physique teares
If this be all the fruite my love tree beares.

In *The Death of Shakespeare - Part Two*, the painting will be commissioned by Oxford and given to Elizabeth as part of his efforts to find out if the Earl of Southampton is their son.

Edward Vere grew up in Sir Henry Lee's household, and was apparently treated well by Sir Sidney, as was Anne, although some of the Sonnets may have been written in anger that Edward was being raised in a house where Edward's mother lived in sin with Sir Henry. Edward may have studied at Leiden University. He later became a famous soldier. He was knighted by his uncle, Sir Horace Vere, and fought alongside Sir Horace and the Earl of Southampton, as well as his half-brother, Henry de Vere, the 18th Earl of Oxford, in the Low Countries. Edward Vere was born in 1581; Henry de Vere, 18th Earl of Oxford, was born in 1593, so they were twelve years apart. Edward Vere died in 1629 of a wound to the back of his head while he was fighting in the Lowlands.

I saw a fair younge ladye come her secret teares to wail is a poem Oxford wrote about Anne Vavasor. The reference Oxford makes to his bad angel/good angel is from Sonnet 144.

My Mistress' eyes are nothing like the sun is Sonnet 130. There is no evidence that Oxford wrote this sonnet with Anne Vavasor in mind, although Charlton Ogburn thinks so. Ogburn, p. 614. It may be a parody of the love sonnets that were the craze in the late 1500s. Compare this sonnet with Thomas Watson's seventh poem in his *Passionate Century of Love*, published in 1582:

W: *Her yellow locks exceed the beaten gold*

S: *If hairs be wires, black wires grow on her head.*

W: *Her sparkling eyes in heav'n a place deserve*

S: *My Mistress' eyes are nothing like the sun*

W: *Her words are music all of silver sound.*

S: *I love to hear her speak, yet well I know,*

W: *On either cheek a rose and lily lie.*

S: *I have seen roses damasked, red and white,*
But no such roses see I in her cheeks.

W: *Her breath is sweet perfume, or holy flame.*

S: *And in some perfume is there more delight*
Than in the breath from my mistress reeks.

W: *Her lips more red than any coral stone,*
Her neck more white than aged swans that moan.

S: *Coral is far more red than her lips red,*
If snow be white, why then her breasts are dun.

Shakespeare's sonnet seems to be a direct parody of Watson's. But the last couplet of Shakespeare's sonnet implies that Shakespeare may not have been painting his love with black wires to defame her:

And yet by heaven I think my love as rare,
As any she beli'd with false compare.

Oxford's use of the 'black wires' sonnet in *The Death of Shakespeare*, therefore, may not be a fair use of the sonnet when the poem is examined as a whole.

Oxford's relationship with Thomas Watson deserves more thought. In an article in Shakespeare Oxford Newsletter, Fall 2004, Eric Lewin Altschuler, M.D., Ph.D. and William Jansen explore "the possibility that the remarkable English poet and translator Thomas Watson (d. 1592) may have been Oxford's primary pseudonym immediately preceding the use of 'Shake-speare.' In addition to the authorship question, they also present evidence about "Watson's genius and place in Elizabethan literary and intellectual history." Beginning on page 14, they compare another poem by Oxford[66] *(Love Thy Choice)* with one attributed to Watson as poem 60 in his *Tears of Fancie*. The two appear to be very similar. Of greater interest is that they include a photographic reproduction of the hand-written copy of *Love Thy Choice* in the Bodleian Library at the University of Oxford which is signed "Earle of Oxenforde." It would be interesting to know whether anyone who has studied Oxford's hand-writing has concluded that Oxford wrote the copy in the Bodleian Library, and whether the hand-writing in this document has been compared to any other hand-writing examples that might bear on the authorship question, including a part of *Thomas of Woodstock* that some believe was written by Shakespeare.

Although the word 'hate' is used extensively in the works attributed to William Shakespeare, as well as by other poets, there may be an interesting connection between a poem attributed to Anne Vavasor and Sonnet 144.

One of the poems found in the Anne Cornwallis papers is attributed to Anne Vavasor and is placed opposite the 'echo' poem attributed to Oxford that begins "*Oh heavens, who was the first that bred in me this fever? Vere.*"

> *Though I be strange, sweet friend, be thou not so;*
> *Do not annoy thyself with sullen will.*
> *My heart hath vowed, although my tongue say no,*
> *To rest thine own, in friendly liking still.*

---

66 *Fuller's* #13; *JTL* #2; Rawlinson MS 85 folio 16.

Thou seest we live amongst the lynx's eyes,
That pries and spies each privy thought of mind;
Thou knowest right well what sorrows may arise
If once they chance my settled looks to find.

Content thyself that once I made an oath
To shield myself in shroud of honest shame;
And when thou list, make trial of my troth,
So that thou save the honor of my name.

And let me seem, although I be not coy,
To cloak my sad conceits with smiling cheer;
Let not my gestures show wherein I joy,
Nor by my looks let not my love appear.

We silly dames, that false suspect do fear,
And live within the mouth of envy's lake,
Must in our hearts a secret meaning bear,
Far from the show that outwardly we make.

So where I like, I list not vaunt my love;
Where I desire, there must I feign debate.
One hath my hand, another hath my glove,
But he my heart whom most I seem to hate.

Thus farewell, friend: I will continue strange;
Thou shalt not hear by word or writing aught,
Let it suffice, my vow shall never change;
As for the rest, I leave it to thy thought.

http://politicworm.com/articles/plays-poems-other-em-texts/ann-vavasors-poem/

Anne Vavasor's last words to Oxford are taken from the above poem.

Anne's reference to giving Oxford her heart, "a double heart for your one," is from *Much Ado About Nothing* where Benedict[67]

---

[67] The First Folio spells the character's name 'Benedick,' and this is how he is known. However, the Ogburns point out on p. 480 that Beatrice says "Benedictus! Why Benedictus?" and that there was an early 1600 play called *Benedicte and Betteris*. The Ogburns argue that Benedict was intended, i.e., 'well-

sees Beatrice coming toward him and complains to Don Pedro that Beatrice has wronged him. He exits before Beatrice comes on stage. Don Pedro is naturally curious and says to Beatrice "Come, lady, come; you have lost the heart of Signior Benedict." Beatrice responds:

> *Indeed, my lord, he lent it me awhile; and I gave*
> *Him use for it, a double heart for his single one:*
> *marry, once before he won it of me with false dice,*
> *therefore your grace may well say I have lost it.*

Act II, Scene 1.

As noted above, there is information that Anne Vavasor may have been twice impregnated by Oxford. Nelson, p. 232. No one knows what happened to the first pregnancy; the second pregnancy resulted in the birth of Edward Vere. This second pregnancy was the one that landed Oxford, Anne, and the baby in the Tower. No one doubts that Edward was Oxford's son by Anne. On the other hand, there is no hard evidence that Oxford accepted Edward as his son.

In *Much Ado,* Beatrice tells Don Pedro that Benedict 'lent it [Benedict's heart] me awhile,' meaning that Benedict loved Beatrice for a period of time in the past, and in return 'I [Beatrice] gave him use for it.' 'Use' has many definitions. One is "the employment or maintenance of a person for sexual intercourse." Another is a legal term: "holding of … property by one person for the use or benefit of another." Oxford English Dictionary. The reference implies that Beatrice and Benedict were intimate. The preposition 'for' is interesting. Beatrice is

---

spoken,' not Benedick, meaning 'well-wished.' Knowing Oxford's pride and his love of hidden meanings, it is almost impossible to believe that he would have written a play about Anne Vavasor and referred to himself as 'well-blessed' (obviously by her, if that was the name intended) instead of 'well-spoken.' This may be an example of where ignorance of the true author has prevented scholars from correcting an error that is as important as the name of one of the leading characters in one of the author's better plays.

saying that in exchange for his love, she gave him something in return, 'a double heart.'

The 'double heart' can be read as referring to the baby Anne Vavasor delivered in the chamber next to the Queen's, giving back to Oxford 'a double heart for his single one.' Beatrice goes on to say that 'once before he won it,' i.e., her heart (meaning her bed), but 'he won it of me with false dice,' meaning he tricked her. Beatrice may have been referring to an earlier pregnancy and speaking for Anne Vavasor.

As with many 'coincidences' between Oxford and the plays, Beatrice's comment seems to refer to the relationship between Oxford and Anne Vavasor. This is a much more specific link between the play than the realization that the author's characterization of Beatrice and Benedict in *Much Ado About Nothing* seems to show him and Anne Vavasor on stage.

The reference to a 'double heart' in *Much Ado* may have been a sly reference to a similar poem by Sir Philip Sidney called *My True Love Hath My Heart and I Have His*:

> *My true love hath my heart and I have his,*
> *By just exchange one for another given;*
> *I hold his dear, and mine he cannot miss,*
> *There never was a better bargain driven.*
> *My true love has my heart and I have his.*
>
> *His heart in me keeps him and me in one,*
> *My heart in him his thoughts and senses guides;*
> *He loves my heart, for once it was his own,*
> *I cherish his, because in me it bides.*
> *My true love hath my heart and I have his.*

Since we know Sidney was dead by 1587 and that *Much Ado* is almost certainly later, this 'double heart' may be a footprint left over from an earlier version. Some Oxfordians believe so. See, the Ogburns at p. 480. Whenever this reference was coined, it appears that Oxford was having fun with Sidney. The two of them did battle with each other over the question of whether Oxford should have a kingdom, a cottage or a grave. See, below.

Oxford's comment to Robin that his 'good angel had to fire my bad angel out' is from Sonnet 144:

Two loves I have of comfort and despair,
Which like two spirits do suggest me still:
The better angel is a man right fair,
The worser spirit a woman colour'd ill.
To win me soon to hell, my female evil
Tempteth my better angel from my side,
And would corrupt my saint to be a devil,
Wooing his purity with her foul pride.
And whether that my angel be turn'd fiend
Suspect I may, but not directly tell;
But being both from me, both to each friend,
I guess one angel in another's hell:
Yet this shall I ne'er know, but live in doubt,
Till my bad angel fire my good one out.

In *Henry VI, Part One*, Talbot is invited to the castle of a French countess who intends to trap him. When she sees him, she evinces surprise that he is so small and un-heroic looking. She tells him he is in her power because she has kept a picture in her gallery, making him 'thrall' to her. Talbot laughs. (His army is waiting outside and eventually comes in to make him the captor and not the captive.) He tells the lady "my substance is not here, for what you see is but the smallest part and least proportion of humanity." The countess is puzzled: "He will be here, and yet he is not here." Act II, Scene 3. Oxford was obviously ruminating in *Henry VI* on how a person of otherwise small in stature can have such a disproportionate effect on those around him. Alexander the Great was such a man; it seems Talbot was also. Oxford, a man of no great height or girth, may have been advertising himself in this scene.

Oxford was in love with the idea that two words can have multiple meanings at the same time. Witness Mercutio's sardonic comment to Romeo after he is stabbed by Tybalt: "[A]sk for me to-morrow, and you shall find me a grave man." *Romeo & Juliet,* Act III, Scene 1. This is a classic Oxford fingerprint. The man could not pass up a pun until he got quite far into his career of writing dark tragedies. A useful study might be to compare the puns in the plays. There are many of them in the early plays (*Comedy of Errors, Two Gentlemen of Verona)* and very few, if any, in the later plays. A graph with the number of puns on the vertical axis and time along the horizontal axis may be of some value.

In *Love's Labour's Lost*, there is a Masque of the Nine Worthies in the last act which sounds suspiciously like the author was aware of Robert Greene's *Alphonsus*. The worthies were women in *Alphonsus,* and men in *Love's Labour's Lost* (although only three playing multiple parts), but the similarities are there.

Oxford is credited with writing a poem about whether he preferred a kingdom, a cottage, or a grave. The poem is reproduced in Looney as #18:

> *Were I a king I might command content;*
> *Were I obscure unknown* **would** *be my cares,*
> *And were I dead no thoughts should me torment,*
> *Nor words, nor wrongs, nor love, nor hate, nor fears*
> *A doubtful choice of* **these things which** *to crave,*
> ***A kingdom or a cottage or a***
> ***grave.*** *Vere*

Fuller reproduces it as #22 with a slight variation:

> *Were I a king I might command content;*
> *Were I obscure unknown* **should** *be my cares,*
> *And were I dead no thoughts should me torment,*
> *Nor words, nor wrongs, nor love, nor hate, nor fears*
> *A doubtful choice for me of* **three things one** *to crave,*
> ***A kingdom or a cottage or a grave.*** *Vere*

In the Chetham MS.8012 is Philip Sidney's reply:

> *Wert thou a King* **yet not** *command content,*
> *Since empire none thy mind could yet suffice,*
> *Wert thou obscure still* **cares** *would thee torment;*
> *But wert thou dead, all care and sorrow dies;*

An easy choice of these things which to crave,
No kingdom nor a cottage but a grave.[68]

Greene's rendition, the part of *Alphonsus* that startled Robin, (or, which startled Robin in a part of Chapter 12 that was cut from the final manuscript of *Part One*) was:

A prince at morn, a pilgrim ere it be night.
I, which erewhile did dain for to possess
The proudest palace of the western world,
Would now be glad a cottage for to find
To hide my head.[69]

An echo is heard in Richard II, Act III, Scene 3, when Richard asks:

What must the king do now? must he submit?
The king shall do it: must he be deposed?

---

[68] Sidney's version reflects the well-known fact that the Queen continually denied Oxford a command and that, no matter what happened, Oxford would still be tormented by cares. The last line might be described as the opposite of wishing someone bon voyage. The relationship between Oxford and Sidney deserves more study. Everyone focuses on the tennis court quarrel years earlier, but Oxford was apparently close with Sidney's sister, Lady Pembroke, the dame aux belles-lettres of England during her life, who was the mother of the "incomparable brethren" of the First Folio, one of whom married Oxford's youngest daughter, Susan. Susan may have been the 'Grand Possessor' of the plays and poetry, although that reference in the 1609 quarto of *Troilus and Cressida* was in the plural.

[69] Sidney and Oxford were obviously going after each other in the 'kingdom, cottage, or a grave' poems. It does not seem a stretch to conclude, as Robin does during the performance of *Alphonsus*, that Greene was having fun with Oxford, but was Greene referring to Oxford as well as the character in the play when he describes the character as a prince at morn and a pilgrim at night who in the past had "*dain[ed] for to possess the proudest palace of the western world*? (By the way, we all use 'disdain' in our daily conversation, but who has ever heard its opposite, dain? Maybe 'deign.') Doubtful, of course, but one of the wonderful aspects of Elizabethan literature is that there are enough certifiable references to events or people buried in the plays and poetry that there is always the tantalizing prospect that something you have just read has a hidden meaning, or that something viewed for 400 years as unnecessary text will open up when someone looks at the lines with new eyes.

The king shall be contented: must he lose
The name of king? o' God's name, let it go:
I'll give my jewels for a set of beads,
My gorgeous palace for a hermitage,
My gay apparel for an almsman's gown,
My figured goblets for a dish of wood,
My sceptre for a palmer's walking staff,
My subjects for a pair of carved saints
And my large kingdom for a little grave,
A little little grave, an obscure grave;
Or I'll be buried in the king's highway,
Some way of common trade, where subjects' feet
May hourly trample on their sovereign's head;
For on my heart they tread now whilst I live;
And buried once, why not upon my head?

Richard's three choices are a kingdom, a *little little* grave, and burial under the king's highway. It's sort of like Oxford saying to Sidney (who was probably dead when *Richard II* was written) 'not just a grave, Philip, but a little little grave, and not in consecrated ground but under a highway where people walk over you.' You can almost hear Oxford, when he writes these lines, asking Sidney: "What do you think of this? Have I bettered you?"

Chapter 13
Billesley Hall

Harold Bloom, the noted Yale Shakespeare professor, once said he would never see *Titus* again unless Mel Brooks staged it. The professor may have been on to more than he knew. T.S. Eliot said it was "one of the stupidest and most uninspired plays ever written, a play in which it is incredible that Shakespeare had any hand at all, a play in which the best passages would be too highly honoured by the signature of Peele." "Seneca in Elizabethan Translation," *Selected Essays 1917-1932* New York: Harcourt, Brace & World, 1950, at p. 67.

The Stratfordians believe Shakespeare wrote parts of *Titus Andronicus* in the early 1590s. A bad quarto of the play was published in 1594 and then an improved version in the 1623

First Folio. The play is famous for being the only one from which a drawing of action on the stage has survived. The drawing was supposedly made by Henry Peacham; the name "Henricus Peacham" is written in elegant script in the lower left-hand corner of the document with notations beneath the signature. (The signature and date of 1595 on the right edge of the document is by John Payne Collier, an 18th century forger.) Stratfordians believe the document was created by Henry Peacham, Jr. in 1595 after he witnessed a performance of *Titus Andronicus*.

However, a number of details don't fit. First, the notations beneath Peacham's signature can be interpreted to mean 1575, not 1595. Second, the text below the drawing doesn't fit either the 1594 Quarto or the 1623 Folio text. Third, another hand has written at the top of the document "Written by Henry Peacham, author of *The Compleat Gentlemen.*" *The Compleat Gentleman* was published in 1622 by Henry Peacham, Jr., born in 1576 to Henry Peacham, Sr., a curate at a church that adjoined Hatfield House, one of Lord Burghley's homes.

David Roper makes a compelling argument in an article published in *The Shakespeare-Oxford Newsletter*, Vol. 37, No. 3, Fall 2001,[70] that the drawing was made in 1575 by the father, not the son. He relies on the differences in the text below the drawing and the texts published later on to argue that Peacham père saw an earlier version. Why would he record words and scenes that did not agree with what he saw in 1595? The notations below his signature confirm the date; the use of a Latinized first name would have been consistent with the father's writing and out of use by 1595. The drawing was found in papers that came from those kept by Sir Michael Hicks, principal secretary to Lord Burghley. Roper thinks Hicks, an ardent collector of things Roman, asked his friend, Henry Peacham, Sr., to record part of a

---

[70] Roper's full article can be found at:

http://www.dlropershakespearians.com/The%20Testimony%20of%20the%20Reverend%20Henry%20Peacham.pdf performance of an early version of *Titus* put on at Hatfield House.

Of further significance is that *The Compleat Gentlemen*, published one year before the 1623 First Folio, lists the Earl of Oxford as first among poets. William Shakespeare is not mentioned. The book went through two further printings but the absence of Shakespeare's name was not corrected. Roper asks how Stratfordians can explain how the man who saw Shakespeare's *Titus Andronicus* could leave him out of a book about poets?

The younger Peacham wrote an emblem book called *Minerva's Brittana*, which sports the following cover:

The design has been thought by some to be a cipher about a playwright who has hidden himself from the world. "Mente, Vide Bori," can be roughly translated as "by the mind shall I be seen." Is this is an anagram for "Tibi Nom. De Vere?" Was Peacham thinking of Oxford?

Chapter 14
The Return to Oxford Court - March 28, 1589

Chapter 15
Oxford's Hand in *Titus Andronicus*

Act and scene divisions were not present in all the early scripts. There are five plays with no divisions (Henry VI, Part 3, Troilus & Cressida, Romeo & Juliet, Timon of Athens, and Anthony & Cleopatra); nine plays with only act divisions (Comedy of Errors, Much Ado About Nothing, Midsummer Night's Dream, All's Well That Ends Well, Henry VI Part 2, Coriolanus, Titus Andronicus, and Julius Caesar), thirteen with act and scene divisions, and nine with divisions that are "regarded as ranging from poor to abominable." The Applause First Folio, p. xxi, footnote 9, and p. lix, footnote 2.

The words 'hand' appears 76 times in Titus Andronicus.

Chapter 16
Titus Andronicus at the Rose

There is no evidence that Marlowe ever met Shakespeare or Oxford or that *Titus* was intentionally written to fail. It was obviously an attempt to capitalize on the success of *The Spanish Tragedy* and does show evidence that Marlowe's language in *Tamburlaine* and *Faust* was stolen and parodied. However, one of the problems in trying to see links between the plays and current events is that there were many later additions to many plays. These additions tend to skew the true date of a play's completion, which ultimately means that it is almost impossible to tell when many plays, or parts of many plays, were written. And, the bias that William Shakespeare could not have appeared in London until around 1590, prevents scholars from seeing links between the plays and earlier events. See, Clarke, for example.

In *The Death of Shakespeare*, Marlowe quotes Aaron the Moor to Shackspear:

Oft have I digg'd up dead men from their graves,
And set them upright at their dear friends' doors,
Even when their sorrows almost were forgot;
And on their skins, as on the bark of trees,
Have with my knife carved in Roman letters,
'Let not your sorrow die, though I am dead.'

which mimics what Marlowe had Barabas speak in *The Jew of Malta* (Act II, Scene 1):

And kill sick people groaning under walls:
Sometimes I go about and poison wells;

...

And every moon made some or other mad,
And now and then one hang himself for grief,
Pinning upon his breast a long great scroll
How I with interest tormented him.

"Circe's charm hath turned them all to swine" is from *Satire VIII: A Cynicke Satyre"* by John Marston. Marston and Ben Jonson got into the 'Poet's War' in 1599-1601. *Hamlet*, published in 1603, seems to be referring to this dust-up which involved the children's players who performed at Blackfriars. (John Lyly and Oxford were associated at various times with the children's players who performed at Blackfriars.)

Rosencrantz:

here is, sir, an aery of children, little eyases,
that cry out on the top of question, and are most
tyrannically clapped for't: these are now the
fashion, and so berattle the common stages--so they call them--that many wearing rapiers are afraid of goose-quills and dare scarce come thither.

Hamlet:

What, are they children? who maintains 'em?
how are they escoted? Will they pursue the

quality no longer than they can sing? will they not say afterwards, if they should grow themselves to common players--as it is most like, if their means are no better--their writers do them wrong, to make them exclaim against their own succession?

Rosencrantz:

'Faith, there has been much to do on both sides; And the nation holds it no sin to tarre them to controversy: there was, for a while, no money bid for argument, unless the poet and the player went to cuffs in the question.

Hamlet:

Is't possible?

Guildenstern:

O, there has been much throwing about of brains.

Hamlet:

Do the boys carry it away?

Rosencrantz:

Ay, that they do, my lord; Hercules and his load too.[71]

Marston will appear in Chapter 40. Although there is no evidence he worked for Oxford, one of the poems in *The Scourge of Villany* appears to praise Oxford:

---

[71] Some think *Hercules and his load too* is a reference to the Globe Theater because supposedly the globe on top was held up by a model of Hercules and, thus, Oxford is indicating the little eyases are taking business away from the adult actors.

John Marston Satyre IX.

Here's a Toy to mocke an Ape indeede.

My soule adores judiciall schollership;
But when to servile imitatorship
Some spruce Athenian pen is prentized,
Tis worse then apish. Fie! be not flattered
With seeming worth! Fond affectation
Befits an ape, an[D] mumping Babilon.

0 wh[A]t a tricksie, lerned, [N]icking strain
[I]s this applauded, sensel[E]se, modern vain!
When [L]ate I heard it from sage Mutius lips,
How ill, me thought, such wanton jiggin skips
Beseem'd his graver speech. "Farre fly thy fame,
Most, most of me beloved! whose silent name
One letter bounds. Thy true judiciall stile
I ever honour; and, if my love beguile

Not much my hopes, then thy unvalued worth
Shall mount faire place, when apes are turned forth."
I am too mild, Reach me my scourge againe;
O yon's a pen speakes in a learned vaine,

"[W]hose silent name One letter bounds" identifies the object of his praise. "Edward de Vere" seems the only name that would solve this puzzle. (Are the "apes … turned forth" Shakespeare?)

Compare the lines between Speed and Valentine in *Two Gentlemen of Verona,* which are discussed in Chapter 23:

Speed:	*To yourself: why, she woos you by a figure.*
Valentine:	*What figure?*
Speed:	*By a letter, I should say.*

The only figure - number - that is also a letter is the letter "O", which may stand for Oxford.

Speed and Valentine are talking about Sylvia, who scholars recognize as a reference to Queen Elizabeth. Valentine, one of the two gentlemen of Verona, is one-half of Oxford (the two gentlemen are *The Two Gentlemen of Ver-One-A*). Valentine is a rather dull character, and Speed is having fun with him. The allusion to Oxford would have been easily recognized by Elizabeth.

Why does Marston refer to the object of his praise as "Mutius?" Mutius was the name of one of the sons of Titus Andronicus. So the reference must be to the play by the same name. But if Mutius is Oxford, doesn't it seem like Marston is saying he dislikes Shakespeare for being an ape and loves Oxford as a "sage?"

It has been pointed out by Gary Wills in *The New York Review of Books*, November 24, 2011, in *Shakespeare and Verdi in the Theater* (excerpted from his upcoming book, *Verdi's Shakespeare: Men of the Theater* (Viking)), that the playwright had to be aware of who the actors were and what their limitations were: "An aspiring playwright had to bring his idea to these actors (or their representatives) with a plot accommodated to the number and talents of the particular troupe. The parts he was describing had to be so arranged as to allow for multiple doublings. A man playing two roles could not meet himself on stage, or even come back in as someone else too soon to allow for costume and other changes (a beard, wig, spectacles, padding, and so on)."

This means that Oxford had to be aware of where Henslowe was going to get two sets of twins to put on *A Comedy of Errors.*

Wills also argues that it was the players who worked with the playwright and the promoter only got involved later on. He may be right. However, his claim that "Lord Bacon or the Earl of Oxford, writing in their homes, could not have known such things [who the actors were, what the human resources were]" is probably wrong unless he knows that Oxford was indeed writing in his home. (And larding in Bacon with Oxford (pun intended) is a standard Stratfordian ploy to limit the growing awareness that Oxford wrote the plays. At least Professor Wills didn't mention Thomas Looney.)

Chapter 17
Gray's Inn

There was a performance of *The Comedy of Errors* at Gray's Inn (not Grey's Inn) that became known as the Night of Errors because of the rowdiness of the students and the collapse of scaffolding on which they were standing, but that performance occurred in 1594. Most scholars believe *The Comedy of Errors* is one of Shakespeare's earliest plays, if not his first. Unlike any other Shakespeare plays, it slavishly follows the rules set down by Aristotle. It's plotting and versification give it away as an early play. The title may even be an homage to Donatus, a 4th century grammarian, who set down a five-part formula for comedy. Donatus thought there should always be 'something towards error' in a comedy, to quote Tony Tanner at p. 16, or "aliquod ad errorem." Oxford's incessant punning in his early plays, combined with his talent in mixing current events and mythology, all the while speaking on multiple levels (see the discussion of *Much Ado About Nothing*) makes it almost certain that he had Donatus in mind when he wrote *The Comedy of Errors.*

Chapter 18
A Summons from the Queen

The deal the Queen strikes with Shackspear and Oxford to give him £1,000 a year in return for plays about English history and help against Martin Marprelate is not supported by any evidence.[72] Many scholars have hypothesized that the grant was given to Oxford (which actually occurred in 1586, not 1589) for writing history plays to bolster the crown during the years Spain threatened invasion. Nashe implies this in *Pierce Penilesse* (1592).

> *"What if I prove plays to be no extreame; but a rare exercise of vertue? First, for the subiect of them (for the most part) is borrowed out of our English Chronicles...How it would have ioyed brave*

---

72 The document read to Oxford in *The Death of Shakespeare* is a verbatim copy of the patent granting him £1,000 a year, except that the year has been altered to reflect 1589 instead of 1586. There was no signature line on the original document.

Talbot (the terror of the French) to think that after he had lyne two hundred years in his Tome, he should triumphe againe on the Stage, and have his bones newe embalmed with the teares of ten thousand spectators at least (at severall times), who, in the Tragedian that represents this person, imagine they behold him fresh bleeding".

The Works of Thomas Nashe, Edited From the Original Texts by Roland Mckerrow (London: Sidgwick & Jackson, 1910), vol. I, p. 212.

Unfortunately, there is no hard evidence to support the scenario put forward in Chapter 18 that the £1,000 was given to Oxford in return for plays. However, the annuity Elizabeth gave Oxford was the largest pension she granted to anyone during her long reign except for secret grants to King James in Scotland. Also, there were no strings attached to it as there were with other grants. See, Appendix C in Ward. Richard M. Waugaman, in his article *The Bi-Sexuality of Shakespeare's Sonnets and Implications for De Vere's Authorship*, in The Psychoanalytic Review, Vol. 97, No. 5, October 2010, states, without giving his source, that at around the time Elizabeth gave Oxford the £1,000 annual pension, "the annual budget of the Revels Office … dropped from £1,300 annually to £300 per year." Henry Howard was awarded £200 a year in 1599;[73] Southampton's income was £1,145 a year, of which he had free use of only £750. Ward, p. 259. The £1,000 annual pension would be worth more than £200,000 in today's money. *www.measuringworth.com/ukcompare/*. The £1 price of the First Folio in 1623 was equivalent to £150 today.

---

[73] The same Howard who, with Arundel, made the allegations from the Tower against Oxford that are repeated as gospel by Nelson in his biography of Oxford. The grant to Howard would continue "as long as lands of the late Earl of Arundel remain in the Queen's hands." Ward, p. 259. Arundel had been beheaded and his lands seized. Had he lived and died a natural death, Howard would have inherited Arundel's property, so the £200 must be seen in a different light from other grants listed by Ward in Appendix C.

Oxford would appear to have been out of money in 1586. *This Star of England* discusses the history of the sale of Oxford's estates at length at pp 705; 781-783. See, Appendix B in Ward, which is a table of lands Oxford bought and sold from 1571 to 1601. Both sources show that most of Oxford's sales of the lands he inherited from his father occurred by 1585. 47 had been sold by then; he only sold 7 more over the remainder of his life.

The plays are rife with references to £1,000. See, the extensive discussion of the use of the word "a thousand pounds" in the plays in footnote 136 at p. 337 in Roger Stritmatter's *A Law Case in Verse: Venus and Adonis and the Authorship Question*, Univ. of Tennessee Law Review, Vol. 72:307. Dr. Stritmatter also discusses the presence of the words 'kiss' and 'thousand' in Venus and Adonis ("A thousand kisses buys my heart from me – line 517, at p. 338, among others) and points out that Endimion danced around "kisses" and Oxford's "thousand-pound annuity" as well. At p. 337.

Borrowing money was commonplace among the noble class in England in the 16th century. Oxford was not the only noble to waste his patrimony. See, Hickes, beginning at p. 149, in which Alan Smith discusses the lending business carried on by Michael Hickes, who was secretary and agent to Lord Burghley as well as Sir Robert Cecil.

The Arte of English Poesy was published in September, 1589, by Richard Fields, who would publish *Venus and Adonis* in 1593 as well as other works attributed to Shakespeare. Fields was from Stratford-upon-Avon and must have known Oxford (and Shackspear). He came to London to apprentice for a Frenchman named Thomas Vautrollier who was an excellent printer. Vautrollier died in 1587 and Fields married his widow the next year.[74] The words quoted by the Queen are verbatim from *The*

[74] Fields' life parallels the events of the life of the Count de Beaumarchais 200 years later in Paris. Beaumarchais was an apprentice watchmaker whose patron suddenly died. Beaumarchais married his patron's widow and acquired the dead man's title and watch-making business. Beaumarchais' watches made him famous (he invented some critical clock

Arte of English Poesy. The author remains unknown. It could have been Oxford. It was not unusual for him to tout himself as the best for comedy. He had not yet written any tragedies, *Titus* notwithstanding.

Fields printed many pamphlets and books in Spanish for dissemination in Spain, an unusual market for him, which gives rise to the thought he must have been working for Burghley who used the pamphlets to sow discord in Spain.

Martin Marprelate was the name of the author who wrote scathing pamphlets attacking the Church of England. He may not have wanted to bring back the Catholic Church but his racy style of challenging the Church caused a great deal of concern for Elizabeth. Countering him was a difficult and lengthy process and Oxford's grant may have been given to him to combat Martin. This corner of Elizabethan history is incredibly complicated. An excellent book on the subject is *An Anatomy of the Marprelate Controversy 1588-1596: Retracing Shakespeare's Identity and that of Martin Marprelate*, by Elizabeth Appleton, The Edwin Mellen Press 2001.

"My soul will be in my words, so give me my soul now, and be damned with it hereafter!" This is a parody of Robert Greene's statement in *A Groatsworth of Wit Bought with a Million of Repentance* as to how he used to think about religion and his life: "If I may have my desire while I live, I am satisfied; let me shift after death as I may." Greene died September 3, 1592; *Groatsworth* was published shortly after his death.

Laying the snake before the fire was a comment actually made by Sir Walter Raleigh (he preferred 'Ralegh') in a letter written in 1583 to Burghley in response to Burghley's request that Raleigh intercede with the Queen to restore Oxford to favor

---

components that were used in watches until motorized mechanisms came along in the 20th century) and he became close to the French king who set Beaumarchais up as the conduit for French efforts to fund the American Revolution. Beaumarchais is more famous, however, for having written *The Marriage of Figaro* and *The Barber of Seville.*

at court. Raleigh is quoted in Anderson at p. 193 (quoting Edwards, Life of Raleigh, 2:22), as having written "I am content, for your sake, to lay the serpent before the fire [meaning Oxford], as much as in me lieth, that having recovered strength, myself may be most in danger of his poison and sting." Raleigh was apparently referring to the fear that Oxford might hurt Raleigh's chances at court if Oxford were restored to favor.

Was Raleigh quoting Oxford? Oxford wrote a poem under the name "*meritum patere, grave*" which is considered to be Oxford's, in which he said the following:

> *To a gentlewoman who blamed him for writing his friendly advice in verse unto another lover of hirs.*
>
> *Amongst old written tales, this one I beare in minde,*
> *A simple soul much like myselfe, did once a serpent finde,*
> *Which (almost dead for colde) lay moyling in the myre,*
> *When he for pittie toke it up and brought it to the fyre.*
> *No sooner was the Snake, cured of hir grief,*
> *But straight she sought to hurt the man, that lent hir such relief.*
> *Such Serpent seemeth thou, such simple soule am I,*
> *That for the weight of my good will, am blamed without cause why.*
>
> . . . .
>
> *I must and will endure, thy spite without repent,*
> *The blame is mine, the triumph thine, and I am well content.*
> *Meritum petere, grave.*

Ogburns, Chapter 1582-1583, quoting from *A Hundreth Sundrie Flowres.*

Since *A Hundreth Sundrie Flowres* was published in 1573, and Raleigh's letter was written ten years later in 1583, it seems Raleigh (who was talking about Oxford when he wrote his letter to Burghley) was thinking of Oxford's poem when he mentioned the snake.

The ipse reference is from *As You Like It,* Act IV, Scene 3:

> *William:* *Good even, Audrey.*
>
> *Audrey:* *God ye good even, William.*

William:	*And good even to you, sir.*
Touchstone:	*Good even, gentle friend. Cover thy head, cover thy head; nay, prithee, be covered. How old are you, friend?*
William:	*Five and twenty, sir.*
Touchstone:	*A ripe age. Is thy name William?*
William:	*William, sir.*
Touchstone:	*A fair name. Wast born i' the forest here?*
William:	*Ay, sir, I thank God.*
Touchstone:'	*Thank God;' a good answer. Art rich?*
William:	*Faith, sir, so so.*
Touchstone:	*'So so' is good, very good, very excellent good; And yet it is not; it is but so so. Art thou wise?*
William:	*Ay, sir, I have a pretty wit.*
Touchstone:	*Why, thou sayest well. I do now remember a saying, 'The fool doth think he is wise, but the wise man knows himself to be a fool.' The heathen philosopher, when he had a desire to eat a grape, would open his lips when he put it into his mouth; meaning thereby that grapes were made to eat and ips to open. You do love this maid?*
William:	*I do, sir.*
Touchstone;	*Give me your hand. Art thou learned?*
William:	*No, sir.*
Touchstone:	*Then learn this of me: to have, is to have; for it is a figure in rhetoric that drink, being poured out of a cup into a glass, by filling the one doth empty the other; for all your writers do consent that ipse is he: now, you are not ipse, for I am he.*

William:	*Which he, sir?*
Touchstone:	*He, sir, that must marry this woman. Therefore, you clown, abandon,--which is in the vulgar leave,--the society,--which in the boorish is company,--of this female,--which in the common is woman; which together is, abandon the society of this female, or, clown, thou perishest; or, to thy better understanding, diest; or, to wit I kill thee, make thee away, translate thy life into death, thy liberty into bondage: I will deal in poison with thee, or in bastinado, or in steel; I will bandy with thee in faction; I will o'errun thee with policy; I will kill thee a hundred and fifty ways: therefore tremble and depart.*
Audrey:	*Do, good William.*
William:	*God rest you merry, sir.*

Exit

Stratfordians pass over this scene because it is difficult to explain why Shakespeare would name a character after himself and then treat the character (himself) so badly. William is obviously a dolt and a coward here and Touchstone is enraged that William is thinking of marrying Audrey.

Oxfordians have no problem with William's treatment. If Oxford wrote the plays, Oxford is sending up Shakespeare (with no less ill-treatment than Jonson treated Shakespeare when he parodied him as the character Sogliardo in *Everyman Out of His Humour*).

Audrey may represent the plays. This scene may have been one of the 'pounds of flesh' Oxford extracted from Shakespeare for having to put up with the man from Stratford being identified as the author of the plays.

This is the same play where Touchstone says:

> *When a man's verses cannot be understood, nor a man's good wit seconded with the forward child Understanding, it strikes a man more dead than a great reckoning in a little room.*

This is almost as difficult to understand what the author "Shakespeare" was trying to accomplish here as the ipse statement. Was this a sensitive poet complaining that his verses "cannot be understood?" An author whose work cannot be identified as his? Why would Shakespeare write this, when his name was on the plays and poems and sonnets? (Many scholars believe that the reference to "a great reckoning in a little room" refers to Marlowe's murder in a little room. That may be so, but the question as to why Shakespeare, if he was the author of *As You Like It*, would write these lines remains unanswered.)

Notice that William is 'five and twenty' in the scene quoted above from *As You Like It.* Shakespeare was twenty-five in 1589, just about the time he made his appearance in London. (Close analysis of Nashe's Preface to *Menaphon*, published in 1589, does not support a conclusion that Nashe was referring to Shakespeare. See, *The Reader's Companion*, Chapter 21.)

Mark Anderson in *Shakespeare By Another Name* makes two very interesting comments about this scene. First, he points out that "to have is to have" is *Avere è avere* in Italian, or, "a Vere is a Vere." At p. 327. This may be a stretch but is not beyond the puns on Oxford's name that appear in Oxford's writings and throughout the plays. See, below, for example, a discussion of the Latin poem Oxford sent his wife, Anne, from Paris in 1575, which is discussed below on the next page. However, Anderson's second comment appears to be spot-on. He points out that Oxford was obviously thinking of Socrates when he wrote the lines for Touchstone. He quotes Socrates from Plato's *Symposium:*

> My dear Agathon, Socrates replied as he took his seat beside him, I only wish that wisdom *were* the kind of thing one could share by sitting next to someone—<u>if it flowed, for instance, from the</u>

> one that is full to the one that is empty, like the water in two cups finding its level through a piece of worsted [Anderson adds *fine woolen fabric*]. If that were how it worked, I'm sure I'd congratulate myself on sitting next to you, for you'd soon have me brimming over with the most exquisite kind of wisdom. (Emphasis added.)

Anderson concludes: "In plain English, then, Touchstone tells William: Know this, kid. I am he himself, the author, a Vere. ... You are only pretending to be me. You are not me. You never will be me."

Oxford constantly punned on his name. He sent his wife, Anne Cecil, a Greek Bible from Paris while he was on his way to Italy which contained a Latin poem written on the fly-leaf. The poem was filled with puns on 'truth' – *Vera, Veritas,* and *Vere.* Clark, p. 118 has a translation in English. One of the lines reads "... and may thy *true* motto be *Ever Lover of the Truth,*" which Ms. Clark translates as a double pun meaning, to Anne, "E. Ver, Lover of the Truth." See, also, *This Star of England*, p. 85.

In *All's Well That Ends Well,* Bertram makes the same pun in a letter to Helen: "When thou canst get the ring upon my finger which never shall come off, and show me a child of my body that I am father to, then call me husband; but in such a 'then' I write a 'never.'" ("never" could be taken to mean "An E. Ver.)[75]

---

[75] This leads to the interesting connection between the bed-switch plays (*All's Well* and *Measure for Measure*) and Oxford's initial belief, when he returned from Italy, that his oldest daughter, Elizabeth, was not his child. It is reported that he was eventually convinced Elizabeth (Lisbeth in *The Death of Shakespeare*) was his child by being told he had unknowingly slept with Anne, his wife, before he left for the continent. (Was he drunk? Did he not remember? Most people have difficulty accepting the possibility that Oxford could have slept with his wife and not recognize her.) Wright's *History of Essex,* p. 517, states that "the father [meaning Oxford] of Lady Anne [not Elizabeth] by stratagem, contrived that her husband should unknowingly sleep with her, believing her to be another woman, and she bore him a son [sic] in consequence of this meeting." Clark, at p. 119, quoting Wright's

A copy of one of Oxford's signatures is:

(Another facsimile, one of many that are extant, is on a letter reproduced at p. 654 in *This Star of England.* Beauclerk has an excellent reproduction of one.)

There are only seven checks on the lower line of Oxford's signature, not seventeen. The horizontal line does not add the missing ten. The bar through the crown is a statement that either no crown was awarded or it was taken away.

Oxford signed his name this until Elizabeth died in 1603. He then dropped the crown and hash marks.[76] Had he become king he would have been Edward VII.

There is no evidence that Oxford was offered or awarded a crown or a coronet (a small crown worn by some nobles below the royal family). The line through the crown on Oxford's signature seems to indicate that Oxford felt he had been denied the crown, a cheeky statement in a time when commenting on the succession could get your hand cut off.[77]

History of Essex, p. 517. There are other references to this connection that are equally as erroneous in the details as this reference, and the bed-switch was a device known in Italian theater at the time, so there is no hard evidence that Oxford was the object of a bed-switch trick before he left for Italy. This is discussed in more detail in Chapter 52 while Oxford is writing *All's Well.*

[76] Pearson has a copy of the last signature, with a knot below his name, and no crown, as well as another Oxford signature with the crown. (unnumbered pages.)

[77] In 1579, Hatton arranged to have the hand of John Stubbe and his publisher, William Page, cut off for writing and printing a tract that argued against Elizabeth marrying the Duke d'Anjou. Stubbe [what an awful name for a man who would lose his hand] wrote: 'The Discoverie of a gaping gulf whereinto England is like to be swallowed by another French marriage, if the Lord forbid not the banes by letting her majestie see the sin and punishment thereof.' For this he and Page had their hands cut off. Stubbe and Page were

An interesting discussion of what Oxford was doing by signing his name this way is in Pearson, Daphne (2005), *Edward de Vere (1550–1604): The Crisis and Consequences of Wardship*, Ashgate Publishing Ltd., at p. 181, and also in her article *Rough Winds Do Shake: A Fresh Look At The Tudor Rose Theory*, which can be read at *http://www.elizabethanreview.com/price.pdf.* In finding the Tudor Rose Theory wanting, Ms. Pearson displays drawings of the crowns for a monarch, duke, marquis, earl, baron, and viscount (p. 17) and effectively argues that Oxford's signature reproduced the crown of an earl. Oxford's friend, Edward Baynam, played with his signature in a similar way. Baynam signed his name with a horizontal line crossed four times, presumably to indicate he was the fourteenth in his line. Pearson, at p. 181. If so, it may have been a joke between the two earls and the reason Oxford was never punished by the Queen for using his signature.

While history may come down on the side of concluding that Oxford was not broadcasting to the world that he was 'not' king of England, support for concluding that he was doing just that comes from, of all people, Sir Philip Sidney. Mary E. Hazard, in

---

brought from the Tower to a scaffold set up in the market-place at Westminster. Before the barbarous sentence was carried out Stubbe addressed the bystanders. He professed warm attachment to the Queen and stated that the loss of his hand would in no way impair his loyalty to her (see his speech in Harrington's *Nugæ Antiquæ*). When he ceased speaking he and Page 'had their right hands cut off by the blow of a butcher's knife (with a mallet) struck through their wrists.' The chronicler Stow was present. "I can remember, "he wrote, "standing by John Stubbe [and] so soon as his right hand was off, [he] put off his hat with his left, and cryed aloud 'God save the Queen.' The people round about stood mute, whether stricken with fear at the first sight of this kind of punishment, or for commiseration of the man whom they reputed honest." (Stow, *Annales*, 1605, p. 1168). The second man, Page, when his bleeding stump was being seared with hot iron, exclaimed, 'There lies the hand of a true Englishman.' Stubbe apparently passed out after his brave speech; whether Page was able to walk away is not known. *Dictionary of National Biography, 1885-1900*, Volume 55, *Stubbs, John,* by Sidney Lee.

Elizabethan Silent Language,[78] writes about the way Elizabethans communicated nonverbally (the 'silent language').

> Courtiers and other members of the upper social classes distinguished themselves through use of devices, … designed both to conceal and to reveal. … Camden's long discussion of impresas in the *Remains* [*Concerning Britain*, Ed. R. D. Dunn, Univ. of Toronto, Toronto, 1984] demonstrates both the usual possibility of identifying the bearer and the occasional confusion caused by ineptitude or ambiguity … Hazard, p. 41.

One of the examples Hazard cites from Camden is the following:

> Sir Philip Sidney, who was a long time heire apparent to the Earle of Leicester, after the said Earle had a sonne borne to him, used at the next Tilte-day following ~~SPERAVI~~, thus dashed through, to shew his hope therein was dashed."[79] (Emphasis added.)

This occurred in 1581 when Leicester's second wife, Lady Essex (née Lettice Knollys, who was the widow of the First Earl of Essex and the mother of the Second Earl of Essex, who would be beheaded in 1601), gave birth to a son named Robert Dudley after his father.[80] Oxford, thirty-one years old in 1581,

---

[78] University of Nebraska Press, Lincoln and London, 2000.

[79] Hazard, p. 42. "Speravi" is translated as "I have hope" from "spero", to look forward to, hope for; hope; anticipate. Oxford Latin Dictionary. Stone, Jon R., *The Routledge Dictionary of Latin Quotations – The Illiterati's Guide to Latin Maxims, Mottoes, Proverbs, and* Sayings, Routledge, New York and London (2005), p. 208. Was Camden punning here when he said Sidney used dashes to express his feeling that his hopes of inheriting Leicester's wealth had been 'dashed'?

[80] Leicester had fathered another son named Robert Dudley in 1574 by Lady Douglas Sheffield. Leicester never married Lady Douglas. Thus, this first son was illegitimate. His second son and namesake, born in 1581, was the child who 'dashed' Sir Philip's hopes. However, Sir Philip despaired too early. The Earl's second son died at three. Sidney followed him in 1587. See, *The Reader's Companion*, Chapter 73, as to Leicester's second wife, Lettice Knollys,

had been using his 'Edward the 7th' signature for quite some time. Therefore, Sidney was, if anything, imitating Oxford, not the other way around.

The line with seven checks on it in Oxford's signature imitate the score-keeping table in a jousting tournament. See, Figure 6 in Nelson as an example of a jousting table. Beauclerk has an excellent reproduction of the 1571 table.[81] Oxford won the tournament a number of times. The last time was in 1581 as Sidney was silently expressing his disappointment at the birth of a legitimate heir who he thought would dispossess him of Leicester's fortune.[82]

Oxford's signature is worthy of more attention than it has gotten. It seems that his signature is a graphic announcement that he had not become Edward VII. If so, it was an outrageous 'silent communication,' and an insight into who he was. The man who would get Anne Vavasor pregnant twice under the Queen's nose, who would blister people with one-liners and fill his plays with characterizations that left them as laughing-stocks for all time to come, was perfectly capable of signing his name 'Edward-the-not-king.' His love of words, is dizzying at times.

---

and the litigation over whether the illegitimate Robert Dudley by Lady Douglas Sheffield was, in fact, legitimate and thereby dispossessed Lettice Knollys, Leicester's widow, of Leicester's inheritance.

81 Ward has an excellent discussion beginning at p. 56 about the records of the tournaments Oxford participated in and the procedures involved.

82 The other contestants were, aside from Oxford and Sidney, Sir Henry Lee, who was keeper of the Tower and Oxford's jailer when Oxford, Anne Vavasor, and their new-born son were committed to his custody in 1581. Sir Henry became so enamored of Anne that he had a suit of armor made with her initials all over it. His pursuit paid off. He induced Anne to live with him ten years later and they apparently had a good relationship that lasted the rest of Sir Henry's life. Oxford's son, then, named Edward Vere was raised by Anne and Sir Henry. Edward Vere became Sir Edward when, as a young man, he was knighted for bravery in fighting in the Lowlands by none other than Sir Horace Vere, his great uncle and Oxford's cousin. (And, with little doubt, the role model for Horatio in *Hamlet*. Sir Horace was sometimes referred to as Sir Horatio.)

The first time Oxford won the tournament was in 1571, for which "Oxford himself [received] a tablet of diamonds." Nelson, p. 69. Sonnet 122 may allude to this gift:

Thy gift, thy tables, are within my brain
Full character'd with lasting memory,
Which shall above that idle rank remain
Beyond all date, even to eternity;
Or at the least, so long as brain and heart
Have faculty by nature to subsist;
Till each to razed oblivion yield his part
Of thee, thy record never can be miss'd.
That poor retention could not so much hold,
Nor need I tallies thy dear love to score;
Therefore to give them from me was I bold,
To trust those tables that receive thee more:
To keep an adjunct to remember thee
Were to import forgetfulness in me.

Are the "tables" the "tablet of diamonds" Oxford received in 1571? Sonnet 122 tells a story that a "table" received as a gift by the author was given by him to a third person. The gift-giver was irked by this. The author responds that he has no need for the gift to remember the gift-giver. In fact, the author chides the gift-giver for thinking the author would forget what was in the tables simply because he gave them away.

Knowing that the Earl of Oxford was given a "tablet of diamonds" for winning the 1571 tournament casts Sonnet 122 in an intriguing light, and raises another interesting question. If the gift was the "tablet of diamonds" Oxford received in 1571, did he pass them on as a gift to Anne Vavasor? Was the "tablet of diamonds" discovered in Anne's bedroom when Anne gave birth to Oxford's son in 1581, the same year he won the tournament again? The room in which Anne delivered Oxford's son was next to the Queen's bedroom. This compounded their violation of Elizabeth's rule that her ladies-in-waiting were to remain chaste. Historians believe the Queen consigned all three (the new baby included) to the Tower because the fault was committed so close to the royal bedchamber, but what if the tablet of diamonds was discovered in Anne's room at the same time? If so, the discovery would have infuriated the Queen even more. And, thus, is Sonnet 122 an attempt on Oxford's part to earn reinstatement at court? If it was, it probably did not succeed. Chiding the gift-giver for thinking the tablet of diamonds were needed to help the poet remember the Queen, if the Queen gifted the tablet to Oxford, is a telling look into the personality of a man who believed words could be twisted to mean anything. He was, after all, one of the highest lords in the land and never needed to apologize for anything. It would be interesting to explore what the other sonnets show about this part of the poet's personality.

Of course, the above string of thoughts does not cement the conclusion that Sonnet 122 was written by Oxford for having given the tablet of diamonds he got in 1571 to Anne Vavasor but, as with so many of the sonnets, what was Sonnet 122 about?

Timothie Bright published *Characterie* in 1588 and is credited with inventing modern shorthand. Elizabeth, to whom the book was dedicated, rewarded him with monopolies and sinecures.

"Nothing" was another word for vagina in Elizabethan times. Kiernan, *Filthy Shakespeare,* p. 69, *et seq*. She cites the following scene between Hamlet and Ophelia (Act III, Scene 2):

Hamlet: *Lady, shall I lie in your lap?*

Ophelia: *No, my lord.*

Hamlet: *I mean, my head upon your lap?*

Ophelia: *Ay, my lord.*

Hamlet: *Do you think I meant country matters?*

Ophelia: *I think nothing, my lord.*

Hamlet: *That's a fair thought to lie between maids' legs.*

Ophelia: *What is, my lord?*

Hamlet: *Nothing.*

Ophelia: *You are merry, my lord.*

Chapter 19
The Boar's Head

Dick Tarleton did a bit with a dog and was a famous clown on stage. Falstaff may have been the outgrowth of something Tarleton started. Tarleton's death in 1588, as well as that of William Knell the year before (whose widow married John Heminges—see Chapter 32—Christmas at the Boar's Head), cause Stratfordians problems with *Famous Victories* because they both are noted as having played in it. That means *Famous Victories* was on the boards before 1587. Every plot event in *Famous Victories* is present in *Henry IV* and *Henry V*, and in the same order. Stratfordians argue that Shakespeare used *Famous Victories* for *Henry IV* and *Henry V*. Similarities, however, imply that the same author wrote them all. If Shakespeare wrote the *Henry* plays, he must have written *Famous Victories*, but this argument is not available to the Stratfordians Shakespeare would have been too young to have had such a play on the stage before 1587. If Oxford is the author of the plays, there are no problems. See, *The Reader's Companion*, Chapter 9 – *Procne's Revenge.*

Chapter 20
The Next Day - Oxford Court

As to Richard Field, the best treatment is in Nicholl, *The Lodger Shakespeare*, p. 175 ff. Field was older than Shakespeare but not by much. Both were from Stratford, and there are records that show the two families interacted. Field apprenticed to a Frenchman, Thomas Vautrollier, who was a high-class printer. Field completed his apprenticeship in February 1587. Conveniently, Vautrollier died in July. In 1588, Field published his first book with Vautrollier's widow, Jacqueline, and married her on January 12, 1589.

Field published *Venus and Adonis* in 1593, which marked the first appearance in print of the name "William Shakespeare." This was a spelling not used by the man from Stratford. See, footnote 3 above. Fields published other publications over the next decades, and must have known Oxford. He also printed a new edition of Ovid's *Metamorphoses* in 1589. Since Oxford had "helped" his uncle, Arthur Golding, translate the original version while Oxford was living at Cecil House and Arthur was Oxford's tutor, Oxford would naturally been keen to find out whether Fielding had altered the original translation. Ovid was Oxford's greatest influence after the Bible. Golding was a Puritan, and published nothing but dry, translations and religious works after he published the *Metamorphoses*, which was, in contrast, full of racy translations that bore little resemblance to the original Latin. Thus, some believe that Oxford was the translator of the *Metamorphoses.* Anderson, p. 25-29.

Endimion - The Man In The Moon was published in 1591 but probably performed earlier. The statement on the Quarto title-page concerning the royal performance "agrees with the record of payment to Thomas Giles, Master of the Children of Paul's for a play presented before the Queen at Greenwich Palace, Feb. 2, 1588, and this doubtless dates *Endimion.* ... Cynthia is the Queen, and Tellus ... must have recalled Mary Queen of Scots[83] .... Some favorable picture of the Earl of Oxford would be expected, and a case has been made out for him as Endimion; but consistent reproduction of actuality would have been impolitic, and the critics who have sought to find it have unduly disregarded the caveat in Lyly's Prologue to the play." (The Prologue simply says that "it is a tale of the Man in the Moon" and nothing else.) *English Drama - 1580 - 1642*, p. 40. Here, the professors (in this case, in 1933) are evidencing concern about labeling the main character as Oxford. They can't avoid naming Cynthia as Elizabeth but cannot bring themselves to identify Oxford as Endimion.

Anderson, p. 212, thinks *Endimion* was a gift to the Queen for reviving Oxford as an author. See also Roger Stritmatter's *"A Law Case In Verse: Venus and Adonis and the Authorship Question,*

---

83 Stritmatter thinks Anne Vavasor inspired the character of Tellus, which might be a better connection since Anne fell in love with her jailer, Sir Henry Lee (or he with her), and Tellus falls in love with her jailer as well. At p. 330. See, also, Clark, *Hidden Allusions,* at 151.

Tennessee Law Review, Vol. 27, 307, at pp. 329-330. It is interesting that the law censoring publications and restricting printing presses in England became effective June 23, 1586, only three days before Oxford received his £1,000 annuity. Stritmatter thinks *Endimion* was written in 1586. It may have been performed in November, less than six months later. The title page (See, *Hidden Allusions*, p. 149) states that it was "play'd before the Queenes Majestie at Greenwich at Candlemas at night" but doesn't say which year. The title page shows the play was published in 1591.

It seems likely that the "pinch him blue" lines in *A Comedy of Errors* are from *Endimion* (and not vice-versa). In *Endimion,* the lines are:

> *Pinch him, pinch him, black and blue,*
> *Saucy mortals must not view*
> *What the Queen of Stars is doing,*
> *Nor pry into our fairy wooing.*

Act IV, Scene 3

In *Comedy of Errors*, the lines are:

> *We talk of goblins, owls, and elvish sprites:*
> *If we obey them not, this will ensue,*
> *They'll suck our breath, or pinch us black and blue.*

Act I, Scene 2.

The idea of fairies biting people black and blue was apparently an idea worth stealing, at least for Ben Jonson who, in 1603 wrote a masque for the newly crowned King James originally titled *The Entertainment at Althorp* in which Queen Mag says:

> *Fairies, pinch him black and blue.*
> *Now you have him, make him rue.*

To go back to *Endimion,* Sir Tophas and the servants whom he threatens are prototypes of Falstaff and the servants in *Two Gentlemen* and *Comedy of Errors*. Bullough thinks so. P. 172.

Lyly was Oxford's secretary for many years. In *Pierce's Supererogation* (1593), Gabriel Harvey said, "*young Euphues hatched the eggs that his elder friends lay*." He published eight plays before his work stopped in the early 1590s, even though he lived on for some time. See, *The Reader's Companion*, Chapter 1.

Looney, in Chapter XI-IV & V of *Shakespeare Identified*, has an extensive discussion of John Lyly and his relationship with Oxford. He quotes Stratfordians to the effect that Lyly was even more of an influence on Shakespeare than Marlowe, and that Lyly created the Elizabethan play. He asks sensibly how much of what we think is Lyly's work was actually Oxford's.

Lewis, in his *English Literature in the Sixteenth Century excluding Drama*, veered away from non-dramatic literature into Lyly's plays because they "cannot be passed over in silence without crippling the whole story that this book sets out to tell." P. 312, *et seq*. Lewis found the courtly scenes of *Endimion* delightful for five full acts but not the "weak foolery" of Sir Tophas. He concluded that Lyly was weak when he came to comedy. However, Lewis' comments on the songs in Lyly's plays are very interesting. "It is on these bubble-like comedies [Lewis wrote], not on *Euphues* nor on his anti-Martinish pamphlet *Pappe with a Hatchet*, that Lyly's fame must rest. It is the perfect instrument for his purpose, and he can make it pert, grave, tragic, or rapturously exalted. If, as most scholars think, he did not write the admirable songs which appeared in the 1632 collection of *Six Court Comedies*, he certainly wrote plays exactly fitted to contain these songs." (Lewis does not identify the scholars who think Lyly did not write the songs. If Lyly didn't, who did? Oxford?)

Lewis begs the question as to why the songs in Lyly's plays were not published earlier. And, as Ward points out, the situation is even more curious because Lyly's plays were published anonymously during his lifetime. Ward asks, understandably, if it is possible "to believe that a professional playwright, who was hoping to be appointed to the Mastership of the Revels [an office that Edward Tilney held from 1579 until his death in 1610], should have objected to having his name printed on the title-pages of his own plays[?]" Ward, p. 278. Lyly had signed both of his immensely popular *Euphues* allegories. As one of the most talked-of writers of his era, his name would have been of recognized value on any publication. Yet it was conspicuously omitted from these early quarto editions of the comedies such as *Endimion*. Lyly's eight plays were published and republished in his lifetime and for almost 50 years thereafter but without the songs that had been written for them. The script only indicated their positions in the plays. The songs were finally published in 1632 in *Six Court Comedies* but nine had gone missing. Lyly's biographer was puzzled. He even has an appendix beginning at p. 367 devoted to Lyly's songs and their history. Looney wonders if the missing songs had appeared in the plays attributed to Shakespeare because their true author was Oxford. Lyly's work and his relationship to the Earl of Oxford needs a scholar's examination beyond that given in Albert Feuillerat's *John Lyly* (in French) or works so far published by Stratfordian or Oxfordian scholars, such as Hunter.

The Cambridge History of English and American Literature in 18 Volumes (1907–21). Volume V. *The Drama to 1642, Part One; VI. The Plays of the University Wits*; § 6. *Authorship of the songs in Lyly's plays* (Available at *http://www.bartleby.com/215/0606.html*) has this to say about Shakespeare and Lyly:

> Whoever knows his Shakespeare and his Lyly well can hardly miss the many evidences that Shakespeare had read Lyly's plays almost as closely as Lyly had read Pliny's *Natural History*. It is not merely that certain words of the song of the birds' notes in *Campaspe* gave Shakespeare, subconsciously, probably, his hint for "Hark, hark, the lark"; or that, in the talk of Viola and the duke [footnote omitted] he was thinking of Phillida and Galathea; [footnote omitted] but that we could hardly imagine *Love's Labour's Lost* as existent in the period from 1590 to 1600, had not Lyly's work just preceded it. Setting aside the element of interesting story skilfully developed, which Shakespeare, after years of careful observation of his audiences, knew was his surest

appeal, do we not find *Much Ado About Nothing* and *As You Like It,* in their essentials, only developments, through the intermediate experiments in *Love's Labour's Lost* and *Two Gentlemen of Verona,* from Lyly's comedies?

Lyly and others participated in the Martin Marprelate controversy, a barrage of pamphlets attacking the writers who had attacked the Church of England. The identities of the various authors is another industry spawned by the interest in Shakespeare and the works attributed to him.

As to the connections between *Endimion* and Elizabeth, Mary, Queen of Scots, the Earl of Leicester, and Elizabeth's court, see *The English Drama - 900 -1642,* Parks, Edd Winfield, and Beatty, Richmond Croom, W.W. Norton & Co., Inc., New York, 1935, p. 170. Also, Roger Stritmatter's *"A Law Case In Verse: Venus and Adonis and the Authorship Question*, Tennessee Law Review, Vol. 27, 307, 331. Putting Endimion to sleep may have been an allusion to Elizabeth barring Oxford from writing plays; kissing Endimion may have been an allusion to an order that Shakespeare be a front man for Oxford and/or the £1,000 pension the Queen gave him in 1586.

Chapter 21
The Trunk of Plays

As to Nashe, see Sams, p. 72 ff. *Menaphon*, written by Robert Greene, was published in September, 1589, but it is the Preface written by Thomas Nashe that has always attracted the greater attention. See, *The Reader's Companion* to the previous chapter.

As to the scholars mistaking Nashe's target as Shakespeare when it was Kyd and Oxford, see Sams beginning page 68.

Sams points out that to bodge a line with 'and' applies to *The Spanish Tragedy* where there are four consecutive lines that begin with 'and':

> ***And*** *with that sword he fiercely waged war,*
> ***And*** *in that war he gave me dangerous wounds,*
> ***And*** *by those wounds he forced me to yield,*
> ***And*** *by my yielding I became his slave:*

[Act II, Scene 1]

but also in *Titus:*

> *Go pack with him,* **and** *give the mother gold,*
> **And** *tell them both the circumstance of all;*
> **And** *how by this their child shall be advanced,*
> **And** *be received for the emperor's heir,*
> **And** *substituted in the place of mine.*
>
> *[Act IV, Scene 2]*

Timon of Athens is "pessimism ... sardonic and unrelieved." Durant, p. 95. "Timon denounces all, high and low, and curses civilization itself as having demoralized mankind." There is no happiness in this play and Durant, shaking his head in disbelief, finds the play "unreal; we cannot believe that Shakespeare felt this ridiculous superiority to sinful men, this cowardly incapacity to stomach life." At p. 96. Clark believes *Timon* first appeared as *The Solitary Knight* in 1576, and makes interesting comparisons between Oxford's life and the plot of the play. P. 30, *et seq.*

The Famous Victories of Henry the Fifth is obviously a precursor to the *Henry IV* and *Henry V* plays, not the least because every major scene in the later plays can be traced back to *The Famous Victories*, including the Gad's Hill robbery, Sir John Oldcastle, and numerous other incidents. Traditional scholarship has difficulty deciding whether or not this is an early work of Shakespeare, or whether Shakespeare borrowed someone else's work. See Sams, p. 74, in which Nashe's comments are discussed, and p. 180 ff. The problem for those who believe that Shakespeare wrote *The Famous Victories* is that it may have been written as early as 1587, far too early for the man from Stratford to be penning plays for the Queen. Some put it as early as 1573 because of the connections to a robbery Oxford was involved in that year. *Shakespeare and the Trussells of Billesley*, Gwynneth Bowen, The Shakespeare Fellowship Newsletter, 1958, available online at:

http://www.sourcetext.com/sourcebook/library/bowen/05trussells.htm

This problem also exists for *The Contention Between the Two Famous Houses of Yorke and Lancaster*, which is recognized as one of the sources for the three *Henry VI* plays. See the extensive discussion in Sam's, beginning at p. 154. There is no problem if Oxford is recognized as the author of these plays and the later plays that are derived from it.

It is apparent that *The Famous Victories* was written no later than 1588 because there is a reference to Tarlton playing the judge who gets his ears boxed by Prince Hal in *Tarlton's Jests: drawn into these three parts*, printed by J. H[aviland] for A. Crook, 1638, as quoted in Bullough, vol. 4, p. 290:

> An excellent jest of Tarlton's suddenly spoken at the Bull at Bishops-gate, was a play of Henry the fift, wherein the judge was to take a box on the eare; and because he was absent that should take the blowe, Tarlton himselfe, ever forword to please, took upon him to play the same judge, beside his owne part of the clowne: and Knel [William Knell, one of the Queen's Men, who was killed in a fight in 1587, and whose widow married John Heminges], then playing Henry the fift, hit Tarlton a sound boxe indeed, which made the people laugh of more, because it was he. But anon the judge goes in and immediately Tarlton in his clownes' cloathes comes out, and askes the actors what newes. O, saith one, hadst thou been here, thou shouldst have seene Prince Henry hit the judge a terrible box on the eare: What, man, said Tarlton, strike a judge! It is true, yfaith, said the other. No other like, said Tarlton, and it could not be but terrible to the judge, when the report so terrifies me, that me thinkes the blow remaines still on my cheeke, that it burnes againe. The people laugh at this mightily.[84]

---

84 Notice that Tarlton's remarks were not part of the script. Actors commonly think they know better than the playwright what lines their characters should speak. This was not just a problem in the Elizabethan theater; George Kaufman is reported to have interrupted a rehearsal for one

The Gad's Hill robbery is one of those 'coincidences' that Orson Welles may have been thinking of when he said Oxford may have written the plays attributed to William Shakespeare. Oxford was 23 when he was involved in an attempted 'robbery' that took place on May 20, 1573. The date is known from a letter written by two servants to Lord Burghley who complained that three of the Earl of Oxford's men had assaulted them on the road between Rochester and Gravesend. Ward, p. 91. The Gad's Hill area is as well-known today as it was then. In fact, there are a number of inns in the area that celebrate the fame brought to this part of the road from London to Dover by the description of the fictional robbery that occurs in *Henry IV, Part One.*

The reference to the robbery in *The Famous Victories* states that it occurred on May 20 in the 14th year of the reign of Henry IV. Henry died in the 14th year of his reign but *before* May 20. The letter by the two servants to Lord Burghley makes clear that the robbery took place on May 20, 1573, *in the 14th year of the reign of Queen Elizabeth.* Oxford was, therefore, making a clear reference in *The Famous Victories* to a caper that he had been involved in, which his audience would have easily recognized because they would have known that there had been no May 20 in the 14th year of the reign of Henry IV.

Most scholars, unaware of the connection to Oxford, or unwilling to acknowledge the connection to Oxford, surmise that the robbery in *Henry IV* was taken from Stow's *Annals,*[85] which has the following reference to Prince Hal, the major character (after Falstaff) in *Henry IV*:

> *Whilst his father lived, beyng accompanyed with some of his yong Lords and gentlemen, he would waite in disguised array for his owne receyvers, and distresse them of theyr money: and sometimes at such enterprices both he and his company were surely beaten: and when his receivers made to him their complaints, how they were*

---

of the Marx brothers' movies because he was so surprised to hear a line he had written.

85 Quoted in Bullough, vol. 4, 219.

robbed in comming unto him, he would give them discharge of so much money as they had lost, and besides that, they should not depart from him without great rewards for their trouble and vexation, especially they should be rewarded that best hadde receyved the greatest and most strokes.[86]

Compare the relevant portion of the letter from the two servants to Burghley complaining about what happened to them in 1573:

So it is, Right Honourable [Burghley], [John] Wooton and myself [William] Faunt] riding peaceably by the highway from Gravesend to Rochester, had three calivers [an early form of rifle] charged with bullets, discharged at us by three of my Lord of Oxford's men; Danye Wylkins, John Hannam, and Deny the Frenchman,[87] *who lay pviily [hiding] in a ditch awaiting our coming with full intent to murder us; yet (notwithstanding the all discharging upon us so near that my saddle having the girths broken fell with myself from the horse and a bullet within half a foot of me)*[88] *it pleased God to*

---

86 There does not appear to be any reference to this colorful event in either edition of Holinshed. Bullough has a few pages devoted to what the author of *Famous Victories* took from the earlier sources beginning at page 159. Titus Livius, an Italian scholar who came to England in the 1400s, penned one such account of Henry V. A scholarly discussion of all the sources for these Prince Hal stories can be read at:

https://archive.org/details/cu31924027928047

including the full text of Livius' *The First English Life Of Henry V*. Stow's *Annales* can be read at:

http://www.archive.org/stream/cu31924027928047/cu31924027928047_djvu.txt

The language about robbing his own receivers is found at p. 557.

87 Deny (probably Denny) the Frenchman crops up in other places in Oxford's life and appears to be a model for some characters in the plays. He is worth a research project on his own and may provide evidence of a connection between Oxford's life and the plays.

88 Does this sound like Falstaff? Was William Faunt fat? What broke the girth of Faunt's horse, toppling him and the saddle onto the road? If a bullet had hit the saddle, he would have reported it. It is obvious that the bullets were intended to miss. Wylkins, Hannam, and Deny the Frenchman must

deliver us from that determined mischief; whereupon they mounted on horseback and fled towards London with all possible speed.

Ward, p. 91.

The only problem with Stow's portrait of Prince Hal is that Stow published his *Survey of London* in 1598, and the story of Prince Hal did not appear until the second addition in 1600 (the preface is dated 1600 – the actual publication may have been 1603). This was almost 40 years after the letter from the two servants was written to Burghley complaining about Oxford robbing them. (The letter was not discovered in Burghley's files until the 1800s.) Edward Hall's *The Union of the Two Noble and Illustrate Families of Lancastre and Yorke*, first published in 1542, and *The Chronicles of England, Scotland, and Ireland* by Raphael Holinshed (who is apparently listed as a member of the jury who returned a verdict of *felo de se* in the coroner's inquest into the killing of Thomas Brincknell by Oxford in 1567 – see *The Reader's Companion*, Chapter 35), which was published in 1577, have been shown to be the sources for *The Famous Victories* and the three *Henry* plays. Neither mentions anything related to Prince Hal robbing his father's receivers. The suspicion is that Stow added a good story to his chronicle that, in the 40 years since the actual robbery, had become a well-known tradition which augmented the collective memory of *Famous Victories* and Falstaff's fame in the *Henry IV* plays.

F. Solly-Flood, Q.C., M.A. Camb., F.R.Hist.S., H.M. Attorney-General at Gibraltar, took a dim view of the antics attributed to Prince Hal in the historical record. His criticism went far beyond stories about robberies on Gad's Hill. Mr. Solly-Flood was exercised over the allegations that the Prince had boxed the ears of the Lord Chief Justice and carried on with

---

have been good enough shots for one of them to hit something at such a close range (and calivers were more like shotguns than rifles). If not, they would have continued their attack. Instead, they immediately "mounted on horseback" and fled to London. Faunt says nothing that he or Wooton did to drive the three men away. Thus, the three attackers clearly intended to scare Faunt and Wooton and not harm them.

ne'er-do-wells. He vented his displeasure in a 100-page paper presented in 1855 to the Royal Historical Society in which he sifted through every historical account that had been published about English history as well as the court rolls to argue that Prince Hal has been done wrong by history and Shakespeare. *Transactions of the Royal Historical Society*, Vol. III, London, Longmans, Green & Co. 1886. The author wrote that there are no records of the Prince boxing the Lord Chief Justice's ears.[89] Being a detail-driven lawyer, he argues that there surely would have been something in the rolls if the event had happened. More importantly, he shows that Sir John Oldcastle was the Prince's companion before the Prince became Henry V, that Oldcastle's martyrdom was done while the Prince, now king, was in France, and that these events and the Prince's redemption may have been related to a fear that Oldcastle's Lollardism was a threat to the throne. The footnotes and summaries of English chroniclers are worth the reading.

A third possibility is that Burghley, embarrassed by his son-in-law's blatant description of the 1573 event in *The Famous Victories*, induced Stow to embellish the *Chronicles* by borrowing from Oxford's caper. Why? So that the scandalous conduct of Prince Hal in *Henry IV*, which the theater-goers would be laughing at, knowing that it was based on Oxford's caper in 1573, would be somewhat muted if Stow said 'tush', 'tis based on history, not Oxford.

That Burghley was fully capable of doing this is shown by his manipulation of the records of who participated in the defense of the realm against the Spanish Armada (drafts of a famous pamphlet and other documents have been found in Burghley's handwriting). See Professor Nelson's excellent analysis and discussion of this manipulation by Burghley, who was interested in presenting a united front to the Spanish. *Monstrous Adversary*,

---

[89] Holinshed's recounting of this event can be read at pp. 557-559, www.archive.org/stream/annalsofenglandt00stow#page/n582/mode/1op.

p. 311, *et seq.* Stow, as well as Camden, were given access to Burghley's documents. Research has shown they were not as objective as assumed on other matters. Thus, it is very possible that Stow added this caper to his story about Prince Hal in order to help Burghley.

There seems little doubt that Oxford's men attacked the receivers on Gad's Hill. The date is fixed: May 20, 1573, in the fourteenth year of Queen Elizabeth's reign (not in the fourteenth year Henry IV's reign, as is stated in *The Famous Victories*). What are the odds that the author of *Famous Victories* would have settled on the exact date of Oxford's caper if the author was not Oxford? *Famous Victories* appears to have been written by Oxford; it also seems that *The Henriad* is an extension of this earlier immature work.

One of the difficulties in tracking the connections between Oxford's life and the plays is that the information comes from so many different sources. Connections are thereby lost, or not seen. On the other hand, when other events are remembered, the connections jump off the page. As Hal says in *Henry IV, Part 1*, the Gad's Hill robbery is "a good jest for ever." II, 2.95. For whom? For "E. Ver." In other words, Hal is telling the audience the robbery is a good jest for the Earl of Oxford. Oxford loved to pun on his name. Examples are rife. The Latin poem he sent his wife from Paris when he learned she was pregnant is full of puns on his name. Ogburns, p. 85. Once an astute reader begins to see the footprints left behind by the Earl ("*Two Gentlemen of Ver-ona" = "One Vere"?)*, the links between the plays and Oxford become more and more obvious.

Another example is in *Henry IV – Part One.* Falstaff has just dusted himself off after faking his death and giving his famous "discretion is the better part of valor" speech, when he sees Hotspur lying on the ground near him. He decides to stab Hotspur in the leg: "[W]ith a new wound in your thigh, come you along with me." If Falstaff was worried that the "gunpowder Percy, though he be dead … should counterfeit too and rise," why would he stab him in the thigh? If Hotspur were still alive, he'd probably roar like the lion he was. But if it were known that the author at the age of seventeen killed Thomas Brincknell, an undercook at Cecil House, by stabbing the poor man *in the thigh*, the scene suddenly takes on a different light. Was this an homage to Brincknell and not just another bumbling moment for Falstaff? Brincknell took 20 minutes to die after Oxford severed the artery in the undercook's leg. See, Chapter 35.

The coroner's inquest into the undercook's death found that Brincknell had committed *felo-de-se* by running on the end of Oxford's sword. Having "killed" himself, Brincknell disappears from history. But people who committed suicide were customarily denied burial in sacred ground. If Brincknell had a wife and children, they were probably thrown into the street. Knowing this connection between Oxford's youth and Falstaff's bravado in *Henry IV, Part 1*, does the grave-diggers' scene in *Hamlet*, where there is a debate as to whether Ophelia can be buried in hallowed ground, take on a different light? Can you imagine the froth that would be generated by main-stream scholars if William had killed a man when he was a young lad in Stratford by stabbing him *in the thigh*? Gone would be the arguments that no one needs to know who wrote the plays. In its place would be hosannas praising the rich personal history that Shakespeare had so skillfully shaped into *Henry IV* and *Hamlet.*

Oxford's reaction to his killing of Thomas Brincknell is unknown, but it would be a mistake to assume that the man's death had no effect on him. *The Labouring Man That Tills The Fertile Soil* makes it probable that Oxford did not escape the event unscathed:

> *The labouring man, that tills the fertile soil*
> *And reaps the harvest fruit, hath not indeed*
> *The gain but paine, and if for all his toile*
> *He gets the straw, the Lord will have the seed.*
> *The manchet fine falls not into his share;*
> *On coarsest cheat his hungry stomach feeds.*
> *The landlord doth possess the finest fare;*
> *He pulls the flowers, plucks but weeds.*
> *The mason poor that builds the lordly halls,*
> *Dwells not in them; they are for high degree,*

His cottage is compact in paper walls,
And not with brick and stone, as others be.

Looney, # 8; Fuller, # 21; *The Earl of Oxford to the Reader* in Bedingfield's *Cardanus's Comfort* (1576).

There is one more aspect of *Famous Victories* that needs to be addressed: why did Oxford create Jockey, the precursor to Falstaff, and name him Sir John Oldcastle? Oldcastle was a Protestant martyr executed in Henry V's reign for his belief in the views of Wycliffe. Only a Catholic would have made him the butt of jokes, or do it to irritate descendants Oldcastle descendants. Were there any around at the time? Yes there were. William Brooke was 10th Lord Cobham. He became Lord Chamberlain in 1596-1597, about the time *Henry IV* was being edited to change Oldcastle to Falstaff. Brooke's daughter Elizabeth married Robert Cecil in 1589 and died in January, 1597. It seems likely that the name had to be changed because of opposition from Lord Brooke. An exhaustive study of the Oldcastle question is contained in Brooks, Douglas A. "Sir John Oldcastle and the Construction of Shakespeare's Authorship", *Studies in English Literature*, Spring 98, 38: 2 (333-62).

Lord Willoughby de Eresby married Oxford's younger sister, Mary. His given name was Peregrine Bertie. His mother and father were famous Protestants who fled England during Queen Mary's reign. Peregrine got his name because he was born in a church in Germany while his parents were trying to find a place to live.

The connections between the Earl of Oxford and Lord Willoughby, however, are far more extensive than the marriage of Lord Willoughby to Oxford's sister. See the lineage chart for *Peregrine Bertie* at the end of *The Death of Shakespeare*. Aside from Lord Willoughby's embassies to Denmark in the 1580s, making him the likely source for much in *Hamlet* (Fortinbras appears to be modeled on Willoughby), there is the interesting fact that the woman considered by many scholars to be the dark lady of the sonnets was also intimately connected with the Berties. Aemilia Bassano was born into a family of Italian court musicians on

January 27, 1569, in Bishopsgate, London. At age seven (1576), she began living with the Bertie family under the tutelage of Lady Susan Bertie. Bassano knew Susan's mother, Lady Catherine, who had convinced Henry VIII to let women read the Bible. Upon the death Bassano's mother in 1587, Bassano became Lord Hunsdon's mistress (yes, he who was Lord Chamberlain until his death in 1596, and patron of the Lord Chamberlain's Men), by whom she had a son in 1592. He was 45 years older than she was. See, the lineage chart *The Lords Hunsdon* at the end of *The Death of Shakespeare.* After she gave birth to her son, Bassano was married off to her cousin, Alfonso Lanier, who died in 1613. In 1611, Bassano published a book of poetry, *Salve Deus Rex Judaeorum,* becoming the first English woman to do so. She lived the rest of her life at the estate of Susan Bertie, who had become the Countess of Kent. Forman, p. 101; Kermode, p. 157.

The trunk of plays is fiction.

Chapter 22
Late September, 1589 – Oxford Court

There is no record of when *The Two Gentlemen of Verona* was written or performed. It makes its first appearance in the *First Folio* in 1623 where it was placed second behind *The Tempest.* The play has never enjoyed much success, primarily because of the ending where Valentine interrupts Proteus as Proteus is about to rape Silvia, Valentine's betrothed. Proteus apologizes profusely and Valentine, in a heartbeat, offers to give Silvia to Proteus:

> *Then I am paid;*
> *And once again I do receive thee honest.*
> ...
> *And, that my love may appear plain and free,*
> *All that was mine in Silvia I give thee.*

Two Gentlemen is not a deep play but, like everything else Oxford wrote, has many layers. Shakespearean scholars discuss the play as an exercise in Renaissance friendship and courtly love. "Much modern writing about the play has concentrated on attempting to explain this gesture [Valentine's attempt to give Silvia to Proteus who has just tried to rape her], whether in terms of Renaissance views on the relative claims of friendship, love, and gratitude, or in terms of the conventions of courtly romance." *The Oxford Companion to Shakespeare,* p. 498.

Harold Bloom admits that, "[e]ven the most solemn of Shakespearean scholars are aware that everything is amiss in the *Two Gentlemen,* but Shakespeare evidently could not have cared less. The cad and the booby, sent off to the Emperor's court by their severe fathers, somehow end up in Milan, or are they still in Verona? Clearly, it does not matter, nor do they matter, nor their unfortunate young women. Launce and his dog Crab matter; for the rest, I have to conclude that Shakespeare cheerfully and knowingly travesties love and friendship alike, thus clearing the ground for the greatness of his high romantic comedies..." Bloom, p. 40.

Marjorie Garber, in *Shakespeare After All,* finds value in the play because it introduces situations that will be expanded or refined in later plays. She thinks it a "lively and often funny play," and goes on to discuss male-male friendships that were strong in England and Europe at the time. P. 43-45. See, also, Tanner, p. 58, *et seq.*

Everything is "amiss" in the *Two Gentleman* because the scholars assume that Shakespeare wrote the play and thereby miss valuable information about who the author was. Bloom senses this: "The peculiar relationship between Valentine and Proteus *is* the play; one ought never to underestimate Shakespeare, and I uneasily sense that we have yet to understand *The Two Gentlemen of Verona*, a very experimental comedy." Bloom, p. 36.

Because Shakespeare could not have appeared in London prior to the late 1580s, events prior to that decade have been ignored. However, it can be easily shown that the play is a reworking of the marriage negotiations between Queen Elizabeth and the Duc d'Alençon in the late 1570s and 1580s. The connections are too detailed and complex to be visited here.

See, Clark, p. 298, *et seq.*, for an in-depth discussion. And, if scholars could be brought around to see that Oxford is the "two gentlemen" of Ver-One-A, they might begin to see how many rich connections they are missing when they assume William was the author.

This stubborn refusal to look at the evidence as scholars rather than as individuals protecting turf and reputations (as well as tourism earnings) has hobbled efforts to evaluate the early plays and determine whether they were precursors to the Shakespearean plays we know. For example, a play titled *The Duke of Millayn and the Marques of Mantua* was presented to the court in 1579 and appears to be a predecessor to *The Two Gentlemen of Verona.* Early plays cannot be properly evaluated until it is accepted that Oxford wrote the plays that appeared in the 1623 First Folio. Oxford was noted by many scholars of his time as being first in comedy and poetry. If he wrote the plays that are now attributed to Shakespeare, he was writing in a time period that preceded the arrival of William in London, and the possibility arises that many of the plays we now know are reworkings of Oxford's earlier work. For example, *The Taming of the Shrew* may be a reworking of the earlier *The Taming of a Shrew.* The Stratfordians have to say the later play was a reworking of the earlier one because William hadn't arrived in London early enough to have written the first one. This examination of earlier plays will deepen the understanding of how the theater evolved in the 16th-century as well as where particular plays came from. Whatever the value of that endeavor, there was no room in *The Death of Shakespeare* to deal with the earlier plays Oxford and others wrote that may have ended up in the later ones we now know and cherish.

Scholars recognize that *The Two Gentleman of Verona* owes much to John Lyly, who was, of course, the Earl of Oxford's secretary for many years. Garber, p. 50. But *Two Gentleman* is much more than a reworking of *The Duke of Millayn* or something that John Lyly wrote. It is the first play to contain clues that Oxford was its author. The title tells the reader that the play is going to be about the two sides of Edward de Vere.

See, Dorothy Ogburn, p. 971. But it is not just a clever play strewn with clues as to who wrote it. It is clear that Silvia is the Queen. This was a name commonly used to identify her. Julia describes Silvia's hair as auburn, which was the color of the Queen's hair. Act IV, Scene 4. The nonsensical banter between Speed and Launce is really about whether the Queen would marry.

If Silvia is the Queen, Julia is Anne Cecil, Oxford's first wife. He married her in December of 1571 but carried on an affair with Queen Elizabeth after his marriage. It was so intense that the Queen made it known that she didn't want Anne at court. Mary Stuart, Queen of Scots, said as much in a letter she wrote Elizabeth in 1584:

> *"[T]hat even the count of Oxford dared not reconcile himself with his wife for fear of losing the favour which he hoped to receive by becoming your lover."* *This Star of England*, Appendix, Note 1, p. 1249.

Oxford and the Queen may have exchanged rings, the way Proteus and Julia do in *The Two Gentleman.* The play may be interpreted as an apology by Oxford to the Queen for his bad behavior (as Proteus) and his recognition that he would have to settle for Anne as his partner and become more like the other side of his personality represented by Valentine (who, in the play, in a sly suggestion, ends up with Sylvia – the Queen).

Two Gentlemen is the first of the 'Italian' plays. See Richard Roe's *The Shakespeare Guide to Italy*. The Italian plays are:

Two Gentlemen of Verona (Verona)
Much Ado About Nothing (Messina)
The Taming of the Shrew (Pisa)
Romeo and Juliet (Verona (again-to quote the maid in *Shakespeare in Love*)
The Merchant of Venice (Venice)
The Winter's Tale (Palermo)
Othello (Venice)
The Tempest (The Island of Vulcano off Sicily)

Oxford traveled to Italy. His itinerary was:

01-24-1575 License issued for Oxford to travel for one year

02-07-1575 Letter from Edward Bacon: "My Lord of Oxford is gone beyond the seas."

03-05-1575 Oxford recorded as being in Paris

03-17-1575 Oxford recorded as leaving Paris (but see next)

03-26-1575 English Ambassador reports Oxford meeting with portraitist 'tomorrow' although earlier he noted that Oxford had left for Germany

04-26-1575 Oxford leaves Strasbourg (where he met John Sturmius)

05-??-1575 Oxford in Venice (presumably via the Brenner Pass)[90]

09-23-1575 Oxford reported as 'coming from Genoa' and hurting 'his knee in a galley'

10-06-1575 Oxford reported as arriving safe 'from Milan'

11-27-1575 Oxford writes from Padua

12-11-1575 Oxford gets money from England in Venice and is to Florence

01-03-1576 Oxford writes from Siena

03-02-1576 Oxford's license renewed by the Queen for one more year

03-05-1576 Oxford leaves Venice

03-??-1576 Oxford reportedly intent on returning home through Lyon

---

[90] *Revenge of Bussy d'Ambois*, 1616, describes Oxford 'comming from Italie, in Germanie.' Nelson, p. 126.

03-??-1576 Oxford passes through Milan

03-21-1576 Oxford is in Paris

03-31-1576 Oxford waits for the arrival of Monsieur

04-10-1576 Oxford leaves Paris

04-15-1576 Privy Council notes Oxford seized by pirates from Flushing

04-20-1576 Oxford arrives at Dover

04-21-1576 French Ambassador reports that Oxford was stripped to his shirt and would have suffered worse had he not 'been recognized by a Scotsman.'[91]

Nelson, pp. 121-137.

Although Sir Henry Wotton would recall in 1617 that "Oxford took no trouble to see the rest of the country [outside Venice]...and even built himself a house," it is clear from the above list that he visited Padua, Milan, Florence, and Siena. Nelson, p. 137. A report dated December 11, 1575 notes that Oxford was in good health and "resolved to see the rest of Italy if he can travel with safety." Nelson, p. 313. In 1590, Edward Webbe published an account in which he was told in Palermo that the Earl of Oxford issued a challenge to defend his queen and country. Nelson, p. 131. A letter from a man who had been accompanying Oxford in Italy, written from Strasbourg after they had parted company, stated that the writer did not know whether Oxford "has started for Greece, or whether he still tarries in Italy..." This letter is dated July 4, 1575. Nelson, p. 128.

The September 24, 1575 letter Oxford wrote to Burghley may or may not express Oxford's true feelings about Italy, but needs to be quoted in full to hear what he said, even if he may not have believed it:

---

[91] Compare Hamlet being captured by pirates on his way to England. *Hamlet,* Act IV, Scene 6. Another 'coincidence?'

> For my liking of Italy, my Lord, I am glad I have seen it, and I care not ever to see it any more, unless it be to serve my Prince and country. For mine intention to travel, I am desirous to see more of Germany, wherefore I shall desire of your Lordship, with my Lord of Leicester, to procure me the next summer to continue my licence, at the end of which I mean undoubtedly to return. I thought to have see Spain, but by Italy I guess the worst.

Oxford goes on to complain that sickness has 'taken away this chiefest time of travel,' and thus needs to stay in Europe. Ward p. 107; Nelson, p. 129.

It is obvious that there are significant links between Oxford's visit to Italy and the plays. Roe is sufficient evidence of that. But there is the interesting question of what Oxford would have learned as he traveled to and from Venice, not just what happened while he was in Italy. (The connections between events in Florence and *All's Well*, for example, and between Palermo and *The Winter's Tale*). Did he stop by the Castle of Tournon when he traveled home up the Rhone Valley? He expressed an intention to pass through Lyon, which is not far away. Did he meet the Dowager Countess of Roussillon and her daughter, Hélène de Tournon, who may be the inspiration for Helena in *All's Well*? Was the daughter's death in 1577 the seed for the graveyard scene in *Hamlet*? *Hidden Allusions*, p. 121.

It seems clear that events that occurred in southwestern France the following year, 1578, formed the greater part of *Love's Labour's Lost*. In 1572, Catherine de Medici, Queen Mother and the real power in France, married her daughter, Marguerite de Valois, to Henri III of Navarre. Henri was Protestant and Catherine hoped the marriage would heal the rift between Catholics and Protestants (Huguenots). Six days after the wedding, however, the Massacre at Paris broke out and Catholics slaughtered as many as 5,000 Protestants. Henri would have been one of the victims if his new wife, Marguerite, had not forced her way into the presence of her brother, King Henri III of France, and made him promise to protect her new husband.

Her brother agreed, provided Henri of Navarre became Catholic. Marguerite's new husband swore he was now a Catholic and was spared execution.

This didn't secure his release, however, He was kept from leaving Paris until he managed to escape in 1576. (With Oxford's help - See Chapter 93-which is fiction.) Another year went by before negotiations resulted in the release of Marguerite to join her husband. Catherine de Medici and Marguerite rode to Navarre, accompanied by a group of beautiful maids of honor, *l'escadron volant*, where great festivities and wit games were waged. See *Hidden Allusions*, pp. 127-131 for other connections.

Notice that Oxford was in Paris while Henri was a 'velvet' prisoner of the French court. There is no evidence they met but there are later connections that suggest they did. For example, Lord Willoughby, Oxford's brother-in-law, commanded troops in the late 1580s that put Henri on the French throne. And Henri, now Henri IV and King of France, wrote a letter in 1595 thanking Oxford "for the good offices [Oxford had] performed on [Henri's] behalf in her presence." *Hidden Allusions*, p. 132.[92] Any friendship between the two men would have brought with it inside knowledge of the events that occurred in Navarre in 1576

---

[92] Nelson dismisses the importance of the letter by stating, at p. 349, that "[s]imilar letters sent on the same day to Burghley and the Lord Admiral, and an even longer letter to Essex, suggest that Oxford's letter had no personal significance." No, except that the King of France wrote him personally. And this occurred while Oxford was out of favor and virtually 'dead.' (The title of the very next chapter in *Malicious Adversary* that follows the above quote is *Some Say my Lord of Oxford is Dead.*) How much more does the poor guy (Oxford) have to do to get any credit? And what was he doing in 1601 watching the Queen as she played the virginal and quipping, when news came that the Earl of Essex had been executed, that "when jacks go up heads go down?" Wasn't he out of favor, if not dead? The French records of Henri's letter (and maybe the period Henri was prisoner in the Louvre) may shed some interesting light on why Oxford was included in the list of people to whom Henri wrote in 1595. The letter was penned September 25, 1594, 3 months before Oxford's oldest daughter married the Sixth Earl of Derby. Was there a connection?

and the basis for *Love's Labour's Lost.* See, Chapter 93 – *A Double Maske.*

Mrs. Frummage is fiction. The 'madman's rags' is from *Lear,* Act V, Scene 3, and seemed appropriate given that Bedlam Hospital was directly across the street from Fisher's Folly.

Robin's suggestion that Julia put on male clothing and go to Milan to be with Proteus is fiction and not new. The sources for *Two Gentlemen (The Seven Books of the Diana* by the Portuguese writer, Jorge de Montemayor, and Thomas Elyot's *The Boke Named the Governour*) contained the idea of Julia adopting male clothing.

Chapter 23
Two Gentlemen of Verona

Oxford rode into London with four-score (80) men on horseback. He was also escorted by 100 yeomen dressed in reading tawny with a blue boar on their left shoulders who were wearing gold chains. (Stow says 180 men; Machyn says 140. Nelson, p. 34.) Oxford's father, Earl Joh, had been buried four days later on September 3. Clark, p. 113.[93] The sending away of Oxford's retainers may have been the seed from which Lear is stripped of his retainers, or it may have been the £10,000 Henry VII fined the 13th Earl of Oxford when, after being fêted at Hedingham, Henry thought the Earl had more retainers than he was allowed. *This Star of England*, p. 429, quoting the Duchess of Cleveland. Or, the objections Lear's daughters have to his retainers may have been based on the objections of Oxford's step-mother, Dorothy, who apparently left Oxford's father, Earl John, because of the way she was treated by the retainers Earl John kept.

The story of the Sixteenth Earl killing a boar in France may be a myth. The story is from Markham, Gervaise, *Honour in his*

[93] The Ogburns have him in 1570, when he was 20, with 80 men with a blue boar on their shoulders when he returned from the border skirmishes. DO, p. 30; *Stow's Annals,* p 34.

Perfection, 1624, quoted in Ward, pp. 9-10, but doubted by Professor Nelson. p. 13. Ogburn quotes a lengthy description of the Earl's encounter with the boar, Ogburn, p. 430, as does Allen, pp. 16-18. The statement by Earl John that any schoolboy would know not to flee a boar is from Richard III, Act II, Scene 2. "*To fly the boar before the boar pursues / Were to incense the boar to follow.*" Markham has Earl John saying the following: "*My lords, what have I done of which I have no feeling? Is it the killing of this English pig? Why, every boy in my nation would have performed it. They may be bugbears to the French, to us they are but servants.*" That he would have uttered this statement in front of a group of French knights is doubtful.

The description of the heads of animals hung in the hall at Oxford Court is fiction.

"Traipse" makes its appearance in the English language in 1593.

As to Falstaff's comment 'I am that I am,' see *The Reader's Companion*, Chapter 3.

Earl John, Fifteenth Earl, was the grandfather of the fighting Veres, Horace and Francis. Horace was also known as Horatio. Nelson, p. 12; p. 444, fn 14. Some scholars have recognized him in the character Horatio in *Hamlet.* He is described in the play as one with an even disposition:

> *or thou hast been*
> *As one, in suffering all, that suffers nothing,*
> *A man that fortune's buffets and rewards*
> *Hast ta'en with equal thanks: and blest are those*
> *Whose blood and judgment are so well commingled,*
> *That they are not a pipe for fortune's finger*
> *To sound what stop she please. Give me that man*
> *That is not passion's slave, and I will wear him*
> *In my heart's core, ay, in my heart of heart,*
> *As I do thee.*

Act II, Scene 2.

This Star of England at p. 636 quotes *Fuller's Worthies* on Horace Vere's character: "As was true of him [Horace Vere] what is said of the Caspian Sea, that it doth never ebb nor flow, observing a constant tenor neither elated nor depressed ... returning from victory in silence ... in defeat [with] cheerfulness of spirit."

It may seem to be a stretch to say that Julia is tearing up Oxford's plays and that Valentine is writing them to himself, but the only letter that is also a figure is "O", which is an interesting 'coincidence,' á la Orson Welles. It is a flip remark that has no bearing on the play, another example of the clues left behind by Oxford, like Spring being referred to as "Ver," which is spring in French, in the concluding song to *Love's Labour's Lost.*

There are many examples of Oxford punning on his name. The Latin poem written in the margin of a page in a Greek Bible he sent her after finding out that she had delivered his first daughter Elizabeth is filled with puns on Vere, *vera*, and *veritas*, such as "thy true motto be Ever Lover of the Truth," which can be read as "E. Ver, Lover of the Truth." Translated by Ward, p. 108. *This Star of England* (at page 118) recognized that Bertram makes the same pun upon the name "E. Ver" in *All's Well*:

> *When thou canst get the ring upon my finger which never shall come off, and show me a child begotten of thy body that I am father to, then call me husband: but in such a 'then,' I write a 'never.'*

Act III, Scene 2.

Whatever the dating of *Two Gentlemen*, it must have preceded the 1599 publication of John Marston's *The Scourge of Villanie,* in which the following lines occur (quoted in Ward, p. 329):

> *Far fly the fame*
> *Most, most, of me belov'd, whose silent name*
> *One letter bounds. Thy true judicial style*
> *I ever honour, and if my love beguile*
> *Not much my hopes, then thy unvalued worth*
> *Shall mount fair place, when Apes are turned forth.*

See, *The Reader's Companion*, Chapter 40, for how this enigmatic encomium obviously refers to Oxford, whose name is bounded by the letter "e." No other Elizabethan poet's name is bounded by one letter: John Greene? Anthony Munday? John Lyly? Gabriel Harvey? Christopher Marlowe? Thomas Watson? John Donne? Thomas Heneage? Walter Raleigh? None fit Marston's reference.[94]

Marston seems to be referring to *Two Gentlemen,* where Speed is talking to Valentine:

Speed:	*To yourself: why, she woos you by a figure.*
Valentine:	*What figure?*
Speed:	*By a letter, I should say.*

To say that Sylvia is wooing Valentine "by a letter" makes sense; "by a figure" makes no sense. The two together solve the puzzle. Oxford's title begins with "O" which is also a figure – zero (or zed).

Marston was relying on readers and playgoers to remember Speed's comments to Valentine identifying Oxford as the author. Marston took this idea to show that he had thought of another way of connecting Oxford to the plays. An author whose "name one letter bounds" can only refer to Oxford, whose given name was "Edward de Vere." Marston, it appears, was one-upping Oxford, who was still alive. He must have thought that the Earl would recognize his invention and take it as praise. Taking a phrase from one play and reworking it for another play was common. See, for example, Oxford and Sidney going back and forth over a kingdom, a cottage, and a grave. *The Reader's Companion*, Chapter 12.

The use of the word "silent" to describe the name of the author Marston was referring to cannot refer to Shakespeare,

---

[94] A recent attempt to link the plays to Thomas Sackville fails when the writings of Sir Thomas are considered. Sir Thomas, the author, or co-author of England's first tragedy—*Gorbuduc*—was incapable of writing the works we (currently) attribute to William Shakespeare.

who was not silent in 1599, and whose name is not bounded by one letter. However, if Marston was playing with Speed's comments to Valentine in *Two Gentlemen*, then Marston is implying that the plays were written by Oxford and not Shakespeare. "When apes are turned forth" may, with the modifier "silent" applied to the author's name, be further evidence that Shakespeare was a front for Oxford.

The badinage between Speed and Valentine is not the only occasion where "Shakespeare" makes allusions to his "silent" name. There are the following lines in Sonnet 76:

> *Why write I still all one, ever the same,*
> *And keep invention in a noted weed,*
> *That every word doth almost tell my name.*

This sonnet is larded with more hidden references than usual. "Still all one" appears to be a reference to The Earl of Southampton, whose motto was "*un par tout, tout par un* (one for all, all for one)." "Ever the same" can only refer to Queen Elizabeth's motto "*semper eadem*," which should be translated "always the same" but Oxford transforms it by substituting "ever" for "always" (Oxford's motto was "*Vero nihil verius*"), thus bringing him into the same line with Elizabeth and Southampton (and in between Elizabeth and Southampton).[95] How more economical could a writer be?

"Invention in a noted weed" may also bear on the authorship question. Recall the dedication to the Earl of Southampton that prefaces *Venus and Adonis* published in 1593:[96]

---

[95] As Orson Welles said, if it isn't the Earl of Oxford, there are a lot of funny coincidences that need to be explained.

[96] The Stratfordian should explain how William could have written *Venus and Adonis* when he was only 29 (possible, of course), and where he got the obvious knowledge of great classical learning as well as the ability to create a complex masterful poem in a difficult rhyme scheme. Even more importantly, how did the young poet from Stratford escape dire punishment for lampooning the Queen? That she thought Venus was intended to represent her is made clear by a letter William Reynolds, who bought a copy

But if the first heir of my invention prove deformed, I shall be sorry it had so noble a god-father.

Venus and Adonis is the first publication identifying William Shakespeare as an author. The phrase "first heir of my invention" could mean "the first result of my creativity," but this is an odd way to tell the reader that the poem is the first work of the author. (And *Venus and Adonis* is far beyond any author's first effort at writing a long, complicated, technically difficult poem.)

"Invention" is defined in the Oxford English Dictionary [the OED] as having many different meanings. Those that existed in the 16th century and earlier are identified as:

I.1.a. "An act or the action of finding or finding out; discovery."

I.1.b. "The selecting of topics to be treated, or of arguments to be used." Rhetorical.

I.1.c. "The solving of a problem."

I.2. "The faculty of inventing or devising, contriving, or fabricating something."

I.3.a. "An act or the action of devising, contriving, or fabricating something."

---

of the very first edition, wrote the Privy Council in September, 1593. In his letter he said that "there is another book made of Venus and Adonis wherein the queen represents the person of Venus, which queen is in great love (forsooth) with Adonis, and greatly desires to kiss him, and she woos him most entirely, telling him although she be old, yet she is lusty, fresh and moist, full of love and life … and she can trip it as lightly as a fairy nymph upon the sands and her footsteps not seen, and much ado with red and white." Beauclerk, p. 178. Her reaction to the publication of the poem is unknown. Other poets lost their hands (Stubbe and Page - see footnote 77 above) or were imprisoned (Ben Jonson and Thomas Nashe for the *Isle of Dogs*) for far less. Nothing was done to William. Was this because everyone knew he was nothing but a front for someone else?

I.3.b. "<u>The devising of a subject, idea, or method of treatment for a work of art or literature, by means of the intellect or imagination</u>."

I.4. "The manner in which a thing is devised or constructed; design.

I.5. "The contrivance or production of a new art, instrument, process, etc.; origination, introduction."

Knowing these definitions, the author of *Venus and Adonis*, if asked, could claim that he meant that the poem was "the devising of a subject, idea, or method of treatment for a work of art or literature, by means of the intellect or imagination" (I.3.b.) but he (Oxford) might have used the word "invention" to express "the solving of a problem," (I.1.c.), namely, the use of Shakespeare as a mask to hide the true author. However, the OED has a second category of definitions for "invention" that may be even more to the point:

II.6.a. "Something devised; a contrivance, a design, a plan."

II.6.b. "<u>A fictitious statement or story; a fabrication</u>."

II.7. "A work of art or literature as produced by means of the intellect or imagination."

II.8. "A new art, instrument, process, originated by the ingenuity of some person."

The word "invention" may signal the creation of William Shakespeare as the front for the true author. The poem and the name of its author is "a fictitious statement or story; a fabrication," (II.6.b.) and "something devised; a contrivance, a design, a plan." (II.6.a.) If so, *Venus and Adonis* is the first issue ("heir") of the author's "invention," William Shakespeare.

The phrase, "the first heir of my invention," is typical of the maddeningly oblique references that appear so frequently in Elizabethan literature. Hidden meanings not only fed the Elizabethan love of "wit" but fended off targets who might sue under the strict libel laws in England that existed then and still do today. London remains the libel capital of the world because it is so easy to win a judgment and enforce it elsewhere. Efforts are afoot to reform English libel law, which is seen by other countries as interference in the right to free speech, but the English change their laws and customs very slowly and unwillingly.

This discussion ignores the questions raised by the use of the word "heir," a loaded one in Elizabeth's time when she had no heir and any writing or discussion about the subject could land one in jail or worse. In modern times, "heir" raises questions about the connection between Oxford and the Earl of Southampton and the Queen. Some think the Earl was the son of Oxford and Elizabeth (the "Prince Tudor" theory). See, for example, Beauclerk for a recent exposition and *This Star of England* for an earlier one.

"Embrace" is one of the many words Oxford invented. It makes its first appearance in Act I, Scene 1, of *Two Gentlemen.*

The virginal was a keyboard instrument played by the aristocracy in Elizabeth's time. There is an interesting anecdote that Oxford was with the Queen at Hampton Court in 1601 when word was received that the Earl of Essex had been executed. Oxford quipped, probably leaning over the virginal, that "when jacks go up, heads go down," referring to both Essex's fall and the action of the virginal.[97] That Oxford was still quick with words only three years before his death is interesting. However, his presence with the Queen at such a time is even more significant, and to have gotten away with such a remark shows that his relationship with her was deeper than official

---

[97] "[The Queen] was playing on the virginal when the news was brought to her that the deed was accomplished [i.e., Essex's execution], and she did not desist [playing the virginal]. Raleigh [sic] was already in the presence-chamber, and the Earl of Oxford, looking at him with the dislike of a noble to a parvenu, whispered, as the keys rose and fell under the Queen's fingers—'when jacks go up, heads go down.'" *Cameos from English History – England & Spain,* p.393, Cameo XXXVIII, Ballads on Essex, by Charlotte Mary Yonge, London (1895); Ogburns, p. 1106, quoting Ward, p. 336.

records would have shown if the comment or the visit had not been recorded.

The best oysters in England at the time were from Colchester at the mouth of the River Colne, which flowed through Oxford country (Hedingham, Earls Colne, Wivenhoe). Thomas Fuller described the oysters one could obtain from Colchester:

> "The best in England [are] fat, salt, green-finned ... bred near Colchester where they have an excellent art to feed them in pits made for the purpose. King James was wont to say he was a very valiant man who first adventured on eating of oysters. Most probably mere hunger put men first on that trial. Thus necessity hath often been the purveyor to provide diet for delicacy itself famine making men to find out those things which afterwards proved not only wholesome but delicious. Oysters are the only meat which men eat alive and yet account it no cruelty. Sometimes pearls considerable both in bulk and brightness have been found within them."
>
> *The History of the Worthies of England,* London, 1840, p. 493.

Whether the Colchester oysters were being bred in pits in 1589 is unknown but probable, seeing that the oyster has been a delicacy cultivated in "pits made for the purpose" as far back as the Roman Empire.

It was from Wivenhoe that Oxford took ship for the continent when he fled the Queen in the summer of 1574. His reasons have never been made clear. He had been very close to the Queen at the time and the two of them had met with the Archbishop of Canterbury shortly before he took off. She forgave him rather quickly, considering her treatment of other persons who fled without permission.

The 'father' of Henry Wriothesley, the Second Earl of Southampton, also fled the country at the same time, in his case, to Spain. He was also forgiven. Some think the two men fled for the same reason—the birth of the third earl, who was actually Oxford's son by the Queen. Interestingly, the second earl, like Oxford's father, also died young and the third Earl ended up a ward in Lord Burghley's house. With the difference in age, however, Oxford was gone from Cecil House before Southampton arrived.

The urge to use a rope ladder to help Silvia escape from her house may have been based on Earl John's use of a ladder to get his hands on Dorothy Fosser. See, Chapter 9. It may have also been based on Bussy d'Amboise's rescue of the Duc d'Alençon from the Louvre in Paris on Valentine's Day, February 14, 1578. Eva Turner Clark thinks so in her book, *Hidden Allusions in Shakespeare's Plays.* She argues, beginning at p. 298, that *Two Gentlemen* was based on *A History of the Duke of Millayn and the Marques of Mantua*, performed on December 26, 1579, at Whitehall, which itself was based on the marriage negotiations between Elizabeth and the Duc d'Alençon in 1578. Ms. Clarke makes a case for all the 'coincidences' between the marriage negotiations and the play. For example, d'Amboise met Alençon at St. Généviève's wall, while Valentine plans on meeting Silvia at St. Gregory's well. The difference may have been that St. Gregory was the saint for November 17, Queen Elizabeth's day.

It is difficult, nay impossible, to imagine Shakespeare writing lines that referred to a woman who "hath no teeth to bite." Lance says this to Speed about a maid Speed is interested in. Act III, Scene 1. Everyone at court would have recognized Lance's comment as parodying language in a letter Sir Christopher Hatton had written to the Queen in which he sought her favor over Oxford for the following reasons: "[R]eserve it to the Sheep [Elizabeth's nickname for Hatton], he hath no tooth to bite, where the Boar's tusk [Oxford] may both raze and tear." Ms. Clark thinks Speed is a caricature of Hatton, already identified as the "shepherd-sheep" in Act I, Scene 1.[98] If so,

---

[98] Ms. Clarke completely misses (or ignores?) the sexual puns that litter this play and many others. See, Kiernan, p. 144. The Elizabethans had a much more open attitude about sex than we do. See, for example, *The Choice of*

Hatton would not have let a provincial playwright named Shakespeare escape his wrath if William had written the plays. If the author was Oxford, however, Hatton would have been barred from doing anything about it because of Oxford's status as a lord.

Beowulf was written circa 500-700 B.C. The only copy still in existence was obtained by Laurence Nowell in 1563 while he was living and working in Cecil House. He had been hired as one of the Earl of Oxford's tutors the prior year. Nowell eventually went off to the continent and never came back.[99] Sir Robert Cotton acquired the manuscript at some point between 1585 and 1631. In 1700, Cotton's grandson donated his grandfather's library to the British government which some time thereafter moved it to Essex House and eventually into the British

---

Valentines, which makes it clear that the Elizabethans knew women had orgasms, something the 19th century (men, at least) thought women did not have:

> *With Oh, and Oh, she itching moues hir hipps,*
> *And to and fro, full lightlie starts and skips.*
> *She ierks hir leggs, and sprauleth with hir heeles,*
> *No tongue maie tell the solace that she feeles.*

Anderson calls this poem "a pornographic spoof of Venus." P. 280. Part of this claim may be based on the dedication—"To the right Honorable Lord S."—which Anderson says was 'no doubt' a reference to Southampton. The poem "made *Venus and Adonis'* implicit sex as explicit as one could get." He's right. The manuscript of *The Choice of Valentines* was not published until 1899.

The Stratfordians enthusiasm for Sonnets 135 and 136, in which the word 'Will' appears numerous times and sometimes as a first name (*And then thou lovest me, for my name is 'Will'*), lessened somewhat when scholars learned that the word 'will' in Elizabeth times was slang for male organs, female organs, and sexual desire. See, Kiernan, p. 52.

[99] Not before telling Burghley that "I clearly see that my work for the Earl of Oxford cannot be much longer required." Most people would take this as a statement that Oxford was precocious. Not Professor Nelson: "Perhaps Oxford surpassed Nowell's capacity to instruct him. More likely—since nothing indicated that Oxford was an enthusiastic scholar, and much indicates that he was not—Nowell found the youth intractable." P. 39.

Museum where it remains today. The best source for Beowulf, its history and its interpretation, is *http://ebeowulf.uky.edu/*.

Chapter 24
Lord Willoughby's

Peregrine Bertie was five years younger than Oxford. He was named Peregrine because he was born in Germany while his mother and father were fleeing persecution by Queen Mary. His mother, Catherine Willoughby, was famous among Protestants for having talked Henry VIII into letting women read the Bible. Peregrine married Oxford's full sister, Mary, in 1577. It was apparently a love match. Catherine and Oxford both initially opposed the marriage because Mary and Oxford were already known for being difficult. At the time of the marriage, Thomas Cecil, Lord Burghley's first son, wrote his father that Lady Mary "will be beaten with that rod which heretofore she prepared for others." Nelson, p. 180. Mary has been thought by some to be the model for Katherine in *The Taming of the Shrew*. Peregrine has been identified as the model for Kent in *Lear*. And Sir Horatio Vere as the model for Horatio in *Hamlet*.

Peregrine was sent to Elsinore in 1582 to talk the king of Denmark into lowering tariffs on English ships passing through the Øresund[100] on their way to Russia. He spent four months there. Rosencrantz and Guildenstern (who were real people) visited him in England in 1592. See, Chapter 75. Doubtless (to use a phrase loved by scholars who think they are studying the author of the plays when they are scrabbling for facts about William Shakespeare), Oxford met both.

Willoughby House was located outside the walls of London in the Barbican "fronting the north end of Redcross-street."[101]

---

[100] Øresund is the 2.5 mile wide strait that connects the Baltic with the North Sea. Elsinore and the castle in *Hamlet* are at the tip of the Danish land opposite Sweden.

[101] *The History and Antiquities of London, Westminster, Southwark, and Parts Adjacent*, vol. 3 by Allen, Thomas, Chapter XVIII, History and Topography of

The house was originally a watch-tower called Burgh-Kenning, or Barbican, an advance post for Cripplegate. It was the London residence for Peregrine Bertie.[102] His ancestral home was in Grimsthorpe where he and his sister, Susan Bertie, Countess of Kent, grew up.

All of the lords had London residences. Some were along the Thames: going from east to west, Baynard's Castle (Pembroke); Hunsdon House, Blackfriars (Hunsdon); Essex, later Leicester House (Essex & Leicester); Arundel House, (Philip Howard, Earl of Arundel);[103] Somerset House (the Earl of Somerset, who

---

Cripplegate Yard Without, can be found at the Tufts Digital Library at *http://hdl.handle.net/10427/44306*.

102 The way to Willoughby House was up Wood Street and through Cripplegate. Shakespeare is believed to have lived at a later date on Silver Street, which is off Wood Street. Nicholl, Charles, *The Lodger Shakespeare*.

103 In 1603, Charles Howard, Lord Howard of Effingham and Earl of Nottingham, Lord Admiral of the Fleet during the Spanish Armada and patron of the Admiral's Players, moved into Arundel House. The prior owner, Philip Howard, had been charged with disloyalty. Howard had tried to escape but was apprehended and thrown into the Tower where he later died. Philip was related to Henry Howard who, with Charles Arundel, was accused by Oxford in 1582 of being Catholics working for Spain. Imprisoned, Howard and Arundel counterattacked by penning accusations against Oxford that Professor Nelson found useful in writing his biography of Oxford. He even borrowed the title of his work from their claims against Oxford. Professor Nelson's acceptance of the claims made by Howard and Arundel is somewhat diluted by the fact that Oxford was soon released and eventually restored to court. Arundel, upon being released from the Tower, ran to the continent where he became a paid agent for Spain where he ended up dying there. Howard survived his imprisonment but was re-imprisoned at various times during Elizabeth's reign because she obviously thought Howard was a Catholic sympathizer. He managed to work his way back into Elizabeth's favor by 1600 and survived 14 more years, acquiring titles and lands under James before dying in 1614. His rise under James may have been helped by the very religious sympathies that got him into trouble under Elizabeth. The testimony of the two men, therefore, given under the treat of execution while they languished in the Tower, wouldn't count for much in a court of law, but Nelson's publication of their extensive claims makes for some very interesting reading. Oxford may have been boastful, as they reported, but his boasts may have contained some elements of truth. The list of claims made by all three

fell from power in 1552); Durham House (Sir Walter Raleigh); York House (Sir Nicholas Bacon); and those on Cannon Row upstream of Whitehall, Sussex House (Thomas Radcliffe, 3rd Earl of Sussex); Derby House (Fernando Stanley, Lord Strange, Fifth Earl of Derby). Others were on the Strand, Cecil House (Burghley) or in Holborn, Ely Palace (Sir Christopher Hatton) or outside Aldersgate, Charter House (Thomas Howard, Fourth Duke of Norfolk) or Cripplegate (Willoughby House and Southampton House).[104]

Interestingly, *The History and Antiquities of London, Westminster, Southwark, and Parts Adjacent*) states the following after describing Willoughby House: "Adjoining to the Barbican, on the east, was another stately edifice, called the Garter-House, which was erected by Sir Thomas Wriothesley, garter king at arms, uncle to the first earl of Southampton. On the top of the building was a chapel, called by the name of Sanctissima Trinitatis in alto." Akrigg places Southampton House "south of Holborn and east of Chancery Lane, hence the name 'Southampton Buildings' for the edifice which now occupies this site." At p. 6, fn. 1. But this may not have been next door to Willoughby House.

The salutation by the servant as Oxford enters Willoughby House is taken from the beginning of the preface to the

---

men deserves careful scrutiny. For example, see Chapter 94—*A Nidicock for Lady Lisbeth*—in which Oxford's claim (as reported by Howard and Arundel) "that the cownetesse of Mirondola came fiftie miles to lie w*i*th him for loves" may have been true. The Countess was from a location only 60 miles from Venice but was one of the ladies-in-waiting for Catherine de Medici, Queen Mother of France, when Oxford passed through Paris on his way to and from Italy.

[104] Based on the map "Edward de Vere's London and Environs", and the table "London and Westminster and the Directory – The Earl of Oxford's London and Environs," pp. 534 and 535 in Ward. However, Ward has Willoughby House inside Cripplegate and Southampton House outside Newgate in Holborn. The Agas Map (*The Reader's Companion* to Chapter 8) shows this area was located outside Cripplegate on what became Barbican Street that ran over to Aldersgate Street. The error as to Willoughby House is carried over in the map of London in Anderson.

translation of Castiglione's *Courtier*, which reads: "Edward de Vere, Earl of Oxford, Lord Great Chamberlain of England, Viscount Bolbec, Baron Scales and Badlesmere."

Francis Vere and his brother, Horace or Horatio, were known as the "fighting Veres." Horace is believed to be the model for Horatio in *Hamlet*. See, the quote in *This Star of England* at p. 636 from *Fuller's Worthies*: "As was true of him [Horace Vere] what is said of the Caspian Sea, that it doth never ebb nor flow, observing a constant tenor neither elated nor depressed ... returning from victory in silence ... in defeat [with] cheerfulness of spirit." Horatio is described in *Hamlet*:

or thou hast been
As one, in suffering all, that suffers nothing,
A man that fortune's buffets and rewards
Hast ta'en with equal thanks: and blest are those
Whose blood and judgment are so well commingled,
That they are not a pipe for fortune's finger
To sound what stop she please. Give me that man
That is not passion's slave, and I will wear him
In my heart's core, ay, in my heart of heart,
As I do thee.

Act III, Scene 2.

Francis was the older of the two and was knighted by Peregrine Bertie in the field at Bergan Op Zoom in 1588, not in 1589 while Bertie was in France as is reported in *The Death of Shakespeare*. At the time of the dinner at Willoughby House, Francis was Sergeant Major General of the Army in the Low Countries. Francis died in 1609 and was buried in Westminster Abbey. A slab next to his sarcophagus is marked "unknown." Oxford was supposedly buried in Hackney but his grave has never been found.

Henry Carey, First Lord Hunsdon, was born in 1526. His mother was Mary Boleyn, Anne Boleyn's sister. Although he was said to be the son of Mary's husband, many believed that he was Henry VIII's son, and that Henry married Mary off after he got her pregnant. Hunsdon, then, was Queen Elizabeth's cousin, if not her half-brother. He was a gruff, blunt man who had a distinguished military career. On his death bed, Elizabeth offered him an earldom. He declined the honor, saying that if he wasn't good enough to receive it while alive, he didn't deserve it in death.

Hunsdon was appointed Lord Chamberlain in July 1585, taking over the office charged with the duty of supervising the theaters and the Office of the Revels. He was the patron of the Lord Hunsdon's Men, and, from 1594, the Lord Chamberlain's Men. He had an affair with Aemilia Bassano from approximately 1587 until he got her pregnant in 1592, whereupon he married her off to a man named Alfonso Lanier.

Aemilia Bassano was born January 27, 1569, in Bishopsgate, London, into a family of Italian (possibly Jewish) court musicians. (She appears to have preferred Aemilia as the spelling of her first name.) At age seven (1576), she went to live with the Willoughby family under the tutelage of Susan Bertie, Peregrine's older sister. Aemilia knew Susan's mother, Lady Catherine, who had convinced Henry VIII to let women read the Bible. Upon her mother's death in 1587, Bassano became Lord Hunsdon's mistress. He was forty-five years older than she was. See, the lineage table for the Lords Hunsdons at the end of *The Death of Shakespeare*. When Bassano became pregnant with Hunsdon's son, Henry, she was married off to a cousin, Alfonso Lanier, who died in 1613. A daughter named Odillya lived but ten months. Her son, Henry, lived to 1633. In 1611, Bassano published *Salve Deus Rex Judaeorum*, the first book of poetry written by an English woman. Some people think Bassano was the dark lady of the sonnets. See Rowse and Cook. The notes of Dr. Simon Forman notes show that he treated her and provide interesting information about Ms. Bassano. For example, she told Forman that Lord Hunsdon treated her well.

Virginia Padoano appears to have been Oxford's courtesan while he lived in Venice during his trip to the continent in 1575-76. Professor Nelson's research has turned up a reference to her in a letter from an Englishman who had moved in next to her in 1587, "and Virginia Padoana, that honoreth all our nation for my

Lord of Oxfords sake, is my neighbour on the lefte side," and that she was twice charged ('condanada' – convicted?) with violating the sumptuary laws. Nelson, pp. 138-139. The Italian record, however, does not specify the charge so it may have been for prostitution instead of violating the sumptuary laws. But women at the time had far more freedom in Venice than they did elsewhere. Oxford may have lingered in Venice because of Virginia: "[w]hen he arrived in Venice, [Oxford] took no trouble to see the rest of the country, but stopped here, and even built himself a house." 1617 recollection of Sir Henry Wotton, Nelson, p. 137. If true, Oxford may have stayed in Venice to see more of Virginia Padoano.

Thomas Cecil was Lord Burghley's oldest son and the only child by his first wife, Mary Cheke. Mary died shortly after she gave birth to Thomas. Burghley next married Mildred Cooke, daughter of Sir Anthony Coke, by whom he had Anne Cecil and Robert Cecil. Anne married Oxford in 1571. She had five children, three daughters and two sons. Only the daughters survived childhood. Anne died in June 1588. Thomas Cecil was a playboy in his youth but turned out to be a competent if dull adult, being knighted in 1575 and becoming the second Lord Burghley when his father died in 1598. In 1604, he was created First Earl of Exeter at the same time his half-brother, Sir Robert Cecil was made First Earl of Salisbury. One of the reasons Polonius in *Hamlet* is thought to be Burghley is because the do's and don'ts Polonius recites to his son Laertes before Laertes goes off to Paris mirrors a list Burghley composed to rein in Thomas when Thomas went to Paris as a young man. Burghley's list was not published until after *Hamlet* was written. Of course, William Shakespeare *could* have obtained access to it …

William Knollys, First Earl of Banbury, was 45 years old at the time of the dinner at Willoughby House. In the mid-1590s, William took in Mary Fitton, the daughter of a family friend, to protect her from the wayward influence of courtiers. He fell in love with her himself and wished his wife dead so he could marry her. His infatuation with Mary was the cause of much laughter at court. One song about him went:

Party Beard, party beard...
...the white hind was crossed:
Brave Pembroke struck her down
And took her from the clown

Knollys was derided as "Party Beard" because his beard was three colors: white at the roots, yellow mid-way and black at the ends. Mary refused to share her favors with him. He courted her even while married but she was not interested in him. After his wife died in 1605, Knollys quickly remarried another woman.

Mary Fitton would have been but nine years old at the time of the dinner at Willoughby House but she was a pistol of a young woman who had affairs with different men over the years. One was the Third Earl of Pembroke, William Herbert, who was sent to the Tower for refusing to marry her after she was made pregnant by him. The baby died at birth and Pembroke was released. The Earl took the time to tell Mary in a poem entitled *To a Lady residing at Court* why he could not marry her:

Then this advice, fair creature, take from me
Let none pluck fruit, unless he pluck the tree.
For if with one, with thousands thoul't turn whore.
Break ice in one place and it cracks the more.

A cad never expressed himself better. Mary Fitton's "afflictions," according to Sir John Stanhope, Treasurer of the Chamber, were "a discouragement of the rest." Mary, in disgrace, returned to Cheshire, her career at court in ruins. The Earl of Pembroke, of course, was not disgraced by either impregnating a lady-in-waiting or using a poem to shake her dust from his shoes. The Earl retired to the countryside where he married Mary Talbot and, as the eldest son of Lady Mary, lived to 1630 as the 'noble' patron of many Elizabethan and Jacobean poets and playwrights. He was the Lord Chamberlain in charge of plays when the First Folio was published in 1623 in which he and his brother, Philip Herbert, then Earl of Montgomery, were acclaimed the "incomparable noble brethren" in the dedication. Mary Fitton might have disagreed.

Oxford's thought when he realizes he's in love with Aemilia Bassano, *Who ever loved that loved not at first sight,* is one of Marlowe's most famous lines. Oxford quotes it in *As You Like It,* Act III, Scene 5.

The bantering among the guests about what you call a flock of birds is from *the Book of St. Albans* published in 1486:

birds	A flock of birds
birds	(small)A dissimulation of birds
bitterns	A siege of bitterns
chickens	A peep of chickens
hens	A brood of hens
choughs	(i.e. jackdaws)A clattering of choughs
coots	A covert of coots
cranes	A herd of cranes
crows	A murder of crows
curlews	A herd of curlews
dotterel	A trip of dotterel
doves	A dole/dule of doves
doves	A flight of doves
ducks	A badling of ducks
emus	A mob of emus
goldfinches	A charm of goldfinches
geese	A gaggle of geese
goshawks	A flight of goshawks
guinea fowl	A rasp of guinea fowl
hawks	A cast of (tame) hawks (=2)
hawks	A lease of (tame) hawks (=3)
herons	A siege of herons

jackdaws	A clattering of jackdaws
jackdaws	A train of jackdaws
lapwings	A desert of lapwings
larks	An exaltation of larks
lyrebirds	A musket of lyrebirds
magpies	A tidings of magpies
mallards	A sute of mallards
mallards	A sord of mallards
nightingales	A watch of nightingales
owls	A parliament of owls
partridges	A covey of partridges
peafowls	A muster of peafowl
pheasants	A nide of pheasants
pheasants	A nye of pheasants
plovers	A congregation of plovers
quail	A bevy of quail
ravens	A murder of ravens
rooks	A building of rooks
snipe	A walk or wisp of snipe
sparrows	A host of sparrows
starlings	A murmuration of starlings
swallows	A flight of swallows
swans	A herd of swans
swans	An eyrar of swans
teal	A spring of teal
turtle doves	A dole/dule of turtledoves

vultures	A venue of vultures
woodcocks	A fall of woodcocks
wrens	A herd of wrens

Oxford's march in honor of Lord Willoughby is attributed to the composer John Dowland, although the authorship is not firm. Only part of the march is reproduced in *The Death of Shakespeare.* Wikipedia has a short page on the march, but some interesting comments.

https://en.wikipedia.org/wiki/My_Lord_Willoughby%27s_Welcome_Home

The music and lyrics can be seen at:

http://imslp.org/wiki/My_Lord_Willoughby's_Welcome_Home_(Dowland,_John).[105]

Oxford wrote other music and, of course, the songs in the plays may have been by him as well, so it is but a slight stretch to have him appear as the composer of the march in honor of his brother-in-law.

Harvey praised Oxford in 1578 in a speech he gave before the Queen at Audley End. The Queen and Oxford, among others, were on their way to Cambridge where Oxford would receive a master's degree (along with other awardees). Harvey said: "In thy breast is noble blood, courage animates they brow, Mars lives in thy tongue, Minerva strengthens they right had, Bellona reigns in thy body, within thee burns the fire of Mars." He ended the piece by stating "Thine eyes flash fire, they countenance shakes a spear." (The 'shakes a spear' comment has made some scholars want to connect this with William Shakespeare but William was 14 at the time and still in Stratford.)

---

105 The March is still of interest to modern musicians, such as Sting: *http://www.sting.com/discography/lyrics/lyric/ltr/M/song/545.*

Harvey followed up his praise by seeking the position of secretary to Oxford. Lyly (who graduated from Oxford, not Cambridge) got the job and Harvey never forgave either one for the slight.

In 1580 Harvey published *Speculum Tuscanismi* or *The Mirror of Tuscanism*, which contained a long description of Oxford that included lines such as "No words but valorous, no works but womanish only" and "a passing singular odd man," and the wonderful word portrait of Oxford wearing "a little Apish flat couched fast to the pate like an oyster." Thus Oxford's remark at Lord Willoughby's dinner.

Harvey collaborated with Sir Philip Sidney and the poet Edmund Spenser to try to force English poetry into rigid schemes composed primarily of hexameter verses. Oxford, Lyly, Nashe, Greene, and most of the other playwrights and poets, including Marlowe, argued that poetry should not be strait-jacketed by rules. (The remark by Jonson that Shakespeare abhorred "small beer and grammar rules" may have referred to Oxford's dislike of Harvey's rules.)

Harvey never produced anything of literary value. He became embroiled in the Martin Marprelate controversy and was almost literally run out of town by the vituperation heaped on him in the pamphlet wars of the 1590s, most of which were written by John Marston, Nashe and Lyly.

Harvey feared being skewered by Oxford. In his 1593 pamphlet *Pierce's Supererogation*, Harvey said: "... all of you ... were best to please Pap-hatchet, and see Euphues betimes: for feare less he be moved, or one of his apes hired to make of Play of you; and then is your credit quite un-undone for ever and ever; such is the public reputation of their plays." Nelson, p. 248.[106]

---

[106] Harvey's fear of being mocked on the stage was shared by others. In 1585, another person was instructed to "take heed and beware of My Lord of Oxenfordes man called Lyly, for if he sees this letter, he will put it in print, or make the boys of Paul play it upon the stage." Nelson, p. 248. Since Lyly was

Harvey also said, "I fear the brazen shield and the brazen boots of Goliath and that same hideous spear like a weaver's beam." In *The Merry Wives of Windsor*, Falstaff says that he "fear[s] not Goliath with a weaver's beam." Act V, Scene 1. This phrase is underlined in Oxford's Geneva Bible.[107] Some scholars think Harvey had seen at least a copy of *The Merry Wives*, if not a performance of the play, but 1593 seems too early for the play to have been in existence by then. *The Merry Wives* probably came later, which means Oxford was stealing from Harvey and not the other way around. See the article in *Shakespeare Matters*, Winter 2002, p. 26, and extensive footnotes therein.

Harvey may have seen an early version of *Love's Labour's Lost* in which he is made fun of as Holofernes (Act IV, Scene 2):

> Holofernes:
>
> *The deer was, as you know, sanguis, in blood; ripe as the pomewater, who now hangeth like a jewel in the ear of caelo, the sky, the welkin, the heaven; and anon falleth like a crab on the face of terra, the soil, the land, the earth.*
>
> Sir Nathaniel:
>
> *Truly, Master Holofernes, the epithets are sweetly varied, like a scholar at the least: but, sir, I assure ye, it was a buck of the first head.*
>
> Holofernes:
>
> *Sir Nathaniel: haud credo.*

Oxford's secretary for ten years, and Oxford obviously influenced *Euphues* and the plays Lyly wrote, Oxford may have been feared as well. In light of the allusions to real people in the plays Oxford wrote (Harvey as Holofernes in *Love's Labour's Lost*, Hatton in *Two Gentlemen of Verona*, Burghley as Polonius in *Hamlet*, to name a few), this is not an unwarranted conclusion.

[107] That Oxford owned and referred to the Geneva Bible should be no surprise. The King James Bible was not published until 1611, seven years after Oxford's death. The copy bought for Oxford when he was a ward of Burghley is owned by, or all places, the Folger Museum in Washington, DC.

Dull:

'Twas not a haud credo; 'twas a pricket.

Holofernes:

Most barbarous intimation! yet a kind of insinuation, as it were, in via, in way, of explication; facere, as it were, replication, or rather, ostentare, to show, as it were, his inclination, after his undressed, unpolished, uneducated, unpruned, untrained, or rather, unlettered, or ratherest, unconfirmed fashion, to insert again my haud credo for a deer.

Dull:

I said the deer was not a haud credo; twas a pricket.

Holofernes:

Twice-sod simplicity, his coctus!
O thou monster Ignorance, how deformed dost thou look!

Sir Nathaniel:

Sir, he hath never fed of the dainties that are bred in a book; he hath not eat paper, as it were; he
hath not drunk ink: his intellect is not replenished; he is only an animal, only sensible in the duller parts: And such barren plants are set before us, that we thankful should be, Which we of taste and feeling are, for those parts that do fructify in us more than he. For as it would ill become me to be vain, indiscreet, or a fool, So were there a patch set on learning, to see him in a school: But omne bene, say I; being of an old father's mind, Many can brook the weather that love not the wind.

Or Harvey's remark, made in 1593, may have caused Oxford to invent Holofernes and add him to *Love's Labour's Lost* the following year. The dating of the plays is a game anyone can play, but if Holofernes is Harvey, as almost everyone believes, and his fear of "the weaver's beam" is dated April, 1593, and it is recognized that Oxford could never resist a dig at one of his contemporaries, it is more likely that Harvey's remark in 1593 was the seed for Holofernes as well as for Falstaff's comment in *The Merry Wives* than that Harvey was reacting to either play.[108]

Hunsdon's "I'm for a jig or a tale of bawdry" is from *Hamlet*, Act II, Scene 2, where Hamlet says to the First Player in a comment about Polonius, "he's for a jig or a tale of bawdry, or he sleeps." Aemelia Bassano speaks the last three words.

The kickshaws (appetizers or hors d'oeuvres), English misspelling of the French *quelque chose*, are mostly from *Shakespeare's Kitchen*. The recipe for birds baked in a pie is from *Cindy Renfro - Elizabethan Food*, which can be viewed at:

www.thousandeggs.com/elizabethan.html#recipe.

> Make the coffin of a great pie or pastry, in the bottome thereof make a hole as big as your fist, or bigger if you will, let the sides of the coffin bee somewhat higher then ordinary pies, which done put it full of flower and bake it, and being baked, open the hole in the bottome, and take out the flower. Then having a pie of the bigness of the hole in the bottome of the coffin aforesaid, you shal put it into the coffin, withall put into the said coffin round about the aforesaid pie as many small live birds as the empty coffin will hold, besides the pie aforesaid. And this is to be done at such time as you send the pie to the table, and set before the guests: where uncovering or cutting up the lid of the great pie, all the birds will flie out, which is to delight and pleasure shew to the company. And because they shall not bee altogether mocked, you shall cut open the small pie, and in this sort

---

108 Hunter, Lyly's biographer, remarks that "The order of the composition in Shakespeare's early plays is a vexed question, and to argue the meaning of the details which constitute evidence in this field would take space quite disproportionate to the value." At p. 300. Hunter follows Chambers on this question. (*William Shakespeare*, I. 243-274.) However, dating the plays is a slippery field, ever-changing. Witness

you may make many others, the like you may do with a tart."

This fantastic recipe, the memory of which has been preserved for us in this nursery rhyme, is sure to bring applause and gasps of surprise at any feast. Dishes such as this one were part of the entertainment at a feast, and fell into two broad categories: elaborate spectacular dishes to be looked at and admired, and illusion foods that seemed to be something they were not. The former, called *sotelties*, could be quite large, and were not always constructed of edible ingredients. Castles, arbors, fantastic beasts, and allegorical figures bearing written mottos were paraded around the hall at the conclusion of a course. A feast by John Chandler, Bishop of Salisbury, circa 1417, featured three sotelties: a Lamb of God, a leopard, and an eagle. A feast by John Stafford, Bishop of Bath and Wells, on September 16th, 1425, also had three sotelties: a doctor of law, an eagle, and Saint Andrew. Following this last sotelty came fruit, wafers, and *vyn dowce* [a sweet wine].

Illusion foods, though not always spectacular in appearance, were intended to trick the diner into believing he was receiving something other than what he was actually served. One marvelous illusion is found in *Delights for Ladies*, by Sir Hugh Plat (1609). He describes how to fashion life-size marchpane animals "molded either in plaster from life, or else carued in wood..." and then to "dredge ouer your foule with crums of bread, cinamon and sugar boiled together: and so they will seem as if they were rosted and breaded... By this meanes, a banquet [dessert course] may bee presented in the forme of a supper, being a very rare and strange deuice.

The song children still sing refers to just such a pie:

> *Sing a song of six-pence, a pocket full of rye*
> *Four and twenty blackbirds, baked in a pie*

When the pie was opened, the birds began to sing.
Now wasn't that a tasty dish to set before the king!

"To make Ipocras with red wine, take a gallon of wine, three ounces of cinamon, two ounces of slic't ginger, a quarter of an ounce of cloves, an ounce of mace, twenty corns of pepper, an ounce of nutmegs, three pound of sugar, and two quarts of cream." (From *The Accomplisht Cook*, by Robert May, 1660.)

"The [sweet] potato roots... being tosted in the embers they lose much of their windinesse, especially being eaten sopped in wine. Of these roots may be made conserues no lesse toothsome, wholesome, and dainty than of the flesh of Quinces... They are vsed to be eaten rosted in the ashes. Some when they be so rosted infuse them and sop them in Wine; and others to giue them the greater grace in eating, do boyle them with prunes, and so eate them. And likewise others dresse them (being first rosted) with Oyle, Vineger, and salt, euerie man according to his owne taste and liking. Notwithstanding howsoeuer they bee dressed, they comfort, nourish, and strengthen the body, procuring bodily lust, and that with greedinesse." (Gerard's *Herball*, 1633 edition.)

The song Oxford sings is part of one of his poems: *Come hither, shepherd swain (Fond Desire)* - to be performed by two singers.

Come hither, shepherd swain!
Sir, what do you require?
I pray thee show to me thy name;
My name is Fond Desire.

When wert thou born, Desire?
In pride and pomp of May.
By whom, sweet boy, wert thou begot?
By fond conceit men say.

Tell me who was thy nurse?
Fresh youth, in sugar'd joy.

What was thy meat and daily food?
Sad sighs and great annoy.

What had'st thou then to drink?
Unfeign'd lover's tears.
What cradle wert thou rocked in?
In hope devoid of fears.

What lulled thee to thy sleep?
Sweet thoughts that liked one best.
and where is now thy dwelling place?
In gentle hearts I rest.

Doth company displease?
It doth in many one.
Where would Desire then choose to be?
He loves to muse alone.

What feedeth most thy sight?
To gaze on beauty still.
Whom find'st thou most thy foe?
Disdain of my good will.

Will ever age or death
Bring thee unto decay?
No, no, Desire, farewell;
A thousand times a day.

The, Fond Desire, farewell;
Thou art no mate for me;
I should be loathe, methinks, to dwell
With such a one as thee.

Earle of Oxenforde

Come hither, shepherd swain (Fond Desire) is a poem by Oxford found in *Fuller's* #10; *JTL* #6. A less complete version of this song appeared in the anonymous *Arte of English Poesy* 1589.

If once your lips should lock with mine will come back in *Venus and Adonis* as:

> *but soon she stops his lips;*
> *And kissing speaks, with lustful language broken,*
> *'If thou wilt chide, thy lips shall never open.'*

And

> *But when her lips were ready for his pay,*
> *He winks, and turns his lips another way.*

And

> *'Touch but my lips with those fair lips of thine,--*
> *Though mine be not so fair, yet are they red--*
> *The kiss shall be thine own as well as mine.*
> *What seest thou in the ground? hold up thy head:*
> *Look in mine eye-balls, there thy beauty lies;*
> *Then why not lips on lips, since eyes in eyes?*

And the most famous lines from *Venus and Adonis* that include the word 'lips:'

> *Graze on my lips; and if those hills be dry,*
> *Stray lower, where the pleasant fountains lie.*

The word 'lips' appears 26 times in *Venus and Adonis*, much less than the word 'hand' appears in *Titus Andronicus* (76 times), but Oxford was definitely having a good time with 'lips' when he wrote *Venus and Adonis.* See, Roger Stritmatter's *"A Law Case In Verse: Venus and Adonis and the Authorship Question*, Tennessee Law Review, Vol. 27, 307, 337, 338, 344, *et seq.*

Orazio Coquo accompanied Oxford back from Italy and stayed nearly a year as Oxford's page before returning home. Nelson, p. 155, *et seq.* Coquo was debriefed by the Inquisition when he got back. Professor Nelson provides much of the inquiry. Coquo said Oxford treated him fairly ("he let each person live in his own way), and was fluent in Latin and Italian. Coquo was a good enough singer to attract Oxford's attention and to sing before the Queen, who tried to convert him. He said Oxford never tried to convert him. Coquo mentions five

Venetian brothers "who are musicians of the Queen and play flute and viola." He does not name them, but one of them may have been the father or grandfather of Amelia Bassano, as her relatives were Venetian musicians who played the viola among other instruments.

Hunsdon's dig about Orazio Coquo is from Charles Arundel's accusations made against Oxford after Arundel, Henry Howard, and Francis Southwell were locked up by the Queen on information from Oxford that they were conspiring against her. Ward has the best discussion of the allegations that swirled around Oxford after he made his claims before Elizabeth in December, 1580. See p. 206, *et seq*. Professor Nelson also devotes considerable space to this subject beginning at p. 203. Unfortunately, for both Professor Nelson and his readers, the professor takes the statements of Arundel, Howard, and Southwell at face value, even to the point of adopting Arundel's description of Oxford as the title to his book ("*Monstrous Adversary*"). Prisoners facing the death penalty are not reliable sources as to the character and actions of the person whose accusations have landed them in prison. No attorney with courtroom experience would accept one-tenth of what these men said in their depositions. The history of these three men show that Oxford's information was accurate; the Queen's treatment of Oxford shows that she believed him. These two facts are conveniently glossed over by Professor Nelson in his biography of Oxford and undermine much of what Professor Nelson writes.[109]

"I am with sonnets," is adapted from Don Armado's speech in *Love's Labour's Lost*, Act I, Scene 2, in which he rapturously describes his feelings about love:

> *I do affect the very ground, which is base, where her shoe, which is baser, guided by her foot, which is basest, doth tread. I shall be forsworn, which*

---

[109] Nelson paints a more balanced picture of Howard and Arundel in his notes to the charges made by Arundel, which he reproduces on his website.

is a great argument of falsehood, if I love. And
how can that be true love which is falsely
attempted? Love is a familiar; Love is a devil:
there is no evil angel but Love. Yet was Samson so
tempted, and he had an excellent strength; yet was
Solomon so seduced, and he had a very good wit.
Cupid's butt-shaft is too hard for Hercules' club;
and therefore too much odds for a Spaniard's rapier.
The first and second cause will not serve my turn;
the passado he respects not, the duello he regards
not: his disgrace is to be called boy; but his
glory is to subdue men. Adieu, valour! rust rapier!
be still, drum! for your manager is in love; yea,
he loveth. Assist me, some extemporal god of rhyme,
for I am sure I shall turn sonnet. Devise, wit;
write, pen; for I am for whole volumes in folio.

The poetry Oxford recites on the way back

She hangs upon the cheek of night
Like a rich jewel in an Ethiope's ear;
Beauty too rich for use, for earth too dear!
I ne'er saw true beauty till this night.

is from *Romeo & Juliet,* Act I, Scene 5

The second outburst that starts:

If I could write the beauty of your eyes,
And in fresh numbers number all your graces,
The age to come would say this Poet lies,
Such heavenly touches never toucht earthly faces.

is from Sonnet 17, which reads as follows:

Who will beleeue my verse in time to come
If it were fileld with your most high desserts?
Though yet heaven knowes it is but as a tombe
Which hides your life ,and shewes not halfe your parts:
If I could write the beauty of your eyes,
And in fresh numbers number all your graces,

The age to come would say this Poet lies,
Such heavenly touches never toucht earthly faces.
So should my papers (yellowed with their age)
Be scorn'd,like old men of lesse truth then tongue,
And your true rights be termd a Poets rage,
And stretched miter of an Antique song.
But were some childe of yours alive that time,
You should liue twise in it, and in my rime.

The banter between Oxford and Robin as they walk back to Vere House will be used by Oxford in Act I, Scene 1, and in other scenes in *Two Gentlemen.* Notice that the reference to "Fond Desire" (capitalized in the text of Oxford's poem *Fond Desire)* is repeated in Valentine's speech to Proteus:

But wherefore waste I time to counsel thee,
That art a votary to fond desire?

Which may be a slight but interesting connection between *Two Gentlemen* and Oxford if "fond desire" was not used extensively by other poets.

Chapter 25
Sonnets for Aemilia Bassano

The first sonnet Oxford works on is Sonnet 18:

Shall I compare thee to a Summer's day?
Thou art more lovely and more temperate:
Rough windes do shake the darling buds of May,
And Summer's lease hath all too short a date:
Sometime too hot the eye of heaven shines,
And often is his gold complexion dimm'd,
And every faire from faire some-time declines,
By chance,or natures changing course untrim'd:
But thy eternall Summer shall not fade,
Nor loose possession of that faire thou ownst,
Nor shall death brag thou wandr'st in his shade,
When in eternall lines to time thou grow'st,
So long as men can breath or eyes can see,
So long lives this, and this gives life to thee.

The second sonnet he mentions is Sonnet 55:

Not marble, nor the gilded monuments
Of princes, shall outlive this powerful rhyme;
But you shall shine more bright in these contents
Than unswept stone besmear'd with sluttish time.
When wasteful war shall statues overturn,
And broils root out the work of masonry,
Nor Mars his sword nor war's quick fire shall burn
The living record of your memory.
'Gainst death and all-oblivious enmity
Shall you pace forth; your praise shall still find room
Even in the eyes of all posterity
That wear this world out to the ending doom.
So, till the judgment that yourself arise,
You live in this, and dwell in lover's eyes.

The third sonnet he quotes in full is Sonnet 99:

Some glory in their birth, some in their skill,
Some in their wealth, some in their bodies' force,
Some in their garments, though new-fangled ill,
Some in their hawks and hounds, some in their horse;
And every humour hath his adjunct pleasure,
Wherein it finds a joy above the rest:
But these particulars are not my measure;
All these I better in one general best.
Thy love is better than high birth to me,
Richer than wealth, prouder than garments' cost,
Of more delight than hawks or horses be;
And having thee, of all men's pride I boast:
Wretched in this alone, that thou mayst take
All this away and me most wretched make.

"Puppy" and "puppy-dog" are used a number of times in the plays:

Launce: *When a man's servant shall play the cur with him, look you, it goes hard: one that I brought up of a puppy; one that I saved from drowning, when three or four of his blind brothers and sisters went to it.*

Two Gentlemen of Verona, Act IV, Scene 4.

Fluellen: *By Cheshu, he is an ass, as in the world: I will verify as much in his beard: be has no more directions in the true disciplines of the wars, look you, of the Roman disciplines, than is a puppy-dog.*

Henry V, III, Scene 2

Bastard: *Here's a stay*
That shakes the rotten carcass of old Death
Out of his rags! Here's a large mouth, indeed,
That spits forth death and mountains, rocks and seas,
Talks as familiarly of roaring lions
As maids of thirteen do of puppy-dogs!

King John, Act II, Scene 1

Buckingham:

Pray, give me favour, sir. This cunning cardinal
The articles o' the combination drew
As himself pleased; and they were ratified
As he cried 'Thus let be': to as much end
As give a crutch to the dead: but our count-cardinal
Has done this, and 'tis well; for worthy Wolsey,
Who cannot err, he did it. Now this follows,--
Which, as I take it, is a kind of puppy
To the old dam, treason.

Henry VIII, Act I, Scene 1

Do you hear, master porter?

Porter: *I shall be with you presently, good master puppy.*

Henry VIII, Act V, Scene 4

Stephano:	*Come on then; down, and swear.*
Trinculo:	*I shall laugh myself to death at this puppy-headed monster. A most scurvy monster! I could find in my heart to beat him,--*
Stephano:	*Come, kiss.*

The Tempest, Act II, Scene 2

The back and forth between Robin and Aemilia Bassano will form the seed from which *Twelfth Night* will grow (at least in *The Death of Shakespeare*).

Chapter 26
Blackfriars - The Next Night

Lord Hunsdon lived in Blackfriars. In fact, John Lyly sold the lease to part of the old friary to him in 1585. Lyly had leased it with others in 1576 but the landlord finally forced Lyly and the others out in 1584. Hunter, p. 75.

In November 1596, Hunsdon was one of the residents who opposed James Burbage's plans to use part of the Blackfriars for the performance of plays by the Lord Chamberlain's Men. This opposition is as surprising to us as it was to Burbage; Lord Hunsdon was the Lord Chamberlain in charge of the plays, but he apparently did not want a theater in the same complex of buildings in which he lived. Lord Hunsdon's opposition is an indication of his true attitude toward and involvement in the Lord Chamberlain's Men.

Chapter 27
A Week Later – Newgate Prison

Marlowe was arrested with Watson on Sept 18, 1589. *The Cambridge Companion to Christopher Marlowe,* ed. By Patrick Cheney, Cambridge University Press, 2004, p. xvii. For a description of the prison and Marlowe's imprisonment there, see Bolt, Rodney, *History Play – The Lives and Afterlife of Christopher Marlowe,* Bloomsbury, New York, New York (2004), ps. 151-152. Bolt says Newgate was the worst of the twelve prisons in London.

Bolt, p. 152. See, also, Riggs, David, *Christopher Marlowe*, Henry Holt & Co., New York, New York (2004), ps. 254-255. The coroner's jury ruled that Watson had killed Bradley in self-defense and exonerated Marlowe.

There is no evidence Oxford bailed Marlowe out of Newgate Prison or met with him later, although scholars are uniform in commenting that they obviously influenced each other. Examples of how they borrowed, stole, and twisted lines from each other can be read in "Marlowe and the English literary scene," by James P. Bednarz, in *The Cambridge Companion to Christopher Marlowe,* ed. By Patrick Cheney, Cambridge Univ. Press 2004.

Oxford's belief that Marlowe must have some nobleman's blood in him (*'Else, anyone can write'*) is based on the Bastard's comments about how he was conceived in Act I, Scene 2, of *King John:*

> *Something about, a little from the right,*
> *In at the window, or else o'er the hatch:*
> *Who dares not stir by day must walk by night,*
> *And have is have, however men do catch:*
> *Near or far off, well won is still well shot,*
> *And I am I, howe'er I was begot.*

Chapter 28
Oxford and Marlowe in the Boar's Head

Marlowe's claim that his status as a spy for Walsingham allowed him to get away with many things, including the staging of *Tamburlaine*, is based on the conclusion by many, including Nicholl (see p. 322), that Marlowe was, indeed, a spy working for Walsingham and Cecil.

There is no evidence Marlowe and Oxford ever met.

In 1592, Thomas Nashe published a broadside against Gabriel Harvey (one of many between them) in which Nashe, angry at Harvey for the way Harvey had written about Robert Greene's death in September, said the following:

> I, and one of my fellows Will Monox, (Hast thou never heard of him and his great dagger?) were in company with him a month before he died at that fatal banquet of Rhenish wine and pickled herring (if thou wilt needs have it so), and the inventory of his apparel came to more than three shillings (though thou sayest the contrary).

So Nashe is saying that he and Greene and "Will Monox" dined together on "Rhenish wife and pickled herring a month before Greene died.[110] Who "Will Monox" was has occasioned considerable discussion in both the Stratfordian and Oxfordian camps. Oxfordians are eager to point out that "Monox" is "mon ox" in French, which is "Oxford," and, therefore, the third guest was the Earl. This conclusion is reinforced by Nashe's relationship with Oxford and Nashe's comment: "Has thou never heard of him and his great dagger?" Oxford carried the Sword of State at state functions. But it is doubtful that Nashe would have referred to Oxford as "one of my fellows." The difference in rank was too much. Also, the Stratfordians can legitimately claim that "his great dagger" is intended as a clue that "one of my fellows" referred to Shakespeare.

Literary license allows Oxford to use the moniker in *The Death of Shakespeare* to leave a message for Marlowe to meet him at the Boar's Head.

The Globe First Folio refers to "*Come live with me and be my love*" as Kit Marlowe's "smooth song." P. 687. (Both John Donne and Sir Walter Raleigh also wrote a version of this poem.) The commentator states that, "[t]hough repeatedly quoted, and familiar to every one acquainted with our early poesy, we should be held inexcusable for omitting [to mention that this line was written by Marlowe]." An "imperfect version" of "[t]his beautiful song" appeared in *The Passionate Pilgrim*,

---

110 A site that claims Christopher Marlowe wrote the plays believes that Greene was poisoned at this meal. *http://themarlowestudies.org/z-ule/ch9-128-143.pdf.*

reprinted by the Globe at p. 230. A more "perfect" version is printed in the Globe at p.687.

David Riggs thought Marlowe may have been paraphrasing his famous line, "*Come live with me and be my love,*" when the Elizabethan poet opened *Dido* with "*Come, gentle Ganymede, and play with me.*" Riggs, at p. 121.

The lines, "*Is it not passing brave to be a king/ And ride in triumph through Persepolis?*" are from *Tamburlaine – Part One*, Act II, Scene 5.

"Anyone can write."[111] Anthony Burgess thought so. In defending Shakespeare against claims that Shakespeare did not possess enough education to write the plays attributed to him, Burgess said the following: "[I]t is nonsense to suppose that high art needs high learning. And any peasant can teach himself to write, and write well. Any peasant writer can, by reading the appropriate books and by keeping his senses alert, give the illusion of great knowledge of the world." *Shakespeare*, p. 40.

To such lengths are the defenders of the status quo forced to go. Burgess opined on the same page that the plays of Shakespeare, "through the trickery of the artist, give the illusion that their creator has travelled widely, practised all the learned professions, [and] bent his supple knee in courts domestic and foreign." It is the 'trickery' of the establishment, and so-called scholars like Burgess, who continue to gull the public as to who actually wrote the plays attributed to the man from Stratford.

The Privy Council actually wrote write a letter to Cambridge on Marlowe's behalf, explaining that Marlowe "had done Her Majesty good service, & deserved to be rewarded for his faithful dealing. … it was not Her Majesty's pleasure that anyone employed, as he had been, in matters touching the benefit of his country, should be defamed by those that are ignorant in th' affairs he went about." Quoting from the Council minutes as the

---

[111] With apologies to Chef Gusto in the movie *Ratatouille* who thought that "anyone can cook."

letter itself is missing. Nichol, p. 92. Those present at the meeting were Archbishop Whitgift, Lord Burghley, Lord Hunsdon, Sir Christopher Hatton, and Sir James Crofts. Sir Francis Walsingham was not present. Marlowe must have done significant work to have the civil and religious leaders of England send a letter to Cambridge telling them they should graduate a mere student.

Marlowe's involvement with Bradley's death is known from the coroner's inquest, which can be read at The Marlowe Society website: *http://www.marlowe-society.org/marlowe/life/deptford3.html.* Marlowe was bailed out by Richard Kitchen and Humphrey Rowland. Kitchen did work for Henslowe; Rowland had connections with Burghley. Bolt, p. 153. It appears that Marlowe was released on bail on October 1, 1589, and the charges dropped when he and Watson appeared in the Old Bailey criminal court in early December of that year. Riggs, p. 255. Watson was held over until the January session. There is no evidence Oxford arranged for Marlowe's release.

Watson was related by marriage to Roger (or Robert) Poley, one of the three men in Deptford when Marlowe was killed, Nicholl, p. 183, (and one of the men in the carriage in 1616 when Nicholas Skerres murders William Shackspear in *The Death of Shakespeare*).

The accusations of atheism against Oxford and Christopher Marlowe are very similar. Marlowe and Oxford both went to Cambridge and it is likely that Marlowe heard of Oxford's blasphemies when he was a student there. Oxford and Marlowe were not the only men to be accused of atheism and heresy. See, Nelson at p. 210. Sir Walter Raleigh was accused of atheism in 1594. Oxford and Marlowe never lost their ears, or were hung and then drawn and quartered, as others were, but there is some suspicion that Marlowe's death in 1593 was partly caused by his blasphemies.

Marlowe's comment that Oxford is of no concern to the authorities is based on the reports made by Sir John Peyton in 1603 that, as Queen Elizabeth lay dying, the Earl of Lincoln reported to him that Oxford had suggested that a certain peer should be carried over to France for safe-keeping and placed on the throne of England after Elizabeth died. Sir John reported that he did not put much stock in Lincoln's information because "I knew him [Oxford? Lincoln?]to be weak in body, in friends, in ability, and all other means, to raise any combustion in the state, as I never feared any danger to proceed from so feeble a foundation." Nelson, p. 415.

The meaning of this report turns on who Sir John was referring to when he said "I knew *him* to be ...." Professor Nelson has concluded that Sir John was referring to Oxford (and delights in reading that Oxford was weak in body, friends, ability, and everything to raise a combustion in the state). A close reading supports Professor Nelson's conclusion. The difficulty in understanding Sir John's report is the way he related what the Earl of Lincoln was telling him. The Earl was reluctant to reveal the identity of the peer he was talking about, although the comments that the peer was far above Sir John and lived in Hackney was a good clue it was Oxford. (The Earl, in a separate statement, confirmed he met with Oxford at Oxford's place in Hackney.) However, Sir John tries to string the reader along to recreate the tension he felt while he listened to the Earl of Lincoln but inadvertently sticks the Earl of Oxford's name in the narrative just before he gets to the language quoted above. According to Lincoln, Oxford was pushing for the Earl of Lincoln to send a nephew of blood royal overseas to provide a base against James. (Elizabeth was two days away from dying.) It is difficult to tell whether Sir John meant "him" to refer to Oxford or the nephew, who was only eighteen at the time. On balance, it looks like Oxford was intended.

The Oxfordians like to believe the peer was Southampton. Ogburns, p. 924. At the time, he was a prisoner in the Tower and Sir John was his jailer, but any movement in this direction is not helped by Sir John continuing on to relate how he told Southampton the latest news on the Queen's prospects of living. Had he put this in a separate sentence, it might be claimed that Southampton was intended (he [Southampton] was "weak in body, in friends, in ability, and all other means, to raise any combustion in the state," i.e., because he'd been locked up in the Tower for quite some time) but Sir John tagged this on to the end of a long sentence about Oxford's actions and it is unclear that he saw Southampton as the object of Oxford's maneuvering.

It is possible that a third explanation may fit these facts. Oxford's suggestion to Lincoln to send Lincoln's nephew overseas may have been an opening gambit to see whether there was sufficient "combustion" in the state to support a candidate for the throne of England other than James. If so, Oxford may have been using Lincoln's nephew as a stalking horse who he may have intended to replace, at the proper moment, by Southampton. However, this is more speculation than is present in a biography of William Shakespeare and should be discarded.

Marlowe found most of his material for *Edward II* in the third volume of Raphael Holinshed's *Chronicles* (1587). Oxford will write *King John* from the same source.

Putting a head on a beer was not necessarily considered a good thing in Elizabethan times. Beer-drinkers apparently thought that the practiced reduced the amount of beer the customer was getting, and thereby increasing the tavern-keeper's profit. When Falstaff palms Bardolph off on the Host in *The Merry Wives of Windsor,* the following occurs (Act 1, Scene 3):

Host: *I will entertain Bardolph; he shall draw, he shall tap. … Let me see him froth and lime.*

Falstaff: *Bardolph, follow him. A tapster is a good trade: an old cloak makes a new jerkin; a withered servingman, a fresh tapster. Go, adieu.*

Bardolph: *It is a life that I have desired. I will thrive.*

The note to the Globe edition of *The First Folio* explains:

Froth and lime: The folio reads *live*, for lime. *Froth and lime* was an old cant term for a tapster, in [sic] allusion to the practice of frothing beer, and

> adulterating sack. The host means, let me see thee turn tapster. "To keep a tapster from frothing his pots—Provide [sic] in a readiness the skin of a red-herring, and when the tapster is absent, do but rub a little on the inside of the pots, and he will not be able to froth them, do what he can in a good while after."—Cotgrave's *Wit's Interpreter*, 1671, p. 92. *ap. Halliwell.*

Marlowe's suggestion that "the less the king deserves, the more merit will be the bastard's bounty," will reappear in *Hamlet*, Act II, Scene 2, in Hamlet's angry instructions to Burghley to treat the players well, for "*the less / they deserve, the more merit is in your bounty.*"

Chapter 29
Two Gentlemen Finished

The earldom of Wessex was one of the four earldoms of Anglo-Saxon England and extended in the west of England to Cornwall and Wales. The earldom died out when Roger de Breteuil was convicted in 1071 of rebellion against William the Conqueror. It was not revived until 1999 when Prince Edward was made Earl of Wessex upon his marriage to Sophie Helen Rhys-Jones.

Therefore, there was no Earl of Wessex in 1589 when Nigel informs Oxford that the Earl of Wessex is at the door asking to marry Oxford's oldest daughter. An earl would never broach the subject in this fashion, of course, but *The Death of Shakespeare* is fiction. The Earl of Wessex in the movie *Shakespeare in Love* is also fiction since the title was vacant when the movie was made in 1998.

Shakespeare in Love was made one year before the real-life Prince Edward was made the Earl of Wessex. The newspapers reported that Edward, an avid theater fan involved in theater and movies, asked his grandmother, Queen Elizabeth, to give him the title, no doubt because of his love for the Earl of Wessex in *Shakespeare in Love.*

The theme of constancy, as expressed in Robin's suggested lines about men, will be at the center of *A Midsummer Night's Dream*. See Tanner, p.129, *et seq*.

The ending of *Two Gentlemen* has distressed scholars and commentators for over 400 years.

Chapter 30
More Sonnets for Aemilia Bassano

Chapter 31
Two Gentlemen before the Queen

Two Gentlemen of Verona was printed second in the Folio after *The Tempest.* Since all critics agree that *Two Gentlemen* was an early effort and *The Tempest* one of Shakespeare's last, the order of the plays in the First Folio makes no sense. (Unless, Ben Jonson had something to do with the completion of the play and wangled to place it first because of his ego. See, *The Death of Shakespeare - Part Two*.)

The First Folio had Launce arriving in Padua, not Milan, which the scholars have concluded was a misprint since everyone was in Milan. But was it? A misprint of a letter is understandable, or even a word, but the name of a city? Changing text is not limited to substituting Milan for Padua. Because of poor original drafts and bad printing, some scholars think they know what was meant and change the text of a play. "School of night" in *Love's Labour's Lost*, is a good example. The original may have been "suit of night" or "scowl of night." Richard Roe, in his excellent examination of the connections between the plays and Italy in *The Shakespeare Guide to Italy: Retracing the Bard's Unknown Travels*, points out that editors have lower-cased 'City' in *All's Well That Ends Well* and 'Temple' in *Midsummer Night's Dream*, thereby missing essential information about where the action is taking place in those plays. Was Oxford playing with Launce here? Sir Christopher Hatton was a favorite of the Queen. He had risen to high positions, it was said, because he could dance well. See, *The Reader's*

Companion, Chapter 2. He and Oxford were competitors for the Queen's favor in the 1570s. Hatton was obviously the object of the references in *Two Gentlemen* to sheep and the woman who has no teeth to bite. It is likely that he is also Malvolio in *Twelfth Night.* Hatton acquired the right to sue Oxford for Oxford's debts to the Court of Wards in 1590. See, *The Reader's Companion*, Chapter 32.

Lord Hunsdon lived in Blackfriars and Aemilia Bassano was probably living with him there in 1589. There is no evidence that she had a relationship with either Oxford or Shackspear.

Carriages came into fashion during Elizabeth's reign. She had one in 1556 and was so bounced around in one in 1585 that she retired from court for a few days to recover. A hollow turning coach had the front scooped out to let the front wheels turn in a tighter circle. It would have been the latest design in 1589. Norris, p. 798.

Falstaff's claim that he is a 'tuner of hounds' is fiction. His comments about Lord Rich's hounds comes from the colloquy between the Theseus, the Duke of Athens, and Hippolyta, his bride, in *A Midsummer Night's Dream,* Act IV, Scene 1:

Theseus:

Go, one of you, find out the forester;
For now our observation is perform'd;
And since we have the vaward of the day,
My love shall hear the music of my hounds.
Uncouple in the western valley; let them go:
Dispatch, I say, and find the forester.

[Exit an Attendant]

We will, fair queen, up to the mountain's top,
And mark the musical confusion
Of hounds and echo in conjunction.

Hippolyta:

I was with Hercules and Cadmus once,
When in a wood of Crete they bay'd the bear

With hounds of Sparta: never did I hear
Such gallant chiding: for, besides the groves,
The skies, the fountains, every region near
Seem'd all one mutual cry: I never heard
So musical a discord, such sweet thunder.

Theseus:

My hounds are bred out of the Spartan kind,
So flew'd, so sanded, and their heads are hung
With ears that sweep away the morning dew;
Crook-knee'd, and dew-lapp'd like Thessalian bulls;
Slow in pursuit, but match'd in mouth like bells,
Each under each. A cry more tuneable
Was never holla'd to, nor cheer'd with horn,
In Crete, in Sparta, nor in Thessaly:
Judge when you hear. But, soft! what nymphs are these?

The phrase "A cry more tuneable was never holla'd to" may be a reference to the performance of *Palamon and Arcitie* at Oxford University in 1566 while Oxford was getting his second master's degree.[112] In the 1566 performance, the "stage-manager had arranged a cry of hounds for Theseus [yes, he was in this play, as was Hippolyta, and both were in the retelling of this story in *The Two Noble Kinsman*] and the artless lads who were new to plays thought it was a real hunt and started hallooing from windows." Ogburn at p. 460 quoting Elizabeth Jenkins, author of *Elizabeth the Great*, New York, Coward-McCann (1959). The enthusiasm caused a wall and a staircase to collapse which killed three students and injured many more. The play was stopped but renewed the next day. Ogburn, p. 442.

---

112 Oxford's first degree, his B.A., had been given two years earlier at Cambridge where a performance of a play by the students was so anti-Catholic that Queen Elizabeth rose in anger and walked out. The servants holding torches followed her and left everyone else in darkness, the seed, obviously, of Claudius' call for lights upon becoming upset with the play being performed before him in *Hamlet.*

Oxford, had he become king, would have been Edward VII. As noted in Chapter 18, Oxford signed his name as Edward VII. Of course, Oxford knew, as did everyone else did, that even if Elizabeth married him, he would be her consort and not king.

Chapter 32
Christmas at the Boar's Head

The food comes from Segan, Francine, *Shackspear's Kitchen*, and Singman, Jeffrey L., *Daily Life in Elizabethan England.*

The guests at the dinner were the following ages as of Christmas 1589:

Playwrights and Poets

John Lyly (35)

Anthony Munday (29)

Thomas Nashe (22)

Robert Greene (31)

Playwrights who were too young at the time were: Beaumont (4); Decker (17); John Donne (17); Fletcher (10); Gervase Markham (21); Middleton (9); Henry Peacham (13).

Actors and Managers

Edward Alleyn (23)

William Kemp (d. 1603)

Augustine Phillips (d. 1605)

John Heminges (23)

Philip Henslowe (34)

Players too young: Henry Condell (13); Nathan Field (2);

Not present or mentioned were: Barnabe Rich (49); Giles Allen; Francis Langley (42); Burbages (James, Cuthbert, and Richard); George Peele (33); Robert Armin (21); Richard Tarlton (d. 1588);

Mentioned but not present

Thomas Heywood (26) (writing plays – he claimed he wrote 220)

Christopher Marlowe (25) (on the continent for Walsingham)

Others

Giovanni Florio (35)

For Anthony Munday, see, *The Reader's Companion*, Chapter 1.

William Kemp was the comic who replaced Dick Tarlton, who had died the previous year. Kemp became a founding member of the Lord Chamberlain's Men in 1594. He retired from acting and made himself famous by dancing a jig to Norfolk in 1600. He died in 1603

Augustine Phillips was also a founding member of the Lord Chamberlain's men and became one of their managers. He acquired considerable wealth and retired to a London suburb. He died in 1605.

According to the *Oxford Companion to Shackspear*, "Heminges" is the modern spelling of the name of the man identified as "John Hemynges" in Shackspear's will. See, *The Reader's Companion*, Chapter 1. Heminges was recorded as a member of Lord Strange's Men by 1593 but was a player long before that. He married Rebecca Knell sometime after March 10, 1588 when her first husband, William Knell, a player, was killed in a fight while he was on the road in the provinces. Heminges migrated with other players to the Lord Chamberlain's Men in 1594 and became a sharer in the company. Quite a bit is known about Heminges, who became financially successful. "Judging by the ballad on the burning of the Globe, he was afflicted with a stutter, an unfortunate handicap for an actor." Wells, *Shackspear and Co.,* p. 50. Thus, Heminges is the actor in *Shackspear in Love* who comes out at the beginning of *Romeo and Juliet* and puts fear into the hearts of the audience by stuttering his way through the beginning of the introduction to the play.

Heminges and Henry Condell appear to have shepherded the First Folio through production in 1623. Heminges signed the Dedication "to the Most Noble and Incomparable Paire of Brethren" (referring to the Earl of Pembroke and his brother, the Earl of Montgomery) and the "To the great Variety of Readers." Ben Jonson may have played a bigger part in producing the First Folio than adding two poems to the preliminary matter. Heminges is listed as "John Hemmings" in the names of the principal actors and "John Heminge" where he signed his name. Henry Condell's name is spelled the same throughout the First Folio.

Kemp's toast referring to the Heliconian imps is from a sonnet Edmund Spenser appended to *The Faerie Queen*, published in 1590, which was addressed to Oxford: "*The love which thou dost bear/ To th' Heliconian imps and they to you.*"

Oxford's toast "I drink to the general joy o' the whole table," is from *Macbeth,* Act III, Scene 4. The next line is "*and to our dear friend Banquo, whom we miss.*" Macbeth is distracted because he has just seen Banquo's ghost. His friends, not knowing this, urge Macbeth to join them at the table.

"*The charge and thanking shall be for me,*" is from *All's Well That Ends Well,* Act III, Scene 5.

Lyly gives the guests a quote from *Euphues, the Anatomy of Wit* (1578) as his contribution to the feast (as to John Lyly, see, *The Reader's Companion*, Chapter 1 and 7):

> *It is virtue, yea virtue, gentlemen, that maketh gentlemen; that maketh the poor rich, the base-born noble, the subject a sovereign, the deformed beautiful, the sick whole, the weak strong, the most miserable most happy.*

The song Anthony Munday sings is from *Campaspe* by John Lyly, found in Bond, R. Warwick, M.A. *The Complete Works of John Lyly*, Vol. III. Oxford: Oxford University Press, 1902, 1967. The song Falstaff sings is also from *Campaspe.*

Philip Henslowe is known for his diary, one of the key sources for the theater in the 1590s. He also founded the

Fortune Theater north of London when the Globe began eating into his profits after 1599.

Edward Alleyn married Henslowe's daughter and became the leading actor of his time. He became rich and founded Dulwich College with the money he made from the theater.

Robert Greene was the leading playwright and poet until Marlowe came along. He is famous for his reference to *Henry VI* in his *Greene's Groatsworth of Wit* published in 1592. Professor Wells, among others, cites this work as containing the first reference to Shackspear in print. Other scholars disagree. Harvey says that Greene had a son by "a sorry ragged queane" whose brother was named Ball. Greene employed Ball to protect him from arrest for debt. Nashe says in *Strange Newes* that he once saw Greene make an apparitor (one who serves suit papers) eat his own citation, 'wax and all very handsomely served between two dishes.' In the apologetic play about Lord Cobham,[113] *The first part of the true and honorable historie of the Life of Sir John Oldastle, the good Lord Cobham*, Lord Cobham's man, Harpoole, makes the process server eat his summons. Oxford may have been parodying Greene, and his man, Ball, when he has Fluellen make Pistol eat his leek in *Henry V*, Act V, Scene 1.

The song sung by Kemp is *Hold Thy Peace,* a three-part round; Robin's song is *Of All The Birds That Ever I See.* Both are found in Singman, on p. 175 and 176.

---

113 In the epilogue to *Henry IV, Part Two,* the audience is told that Falstaff "is not Oldcastle; for Oldcastle died a martyr, and this is not the man." There is reason to believe that Falstaff was originally called Sir John Oldcastle, a Protestant martyr known as Lord Cobham. Lord Cobham's descendant was Lord Brooke, 7th Lord Cobham, who became Lord Chancellor in 1596. As the man in control of the plays, Brooke may have ordered the change in Oldcastle's name. He died in 1597; Oxford and his wife, Elizabeth Trentham, purchased Brooke House in Hackney in the same year but not from the Lord Brooke who had been Lord Chancellor for less than a year. The House became known as Brooke House after a later owner of the property.

Hold Thy Peace is referred to in *Twelfth Night*, Act II, Scene 3, when Sir Toby says to Sir Andrew Aguecheek, engaging in badinage similar to the "boots" sequence in *Two Gentlemen,* says:

> *Shall we rouse the night-owl in a catch that will draw three soul out of one weaver? Shall we do that?*

To which Sir Andrew answers:

> *An [If] you love me, let's do it: I am dog at a catch.*

The Clown:

> *By'r lady, sir, and some dogs will catch well.*

Sir Andrew:

> *Most certain. Let our catch be Thou Knave.*

The clown knows that each person in this round will have call another 'knave' and wants to make sure Sir Andrew understands this. The clown asks him:

> *'Hold thy peace, thou knave', knight? I shall be constrained in 't to call thee 'knave,' knight.*

Sir Andrew, not realizing what the clown is telling him, admits that:

> *'Tis not the first time I have constrained one to call me knave. Begin, fool; it begins 'Hold thy peace.'*

To which the clown answers:

> *I shall never begin, if I hold my peace.*

See, Illustrative Comments to *Twelfth Night*, *The Globe Illustrated Shackspear*, Act II, Scene III, p. 1028: "[T]he fun consists in the parts being so contrived that each singer in turn calls his fellow *knave*."

Thus, the love of weak puns seen in the early plays is alive and well (or unwell) in the later ones.

Fox and Geese was a traditional game played at Christmas time, modified here to make it Boar and Hounds. Singman, p.

164. The board is in the shape of a quincunx, in which four points have a fifth point in the middle.

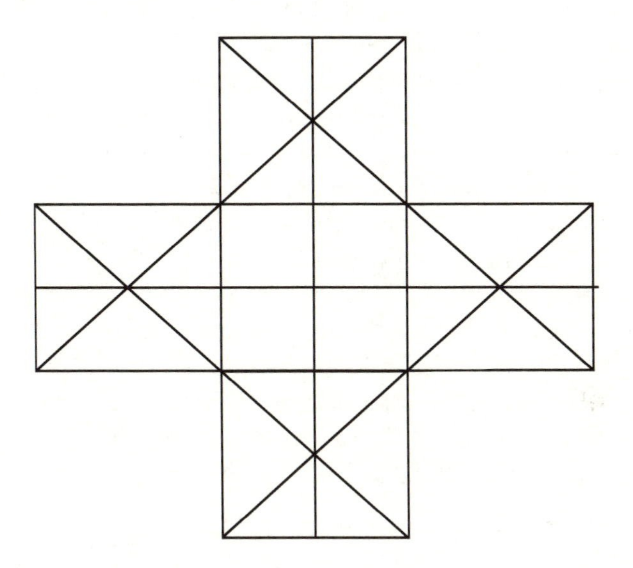

See the site plan for Cecil House in Chapter 4 above where this word is used to describe the orchard to the rear.

The Ogburns say that Oxford owed the Master of Wards £22,000 in 1590. *This Star of England,* p. 781. They cite John Strype, *Annales,* 1631; III.ii.191.

Forfeitures, in the Court of Wards	11,000
Forfeitures of Covenants upon the livery	4,000
Upon his wardship	3,000
Other Obligations	4,000
Total:	£22,000[114]

[114] Nelson, relying on a letter written in 1593 by Oxford to Burghley, which contains Burghley's marginal notes, states that Oxford owed about £11,000. Nelson, p. 334. Nelson makes no mention of Strype or Hatton forcing Oxford to pay up money Oxford owed to the Court of Wards. For a detailed analysis of Oxford's indebtedness, see Green, Nina, *An Earl in Bondage,*" in *Report My Cause Aright,* The Shakespeare Oxford Society (2007), p. 125.

This was an enormous amount of money. It is difficult for us to believe today that a young man coming of age in 1572 would owe money to the Court of Wards for his expenses and to the Queen for the "[de]livery" of title to his lands. His lands had been given to Leicester in trust while he was still a ward (which lasted for nine years); the Queen had awarded Burghley, as master of the Court of Wards, possession and control of Oxford. (Technically, unlike other cases of wardship, the Queen never sold Oxford's wardship; she directed Burghley to handle it.) Burghley's wealth grew while Oxford's shrank. Oxford was a spendthrift but it is unclear where all of Burghley's wealth came from. (*That* would be an interesting research project.) Oxford was not the only minor in Burghley's custody and there were other sources for Burghley's aggrandizement, but suspicions abound that Burghley built himself a fortune by stealing from others, including Oxford.

Also, the involvement of the Earl of Leicester in the dissipation of Oxford's assets while Oxford was a minor is only now being investigated. See Nina Green's *The Fall of the House of Oxford* in Volume 1 of *Brief Chronicles* 2009.[115] Leicester was involved in negotiations with Earl John about marrying off his children before Earl John died. Leicester is one of the executors named under Earl John's will. Another, Robert Christmas, who actually managed Oxford's estates, became a servant of Leicester. Green surmises that the Queen did this to flesh out Leicester's coffers, empty because Leicester was 'propertyless' because his father had been executed in 1552 and the father's property attainted. Given that Leicester was suspected of poisoning more than one person during his life, and may have died from a draught intended for his second wife, Leicester may have had a hand in Earl John's sudden death from unknown causes when the records show Earl John was otherwise a healthy

---

115 See, Gwynneth Bowen's article *What Happened at Hedingham and Earls Colne?* 1970-1971, in the *Shakespeare Authorship Sourcebook*, available online *http://www.sourcetext.com/sourcebook/library/bowen/22colne1.htm and /23colne2.htm.*

man. Burghley may have had physical custody of Oxford as a ward but it seems that Leicester was the one who controlled Oxford's properties. Green notes that others thought Leicester "despoiled" lands that he had been given in trust to administer. At page 82, quoting *Leicester's Commonwealth*, which can be read at *www.oxford-shakespeare.com/ leicester.html.*[116]

Whether Oxford repaid what he owed Burghley and the Court of Wards is unknown. The Ogburns in *This Star of England* claim that "Christopher Hatton ..., as Lord Chancellor in 1590 ... forced the settlement of Oxford's debts to the Master of Wards, Lord Burghley." *This Star of England*, P. 783. The next year the Queen "retaliated [against Hatton for forcing the settlement of Oxford's debts] by vigorously demanding of Hatton what he had forced from Oxford, the payment of an enormous indebtedness, 'representing arrears of tenths and first-fruits,' amounting in all to £42,139, which was nearly twice the amount of Oxford's debts." *This Star of England,* p. 705, quoting Eva Turner Clark, *The Man Who Was Shakespeare*, pp. 141-2.

Ward does not have this information. Clark's source was John Strype, *Annales*, 1631; III.ii.191. In footnote 1 to Chapter XI of *The Man Who Was Shakespeare*, Ms. Clark appears to quote Strype: "Debts to the Queen. Forfeitures, in the Court of Wards, 1000*l.* Upon his wardship, 3000*l.* And other obligations." However, there is nothing to support her statement at p. 142 that the Queen's demand "so vexed Hatton, it is said, that his disease [which Clark believed was diabetes] was aggravated to the point of serious illness causing his death on November 20, 1591." Furthermore, nothing in Clark supports the Ogburns' claim that the Queen forced Hatton to disgorge what he had forced Oxford to pay.

---

116 *Leicester's Commonwealth,* it must be pointed out, is believed to have been written by the Earl of Arundel, who libeled Oxford to the Queen in 1581 and then ran to the Continent. Arundel was a spy for the King of Spain. The allegations in the *Commonwealth* are believed to be baseless and part of a campaign to denigrate Leicester, but there may have been some truth to the claims that Leicester stole from others.

It appears that the £42,139 Hatton owed the Queen had nothing to do with whatever action Hatton took against Oxford. The Queen had appointed Hatton receiver of Tenths and First Fruits in 1576. This was a tax originally collected from the clergy by the Catholic Church which, after Henry VIII's break with Rome, was paid to the crown by an act of 1534 instead. (The amount collected in 1534 was £14,000.) By 1591, the Queen claimed Hatton owed her more than £40,000, which must have been the amount he didn't pass on to her from the taxes he collected from the clergy. One of Hatton's biographers comments: "[At the time that] Hatton was seized with his last illness, ... [h]is mind had been harassed by the Queen's insistence upon a large sum of money which he owed to the crown from the receipt of Tenths and First Fruits, amounting, it is said, to £42, 139, 5 s, for which, after his decease, an extent was laid on his house in Hatton Garden." Nicolas, [*sic*], Sir Nicholas Harris, *Memoirs of the Life and Times of Sir Christopher Hatton, K.G.*, Richard Bentley, London, 1847, p. 495, citing Camden's *Annals*, b, iv. p 34. Therefore, it seems that the Queen's demands on Hatton had nothing to do with Oxford.

There is no evidence that Hatton sued Oxford to gain money to pay off his even more substantial debts,[117] but *something* more than just being an annoying presence at court must have driven Oxford to lampoon Hatton in *Two Gentlemen* and *Twelfth Night.* Hatton had been a long-time rival of Oxford when they were both courting the Queen. Oxford owed Burghley money; Hatton disliked Oxford and needed money himself. What better solution than that Burghley would assign his claims against Oxford to Hatton and let Hatton annoy the father of Burghley's grandchildren? If so, Pondus would probably tsk-tsk this unfortunate turn of events (for Oxford) and claim he had

---

117 The immense debt Hatton incurred shows that Oxford was not the only Elizabethan nobleman who mismanaged money. Nelson and others have railed against Oxford for his wastefulness but the biographies and national entries relating to Hatton and others show that many of those who attained rank in England could not hold onto what they had inherited, earned, or been gifted by others.

nothing to do with it. In the end, neither Oxford nor Hatton repaid the people who had financed them during their lives.

One of the egregious actions Oxford is charged with is dismantling much of Castle Hedingham at the time it was deeded over in trust for his daughters in 1593. "Before Burghley could take possession on behalf of his grand-daughters, however, the castle, its appendages, and many outbuildings were stripped or razed at Oxford's direction and on his warrant." Nelson, p. 335. Professor Nelson's source is *An Account of Castle Hedingham* by Lewis Majendie written in 1796. The date of the publication, 206 years after the event being spoken of, and coming after the tumultuous events of the 17th century, somewhat erodes the support for Majendie's claim and Professor Nelson's eager support of it.[118]

Professor Nelson goes on to cite another source written closer to the transfer of the Castle:

> … [T]he Earl of Oxford, who in the year 1575 was rated at 12,000 a yeare sterlinge, within 2 [sic] following was vanished and no name of him found, having at that time prodigally spent and consumed all even to the selling of the stones timber and lead of his castles and howses, and yett he liveth and hath the first place amongst Earles, but the Queen is his gracious Mistress and gives him maintaynance for his nobility sake, …"

Nelson, pp. 379-380, quoting from *State of England Anno dom. 1600,* Thomas Wilson. However, a closer look at Wilson's account does not support a finding that Oxford stripped Castle Hedingham when it was deeded to Burghley in trust for

---

118 Professor Nelson does not cite the expansion of this story contained in *The History and Topography of the County of Essex*, Thomas Wright, published in 1836, quoted in Appendix H to Ward, p. 387, which records that the Seventeenth Earl of Oxford would not lie with his wife so she tricked him into sleeping with her and gave birth to a *son.* This may be a case of the plays (*All's Well That Ends Well* probably more than *Measure for Measure*) seeping back into local traditions.

Oxford's daughters. Wilson states that Oxford had "vanished" from the records of the earls of the realm "within 2 years" of 1575 because of his prodigious spending, "even to the selling of the stones timber and lead of his castles and howses." The period covered is 1575-1577, long before the Castle was deeded over to Burghley in 1591.

Professor Nelson's claim, therefore, is unsubstantiated. And it would have made little sense for Oxford to strip Castle Hedingham when he turned it over to his father-in-law for the benefit of his three daughters. He was marrying Elizabeth Trentham, who brought a considerable dowry with her. He was receiving £1,000 a year from the Queen. He didn't need the profits from stripping Castle Hedingham (although stranger things have happened). If he had stripped the Castle, his actions would have been taken as directed against his daughters more than Burghley. More importantly, however, there is little doubt that Burghley would have recorded Oxford's spoliation to further denigrate his son-in-law's reputation and there is nothing in the Burghley papers that support the claim by Majendie 200 years later that Oxford ordered the Castle stripped or razed. As Ward suggests, the Castle may have fallen into "sad repair" and the order was to pull down those parts that were dangerous. Ward, p. 806.

However, Wilson's claim that Oxford's spendthrift actions included "selling of the stones timber and lead of his castles and howses" may be true in his earlier years, although the true extent of the damage may not have been done by him. Oxford went through a lot of money in his early years. Many of his estates were sold and may have been stripped to finance his trip to Europe and other endeavors. See Appendix B to Ward, which shows that Oxford's lands were nearly all gone by 1586 when the Queen granted him £1,000 a year. But Oxford did not have control of his lands until long after he turned twenty-one in 1571. As shown by Green, discussed above, Sir Robert Dudley, later made Earl of Leicester, may have been the one who "despoiled" Oxford's lands in order to fund the lifestyle expected of him as the Queen's favorite and an earl of the kingdom. Oxford would have little noticed whether an order to sell property or assets to provide money to him was carried out in a trustworthy manner. Money seemed to be something he never understood.[119] Such people are always easy marks for those who, like Leicester and Burghley, lusted after it. Burghley may have wanted to keep Oxford afloat because Oxford was the father of his grandchildren, but Leicester would have no reason to refrain from profiting from the spoliation of Oxford's property. Earl John, Oxford's father, had not backed Leicester's father in 1550-1552 when the latter fell from power and was beheaded. The lands and titles owned by Leicester's father, which should have gone to Leicester, were instead forfeited, leaving Leicester, then merely Robert Dudley, 'propertyless.'

The Queen must bear some responsibility in Oxford's financial difficulties. She apparently did not handle his wardship properly. See Green, cited above. The Queen allowed Earl John's estate to be administered by Leicester when Leicester was "propertyless." Nina Green's thought that the Queen used Earl John's estate to finance her lover has merit. Oxford was only twelve when his father died in 1562 and Leicester in ascendance. The Queen would not become involved with Oxford until the 1570s. In 1562, she seems to have viewed the Oxford estate as a cash cow that could be used more usefully elsewhere. The Seventeenth Earl does not seem to have been a factor in anyone's decisions at that time.

Even when Oxford came of age, however, and even after he was close to the Queen, she did not take advantage of opportunities to help Oxford. Oxford's continual attempts to get commands when he was young and obtain land and offices

---

119 Witness his offer to the Queen in a letter dated May 18, 1591 that he exchange his £1,000 a year for a lump sum of £5,000. He was 41 years old at the time. Anyone with any financial sense would have counseled him not to make the offer. One of her gracious acts in his favor may have been her refusal to accept his offer. The £1,000 a year was continued through her reign and affirmed by King James. Oxford's widow was given a reduced annuity by James after Oxford's death.

when he was older were frustrated by the Queen. More significantly, she did nothing to help him when his half-sister Catherine sued him in 1568 to declare Earl John's marriage to Margery Golding invalid. If, as some Oxfordians believe, Oxford and Elizabeth were the parents of the Earl of Southampton, her behavior is difficult to understand. She may not have been Southampton's mother, even if Oxford came to believe it. Or, if she had a child by Oxford she may not have known what happened to it. The record indicates that she and the Earl were an item in the early 1570s and then she moved on to other men.

The Queen did, however, grant him £1,000 a year in 1586. Was this because he was on the verge of becoming destitute? (The grant was not for a term of years but *until such time as he shall be by Us otherwise provided for to be in some manner relieved.*) Did she finally realize that letting Leicester handle Oxford's property had led to Oxford's ruin?

"Samphire" or "rock samphire" or "sea fennel" (Schmidt) grew on rocky cliffs near the sea and was used as a condiment when pickled and in salads when fresh. In *King Lear*, Act IV, Scene 6, Edgar looks over the Dover cliff and tells Lear that "half way down hangs one that gathers samphire – dreadful trade!" Winter, *Shackspear's England,* p. 168.

Chapter 33
William the Conqueror

To imagine Oxford as the bard is no great leap; to imagine that the dark lady is Aemilia Bassano is not much more; to imagine that Shakespeare wangled the dark lady away from Oxford because she thought Shakespeare wrote the plays is a greater leap. On the other hand, if Oxford was Shakespeare's muse, and others thought Shakespeare was the true author, is it unrealistic to imagine that Aemelia Bassano thought so too?

The evidence is otherwise. Sonnet 41 seems to be a lament that the young man the author loves has been taken from him by a woman the author loves. These possibilities have bothered scholars for centuries, but even if the homosexual and bi-sexual nature of some of the rival poet sonnets are put aside, who these sonnets are talking about remains a problem that has not yet been solved. Scholarship aside, however, having Oxford lose Aemilia Bassano to the monster Oxford had created was too delicious to pass up.

When the theater returned after the restoration, people recognized that the plays by Shakespeare were extraordinary. The theater-going audience was in a lather to come up with stories to fill the empty record of William Shakespeare's life. One of those stories, now discredited, is that a young lady became so enamored of Richard Burbage, who was playing Richard III at the time, that she left a note asking Burbage to meet her after the play by knocking three times and announcing he was Richard III. Shakespeare intercepted the note and went ahead of Burbage. Shakespeare claimed he was Richard III and was admitted. When Burbage arrived later, Shakespeare popped his head out of a window and bid Burbage be gone "for that William the Conqueror had reigned before Richard III." Schoenbaum offers this anecdote "for the sake of the entertainment it may afford the reader" but dismisses it as he does much else that others have claimed reflect the actual doings of the Bard. Schoenbaum, p. 205 (where he quotes the entire description of the incident).

Schoenbaum's handling of this incident may be restrained scholarship, driven in part by a certain amount of prudishness, but his conclusion that the story must be rejected is based, in part, because the facts are too good to be true. In real life, however, the very outrageousness of a story may be proof that the event actually happened. Schoenbaum's handling of another story about Shakespeare—the dropped glove Shakespeare returned to the Queen during the performance of a play—is instructive as to how a belief that Shakespeare wrote the plays can skew a scholar's assessment of an event. Schoenbaum relates the story of how Shakespeare was performing before the Queen one evening when she dropped her glove in front of him to see if he would depart from the character he was playing. Shakespeare reportedly picked up the glove and returned it to her with the following ad lib couplet: "And though now bent on this high embassy / Yet stoop we to take up our Cousin's glove!"

Schoenbaum points out reasons why this story is not believable:

> So agreeable is it to have this glimpse of the courtly Warwickshire provincial exercising his extempore wit with his sovereign that one is almost tempted to overlook a few considerations hostile to romance. In Elizabethan theaters performances took place in the afternoon, not at night; the stage afforded no scenery for eavesdroppers to conceal themselves behind; the Queen is not known to have professed admiration for Shakespeare; she was disinclined to expose herself to the multitude by visiting the playhouse; and she restrained herself publicly (as in private) from flirtations with subjects of inferior station.

All of the above is true. However, astoundingly, Schoenbaum misses the most significant fact that gives this story the lie, "Yet *stoop* we to take up our *Cousin's* glove!" It is impossible to believe that any "subject of inferior station," much less a lowly player and "Warwickshire provincial" could get away with referring to himself with the royal 'we' and telling the Queen he was *stooping* to pick up her glove, much less his *'cousin's'* glove. Had the man from Stratford made such a remark, the hand that picked up the glove may well have been separated from the arm it was attached to, in which case the history books would have told of his cheek and not his "extempore wit with his sovereign."

But if the story was about Oxford's wit and not Shakespeare's, the facts suddenly take on credibility. Oxford acted in some of his plays and his plays were performed at court, not just in the playhouse. It is not unreasonable to believe that the Queen arrived late for the performance and that she had done so purposely to annoy him. If so, Oxford would have studiously ignored her. She is reported to have moved across the stage and sat or stood "behind the scenes." Schoenbaum rejects this fact, contending that there was no scenery, but sitting on the stage was a practice engaged in by nobles who attended public theaters that continued into the 1600s, so her doing so does not invalidate the story. Irritated that Oxford continued to ignore her, Elizabeth may have finally stepped in front of him and dropped her glove. He retrieved it and said he was stooping to retrieve his cousin's glove.

None of these facts fit Shakespeare. In fact, it is impossible to believe that he could have been the player in the story. Schoenbaum is right on this point. However, if the player was Oxford, the facts all fit, including the Queen toying with him. They had been lovers in the 1570s and he was her most senior lord. In court parlance, they were 'cousins.' He was being cheeky in saying 'we stoop' to pick up her glove, but this would have been vintage Oxford who was known for his constant wordplay. If she objected to his choice of words, he could defend himself by claiming he was only using the word 'stoop' to describe the physical act of bending over to retrieve it and not that he was lowering himself in station to assist his sovereign.

This anecdote, dismissed by Stratfordians, is a good example of how an event or story may take on new light once Shakespeare is relegated to his player role in the Chamberlain's Men and scholars recognize that Oxford wrote the plays. Reanalysis of stories like this may add flesh to the life Oxford led, both before Shakespeare appeared from his 'lost years' and Oxford disappeared into his.

The bells of St. Bennett will make their appearance in *Twelfth Night* when the Clown refers to them in an (unsuccessful) attempt to get Duke Orsino to give him three coins instead of two. There is an interesting article in an issue of *Shakespeare Matters* in which the author believes the reference was to the three St. Bennett churches in London and that the Clown is referring to the fact that all three could be heard at the same time in certain places. Although the author does not say so, Oxford Court was likely one of those places.

The reference to the dawn will reappear in *Romeo and Juliet*, Act III, Scene 5.

Juliet:

Wilt thou be gone? it is not yet near day:
It was the nightingale, and not the lark,
That pierced the fearful hollow of thine ear;
Nightly she sings on yon pomegranate-tree:
Believe me, love, it was the nightingale.

Romeo:

It was the lark, the herald of the morn,
No nightingale: look, love, what envious streaks
Do lace the severing clouds in yonder east:
Night's candles are burnt out, and jocund day
Stands tiptoe on the misty mountain tops.
I must be gone and live, or stay and die.

Dawning day new comfort doth inspire, slightly modified, comes from *Titus Andronicus*, Act II, Scene 2:

Titus:

The hunt is up, the morn is bright and grey,
The fields are fragrant and the woods are green:
Uncouple here and let us make a bay
And wake the emperor and his lovely bride
And rouse the prince and ring a hunter's peal,
That all the court may echo with the noise.
Sons, let it be your charge, as it is ours,
To attend the emperor's person carefully:
I have been troubled in my sleep this night,
But dawning day new comfort hath inspired.

As to *The Famous Victories of Henry the Fifth*, see, *The Reader's Companion*, Chapter 9.

The night watchmen wore long coats or cloaks that hung to their heels and were belted. They carried halberds or pikes. Globe, p. 742, note 2, describes them.

It appears that Hunnsditche, the spelling of which is taken from the Agas Map (though the intended name was probably 'Houndsditch'), was separated from the city wall at Bishopsgate by fields and houses in the narrow space between the road and the wall. Falstaff, therefore, did not drive along a ditch full of water. See the reference to the Agas Map in *The Reader's Companion,* Chapter 3.

The date of the first performance of *The Famous Victories of Henry the Fifth* is unknown. It was registered in 1594, published in quarto form in 1598, and probably "first performed c. 1586." *The Oxford Companion to Shakespeare*, p. 135.

As to Thomas Trussell and his conviction for robbery on the highway in Kent, the Gad's Hill robbery, and *The Famous Victories of Henry the Fifth,* see, *The Reader's Companion*, Chapters 9 and 22.

The Queen's 'mongrel' remark is not without substance (although fiction here). Charles Arundel reported Oxford saying "that the Quene sayd he was a bastard for which he would never love hir and leve her in the lurche one daye." Nelson, p. 206. Clark, p. 483, quoting Feuillerat, *John Lyly,* p. 123. Oxford's half-sister, Mary, claimed that Earl John's marriage to Oxford's mother was illegal. See, *The Reader's Companion*, Chapter 9, for an overview of Oxford's problems with his half-sister Mary. In real life, Mary's attempt to disinherit Oxford failed. In *The Death of Shakespeare*, the trial occurs in 1593, not 1583.

Oxford, as proud as he was, would not have taken kindly to the Queen calling him a mongrel. In *The Death of Shakespeare*, the comment is moved to 1589 and the Queen calls Oxford a mongrel instead of a bastard. The Queen is not impugning Oxford's legitimacy but his bloodline. To call Oxford a bastard was to impugn his legitimacy; to call him a mongrel was to question his lineage. The Bastard in *King John* may have been his response to her jibe. Clark, p. 482, believes that this is so.

Professor Nelson, of all people, would probably have seconded the Queen's remark. In his book, he says that "Katherine [Oxford's older half-sister] was an uncharacteristic product of the Oxford line, for her mother was an earl's daughter. After [Katherine's mother died] in 1548, Earl John [Oxford's father] took a commoner as his next wife. The difference in lineage between the pure-bred Katherine and her mongrel half-brother would have serious repercussions following [Earl John's] death in 1562." p. 14. (Emphasis added.)

As to the Gad's Hill robbery and its echoes in the lives of Oxford, Prince Hal, *Henry IV*, and Thomas Trussell, see, *The Reader's Companion*, Chapters 10 and 24.

The Queen had nicknames for her courtiers. "Turk" was one she used for Oxford. Its genesis is unknown. See, *The Reader's Companion*, Chapter 82.

Chapter 34
Pericles, Prince of Tyre

As to the "I am that I am" comment, see, *The Reader's Companion*, Chapter 2.

It is unknown whether Thomas Trussell was pardoned by the Queen for his conviction for committing robbery on the highway in Kent. See, *The Reader's Companion*, Chapter 9.

Pericles, of course, opens with the title character being presented with the puzzle Oxford recites in this chapter. If he solves it, he gets the king's daughter; if he doesn't, he dies. This is the puzzle:

I am no viper, yet I feed
On mother's flesh which did me breed.
I sought a husband, in which labour
I found that kindness in a father:
He's father, son, and husband mild;
I mother, wife, and yet his child.
How they may be, and yet in two,
As you will live, resolve it you.

The solution? The king is sleeping with his daughter. Pericles realizes what the answer is. His revulsion is real:

He's no man on whom perfections wait
That, knowing sin within, will touch the gate.

You are a fair viol, and your sense the strings;
Who, finger'd to make man his lawful music,
Would draw heaven down, and all the gods, to hearken:
But being play'd upon before your time,
Hell only danceth at so harsh a chime.
Good sooth, I care not for you.

Pericles also realizes that he can't let the king know that he has solved the riddle. Pericles asks for time. Pericles' request is proof to the king that Pericles has figured out the answer. Pericles escapes and the race is on.

There is no record of *Pericles* being performed or registered with the stationer's office, although there is a 1609 quarto[120] that

---

[120] 1609 is a signal year in Shakespearean studies. Oxford died in 1604. The only plays published between 1604 and the First Folio in 1623 were a clutch of plays published in 1609 and 'The False Folio' in 1619. The 1619 publication appears to have been withdrawn, possibly because the people involved in publishing the plays in a folio wanted the market clear before the First Folio went to print in 1623. The plays published with a date of 1609 on them were *Pericles, Troilus and Cressida,* and *King Lear.* The *Sonnets* were also published in 1609. Elizabeth Trentham moved out of Hackney in that year. Was her move related to the 1609 publications? The preface to the first publication of *Troilus and Cressida* was headed "A never Writer to an ever Reader. Newes." This sounds suspiciously like a pun on Edward de Vere's name as well as a reference to Oxford himself. The body of the preface, which was removed from the second publication that year (so someone in authority may have taken offence and ordered it removed) contained the now famous phrase that the play had been saved by the "grand possessors." The preface is quoted in notes to *The Globe Illustrated Shakespeare*, p. 1787. Who these grand possessors were is the subject of much discussion. Were they the 'incomparable brethren,' the Earl of Pembroke and his brother, the Earl of Montgomery, who was married to Oxford's youngest daughter Susan, and so referred to in the 1623 First Folio? In fairness, it should be pointed out that the same preface makes the statement that "when hee is gone, and his Commediies out of sale, you will scramble for them, and set up a new English Inquisition." This claim does not fit Oxford who was dead in 1609 (although why would there be an 'Inquisition' if the author was Shakespeare?). However, it may have been written earlier, even by Oxford himself, and research has shown that the title pages contained a high percentage of false statements. The claim in Chapter 76—*An Heir for his Lordship*—that Robin kept copies of the plays is not based in fact.

is so corrupt that it is often compared with the 1603 bad quarto of *Hamlet* and thought to be a reconstruction from actors trying to remember the play.

Pericles was not included in the 1623 First Folio. Ogburn, in mincing words, said: "Let us put down to an over-zealous imagination my notion that it may have been the susceptibility of this aspect of the play [the subject of incest] to scandalous inferences that kept *Pericles* out of the First Folio and the Second." P. 596. It was added to the Third Folio in 1664, by which point everyone associated with the plays was dead. Scholars disagree on whether it was written by Shakespeare, written by someone else, or written by Shakespeare with George Wilkins (a witness with Shakespeare in the Belott-Joy lawsuit of 1612).

Little or nothing is said by scholars about the incest presented squarely at the beginning of *Pericles*, perhaps for the same reason that Charlton Ogburn seemed incapable of discussing it directly. It may be Oxford's idea about who impregnated his wife, Anne, while he was in Italy, which would implicate her father, Lord Burghley. Burghley knew that, if Oxford died while he was abroad, Burghley would be left without a descendant Burghley could use in the succession games that would follow Elizabeth's death. See Anderson and Beauclerk on this.

If the idea did not come from Oxford's personal life, it is difficult to imagine where such an idea came from and, if a source is identified, why Oxford would have used such a plot device. Bloom and others believe that George Wilkins was the author of at least the first two acts. P. 603. "The first two acts of the play are dreadfully expressed [whatever that means—the writing? the idea of incest?] and cannot have been Shakespeare's, no matter how garbled in transmission." But Bloom concedes that the play is "quite playable ... even the first two acts." P. 604.

There may be a connection here between the Queen and Marguerite of Navarre. Marguerite was the sister of Francis I of

France. Marguerite was a published author and wrote two works that bear on incest. The first was *Miroir de l'âme pécheresse* (*Mirror of the Sinful Soul*), printed in 1533. (The French work was burned by the authorities; her brother, with whom she may have had an incestuous relationship, saved copies.) Queen Elizabeth of England, aged 11, translated *Miroir* as *The Glass of a Sinful Soul* and gave the translation to Katherine Parr, Henry VIII's widow, with whom she was living at the time. Marguerite also wrote *Heptameron*, which also treated of incest.

The incestuous theme in *Mirrors* arose from the weighing of what it meant for the virgin Mary to be mother, daughter, and spouse of God. Elizabeth compares herself to Mary in her translation. In *Heptameron*, Marguerite wrote a story in which a young man unknowingly has sexual intercourse with his mother (who knows he's his son and initiates the act). The off-spring is a daughter – a daughter and sister, who becomes a spouse when the daughter unknowingly marries her father. They love each other "so much that never were there husband and wife more loving …" Marguerite may have believed that such earthly incest can become the blessing of heavenly incest: "[the mother in *Heptameron*] must have been some self-sufficient fool, who, in her friar-like dreaming, deemed herself so saintly as to be incapable of sin, just as many of the Friars would have us believe that we can become [i.e., reach such a state] merely by our own efforts, which is an exceedingly great error. Without God, fleshly desire will turn to naughty action." *Heptameron.*

This is dangerous stuff. And Elizabeth's choice of the subject is particularly interesting. Many thought her father's relationship with her mother, Ann Boleyn, was incestuous because Henry had slept with Mary Boleyn, Anne's older sister. The Church also thought Henry had never been divorced from his first wife, Catherine of Aragon, when he married Elizabeth's mother, making his second marriage bigamous. And Ann was accused of having sex with her brother, thereby raising the specter that Elizabeth could be a bastard of an incestuous relationship.

There is an introduction to this little-visited area of Elizabethan studies in the article *Elizabeth's Glass* by Charles Boyle in the Winter 2001 issue of the Shakespeare Oxford Newsletter. Boyle makes reference to an article by Harvard professor Marc Shell in the *Journal of the American Academy of Religion*, LXIII, 3, "*The Want of Incest in the Human Family: Or, Kin and Kind in Christian Thought*" (1994), that explores the idea of incest that Marguerite (and possibly Elizabeth) may have been attracted to.

Knowing how Oxford recycled everything, Elizabeth's translation and the poetry of Marguerite of Navarre may be lurking in the background of *Love's Labour's Lost* and *Hamlet*, not to mention *Pericles*. Listen to Isabel in *Measure for Measure* rejecting her brother Claudio's plea that she save him from being executed for his crimes (Act III, Scene 1):

Isabella:

O you beast!
O faithless coward! O dishonest wretch!
Wilt thou be made a man out of my vice?
Is't not a kind of incest, to take life
From thine own sister's shame? What should I think?
Heaven shield my mother play'd my father fair!
For such a warped slip of wilderness
Ne'er issued from his blood. Take my defiance!
Die, perish! Might but my bending down
Reprieve thee from thy fate, it should proceed:
I'll pray a thousand prayers for thy death,
No word to save thee.

Dr. Simon Forman was a poor country boy who made himself into a prominent physician in London. He was also an astrologer. He kept a diary that showed he was a charismatic, volatile, ambitious man, and a womanizer of the first order, having bedded or tried to bed his female patients. He treated, among others, Richard Field, the printer of *Venus and Adonis*, the Jaggard brothers, who printed the 1623 First Folio, Marie

Mountjoy, who was involved in the Mountjoy lawsuit where Shakespeare's sixth signature was found and who was wife of the landlord of the house in London where Shakespeare lived for six years, Bridget Vere, Oxford's middle daughter, who would become Lady Norris when she married the Baron of Rycote in 1599, and Aemilia Bassano, Lord Hunsdon's mistress, who is thought by some to be the Dark Lady of the Sonnets. His diary contains notes of his having seen *Macbeth, The Winter's Tale,* and *Cymbeline. The Oxford Companion to Shakespeare,* p. 151. Cook, Judith, *Dr. Simon Forman- A Most Notorious Physician*, Chatto & Windus, London, 2001.

1590

Chapters 35 – 49

Chapter 35
Billesley Again

In *Love's Labour's Lost*, Sir Nathaniel says: "*Sir, he hath never fed of the dainties that are bred in a book; he hath not eat paper, as it were; he hath not drunk ink: his intellect is not replenished.*" Act IV, Scene 2.

In Act I, Scene 2 of *Henry IV, Part Two*, Falstaff remarks that "he is the cause of wit in others."

> *Men of all sorts take a pride to gird at me: the brain of this foolish-compounded clay, man, is not able to invent anything that tends to laughter, more than I invent or is invented on me: I am not only witty in myself, but the cause that wit is in other men.*

The scholars agree. Harold Bloom, in his chapter on *The Merry Wives of Windsor*, laments that Falstaff is "[n]o longer either witty in himself or the cause of wit in other men [as he had been in the three *Henriad* plays]." Bloom, p. 316.

Looney, in Chapter VII, page 122, says the following:

> Again, we would draw special attention to the following excerpts from the "History of English Poetry" (vol. ii, pp. 312-313) by W. J. Courthope, C.B., [122] M.A., D.Litt. (Professor of Poetry at the University of Oxford):
>
> "Edward de Vere, Seventeenth Earl of Oxford . . . a great patron of literature. . . . His own verses are distinguished for their wit . . . and terse ingenuity. . . . His studied concinnity of style is remarkable. . . . He was not only witty himself but the cause of wit in others. . . . Doubtless he was proud of his illustrious ancestry. . . . He was careful in verse at any rate to conform to the external requirements of chivalry, but in later

> years his turn for epigram seems to have prevailed over his chivalrous sentiments." (Emphasis added.)

It is very interesting that Courthope didn't realize he was using Falstaff's lines to describe Oxford. And Looney gives no indication that he himself caught the connection.

When Oxford was seventeen he stabbed and killed an undercook named Thomas Brincknell. Brincknell left a widow who died in 1578. The widow was apparently supported in her later years by the parish of St. Margaret's in Westminster. Nelson, pp. 47-49.

The record of the coroner's inquest has survived. Translated from the Latin (by Professor Nelson), it reads, in part: "Edward Earl of Oxford [was together with an Edward Baynam, tailor, in the backyard of Cecil House between seven and eight o'clock in the evening], [e]ach with a sword, called a foil, and together they meant to practice the science of defense. Along came Thomas Brincknell, drunk, … who ran and fell upon the point of the Earl of Oxford's foil (worth twelve pence) which Oxford held in his right hand intending to play (as they call it). In the course of which, with this foil Thomas Brincknell gave himself a wound to the *front* of his thigh four inches deep and one inch wide, of which he died instantly. This, to the exclusion of all other explanations, was the way he died." Nelson, p. 47.[121]

The phrase, "to the exclusion of all other explanations," is formula, but of interest in this particular case, since there were other possible explanations. Burghley thought of telling the jury that Oxford had acted in self-defense. *This Star of England*, pp. 13-14; Nelson, p. 48. Professor Nelson points out that Oxford was a skilled swordsman, later winning at least two tournaments in front of the Queen (although these were semi-ritualized jousting, etc., and not events in which one of the participants might die). Professor Nelson also correctly notes that the

---

121 Whether the wound was to the front or the back of the thigh is discussed below.

instantaneous death was a fiction, probably to reinforce the conclusion of suicide, which would be eroded somewhat if the victim had time to repent his own murder. Brincknell more likely cried out against the injustice of his early death. The absence of any burial records for poor Thomas may be confirmation of the coroner's finding. Nelson, p. 48.

The location of the wound the undercook suffered may be important. Paul Streitz, in his book, *Oxford – Son of Queen Elizabeth I,* Oxford Institute Press (2001), quotes from the coroner's inquest which, because it was in Latin, had to be translated into English. Professor Nelson admits that he summarized the report while Streitz relies upon a translation by a third party. The two versions differ in many respects, most significantly in describing where Brincknell was wounded: Professor Nelson says the undercook "gave himself a wound to the *front* of his thigh [not identified as either right or left] four inches deep and one inch wide, of which he died instantly;" Streitz has it that "Thomas struck himself criminally with the same sword called a foil in the *back* of his left thigh, stabbed himself, and there and then gave himself a mortal blow with the aforesaid sword four inches deep and one inch wide." The Latin original reads: "*Thomas cum eodem gladio voc{ato} a ffoyle in ant{er}iore p{ar}te sui ip{s}ius sinistri femoris tunc,*" which can be translated as "Thomas was stabbed in the *anterior* [front] part of his *sinistri femoris* [left thigh]."[122]

A wound in the *front* of the thigh appears to be the correct translation of the Latin. If the wound had been to the rear of the thigh, Brincknell would have had to have run *backwards* onto Oxford's sword, an inconsistent action for someone who is trying to kill himself. Or, Brincknell was trying to get away from Oxford when Oxford stabbed him from behind. The location of the wound is important, therefore, as to the intent of each man

---

122 The Latin transcript can be viewed at: *http://socrates.berkeley.edu/~ahnelson/DOCS/brinck.html*

at the time Brincknell was killed. Bad enough that Oxford stabbed Brincknell in the thigh; it would have been far worse [for Oxford's 21st century reputation] to have stabbed Brincknell as he was running away.

The jury consisted of 17 men. It included at least one of Burghley's servants and possibly Raphael Holinshed, a protégé of Burghley, who was the future author of *The Chronicles of England, Scotland, and Ireland.* Nelson, p. 48. Joseph Satin described *The Chronicles* in *Shakespeare and His Sources* as Shakespeare's "most frequently consulted source [along with Plutarch] for seminal ideas." Satin, p. xi.

No one knows who supplied the idea that Brincknell ran upon the earl's sword and committed *felo de se,* or 'felony upon oneself.' It didn't come from Burghley because he left notes that he thought of having the jury render a verdict that Oxford acted in self-defense. Only Falstaff seems capable of coming up with the idea. Of course, Falstaff is a fictional character, unlike Oxford and the unfortunate man he killed.

Professor Nelson claims that Oxford "learned a lesson which largely determined the next thirty years of his life: "he could commit no act, however egregious, that his powerful guardian Cecil would not personally forgive and persuade others to forget." Nelson, p. 49. Professor Nelson does not cite what those egregious acts were.

Burghley described Brincknell as a "poor man" (meaning unfortunate, not poor in money) and the context of his remark indicates that Burghley must have felt something for him. Professor Nelson uses this remark to claim that Burghley felt sorry for Brincknell's family but there is nothing to support this claim. Whatever St. Margaret's did for the widow after 1567 is no evidence that Burghley felt compassion for Brincknell's family. It might have been Oxford who made the arrangements.

Some interesting comments on Oxford's involvement in the death of Thomas Brincknell may have been left behind by Henry Howard and Charles Arundel in 1580 as part of their defense against Oxford's claim that they were involved in a Catholic conspiracy. Howard said that he would not deal "with the bloodshed of [Oxford's] youth because it is long past although most terrible." This conveys something of the impact Brincknell's death may have had on Oxford's contemporaries, but Charles Arundel was more specific than Howard. He wrote that ""the Earle being grieved in conscience about killing of (blank) about five years since desired [me to help him to conference with] some learned man whereupon I brought him unto (blank)."[123]

Charles Arundel related that Oxford was 'grieved in conscience' about killing a man "five years since." Arundel made this statement while in the Tower. The Queen had committed him around Christmas of 1580, His statement appears to have been made before the end of 1580, which means that the murder he was referring to took place in 1575 or 1576. Thomas Brincknell died in 1567, thirteen years earlier. It is possible that the five years is accurate and Oxford killed someone else in 1575, although there is no record of his having done so. Oxford left England for Italy in February, 1575 and returned in 1576. Did he murder someone while he was in Italy? There is no evidence he did. Arundel may have had the number of years (five as opposed to thirteen) wrong. That he may have been confused is supported by his inability to keep numbered arguments in order, as to which see Chapter 75—*Much Ado About Nothing.*

It is possible that Arundel created this conversation. After all, he and Howard were facing the block at the time and much of what they said is suspect. For example, why would Oxford need Howard to find him a "learned man?" Oxford could

---

[123] These quotes are from the Howard/Arundel libels which can be read on Professor Nelson's website at

http://socrates.berkeley.edu/~ahnelson/LIBELS/libelndx.html.

Professor Nelson believes that the man Howard brought to Oxford was a priest. The spelling of the statements quoted has been modernized. The word 'blank' is in the original.

obviously find someone himself. And why take Arundel into his confidence, unless Oxford was using Arundel, which is not beyond the capability of the man who wrote the plays. Howard reports that Oxford offered him £1,000 to help Howard run to the continent when Francis Southwell confessed all. If Howard had run, Oxford would have looked better in the Queen's eyes since they were all accusing each other of multiple crimes. A close reading of Oxford's offer as told by Howard outlines the faint image of a man (Howard) who could be fooled by the con man Oxford might have been. And where would Oxford get a £1,000 or the bills for money being held by the ambassador from Spain? The story smacks of clever finagling by Oxford and details added by Howard that don't add up.

However, Arundel had nothing to gain by repeating to the Privy Council investigators that Oxford was grieved over the killing of a man. It is difficult to believe that the man who could write the works identified with William Shakespeare was not scarred in some way by Brincknell's death, as well as the ease with which it was swept away. Brincknell's death may be hidden in *Measure for Measure,* for example.

Professor Nelson is dismissive of the claim by the Ogburns that "Brincknell was Burghley's spy, and so (like Rosencrantz and Guildenstern) deserved to die— an argument as unfounded as it is blood-curdling." Nelson, p. 450, footnote 1. However, there is ample evidence that Burghley employed spies. See *This Star of England*, pp. 13-16. Brincknell, like Rosencrantz and Guildenstern, as well as Polonius in *Hamlet*, may indeed have been a spy for Burghley. If Oxford wrote the plays, the dispatch of Rosencrantz and Guildenstern in *Hamlet* and Hamlet's killing of Polonius take on a different light when it is realized that the author at seventeen killed a man spying on him at the bidding of Lord Burghley.

The connection between the killing of the undercook and the stabbing of Hotspur by Falstaff in *Henry IV – Part 1* is also interesting. Both the undercook and Hotspur were stabbed in the thigh, Hotspur by a worried Falstaff imagining Hotspur rising up and killing him. It may be one of the "coincidences"

Orson Welles was referring to when he remarked that, if Oxford didn't write the plays, there were an awful lot of funny coincidences to explain away. Looney put it this way, which is an excellent exposition of how a juror may consider facts that appear to be connected:

> *The predominating element in what we call circumstantial evidence is that of coincidences. A few coincidences we may treat as simply interesting; a number of coincidences we regard as remarkable; a vast accumulation of extraordinary coincidences we accept as conclusive proof.*
>
> Looney, p. 80.
>
> Ethelbert is fiction.

Chapter 36
Robin Is Gone

Ferdinando Stanley was the son of Henry Stanley, Fourth Earl of Derby, and would become the Fifth Earl for a short time when his father died in 1593. Ferdinando was also known as Lord Strange, further confusing matters. He had a group of players known as Lord Strange's Men before he became the Fifth Earl when they became the Earl of Derby's Men. His brother, William, succeeded him as the Sixth Earl of Derby and married Oxford's eldest daughter, Lisbeth.

The Troublesome Reign of King John dates from 1589. Scholars differ as to whether it was written wholly by Shakespeare, whether he wrote it with someone else, or whether Shakespeare adapted a play someone else wrote.

"Dwindle" makes its first appearance in *Henry IV – Part One*, Act III, Scene 3, when Falstaff asks Bardolph, "*am I not fallen away vilely since this last action? Do I not bate? So I not dwindle? Why my skin hangs about me like an old lady's loose gown; I am withered like an old apple-john. Well, I'll repent, and that suddenly, while I am in some liking; I shall be out of heart shortly, and then I shall have no strength to repent.*"

Virginia Padoana was a courtesan who lived in a palazzo not far from the current-day train station in Venice. Nelson, p. 139. (Elspeth Trentham brings her up in Chapter 82.) The Jewish Ghetto, the setting for *The Merchant of Venice* was not far away. Farina, p. 222. Oxford's life in Venice needs more study and reflection. He stayed there longer than in any other area while he was abroad. The culture was far ahead of England's at the time. Women, for example, were allowed to publish their poetry, something that would not occur in England until Amelia Bassano published her poetry in 1611. Women were also allowed to act in plays. Farina, p. 222. Oxford went to an orthodox Greek church, which is unusual, but it may have been because it was not a Catholic church and he was concerned about being labeled a Catholic sympathizer at home, something that had been bruited about when he fled to the Low Countries in 1573. Orazio Coquo, the Italian page Oxford brought with him when he returned to England implied as much when he was interrogated by the Inquisition upon his return to Venice. Nelson, p. 154-177. Orazio, by the way, denied that Oxford had abused him. He told the Inquisition that Oxford let him and others worship in his house as they saw fit. Of course, just as Arundel and Howard may have lied in their libels against Oxford because they were facing the block, Orazio Coquo may not have been forthcoming when the Inquisition examined him about what happened while he was in England.

Chapter 37
John Shackpear

Oxford's encounter with Duke Cassimere is recounted in *The Revenge of Bussy d'Ambois*, by George Chapman, published in 1613. Bussy d'Ambois was a real person. Lord Willoughby, Oxford's brother-in-law, put Henry of Navarre on the French throne with the help of English troops. Bussy used a rope ladder to get Henri out of the Louvre. See the connections between this event and *Two Gentlemen of Verona* in Clark, p. 315, and in *The Reader's Companion*, Chapter 27.

Oxford's encounter with the Duke resurfaces in *Hamlet* when Hamlet reviews Fortinbras' army. As to the real encounter between Oxford and the Duke, see Anderson, p. 109, and *The Revenge of Bussy D'Ambois.*

Sir John Smith was a strange man who served in many countries. He was knighted by the Queen, sent on missions abroad, including France when Oxford was there, and ended up trying to incite a rebellion at home in 1595 for which the Queen put him in the Tower. He was then restricted to his home in Essex for the rest of her reign. Clark has an interesting discussion of how Falstaff's actions in recruiting soldiers in *Henry IV*, Act 4, Scene 2, is based on the writings and common knowledge of Sir John Smith's odd ideas about soldiering. P. 702 *et seq.*

Stratford, like many other towns and villages, was a foul place in 1590. "Stratford [in Elizabeth's reign] contained about 1800 inhabitants, who dwelt chiefly in thatched cottages, which straggled over the ground . . . . The streets were foul with offal, mud, muck heaps, and reeking stable refuse." Richard Grant White, *England Within and Without*, p. 21, quoted in *This Star of England*, p. 940. In 1552, John Shakespeare was fined 1 shilling for making a dunghill in Henley Street. Sams, p. 197.

No one knows what John or Hamnet Shakespeare looked like. The tanning business was an awful trade. Night soil and urine were used with other chemicals to soak hides to alter the protein structure of the skins so that they remained soft, i.e., could not return to rawhide. Tanned leather was made by soaking the hides in lye (wood ash) or lime which rendered them unlikely to decompose. Tannin was usually obtained from the oak tree (the word derives from the German *tanna* meaning oak or fir).

A whittawer was a glove maker who worked only in the 'white' hides, soft white or light-colored leather. Jon Aubrey reported in his *Brief Lives* that John Shakespeare was a butcher but Schoenbaum believed that Will's father was a glover because the two occupations were kept separate for sanitary reasons.

Schoenbaum, pp. 16-17; pp. 74-75. Schoenbaum chose to ignore the reality of what it was to be a tanner or a glover by writing that Will may have experienced the 'clutter' of the 'merchandise of his father's shop, pungent with the aroma of leather, …' thus romanticizing Will's youthful influences. Whether or not John was a glover, there is ample evidence that he engaged in a number of other businesses in Stratford.

The words John Shakespeare use to shoo Hamnet away, "Away, you whoreson upright rabbit, away!" are from *Henry IV, Part 1*, Act II, Scene 2, where Bardolph reacts to something a young page says to him.

Chapter 38
The Earl of Surrey

"I am nothing but a base football player" is adapted from *Lear*, Act 1, Scene 4, where Kent trips Oswald and says, "you base football player."

Henry Howard, Earl of Surrey, married Francis de Vere, John de Vere's sister, and was therefore Edward de Vere's uncle. Howard was known as the Poet Earl. He is credited with introducing blank verse to English literature and, with Thomas Wyatt, the sonnet form of poetry. The first poem in blank verse (Anthony Burgess, *Shakespeare*, p. 37) was:

They he whisted all, with fixèd face attent
When Prince Aeneas from the royal seat
Thus gan to speak, O Queene, it is thy will,
I should renew a woe can not be told:
How that the Grekes did spoile and overthrow
The Phyrgian wealth, and wailful realm of Troy,
Those ruthful things that I myself beheld.

Howard was executed in January 1547, three years before Oxford was born. Henry VIII turned paranoid as he began to die and imagined that conspirators were at work to prevent his son, Edward, from succeeding him. Howard was foolish enough to suggest that his father should be Edward's protector during Edward's minority, but the Duke of Somerset wanted the position and quickly trumped up charges against Howard and his father. Somerset had Henry sign the death warrant for both. Howard was executed six days after he was imprisoned. His father was to follow him the next day but Henry died that night, thus sparing the father. He was released by Mary when she came to the throne at the end of Edward's reign.

The lines Howard speaks to Oxford come from the Ghost in *Hamlet* and Warwick's comments in *Henry VI, Part 1*. The description of the Earl of Surrey being without eyes is from *Henry VI, Part 2*, Act 3, Scene 3, where Cardinal Beaufort, having caused the death of the Duke of Gloucester, describes seeing Gloucester's ghost as Beaufort dies: "*He hath no eyes! The dust hath blinded them.*"

Henry Howard, the poet Earl of Surrey, fathered the Henry Howard who, along with Charles Arundel and Thomas Southwell, accused Oxford of having Catholic sympathies in 1581.

What fool hath added water to the sea, is from *Titus and Andronicus*, Act III, Scene 1. *When to the Sessions of sweet silent thought,* is from Sonnet 30.

William Cecil's early career was spent in the service of the Duke of Somerset who was Lord Protector during the early years of the reign of Edward VI. In 1548, Cecil was described as the Protector's Master of Requests. He also seems to have acted as private secretary to the Protector, and was in some danger at the time of the Protector's fall in October, 1549. The lords opposed to Somerset ordered Cecil's detention on 10 October, and in November he was in the Tower. But Cecil successfully convinced the new powers-that-be that he was innocent of wrong-doing and was released from the Tower in less than three months. In 1550, he was sworn in as one of King Edward's two secretaries of state. In April 1551, Cecil became Chancellor of the Order of the Garter.

Cecil improved his position when Mary came to the throne. He went to Mass, confessed, and met Cardinal Pole on his return to England in December 1554. These shows of Catholic faith, of course, were only superficial as he kept in touch with Elizabeth and earned her gratitude when she succeeded Mary.

There is no evidence that Burghley played a role in the execution of Surrey in 1547.

Howard and Arundel accused Oxford of many crimes, including having sex with a mare. Oxford, here, explains to Surry that the actual words were "sex with a *mère*" [mother in French]. They also said that Oxford had told them that "Charles Tyrrell appereid to him with a whipp, which had made a better shew in the hand of a Carman [cart-driver] then of hobb gobbline and this was in unckle howard's at grenewidge." See, Libels, online, web site address given in Sources to *The Death of Shakespeare.*

An orpharian was a member of the cittern family. It was invented in England during Elizabeth's reign. There is a picture of one that may have been given to Elizabeth on page 8 of *Elizabeth I – The Golden Reign of Gloriana* by David Loades, The National Archives (2003). Howard's ghost is up to date; the orpharian was invented in 1581, 24 years after he was beheaded.

Chapter 39
Thomas Digby

There is no evidence that Oxford was ordered to escort and entertain the Duke of Saxe-Coburg in 1590. Havering-in-the-Bowerie was one of Oxford's estates. The Queen visited Oxford there in 1572 when they were carrying on with each other. It was near Colchester. Its park contained 1,000 acres. In 1574, she spent six days there with him. The 'noble progress' went through Havering in 1578. *The History of Essex,* London 1814, p.113. Nothing remains of it today. Ogburn, pp. 508, 511.

The parallels between King John's reaction to Arthur's death and Elizabeth's reaction to Mary's execution are striking. Like many other plays, it is difficult to accept that William Shakespeare could escape retribution for a play that so blatantly alluded to Elizabeth's role in Mary's death.

King John and the Bastard first appeared in print in the 1623 *First Folio.* It was preceded by the anonymous *The Troublesome*

Raigne of King John of England, which was published in 1591. Scholars do not agree as to which was written first but most conclude that *The Troublesome Raigne* preceded *King John.*[124] The Bastard is probably Shakespeare's first great individual character.

Oxford's return trip from Italy went up the Rhone River in the center of France. The trip spawned at least two plays—*All's Well That Ends Well* and *Love's Labour's Lost.* The former is based on a story in Boccaccio's *Decameron* that tracks Oxford's early life (Bertram is forced to marry a woman beneath him and is tricked into bedding her by mistakenly thinking he is sleeping with a woman he has been trying to seduce) while *Love's Labour's Lost* is based on events that took place, most scholars think, in the court of Navarre in the southeast corner of France at the base of the Pyrenees. However, Abbe le Franc and George Lambin make a convincing argument that the events that influenced the writing of *Love's Labour's Lost* took place at Castle Roussillon in the Rhone River basin, and that Oxford learned of them on his

---

124 The anonymous plays that seem to have provided the seeds for later plays attributed to Shakespeare are numerous—*The Troublesome Raigne of King John, Famous Victories of King Henry V, The First Part of the Contention of the Two Famous Houses of York and Lancaster, The Taming of A Shrew*, and others — not to mention many plays where only the title is known—*The Rape of The Second Helene*, for example. The connection between the plays and the actual events that took place at the time is a fascinating mini-universe of Shakespearean /Oxfordian studies that could not be explored in a novel about all the plays. (For example, read Clark's cogent arguments that much of *Love's Labour's Lost* is about Elizabeth's marriage negotiations with Alençon. P 477, *et seq.*). There was also no room in *The Death of Shakespeare* to treat of the earlier plays, which many believe were written by Oxford. Sams struggles with his conclusion that the earlier plays must have been written by Shakespeare when he knew the man from Stratford could not have been the author: "But what if he had begun in the 1580s, and thus created the stage …? <u>The dramatist best placed to transform shapeless plays would be the one who had written them…and then developed as an artist</u>." At p. 64. Being married to the idea that Shakespeare wrote the plays, he is blind to the proposition that they were written by another dramatist.

trip home from Italy. *Voyages de Shakespeare en France et en Italie*, Librairie E. Droz, Geneva, 1962.

Châteaux Coûtet is a first-growth from the Barsac-Sauterne region of southwestern France. Thomas Jefferson brought some back with him when he completed his tour as the American ambassador to France. It was ranked as one of the premier grand-cru in the 1855 classification. However, there is no evidence that Oxford visited any winery. And, unfortunately, Chateau Coûtet would have been more than a day's ride from Tournon.

Oxford sat on the jury that convicted Mary Queen of Scots in 1586 (as well as the trial that convicted Essex and Southampton in 1601). *King John*, *Macbeth*, and *Hamlet,* among other plays, may have been written in reaction to his participation in the trial that convicted Mary. Oxford may have been able to depict power politics at the top of the English ruling system (and *King John* is a good example of those struggles) but the Seventeenth Earl of Oxford was the last of the medieval courtiers and does not seem to have embraced the 'commodity' so willingly adopted by many of the characters in his plays. The Bastard speaks thus in Act II, Scene 1:

And why rail I on this Commodity?
But for because he hath not woo'd me yet:
Not that I have the power to clutch my hand,
When his fair angels[125] *would salute my palm;*
But for my hand, as unattempted yet,
Like a poor beggar, raileth on the rich.
Well, whiles I am a beggar, I will rail
And say there is no sin but to be rich;
And being rich, my virtue then shall be
To say there is no vice but beggary.
Since kings break faith upon commodity,
Gain, be my lord, for I will worship thee.

---

[125] References to angels in the plays are almost always references to money.

But the Bastard lets the theater-goers know early on that he is made of better metal and only learns how to connive in order to survive:

But this is worshipful society
And fits the mounting spirit like myself,
For he is but a bastard to the time
That doth not smack of observation;
And so am I, whether I smack or no;
And not alone in habit and device,
Exterior form, outward accoutrement,
But from the inward motion to deliver
Sweet, sweet, sweet poison for the age's tooth:
Which, though I will not practise to deceive,
Yet, to avoid deceit, I mean to learn;
For it shall strew the footsteps of my rising.

The Bastard may be the first dramatic character to display the humanity that will mark Falstaff, Hamlet, Richard III, Viola and so many others of the characters that appear in the later plays.

Chapter 40
Oxford Court

As to the fiction of bringing in the Queen as a defendant in a case where the actual defendant owes her money, see Plucknett, Theodore F. T., *A Concise History of the Common Law*, Little, Brown and Company, Boston, Fifth Edition, 1956, p. 161.

The young boy is John Marston, born in 1576. He will go on to become a satirist and one of the poets who engages in the War of the Theaters with Ben Jonson and others in 1599-1600. He will attend Oxford University and the Middle Temple but not practice law. He will write plays for Henslowe and satires for the public but will resign his ownership interest in the Children of Blackfriars in 1609 and become an Anglican priest. He died in 1634.

Jonson later claimed that he beat Marston once and took his pistol, but the two of them went back and forth as critics of each other while writing praise of each other as well so it is unclear exactly what their relationship was.

Marston's works began to appear in 1598. He wrote *The Scourge of Villany* in 1599 in which the following lines occur (quoted in Ward, p. 329):

> *Far fly the fame*
> *Most, most, of me belov'd, whose silent name*
> *One letter bounds. Thy true judicial style*
> *I ever honour, and if my love beguile*
> *Not much my hopes, then thy unvalued worth*
> *Shall mount fair place, when Apes are turned forth.*

Marston seems to referring to *Two Gentlemen* here, where Speed is talking to Valentine:

> *Speed:* *To yourself: why, she woos you by a figure.*
> *Valentine:* *What figure?*
> *Speed:* *By a letter, I should say.*

To say that Sylvia is wooing Valentine "by a letter" makes sense; "by a figure" makes no sense. The two together solve the puzzle. Oxford's title begins with "O" which is also a figure – zero (or zed).

Marston assumed his readers would remember Speed's comments to Valentine and know Speed was alluding to Oxford. Marston took this one step farther. His reference to an author whose "name one letter bounds" can only refer to Oxford, whose given name was "Edward de Vere." It appears, therefore, that Marston was one-upping Oxford, who was still alive, and probably thought the Earl would recognize the imitation as praise. Taking a phrase from one play and reworking it for another play was common. See, for example, Oxford and Sidney going back and forth over a kingdom, a cottage, and a grave. See, *The Reader's Companion*, Chapter 12.

C.S. Lewis thinks little of Marston's work. See his analysis beginning at p. 472 of *English Literature in the Sixteenth Century excluding Drama.*

Chapter 41
The Bastard

Hubert de Burgh, Earl of Kent, the character in *King John* who threatens to put out Arthur's eyes, is buried in the Church of Austin Friars in London, not far from Oxford Court. Edward VI had given the church to the Dutch living in London. Oxford's ancestor, John de Vere, Twelfth Earl of Oxford and his son, Aubrey, are also buried in the church after they were executed on Tower Hill in 1461. In 1593, the infamous "satirical verses" that may have sent Marlowe to his death were nailed up on the church. Walter Thornbury, *Bishopsgate, Old and New London: Volume 2* (1878), pp. 152-170, which can be viewed at:

http://www.british-history.ac.uk/old-new-london/vol2/pp152-170

and which contains a great deal of interesting facts and connections to Oxford in this northern part of old City of London.

Chapter 42
King John before the Queen

Figure 1 in Nelson's *Monstrous Adversary* is a map of Essex showing "places of particular significance to the Earl of Oxford." Sible Hedingham is a village near Hedingham Castle. Wivenhoe is below Colchester on the Colne River. Havering-in-the-Bowerie is further downriver near the mouth of the Colne. It is likely that Oxford met the Queen there on her progress in June 1572. Nelson, p. 84. Havering and other properties had been taken away from him during his minority and he labored mightily during Elizabeth's reign to get them back. Only James, shortly after his ascent to the throne, gave Oxford back his lands. However, not having legal title did not mean Oxford did not use them and control them. It is probably, therefore, that he was there in 1572. His hosting of the Duke of Saxe-Coburg is fiction, however.

The Queen's reference to Oxford as an orange that needs to be squeezed must have been overheard by someone who passed it on to Ben Jonson. In *Everyman Out of his Humour*, 1600, Ben creates two characters named "Clove" and "Orenge" who he describes in the list of characters as "*Geminis* or twins of foppery. ... Orenge is the more humerous [sic] of the two (whose small portion of juice (being squeez'd out:) [sic].

Sonnets 1-17 urge someone (most scholars agree they seem to be directed at Southampton) to procreate. Schoenbaum, *A Compact Documentary Life*, p. 179. Akrigg, in his biography of Southampton, writes the following at page 205:

> In fact Shakespeare, writing *Venus and Adonis*, was already so concerned <u>lest Southampton wreck his career by refusing to marry Lady Elizabeth Vere</u> that, while writing the sort of Ovidian poem popular at this period, he kept slipping into the mouth of Venus the arguments for marriage which he would shortly present more directly in his sonnets. (Emphasis added.)

This is one of the most astonishing sentences ever to be read about the relationship between the Third Earl of Southampton and William Shakespeare. Shakespeare was so concerned that Southampton would wreck his career by *refusing* to marry the Earl of Oxford's daughter that he made Venus speak lines to make sure he didn't pass up the opportunity? Shakespeare to the rescue, then, with *Venus* and his sonnets? Was Shakespeare Southampton's father? Substitute Oxford for Shakespeare and Akrigg's take on what was going on here makes sense. It makes no sense for the man from Stratford-upon-Avon.

The lines Oxford recites in this chapter are the last two lines of Sonnet 17. Earlier lines from the same sonnet are quoted in Chapter 28 when Oxford is returning from Willoughby House after meeting Aemilia Bassano.

The Third Earl of Southampton did not agree to marry Elizabeth Vere, even though Burghley ordered him to do so. Rumor has it that he paid a £5,000 fine for the privilege of remaining single (for a while).

For Oxford to urge Southampton to marry his daughter, Oxford must have believed that Southampton was not his son.

He doubted that Elizabeth was his daughter, but it seems inconceivable that he would have urged her to marry Southampton if he was father to both Elizabeth *and* Southampton. Then again, there were Egyptians who married their siblings. Oxford probably knew about that, but the suggestion that he knew they were both his children and wanted them to marry is not supported by any evidence. If anything, his encouragement of the match shows that he didn't think Southampton was his child.

On the other hand, if Oxford believed Southampton *was* his son, he would be very interested in having his son marry and procreate. Some scholars have recognized that the first seventeen sonnets might have been written by a father: "What man in the whole world, except a father or a potential father-in-law, cares whether any other man gets married?" C.S. Lewis, *English Literature in the 16th Century – Excluding Drama*, p. 503-504.

Henry VI has come down to us as the three parts of *King Henry VI*. They are related to *The First Part of the Contention of the Two Famous Houses of York and Lancaster* (Parts 1 and 2) and *Richard Duke of York* (Part 3) but scholars have been unable to reach agreement in what way (earlier works of Shakespeare? Collaborations? By someone else?). There was insufficient space in *The Death of Shakespeare* to comment on these sources and how they relate to the *Henry VI* plays we know from the First Folio. See, *The Oxford Companion to Shakespeare*, p. 140, and *The Reader's Companion*, Chapters 23, 37, and 55.

Had any part of the *Henry VI* trilogy been the only Shakespeare play to survive, Shakespeare would've been considered a major playwright (despite Harold Bloom's dismissal of the trilogy as written in "Marlowe's mode and rhetoric appropriated with great zest and courage but with little independence, as though the novice dramatist were wholly intoxicated by the *Tamburlaine* plays and *The Jew of Malta*."). Marjorie Garber thinks "they contain … patterns of symmetry, echo, inversion, and opposition that demonstrate their powerful effectiveness as dramatic vehicles, and as stage pictures." Interest in the trilogy is dimmed by the brilliance of the later plays.

Chapter 43
The Queen and Lady Elspeth Trentham

There is no evidence Elizabeth Trentham was called Elspeth (see, *The Reader's Companion* to the Prologue as to the names of the women in *The Death of Shakespeare*) or that she conspired with Queen Elizabeth to snare Oxford as a husband.

In fact, there is little evidence of who Elizabeth Trentham was. There are no paintings of what she looked like. There is only a description of a number of ladies-in-waiting which includes the comment that Elizabeth Trentham was 'fair.' There are a few letters she wrote to Cecil after Oxford died that show a woman who could handle business. And she handled her father's estate, even though she had brothers who were alive at the time her father died.

It was customary for unmarried women to leave their bosom uncovered. "Hentzer, who saw her[the Queen] in 1598 in her 66th year, describes her: —Very majestic, her face oblong, fair, but wrinkled; her eyes small, yet black and pleasant; her nose a little hooked, her lips thin, and her teeth black. [She loved sweets and the sugar apparently rotted her teeth.] She had in her ears two pearls, with very rich drops; she wore false hair, and that red; upon her head she had a small crown. <u>Her bosom was uncovered, as all English ladies have it till they marry</u>; and she had on a necklace of exceeding fine jewels; her hands were small, her fingers long, and her stature neither tall nor low." Notes to Portrait of Elizabeth, No. 619, p. 228, *The Royal Gallery of Hampton Court.*

An "eyrar of swans" is how *The Book of St. Albans*, published in 1486, describes a group of swans on a river. See, *The Reader's Companion*, Chapter 24 - Lord Willoughby's.

The Queen's comment that Oxford is a fool with loose change when it comes to "novelties and predictions of the future" is a paraphrase of what the Earl of Arundel said about Oxford and a book of prophecies in 1581: "… as indeed it was not rare to pick his purse with pretence of novelties and future accidents ..." Nelson, p. 219. Oxford's servant of twenty years, Henry Lok, wrote to Burghley on November 6, 1590 seeking a position of service. Oxford had apparently severed relationships with Lok. In his letter, Lok attempted to a distance himself from "the number of the overmany [sic] greedy horse leeches which had sucked too ravenously on his sweet liberality."[126]

Chapter 44
A Poem for Lady Elspeth

All's Well That Ends Well is an apology for Oxford's treatment of his first wife. See *Hidden Allusions*, p. 110, *et seq.* There is no record of its publication or performance before it appeared in the First Folio in 1623, so it is difficult to determine when it was written. Most scholars consider it an early play. Some (Ogburn, p. 79) think it is a reworked version of *The historie of the Rape of the Second Helene*, performed at Richmond on January 6, 1579. The Applause First Folio notes, on p. 1011, footnote to p. 230, that 'though the opening stage direction refers to her as Helena, most of the F1 textual references call her 'Hellen.' It is unclear whether the stage directions were added by 18th century commentators and the correct name is Hellen. The Globe First Folio has her as 'Helena' with no comment on the name.

The parallels between Oxford and the play are significant. Bertram is a count whose father has died, forcing Bertram to become a ward of the king. The king forces him to marry a woman he grew up with who is far beneath his station. By using the same trick that may have convinced Oxford that he was the father of his first child, Helena tricks Bertram into consummating their marriage by taking the place of another woman Bertram had schemed to bed. This allows for a happy ending.

---

126 "[H]is sweet liberality[?]" Has any biographer quoted Lok, who certainly knew Oxford? And Lok is making this comment to Burghley, who found Oxford wanting in so many areas?

The "switched-bed" trick was not original with Shakespeare. Jacob used it to get Leah into his bed in Genesis. The same trick is in *The Reeve's Tale* by Chaucer and used multiple times in the *Decameron*. Anderson, p. 145.

It is of interest that the bed-trick that appears in *All's Well* (and in *Measure for Measure*) is alleged to have been used on Oxford himself. See below. Imagine the froth that would be generated if someone discovered that Shakespeare had been the victim of a bed-trick and married a woman beneath his station!

The Shakespeare Guide to Italy has a chapter devoted to *All's Well* that tracks Bertram back to Roussillon in the Rhone River valley in central France, not in southwestern France on the Spanish border. His adventures in Florence are carefully identified by Mr. Roe and worth the reading. What is interesting is that Bertram's Roussillon in the play is where the Dowager Countess of Roussillon resided in Oxford's day—the Castle of Tournon. The Countess, a former lady-in-in-waiting to Marguerite of Navarre, was the mother of Helene de Tournon, whose tragic death may be echoed in the grave-digger scene in *Hamlet*. See *Hidden Allusions*, p. 121. Also, *Love's Labour's Lost* was obviously based on the events that took place in France in August, 1578, when Catherine de Medici and her daughter, Marguerite de Valois, met with Henry of Navarre to settle Marguerite's dowry, business that had been left unfinished when the Massacre of Paris occurred six years earlier in 1572. Oxford passed through Paris in 1575 on his way to Italy while Henry of Navarre was held prisoner in the Louvre and probably met him (although he didn't rescue him as Oxford claims to Robin in *The Death of Shakespeare*).

Oxford may never have knowingly gone to bed with his wife in the weeks or months before he left for Italy in February, 1575. He was with her in October and this may explain his acceptance of the news he received in Paris in March that Nan was pregnant. His reaction is certainly proof that he had consummated the marriage. A July 2 birth date would fit an October conception. But there is evidence that Nan was very upset about being pregnant and that she wondered how her husband "would pass on it and her." See an excellent discussion of the facts surrounding the pregnancy and the birth of her baby in *This Star of England*, p. 91, *et seq*. Some take her anxiety as concern that he would think she had cheated on him, but given the way he had treated her, it may be more likely that the young woman, pregnant for the first time, worried that he would abandon her completely when she became a mother.

Oxford was told on his return to England that Lisbeth had been born in September, which would not fit an October conception date. There is no birth certificate, of course, and Ogburn claims (p. 575, without identifying his source) that the child had been baptized on September 29, almost three months after the alleged July 2 birth date. But the Queen signed a warrant to give Anne a gold cup in July, which would confirm a July date, as does a letter written on July 3 to Burghley congratulating him on the birth of a granddaughter. Burghley's memorandum also states that Elizabeth was baptized at Theobalds. Nelson, p. 127-128.

There is no hard evidence Nan or Burghley ever claimed a bed trick to get Oxford back into his marriage. The sources of the story are two reports that are gossip, one of which was written much later, and which may be an example of 'reverse-engineering', i.e., applying the bed-trick in the plays to the author, Oxford. Ogburn has an excellent discussion on the bed-trick as it relates to Oxford that begins on p. 674. He writes that Looney found in *The Histories of Essex* by Morant and Wright, printed in 1836, a claim that "*[h]e [Oxford] forsook his lady's bed, [but] the father of Lady Anne by stratagem, contrived that her husband should unknowingly sleep with her to be another woman, and she bore a son to him in consequence of this meeting*." Clark has this at p. 119.

Ogburn reports a second source for the bed-trick involving Oxford (p. 576) which was found by Barrell in 1943. *Traditional Memoirs of the Reigns of Elizabeth and James I* (publication date not given) was written by Francis Osborne, who lived from 1593 to 1659. He was Master of Horse to Philip Herbert, the Earl of Montgomery, who married Oxford's youngest daughter, Susan. Osborne wrote about a quarrel between Montgomery and a hanger-on at Court named Ramsay in which the Earl was bested by Ramsay in some undisclosed way, leaving "*nothing to testify to his manhood but a beard and children, by the daughter of the last great Earl of Oxford, whose lady was brought to his bed under the notion of his mistress and from such a virtuous deceit she (the Countess of Montgomery) is said to proceed.*"[127]

Both anecdotes get crucial facts wrong, which erode their credibility: if the bed-trick occurred, the result was Lisbeth, Oxford's first daughter, not a son. The second anecdote sounds like it's talking about Nan being brought to Oxford's bed, but the issue would have been Lisbeth, not his third daughter, Susan (unless, Oxford was tricked a second time by Nan, the issue being Susan).

In *The Death of Shakespeare*, Oxford takes the position that Bertram takes in *All's Well*—he did not consummate his marriage to Nan before he left for Italy. In real life, Oxford may have been sleeping with Nan in the fall of 1574. Burghley records that Oxford and Nan were together at Hampton Court in late October, 1574. (See Burghley's memo listing what he thought were significant dates in *This Star of England*, p. 94.) When Oxford heard from Burghley in April of the next year that Nan was pregnant, Oxford sent back two horses, a painting of himself, and a Bible inscribed with a Latin poem that punned on his motto. All of this indicates he had at least slept with Nan at some point before he left. If he had not, he would have immediately known that Nan's child was not his, and there would have been no gifts sent back to London in celebration of the news.[128]

---

[127] "[A] virtuous deceit" captures the sin/or no sin quandary John Marston and Christopher Marlowe find themselves grappling with the question of whether sin is in the heart - Bertram thinks he's sleeping with Diana - or in the deed - Bertram is actually sleeping with his wife!

[128] However, it is very curious that Oxford wrote that he hoped he would have "a son of *his own*." This comment does not bear on Lisbeth's paternity, but does lend weight to suggestions that Oxford had gotten the Queen pregnant and she had given birth to a son.

In *The Death of Shakespeare*, matters are simpler. Oxford never sleeps with Nan and therefore the child could not be his no matter when it was born. However, if, in real life, he had been tricked into sleeping with Nan before he left, then the child born in September could be his. It is easy to believe that Burghley could have engineered this event, not wanting Oxford to go to Europe without leaving an heir behind him. It is extremely difficult to believe that Burghley or his son Thomas slept with Nan to give her a child because Oxford refused to do so, but there are references to incest in the plays (*Hamlet* and *Pericles* to name two) but this may be related to Elizabeth's translation of Marguerite of Navarre's *Miroir de l'âme pécheresse* (*Mirror of the Sinful Soul*) when Elizabeth was only eleven years old.

Parolles ('parole' is 'speech' in French; 'paroles' is 'words' or 'lyrics.') is a mouthy fool who will be eclipsed by Falstaff.

The acrostic poem Oxford dictates to Lyly appeared in *Brittons Bowre of Delights* and was obviously intended for Elizabeth Trentham. It appeared in 1591 around the time she was establishing a relationship with Oxford. The poem is unsigned but has been attributed to Oxford. There are other poems in *Brittons Bowre* that are attributed to him, some signed *Ignoto*. See, Anderson, p. 249-250; *Shakespeare Oxford Newsletter*, Fall 2006, p. 9, *et seq*., for an interesting comparison of phrases from the poem and a number of the plays.

Oxford's description of his daughter Lisbeth's eyes and protruding nether lip is based on his portraits (see two portraits of Oxford following p. 134 in Anderson) and Falstaff's description of Prince Hal (Oxford) in Act II, Scene 4, of *Henry IV – Part One*:

> *That thou art my son, I have*
> *partly thy mother's word, partly my own opinion,*
> *but chiefly a villanous trick of thine eye and a*
> *foolish-hanging of thy nether lip, that doth warrant me.*

See Oxford's reaction when he sees Lisbeth in Chapter 4.

Falstaff's plea that Oxford not pursue Elizabeth Trentham because it will end up banishing Falstaff from Oxford's life is from Falstaff's speech to Prince Hal in Act II, Scene 4 of *Henry IV, Part One*:

Prince Henry:

What manner of man, an it like your majesty?

Falstaff:

A goodly portly man, i' faith, and a corpulent; of a cheerful look, a pleasing eye and a most noble carriage; and, as I think, his age some fifty, or, by'r lady, inclining to three score; and now I remember me, his name is Falstaff: if that man should be lewdly given, he deceiveth me; for, Harry, I see virtue in his looks. If then the tree may be known by the fruit, as the fruit by the tree, then, peremptorily I speak it, there is virtue in that Falstaff: him keep with, the rest banish. And tell me now, thou naughty varlet, tell me, where hast thou been this month?

In *The Death of Shakespeare, Part Two,* Oxford will banish Falstaff at the urging of Elspeth Trentham, which, in turn, will be the cause of Falstaff's banishment in *Henry IV, Part Two.*

Oxford will put Falstaff's claims about staying a bachelor in Benedict's mouth in *Much Ado About Nothing:*

Because I will not do them the wrong to mistrust any, I will do myself the right to trust none; and the fine is, for the which I may go the finer, I will live a bachelor.

Act I, Scene 1.

Chapter 45
Miss Trentham

A number of the Queen's palaces were on the Thames, beginning with Greenwich downriver from London, Whitehall in Westminster, Hampton Court Palace, a half-dozen miles farther upriver, and Windsor Castle, fifty miles farther on. They were all used by the Queen because river transportation was easy and roads were almost non-existent.

There is the poem mentioned in *The Reader's Companion* to the previous chapter and another longer poem, *Willobie His Avisa*, that some have thought described Elizabeth Trentham. *Willobie His Avisa* was printed in 1594 and contains the first reference to 'Shake-speare' aside from the title pages of *Venus and Adonis* (1593) and *The Rape of Lucrece* (1594):

> *Yet Tarquyne pluckt his glistering grape,*
> *And Shake-speare paints poore Lucrece rape.*

Space does not permit including *Willobie* in *The Death of Shakespeare,* at least in 1594.

The information Henry Howard gives to Elspeth Trentham about Oxford at the end of this chapter are from the libels he and Charles Arundel wrote in 1580/1581 while they were under arrest because Oxford had told the Queen they were Catholic sympathizers. The transcripts of their depositions and interrogatories have been posted on the internet by Professor Nelson at:

http://socrates.berkeley.edu/~ahnelson/LIBELS/libelndx.html.

Akrigg describes Howard as, "[t]he serpentine Lord Henry Howard, who enjoyed a reputation as a smooth negotiator...." Akrigg, pp. 73-74. He referred to Anne Vavasor as "the leavings of another man" in *Leicester's Commonwealth.* E. K. Chambers, *Sir Henry Lee,* Oxford 1936, p. 36.

Chapter 46
Henry VI and a Sonnet for the Earl of Southampton

Scholars debate whether the three parts of *Henry VI* were written sequentially or whether the first part was written after parts two and three. For purposes of *The Death of Shakespeare,* the three parts are written in the order of their titles.

The author added much to Holinshed and the other historians he used as sources. A thoroughly dislikeable Joan of

Arc was one addition. The similarities between her attempts to get out of being burned to death and Jesus on the cross is an example of Oxford playing at more than one level at the same time.

Warwick:

And hark ye, sirs; because she is a maid,
Spare for no faggots, let there be enow:
Place barrels of pitch upon the fatal stake,
That so her torture may be shortened.

Joan:

Will nothing turn your unrelenting hearts?
Then, Joan, discover thine infirmity,
That warranteth by law to be thy privilege.
I am with child, ye bloody homicides:
Murder not then the fruit within my womb,
Although ye hale me to a violent death.

York:

Now heaven forfend! the holy maid with child!

Warwick:

The greatest miracle that e'er ye wrought:
Is all your strict preciseness come to this?

York:

She and the Dauphin have been juggling:
I did imagine what would be her refuge.

Warwick:

Well, go to; we'll have no bastards live;
Especially since Charles must father it.

Joan:

You are deceived; my child is none of his:
It was Alencon that enjoy'd my love.

York:

Alencon! that notorious Machiavel!
It dies, an if it had a thousand lives.

Joan:

O, give me leave, I have deluded you:
'Twas neither Charles nor yet the duke I named,
But Reignier, king of Naples, that prevail'd.

Warwick:

A married man! that's most intolerable.

York:

Why, here's a girl! I think she knows not well,
There were so many, whom she may accuse.

Warwick:

It's sign she hath been liberal and free.

York:

And yet, forsooth, she is a virgin pure.
Strumpet, thy words condemn thy brat and thee:
Use no entreaty, for it is in vain.

Joan:

Then lead me hence; with whom I leave my curse:
May never glorious sun reflex his beams
Upon the country where you make abode;
But darkness and the gloomy shade of death
Environ you, till mischief and despair
Drive you to break your necks or hang yourselves!

Exit, guarded

Henry VI – Part 1, Act V, Scene 4.

The history plays are further confused by the existence of other plays that may have been precursors or recollections of actors assembled later for publication. Like the relationship between *Famous Victories* and the *Henriad*, scholars debate how they relate to each other. A concise explanation of the relationship of *Henry VI – Part 2* and *The First Part of the Contention betwxt the two famous Houses of York and* Lancaster, *The true Tragedy of Richard Duke of* York, and *The Whole Contention between the two Famous Houses, Lancaster and* York, can be read in the forward to *Henry VI – Part 2* in the Arden Shakespeare beginning at p. 495.

Trogus Pompeius was a Roman historian who lived in the era of Emperor Caesar Augustus (63 BCE-14 CE), as did the writers Virgil, Horace and Ovid. Pompeius' work was a 44-book history of Greece from early Athens to its conquest by Rome. None of the original survives, but the work lives on in the form of Justin's *Abridgment of Trogus Pompeius*, which epitomized the 44 books.

Very little is known about Marcus Justianius Justinus, but his Latin style suggests that he lived a considerable time after the Augustan age. His abridgment is first mentioned in the early 400s, so he is thought to have lived in the third or fourth century CE. Oxford was clearly familiar with Justin's *Abridgement* in Latin or the translation by Arthur Golding, which was dedicated to Oxford. (Golding's translation came out in 1564 – Oxford was fourteen at the time.) As Charles Wisner Barrell pointed out in 1940, there are at least ten citations in Shakespeare's plays derived from Justin. Shakespeare uses Pompeius' reference to Tomyris as Queen of the Scythians, whereas all Greek historians referred to Tomyris as Queen of the Massagetae:

> *The plot is laid; if all things fall out right,*
> *I shall be as famous by this exploit*
> *As Scythian Tomyris by Cyrus' death.*

Henry VI-Part 1 (2.3.3).

The Folger has a 474-page quarto in its collection bound in brown leather by Francesco Guiccardini entitled *La Historia d'Italia.* The copy in the Folger was published in 1565 with the Oxford emblem—the boar's head—on its front and rear covers.

In *Henry VI, Part One*, Talbot is invited to the castle of a French countess who intends to trap him. When she sees him, she is surprised to see he is small and un-heroic looking. She tells him he is in her power because she has kept a picture in her gallery, making him 'thrall' to her. Talbot laughs. (His army is waiting outside and eventually comes in to make him the captor and not the captive.) He tells the lady "my substance is not here, for what you see is but the smallest part and least proportion of humanity." The countess is puzzled: "He will be here, and yet he is not here." Act II, Scene 3. Oxford was obviously ruminating in *Henry VI* on how a person of otherwise small stature can have such a disproportionate effect on those around him. Alexander the Great was such a man; it seems Talbot was also. Oxford, a man of no great height or girth, may have been advertising himself in this scene.

Chapter 47
Cecil House

The two lines Oxford begins to recite—*From fairest creatures*—are from Sonnet 1. Southampton recites two lines from Sonnet 3 and four lines from Sonnet 19. The first seventeen sonnets were written to encourage someone to marry and have children. Southampton is believed to be the object of these sonnets. Since Sonnet 2 begins *When forty winters have besieged your brow*, Oxfordians believe this supports their claim that the Earl of Oxford was the author of the sonnets since he was forty years old in 1590, the period when most scholars believe the early sonnets were written. Shakespeare was twenty-six at the time. This was also the period when Lord Burghley was trying to marry Oxford's daughter, Elizabeth, to the Earl of Southampton. Traditional scholars are not reluctant to believe the sonnets were addressed to Southampton but rarely, if ever, discuss how Shakespeare, an unknown provincial without formal education, could have written such pointed suggestions to the Earl of Southampton, one of the most senior lords in England. Oxford, as the true poet and father of the intended bride, would have had no such limitation. C.S. Lewis recognized that these sonnets were written by a father: "What man in the whole world, except a father or a potential father-in-law, cares whether any other man gets married?" p. 503-504. *English Literature in the 16th Century – Excluding Drama.*

Southampton refused Lord Burghley's order to marry Lisbeth, Oxford's oldest daughter, and reportedly paid a £5,000 fine for not obeying his guardian. Nelson, p. 323, quoting the Jesuit Henry Garner writing in 1594: "*...the young Earl of Southampton refusing the Lady Vere payeth £5,000 of present money.*" Southampton later married Elizabeth Vernon. His reasons for rejecting Elizabeth Vere are unknown. However, it is very likely that his refusal was based on his unwillingness to become, like Oxford, Burghley's son-in-law. Roger Stritmatter, in *A Law Case in Verse: Venus and Adonis and the Authorship Question*, Univ. of Tennessee Law Review, Vol. 72:307, at 328, quoted another author wondering whether Southampton and Lisbeth "thought of each other as brother and sister," having both been raised in Cecil House, and were reluctant to marry because they regarded the marriage as incestuous.

Chapter 48
The War of the Roses

Scholars have gone from denying that Shackspear wrote the first part of *Henry VI* to believing that he wrote it with the collaboration of others. Their reluctance to attribute the entire play to Shackspear may be based on the "eyeballs as bullets" scene involving Sir Thomas Lucy, who may have been the ancestor of the Sir Thomas Lucy Shakespeare fans want to believe ran Will Shakespeare out of Stratford. *The Oxford Companion to Shakespeare*, at p. 200, discusses *Henry VI, Part I* and surmises it was the play referenced in Henslowe's records as having made quite a bit of money in March, 1592.

Henry VI, Part I was not printed until it appeared in the First Folio in 1623. Many scholars believe that Part II and Part III were rewrites (or cribbed from) *The First Part of the Contention of the Two Famous Houses of York and Lancaster* and *Richard Duke of York* respectively. Furthermore, some scholars argue that Part I was written last. The former was published in 1594 and the latter was published in 1595. Various other authors have been cited as true or partial authors (Greene, Nashe) and that Shakespeare dressed up the versions found in the 1623 First Folio.

Rumors say Shakespeare played the ghost of Hamlet and, from an obscure reference, may have played the old man in *All's Well That Ends Well*, but no there is no claim that he played Sir Thomas Lucy in *Henry VI.*

Chapter 49
John Marston and the Nature of Sin

Scholars and critics have not liked *All's Well That Ends Well.* The author had obviously read *The Ninth Tale* from the third day of Boccaccio's *Decameron* which *All's Well* follows closely. However, the story tracks Oxford's life as well.

Harold Bloom called some of the couplets among "Shakespeare's most rancid." P. 356.[129] Bertram is a most unlikable character and Helena is another strong woman working her way toward what she wants. When Oxford's life is laid alongside the events of this play, the coincidences are startling. Future scholars will go beyond identifying LaFew as Burghley (the king comments that LaFew *special nothing ever prologue*) and wonder where Parolles, the forerunner of Falstaff, came from.

The historie of the Rape of the second Helene was presented at court in January 1579. Some scholars believe that this was an earlier version of *All's Well.*

---

[129] Bloom notes on the same page that "the insufferable Bertram … goes out on the right note of ludicrous insincerity: 'I'll love her dearly, ever, ever dearly,' which is at least one 'ever' too many." The Professor did not go on to say that if the author was Edward de Vere and unable to stop himself from punning on his last name, the 'evers' might have been just right. Listen to Prince Hall in *Henry IV, Part I*, Act II, Scene 2: "*Now could thou / and I rob the thieves and go merrily to London, / it would be argument for a week, laughter for a month / and a good jest for ever.*" For whom? For 'E. Vere.' Bloom comes so close, but there's always that William Shakespeare blocking his view.

1591

Chapters 50-65

Chapter 50
Aemilia Bassano (Again)

Alas! 'tis true, I have gone here and there,
And made myself a motley to the view,
Gored mine own thoughts, sold cheap what is most dear,
Made old offences of affections new;
Most true it is, that I have looked on truth
Askance and strangely; but, by all above,
These blenches gave my heart another youth.

Sonnet 110

Most commentators think that this is Shakespeare expressing his regret that he acted the fool on the stage. However, if the plays are based on Oxford's life, Sonnet 110 may be speaking to something much larger than appearing on stage as an actor. Thus, the Queen's comment that Oxford made himself a motley to the public by dramatizing scenes from his life.

What joy is joy, if Silvia be not by? is from *Two Gentlemen of Verona*, Act III, Scene 1.

Sonnets 135 and 136 are called the 'Will' sonnets. (The words Oxford recites to Aemilia Bassano in *The Death of Shakespeare* are derived from Sonnet 135.) Some scholars thought they were Will Shakespeare's signature until research revealed that 'will' was a smutty reference to body parts and things sexual.

Whoever hath her wish, thou hast thy 'Will,'
And 'Will' to boot, and 'Will' in overplus;
More than enough am I that vex thee still,
To thy sweet will making addition thus.
Wilt thou, whose will is large and spacious,
Not once vouchsafe to hide my will in thine?
Shall will in others seem right gracious,
And in my will no fair acceptance shine?

The sea all water, yet receives rain still
And in abundance addeth to his store;
So thou, being rich in 'Will,' add to thy 'Will'
One will of mine, to make thy large 'Will' more.
Let no unkind, no fair beseechers kill;
Think all but one, and me in that one 'Will.'

Sonnet 135

If thy soul cheque thee that I come so near,
Swear to thy blind soul that I was thy 'Will,'
And will, thy soul knows, is admitted there;
Thus far for love my love-suit, sweet, fulfil.
'Will' will fulfil the treasure of thy love,
Ay, fill it full with wills, and my will one.
In things of great receipt with ease we prove
Among a number one is reckon'd none:
Then in the number let me pass untold,
Though in thy stores' account I one must be;
For nothing hold me, so it please thee hold
That nothing me, a something sweet to thee:
Make but my name thy love, and love that still,
And then thou lovest me, for my name is 'Will.'

Sonnet 136

Like William in *As You Like It,* these sonnets are not kind notes to a man named 'Will.' Oxford riffing on William's name as he recovers Aemilia Bassano from his hated front man is as good a place as any to use them.

And, when thou art away is adapted from Sonnet 97.

If once your lips should lock with mine are lines Oxford quoted to Aemilia Bassano in Chapter 24.

I Modi, (the Ways, or The Sixteen Pleasures) was published in 1524 by Marcantonio Raimondi. They were drawings showing men and women having sex in various positions. They were by the painter and sculptor, Giulio Romano. The Pope imprisoned Raimondi and had all copies destroyed. Romano was not prosecuted because Romano had intended them only for private viewing and had been unaware that Raimondi published them.

Romano was working at the time on a commission for Frederico II's Palazzo dl Te in Mantua. Pietro Aretino saw one of the copies and came to Romano to see the originals. Aretino, one of Renaissance Italy's reigning poets, then composed sonnets to accompany the drawings. He also secured Raimondi's release from prison. A second printing, this time with Aretino's sonnets, was published in 1527 and again suppressed. No copies of either edition survive. A third edition was published in Venice in 1550. It was this copy that Oxford may have seen when he was in Venice in 1575. See ,*The Reader's Companion*, Chapter 90 - A Conference with Venus.

See *https://en.wikipedia.org/wiki/I_Modi* for a discussion of the work and copies of the drawings. Also, an article by John Hamill in Vol 39, No. 3, Summer 2003, of *The Shakespeare Oxford Newsletter* contains a great deal about Romano, Aretino, and the City of Mantua.

Giulio Romano is the only sculptor referred to in the plays attributed to Shakespeare. He is mentioned in *The Winter's Tale* as the sculptor who has crafted a statue of Hermione, the woman wronged by the king in that play:

> *No: the princess hearing of her mother's statue,*
> *which is in the keeping of Paulina,--a piece many*
> *years in doing and now newly performed <u>by that rare</u>*
> *<u>Italian master, Julio Romano</u>, who, had he himself*
> *eternity and could put breath into his work, would*
> *beguile Nature of her custom, so perfectly he is her*
> *ape: he so near to Hermione hath done Hermione that*
> *they say one would speak to her and stand in hope of*
> *answer: thither with all greediness of affection*
> *are they gone, and there they intend to sup.*

Act V, Scene 2.

Scholars initially laughed at Shakespeare because they thought Romano was only a painter, but research has shown that the critics were wrong: Romano was both a painter *and* a sculptor. Ogburn has a whole section on 'Shakespeare's Blunders' beginning at p. 306. For example, Act IV, Scene 3 of *The Winter's Tale* speaks of Autolycus' ship landing on the seacoast of Bohemia. Everyone (Ben Jonson included) thought Bohemia never had a seacoast. It did, beginning in 1526 and up through the time Oxford was in Italy. The critics shook their heads over the characters in *Two Gentlemen* sailing between inland Italian cities, but that's what they did—on canal boats.

There is no evidence that Oxford possessed a copy of *I Modi*,[130] but there is an indirect connection with Romano. Romano sculpted the tomb in Mantua, Italy, for Baldassare Castiglione and his beloved wife, Ippolita. Castiglione wrote *The Courtier*. Oxford wrote an excellent introduction to the Latin translation which the Queen reads to him in Chapter 2. See *The Reader's Companion* to Chapter 2 as to Castiglione.

Chapter 51
Senior Baldini's Love Philtre

Senior Baldini's purple vial of ground penises taken from giant blue spiders found only in the Persian Gulf is fiction.

Chapter 52
The Boar's Head and Christopher Marlowe

The lines about lying to and with each other are from Sonnet 138:

> *When my love swears that she is made of truth,*
> *I do believe her though I know she lies,*
> *That she might think me some untutored youth,*
> *Unlearned in the world's false subtleties.*

---

130 Romano drew the figures in *I Modi* ('The Positions') that graphically show different ways people can have sex. Pietro Aretino, the famous 16th century Italian poet and writer, wrote sonnets to accompany them. They were the most scandalous publications of the Italian Renaissance.

Thus vainly thinking that she thinks me young,
Although she knows my days are past the best,
Simply I credit her false-speaking tongue:
On both sides thus is simple truth suppressed:
But wherefore says she not she is unjust?
And wherefore say not I that I am old?
O! love's best habit is in seeming trust,
And age in love, loves not to have years told:
Therefore I lie with her, and she with me,
And in our faults by lies we flattered be.

Oxford was obviously having a good time with a young woman when he wrote this sonnet. It is a good example of how much he loved to pun. The Ogburns think this was written for Elizabeth Trentham. At p. 906. It might have been.

Sir Thomas Smith was one Oxford's tutors, possibly while Oxford's father was still alive. In 1576, Sir Thomas wished Oxford well in a letter to Burghley "for the love I beare hum, bicause he was brought up in my howse." Nelson, p. 25. See Chapter 63 in which Oxford meets Sir Thomas in Ankerwycke where Oxford was his student. Laurence Nowell was another tutor while Oxford was at Burghley House. He was the first to be recorded as owning the only copy of *Beowulf.* See, *The Reader's Companion*, Chapter 26.

Professor Nelson admits that Oxford, "unlike some of his contemporaries, including Queen Elizabeth herself ... never to the end of his life stinted his penmanship: letters and memoranda in Oxford's hand are among the most accessible of the Elizabethan age." P. 41. A letter discovered in 2000 written by Oxford in his own handwriting. It had been written to King James in 1604 five months before Oxford died. The letter "could be read as effortlessly as a letter from a friend." *The Shackspear Oxford Newsletter*, Spring 2000, Vol. 36; 1, at page 4. The letter itself can be read on page 5.

As to blotting out a word: "*I remember, the players have often mentioned it, as an honour to Shackspear, that in his writing (whatsoever he penned) he never blotted out a line.*" Ben Jonson, *Discoveries*, —

Johnson's Works, xi, 175, Gifford's edition, quoted in the Globe *First Folio*, p. 2355.

The three parts of *Henry VI* have caused many scholarly contortions. Many scholars think Part 1 came after Parts 2 and 3. Hard evidence as to dating is scant, although Robert Greene's comment in *A Groatsworth of Wit* published in September, 1592 shows that Part 3 had already been performed by then because Greene quotes the famous 'tiger's heart wrapped in a woman's hyde' line.

In this chapter, Shackspear complains about the cost of putting on the opening to Part 1. Marchette Chute, in *Shackspear of London,* describes the costs of staging *Henry VI* at pages 96-97. See, also, the costs of the Office of the Revels in *Notes on the History of the Revels Office Under the Tudors,* E.K. Chambers, London (1906), reprinted by Cornell University Library, Digital Collections.

Marlowe's 'twisting' of Herbert Spenser's description of Arthur's Crest in *Fairie Queen* predated the publication of Spenser's poem, so Marlowe must've seen a manuscript of it. These lines were some of the most quoted from Spenser's long poem. Spenser, like Jonson, could not help larding his poetry with Biblical and classical references. Each reference in Spenser can be linked to a well-known line in the Bible or Latin source, which makes Marlowe's recasting of Spenser so interesting. Marlowe not only preempted the *Fairie Queen* but twisted Spenser's description of Arthur's glorious helm into a parody. Spenser's reaction is unrecorded.

As to the "bunch of hairs" evoking a quill pen, see Riggs at page 215.

Marlowe's comment about Oxford's sly allusion in *All's Well* to Helen of Troy is Oxford's 'twist' on Marlowe's famous lines in *Faust.* The commentators in the Globe First Folio comment that this was "perhaps, a snatch of some antique ballad, which the fool craftily corrupts, to imitate, and the enigmatical manner of his calling, that he was not altogether ignorant of the subject which is mistress and her steward had met to speak about." P.

762, comment e. They completely miss that the lines are based on Marlowe's *Faust.*

Marlowe's comment that, "[I]f a man's verses cannot be recast so that they are recognized by a second reader, the first poet is more dead than if he had died alone in a little room" will reappear in *As You Like It*, Act III, Scene 3:

> *When a man's verses cannot be understood, nor a*
> *man's good wit seconded with the forward child*
> *Understanding, it strikes a man more dead than a*
> *great reckoning in a little room. Truly, I would*
> *the gods had made thee poetical.*

Many scholars think this is a reference to Marlowe's murder since the dispute that resulted in his death was supposedly over the 'bill', or 'reckoning' for the food and drink consumed the afternoon of his death. It certainly seems that Marlowe was murdered, possibly for his sacrilegious statements, but more likely for his work as a spy for Burghley and Walsingham. See Nicholl and Riggs. Most scholars agree that *As You Like It* is a strange play for many reasons, not the least of which is Touchstone's words to Audrey quoted above. The author seems to be referring to Marlowe's murder. But is the playwright actually bemoaning that he will be unknown? Is Audrey a personification of the plays?

Marlowe's description of his room at Cambridge is the seed from which Oxford will write Richard II's examination of his prison cell in *Richard II*:

> *I have been studying how I may compare*
> *This prison where I live unto the world:*
> *And for because the world is populous*
> *And here is not a creature but myself,*
> *I cannot do it; yet I'll hammer it out.*
> *My brain I'll prove the female to my soul,*
> *My soul the father; and these two beget*
> *A generation of still-breeding thoughts,*
> *And these same thoughts people this little world.*

Richard II, Act V, Scene 5.

Walt Whitman had doubts that Shackspear wrote the plays. "[O]nly one of the '*wolfish earls*' so plenteous in the plays themselves, or some born descendent and knower, might seem to be the true author of those amazing works." *November Boughs*, quoted in Ogburn, p. 260.

Marlowe's description of women being centaurs from the waist down will appear in *Lear*, Act IV, Scene 6.

Arden of Faversham recounts the true story of the murder of a man named Arden who lived in Faversham, a small town between Gravesend and Canterbury. Arden was murdered by his wife Alice. Michael, her servant, helped her. Some scholars have thought that the play was originally known as *The history of murderous mychaell*, a lost play that was shown before the Queen on March 3 1579. Eva Turner Clark has an entire chapter on *Arden of Faversham* in her book *Hidden Allusions in Shackspear's Plays*. Some scholars have connected the play with Shackspear. Ms. Clark believes that Oxford had a hand in the play. Two of the bungling assistants were named Shakebag and Black Will. Anyone who would rush to the conclusion that the author (Oxford? Marlowe?) added these names to the play to parody Will Shackspear will be disappointed to learn that they were the actual names of two of Michael's accomplices. Was Robert Greene making a reference to 'Shakebag' when he talked of 'Shakescene' in his farewell work written in 1593? Doubtful, since his remark is tied to a line that is taken directly from *Henry VI*.

In 1588, Robert Greene complained in *Perimedes the Blacksmith* that he had been taken advantage of in a play where two 'mad Romans' went at each other with swords. His motto was on their shields and they beat their shields unmercifully. *The Cambridge Companion to Christopher Marlowe,* Patrick Cheney, ed., Cambridge Univ. Press, 2004, p. 95. Cervantes refers to *Perimedes* in *Don Quixote*. See, *The Reader's Companion*, the Prologue. Anthony Munday translated *Perimedes of England* in 1588, but Greene's anger refers to a play, not a prose work.

The Globe First Folio refers to "Come live with me and be my love" as Kit Marlowe's "smooth song." P. 687. The commentator states that, "[t]hough repeatedly quoted, and familiar to every one acquainted with our early poesy, we should be held inexcusable for omitting [to mention that this line was written by Marlowe]." An "imperfect version" of "[t]his beautiful song" appeared in *The Passionate Pilgrim*, reprinted by the Globe at p. 230. A more "perfect" version is printed in the Globe at p.687.

My flocks feed not is poem XVI in *Sonnets to Sundry Notes of Music* printed at p. 2319 of the Globe First Folio as part of *The Passionate Pilgrim. Crabbed age and youth* is poem X printed at p. 2317 of the Globe First Folio as part of *The Passionate Pilgrim.*

"Renying" is not in Shackspear unless poem XVI in *The Passionate Pilgrim* is accepted as Shackspear's. The Globe First Folio does not think so: "That Shackspear had any hand in [this poem] is inconceivable." Footnote c, p. 2319. The Globe comments that poem XVI also appears in *The Unknown Sheepheard's Complaint* and is subscribed *Ignoto*, which some Oxfordians believe is another Oxford *nom de plume*. The Globe thinks the name is one used by Sir Walter Raleigh. P. 2320, footnote e. The Globe thinks 'renying' means 'to forswear.' The *Shackspear Lexicon* supplies the definitions given by Marlowe in this chapter, although their only apparent basis is *The Passionate Pilgrim.*

There a rules when engaging a rhyming exchange. One is that you cannot add just any word to the end of a line to make it rhyme. In *Love's Labour's Lost,* Act I, Biron is resisting the King's idea that he and his courtiers should renounce all pleasures for three years and the following exchange takes place:

King: *How well he's read, to reason against reading!*

Dumain: *Proceeded well, to stop all good proceeding!*

Longaville: *He weeds the corn and still lets grow the weeding.*

Biron: *The spring is near when green geese are a-breeding.*

Dumain:	*How follows that?*
Biron:	*Fit in his place and time.*
Dumain:	*In reason nothing.*
Biron:	*Something then in rhyme.*

Dumain objects to Biron's suggestion—*spring is near when green geese are a-breeding*—because he finds it nonsensical. Biron shrugs and says, well, at least it's *something then in rhyme.*

Chapter 53
A Sonnet for Aemilia Bassano

Chapter 54
The Geneva Bible

Reams of commentary have been written about Falstaff, but much less about the Falstoffe in *Henry VI, Part I.* Was Falstoffe the model for Sir John Falstaff in *Henry IV, Part 1*? Falstoffe was anything but a coward, and so the pundits wonder why Shakespeare made him so. He was a national hero who became famous to a later generation when he was included in Foxe's *Book of Martyrs.*

There is a similar question about the relationship is between 'Sir John Oldcastle' in *The Famous Victories of Henry V* and the character we know as Falstaff. Most scholars agree that the need to change the name from Oldcastle to Falstaff was probably caused by the objection of William Brooke, Lord Cobham, a descendant of Oldcastle. The fact that Robert Cecil married Lord Cobham's daughter may also have had something to do with the name change. Cobham became Lord Chamberlain in 1597 when *Henry IV* was probably being written and staged.

"Ye cannot capture the spirit" is a rewrite of "*Give me the spirit, Master Shallow,*" spoken by Falstaff in *Henry IV, Part 2*, Act III, Scene 2, which may be a reworking of *II Corinthians, 4:18*: *[F]or the things which are seen are temporal, but the things which are not seen are eternal.*" See Anderson's discussion of Oxford's use of *The Geneva Bible* in Appendix A at p. 385.

Sonnet 86 is one of the 'rival poets' sonnets:

Was it the proud full sail of his great verse,
Bound for the prize of all too precious you,
That did my ripe thoughts in my brain inhearse,
Making their tomb the womb wherein they grew?
Was it his spirit, by spirits taught to write
Above a mortal pitch, that struck me dead?
No, neither he, nor his compeers by night
Giving him aid, my verse astonished.
He, nor that affable familiar ghost
Which nightly gulls him with intelligence
As victors of my silence cannot boast;
I was not sick of any fear from thence:
But when your countenance fill'd up his line,
Then lack'd I matter; that enfeebled mine.

Oxford's *Geneva Bible* is in the Folger's collection, having been acquired by its founder in 1925. The receipt for its purchase in 1570 still exists. See, *This Star of England*, p.17, and discussion in Anderson in Appendix A, beginning at p. 381. Roger Stritmatter wrote his Ph.D. dissertation on the connection between the *Geneva Bible* and the plays. Oxford also had a Bible in Italian and he purchased a Greek Bible before he left Venice and returned to England. Anderson, p. 382. See, *The Reader's Companion*, Chapter 3. The *King James Bible* was not completed until 1611, after Oxford was dead, and, therefore, was not available to Oxford when he wrote the plays.

The verse Oxford quotes from *I Samuel* is underlined in the Geneva Bible in the Folger. Anderson, p. 384.

Chapter 55
Robin Returns

The references to Tournon presage the writing of *Love's Labour's Lost*, which most scholars believe is based on events that took place in the court of Henry of Navarre. But Henry's court was located at the base of the Pyrenees in southwestern France. Instead, the events in *Love's Labour's Lost* seem to have been taken from events near Roussillon in the Rhone River valley. See, *The Reader's Companion*, Chapter 22.

Robin's comment that he didn't know what love is will be transformed by Mozart into a lovely aria sung by Cherubino to the Countess in Act II of *Le Nozze di Figaro*: 'Voi che sapete che cosa è amor' ('You who know what love is').

Chapter 56
Ankerwycke

The speech about Cleopatra's 'burnished throne' will appear in *Antony and Cleopatra,* Act II, Scene 2. It is based on the description of Cleopatra's meeting with Mark Antony in Plutarch's "Life of Marcus Antonius," Vol. 9, from *Plutarch's Lives, Englished by Sir Thomas North,* 1579. North's translation can be read online at

> *http://oll.libertyfund.org/index.php?option=com_staticxt&staticfile=show.php%3Ftitle=1811&Itemid=27.*

Oxford will take Falstaff's swim across the Thames and have Mistress Ford refer to him as a whale with so many tuns of oil in his belly:

> *What tempest, I trow,*
> *threw this whale, with so many tuns of oil in his*
> *belly, ashore at Windsor? How shall I be revenged*
> *on him? I think the best way were to entertain him*
> *with hope, till the wicked fire of lust have melted*
> *him in his own grease.*

The Merry Wives of Windsor, Act II, Scene 1. Falstaff's comments that he's as subject to heat as butter will reappear in the same play, Act III, Scene 5.

Sir Thomas Smith was one of many scholars who tutored Oxford when Oxford was a young boy. Professor Nelson thinks that Smith would have tutored Oxford at Hill Hall in Essex but Anderson points out that Hill Hall was under construction during much of the 1550s and it is more likely that Smith tutored Oxford at Ankerwyke.[131] There is an interesting article by Stephanie Hopkins Hughes in the Shakespeare Oxford Newsletter, Vol. 42, No. 3, Fall 2006, p. 1, about Oxford's years with Smith. Ms. Hughes has collected a number of interesting drawings and maps about Ankerwyke.

Smith was no Stratford headmaster. He had been secretary of state to King Edward VI, provost of Eton College, and was described by another student as "the flower of the University of Cambridge." A contemporary referred to Sir Thomas as Plato. A biographer stated that Sir Thomas was "reckoned the best scholar [at Cambridge] University, not only for rhetoric and the learned languages, but for mathematics, arithmetic, law, natural and moral philosophy."[132] Sir Thomas' attitude toward plays is not known.

When Oxford meets Sir Thomas at Ankerwyke, Sir Thomas quotes the first line of the following poem to Oxford:

If care or skill could conquer vain desire,
Or Reason's reins my strong affection stay:
There should my sighs to quiet breast retire,
And shun such signs as secret thoughts betray;
Uncomely Love which now lurks in my breast
Should cease, my grief through Wisdom's power oppress'd.

But who can leave to look on Venus' face,
Or yieldeth not to Juno's high estate?
What wit so wise as gives not Pallas place?
These virtues rare each Gods did yield a mate;
Save her alone, who yet on earth doth reign,
Whose beauty's string no God can well destrain.

What worldly wight can hope for heavenly hire,
When only sighs must make his secret moan ?

131 Nelson, p. 25; Anderson, pp. 5-7. Curiously, neither of the Ogburns mention Sir Thomas.

132 Anderson, p. 7.

A silent suit doth seld to grace aspire,
My hapless hap doth roll the restless stone.
Yet Phoebe fair disdained the heavens above,
To joy on earth her poor Endymion's love.

Rare is reward where none can justly crave,
For chance is choice where Reason makes no claim;
Yet luck sometimes despairing souls doth save,
A happy star made Giges joy attain.
A slavish smith, of rude and rascal race,
Found means in time to gain a Godess' grace.

Then lofty Love thy sacred sails advance,
My sighing seas shall flow with streams of tears;
Amidst disdains drive forth thy doleful chance,
A valiant mind no deadly danger fears;
Who loves aloft and sets his heart on high
Deserves no pain, though he do pine and die.

Finis. E.O.

Sources: *Fuller's* #4 [Coelum non Solum]*; JTL* #17. First printed in *Paradyse of Dainty Devices*, 1576 & updated in 1596 edition. Also called "*Being in Love he complaineth.*"

Sir Thomas' reference to the marginal comments in Thomas Watson's *The Hekatompathia* is based on Mark Anderson's surmise that Oxford wrote them. P. 182-183. If so, they would be "Shake-speare's only known work of literary criticism." P. 182. C.S. Lewis thought the comments more interesting than Watson's sonnets.

The person who wrote the plays attributed to William Shakespeare had an immense vocabulary.[133] He was also

---

[133] The recent effort to bring Shakespeare down to a size that might fit his Stratford upbringing has occasioned efforts to characterize his vocabulary as "average." "The evidence of vocabulary size and word-use frequency places Shakespeare with his contemporaries, rather than apart from them." Hugh Craig. "Shakespeare's Vocabulary: Myth and Reality." Shakespeare Quarterly 62.1 (2011): 53-74. *Project MUSE*. Web. 15 Sep. 2015. *https://muse.jhu.edu/*. Shakespeare was apparently in the middle of the pack,

comfortable in many languages. Edward de Vere had the training, aptitude, and experience to be the person Sir Thomas Smith describes in this chapter. The following from *The Private Character of Queen Elizabeth*, by Frederick Carleton Chamberlin, Dodd Mead & Co., New York, 1922, at p.17, shows how precocious other famous men were at an early age:

There can be no more doubt that Elizabeth was a youthful prodigy than of the truth of such a description of William Wooton, Newton's friend and Swift's doughty antagonist, who was reading Greek and Latin at five, Hebrew at six, and had by then mastered Homer, Virgil, Pythagoras, Terence, and Corderius—who had his B.A. from Cambridge at twelve, was a Fellow of St. John's, Cambridge at fifteen, and a F.R.S. before he was twenty-one; of John Stuart Mill who had mastered the chief Greek authors by eight, the Latin ones by twelve, had written, at that age, a history of the government of Rome, and other histories before he was seven, not to mention a knowledge of higher mathematics, logic, classical literature, and political economy by thirteen.

Chamberlin was defending Elizabeth's prodigious skills, which he described, in part, as follows (at p. 22):

Correspondence between Elizabeth and Edward [her brother] was conducted in Latin, French, and Italian, and they habitually spoke these tongues. The Queen, indeed, when an old woman, confided to one of the French Ambassadors that when she came to the throne she knew six foreign languages better than she did her own.

Chapter 57
Windsor

Oxford spent time convalescing in Windsor, which was obviously the basis for his knowledge of the town and castle which appears in *The Merry Wives of Windsor.* Whether he crossed paths with his former tutor, Sir Thomas Smith, is unknown.

---

which was headed up by John Webster. The Bard was also average in coining new words.

The story about the man who promised not to eat beef without mustard if God saved him from drowning comes from Thomas Nashe's *Pierce Penniless*, published in 1591, in which he writes:

> And when he [goes to sea], poor soul, he lies in brine in ballast, and is lamentable sick of the scurvies; his dainty fare is turned to a hungry feast of dogs & cats, or haberdine and poor-john at the most, and, which is lamentablest of all, that without mustard.
>
> As a mad ruffian on a time being in danger of shipwreck by a tempest, and seeing all other at their vows and prayers, that, if it would please God of his infinite goodness to deliver them out of that imminent danger, one would abjure this sin whereunto he was addicted, another make satisfaction for that violence he had committed, he, in a desperate jest, began thus to reconcile his soul to heaven.
>
> *O Lord, if it may seem good to thee to deliver me from this fear of untimely death, I vow, before thy throne and all thy starry host, never to eat haberdine more wilst I live.*[134]
>
> Well, so it fell out that the sky cleared and the tempest ceased, and this careless wretch, that made such a mockery of prayer, ready to set foot a-land, cried out, *Not without mustard, good Lord, not without mustard*, as though it had been the greatest torment in the world to have eaten haberdine without mustard.

In *Everyman Out Of His Humour*, Ben Jonson has a character (Sogliardo) who has acquired arms. They are described as "a boar without a head, rampant [a descriptive term in the coat of arms field meaning an animal on its hind legs]." Sogliardo's motto in the play is "Not Without Mustard." Records show that Shakespeare's father was awarded a coat of arms consisting of a spear on a shield. The words "Non Sans Droit" were written

---

134 "Haberdine" is salt cod.

above it. It is unclear whether the words meant Shakespeare had no right to the arms (his application was initially rejected) or meant he was entitled to arms, or the words were his motto.

There is no evidence Shakespeare ever used the phrase. Most scholars agree that Jonson was sending up Shakespeare when he created Sogliardo and his motto. However, no one seems to have noticed that Sogliardo/Shakespeare's coat of arms—a boar without a head, rampant—may have been referencing Oxford, whose emblem was the boar.

Furthermore, the drawing of the coat of arms has the following written on it: "Shakespear the Player." (Emphasis added.) Notice it is not "Shakespear the Playwright." Did the Herald Clerks make a mistake, like the clerks who wrote down who Shakespeare was going to marry? How could Shakespeare be described as a player when he was a well-known playwright, if not *the* playwright in London at the time the application was processed?

Chapter 58
Henry VI – Part 2

A number of scholars comment on the expansive staging of the early plays. Marchette Chute has an interesting section in her book, *Shakespeare of London*, beginning at page 96, in which she discusses how Shakespeare used all the resources of the stage, including the balcony as well as special effects such as thunder, a spirit rising up through the trap door on the stage, and four separate heads and a trunkless body in *Henry VI – Part Two*. She imagines that a dummy head was carved with the living actor as the model and then realistically colored. "A head of this kind could even be made to bleed if a little dough kneaded with bullock's blood was pressed against the head and made to look like part of the dead flesh." P.97.

Jack Cade is a character worthy of more thought than he gets. There are moments when Oxford is obviously flashing some thoughts that should've been disturbing to the aristocracy. Why he would do so is impossible to determine, but this is the man who would write a poem in which concern for the servant "who gets the chaff" is clearly evident. Tanner, in his *Prefaces to Shakespeare*, thinks that Shakespeare, having just shown English law and order going to the grave with Humphrey, cannot introduce a reasonable, civilized, and literate mob-leader, as Cade was reported to be. Tanner does admit that Shakespeare "loathed mobs." If Oxford is recognized as the author of the plays, this antipathy toward mobs is not difficult to understand. The more difficult question is why Oxford would have slipped in what could be viewed as a number of socialist concepts.

It was apparently a custom to scour dining tables before significant banquets with aromatic herbs, a business that someone in this modern age, with all our scented candles and background elevator music, will undoubtedly re-create. *Globe,* p. 683. Oxford recounts part of Sonnet 40 in his attempt to bed Elspeth Trentham.

Chapter 59
The Dinner in the Grotto

Oxford's bit of poetry here is stolen, with some modifications, from *Romeo and Juliet*, Act I, Scene 5. The actual words are:

> *If I profane with my unworthiest hand*
> *This holy shrine, the gentle fine is this:*
> *My lips, two blushing pilgrims, ready stand*
> *To smooth that rough touch with a tender kiss.*

"I am weary of an unsettled life" is a quote from a letter Oxford wrote to Burghley in May, 1591. Nelson, p. 332.

Nothing is known about how Oxford and Trentham courted, if at all, although the *Trentame* poem (see Chapter 44) must have been involved.

Only one reference to *Love's Labour's Won* has been found. It appears in a list of plays attributed to Shakespeare in *Palladis Tamia* by Francis Meres published in 1598. Meres lists *Gentlemen of Verona [sic], Errors [sic], Love's Labour's Lost, Love's Labour's Won, Midsummer Night's Dream, Merchant of Venice, Richard the 2 [sic],*

Richard the 3 [sic], Henry the 4 [sic], King John, Titus Andronicus, Romeo and Juliet. Anderson, p. 306. Charlton Ogburn, at p. 614, thinks *Love's Labour's Won* was another name for *Much Ado About Nothing* but it could also have been *All's Well That Ends Well,* which ends with Helena finally snaring Bertram into marriage. (Or do they get married? John Marston thinks the question unanswered. See his objections in Chapter 49.

Chapter 60
A Marriage Contract

There is no record of Oxford receiving a gift of money from Elspeth Trentham before he married her, although there were a number of financial transactions completed before the marriage that were intended to shield Oxford from his debtors, if not provide for his daughters. See, *The Reader's Companion*, Chapter 65.

The Earl of Oxford signed his name "Edward Oxenford" or the "Earl of Oxenford," which was the old way of signing his name. As with most polysyllabic words, the tendency is to drop syllables and make words shorter, despite the efforts of the Malfises in the world.

There may be an interesting connection between "Oxenford" and the body of water that separates Europe and Asia at Istanbul. The "Bosphorus" translates as "oxen – ford", "bos" being an old word for ox, and "phorus" being a derivative of the same antecedent as the word for "ford." The Bosphorus acquired its name from the myth about Europa. Ovid wrote about Europa in Book II in the *Metamorphoses.*

In *Henry IV, Part 1*, Act II, Scene 4, Poins, watching Falstaff, says to Hal: *Is it not strange that desire should so many years outlive performance?*

"Something wicked this way comes" will appear in *Macbeth*, Act IV, Scene 1.

Chapter 61
Oxford Court – A Month Later

The poem Elspeth Trentham refers to is a poem Oxford wrote that begins "*If women could be fair and yet not fond,*" and which concludes:

Unsettled still like haggards wild they range,
These gentle birds that fly from man to man:
Who would not scorn and shake them from the fist,
And let them fly, fair fools, which way they list?[135]

Compare the following lines from *Othello*, Act III, Scene 3:

If I do prove her haggard,
Though that her jesses were my dear heartstrings,
I'd whistle her off and let her down the wind,
To pray at fortune.

Compare also the following from *The Taming of the Shrew,* Act IV, Scene 1, the wedding night of Petruchio and Kate. Petruchio is describing what havoc he is going to wreak to tame his Kate:

Thus have I politicly begun my reign,
And 'tis my hope to end successfully.
My falcon now is sharp and passing empty;
And till she stoop she must not be full-gorged,
For then she never looks upon her lure.
Another way I have to man my haggard,
To make her come and know her keeper's call,
That is, to watch her, as we watch these kites
That bate and beat and will not be obedient.
She eat no meat to-day, nor none shall eat;
Last night she slept not, nor to-night she shall not;
As with the meat, some undeserved fault
I'll find about the making of the bed;

---

135 *Fuller's* #19 [Fayre Fooles] ; *JTL* #19; From Rawlinson MS 85 Folio 16. A variation was printed as a song lyric by Byrd in 1588. This is how Elspeth knows about the poem in this chapter.

And here I'll fling the pillow, there the bolster,
This way the coverlet, another way the sheets:
Ay, and amid this hurly I intend
That all is done in reverend care of her;
And in conclusion she shall watch all night:
And if she chance to nod I'll rail and brawl
And with the clamour keep her still awake.
This is a way to kill a wife with kindness;
And thus I'll curb her mad and headstrong humour.
He that knows better how to tame a shrew,
Now let him speak: 'tis charity to show.

The exchange between Oxford and Trentham over the balcony that projects into the great hall is based on *Romeo & Juliet*, Act II, Scene 2:

Romeo:

Lady, by yonder blessed moon I swear
That tips with silver all these fruit-tree tops--

Juliet:

O, swear not by the moon, the inconstant moon,
That monthly changes in her circled orb,
Lest that thy love prove likewise variable.

Romeo:

What shall I swear by?

Juliet:

Do not swear at all;
Or, if thou wilt, swear by thy gracious self,
Which is the god of my idolatry,
And I'll believe thee.

Romeo:

If my heart's dear love--

Juliet:

Well, do not swear: although I joy in thee,
I have no joy of this contract to-night:

The disappointment on Oxford's part about the date set for his wedding is based on the following exchange between Theseus and Hippolyta in *A Midsummer Night's Dream*, Act I, Scene 1:

Theseus:

Now, fair Hippolyta, our nuptial hour
Draws on apace; four happy days bring in
Another moon: but, O, methinks, how slow
This old moon wanes! she lingers my desires,
Like to a step-dame or a dowager
Long withering out a young man revenue.

Hippolyta:

Four days will quickly steep themselves in night;
Four nights will quickly dream away the time;
And then the moon, like to a silver bow
New-bent in heaven, shall behold the night
Of our solemnities.

Chapter 62
Castle Hedingham

The editors of the Globe describe an eyas as a sparrow hawk, p. 663. Mistress Ford greets Robin, Falstaff's page in *The Merry Wives of Windsor,* Act III, scene 3, with "How now, my eyas-musket! What news with you?" Hawking was a sport of the nobility. The types of hawks, and which one was the best, was an ongoing topic of intense discussion at the time.

Edward de Vere, the Seventeenth Earl of Oxford, was born in 1550 at Castle Hedingham in Essex. The fortifications consist of a Norman moat and bailey castle with a stone keep. The castle and the surrounding Essex countryside may have been owned by a de Vere prior to the arrival of William the Conqueror in 1066. See, *The Life Story of Edward de Vere as "William Shakespeare,* by

Percy Allen. Just when the Veres came to England and which one of them was made the earl of Oxford may be somewhat murky but Hedingham Castle had been the ancestral home of the Earls of Oxford for more than 500 years before Oxford was born. The castle is now a conference center open to the public.[136]

It is not clear where Oxford lived between the time he was born in 1550 and his father's death in 1562. He may have been sent to live with Sir Thomas Smith, Lord Burghley's own former tutor, at the age of four. He may have stayed there until he was twelve when his father, Earl John, died, forcing Oxford to move to Cecil House in London where he became a royal ward of Lord Burghley. See *Oxford's Childhood Part II: The First Four Years With Smith,* Stephanie Hopkins Hughes, *The Shakespeare Oxford Newsletter*, Fall 2006.

Regardless of Oxford's whereabouts between age four and twelve, Oxford rode into London at age twelve at the head of four-score (80) gentlemen on horseback and 100 yeoman dressed in reading tawny clothes with a blue boar on their left shoulders and wearing gold chains. Nelson, p. 15.

At least one author, a descendant of Edward de Vere, claims Edward may have been the son of Elizabeth and Thomas Seymour, and raised as a changeling boy first by Sir Thomas Smith and then by the Sixteenth Earl of Oxford, who conveniently died in 1562 so that Edward could become the ward of Lord Burghley and eventually marry Burghley's daughter Anne. *Shakespeare's Lost Kingdom*, Charles Beauclerk, Grove Press 2010, p. 55, *et seq.*

---

[136] *www.castlehedingham.org*. See also the description in *The Fighting Veres* by Clements R. Markham, Houghton, Mifflin and Company, 1888, beginning at p. 12. While only the tower stands today, it was surrounded in Oxford's time by a great hall and chapel, kitchens, apartments, stables, granaries, butts, a tennis court, and an open area for tournaments. Markham states that the "great keep of Hedingham is the finest relic of Norman civil architecture in England." P. 12.

Edward de Vere was an avid hunter and falconer. Thomas Digby is a fictional gamekeeper. The surname "Digby" is of Danish origin and consistent with the influx of Danes into Essex over many centuries. Just how far they spread into England can be seen from the names of English villages. If they were established by Danes, the town's name ended in "by," which stood for village or town.

Oxford's decision to let the stag go that had been run to ground in the hunt earlier in the day will appear in Act II, Scene 1, in *As You Like It*:

Duke Senior:

Come, shall we go and kill us venison?
And yet it irks me the poor dappled fools,
Being native burghers of this desert city,
Should in their own confines with forked heads
Have their round haunches gored.

First Lord:

Indeed, my lord,
The melancholy Jaques grieves at that,
And, in that kind, swears you do more usurp
Than doth your brother that hath banish'd you.
To-day my Lord of Amiens and myself
Did steal behind him as he lay along
Under an oak whose antique root peeps out
Upon the brook that brawls along this wood:
To the which place a poor sequester'd stag,
That from the hunter's aim had ta'en a hurt,
Did come to languish, and indeed, my lord,
The wretched animal heaved forth such groans
That their discharge did stretch his leathern coat
Almost to bursting, and the big round tears
Coursed one another down his innocent nose
In piteous chase; and thus the hairy fool
Much marked of the melancholy Jaques,
Stood on the extremest verge of the swift brook,
Augmenting it with tears.

Duke Senior:

But what said Jaques?
Did he not moralize this spectacle?

First Lord:

O, yes, into a thousand similes.
First, for his weeping into the needless stream;
'Poor deer,' quoth he, 'thou makest a testament
As worldlings do, giving thy sum of more
To that which had too much:' then, being there alone,
Left and abandon'd of his velvet friends,
"Tis right:' quoth he; 'thus misery doth part
The flux of company:' anon a careless herd,
Full of the pasture, jumps along by him
And never stays to greet him; 'Ay' quoth Jaques,
'Sweep on, you fat and greasy citizens;
'Tis just the fashion: wherefore do you look
Upon that poor and broken bankrupt there?'
Thus most invectively he pierceth through
The body of the country, city, court,
Yea, and of this our life, swearing that we
Are mere usurpers, tyrants and what's worse,
To fright the animals and to kill them up
In their assign'd and native dwelling-place.

Duke Senior:

And did you leave him in this contemplation?

Second Lord:

We did, my lord, weeping and commenting
Upon the sobbing deer.

Duke Senior:

Show me the place:
I love to cope him in these sullen fits,
For then he's full of matter.

(Some scholars have thought Jacques was Oxford. The outcry against the 'fat and greasy citizens' – the fallen deer's 'velvet friends' – who fail to look down as they 'sweep by' the 'poor and broken bankrupt' would fit Oxford well in his later years.)

This is also based on part of a poem by Oxford about a "stricken deer:"

The stricken deer hath help to heal his wound

From *Paradyse of Dainty Devices*, 1576.[137] Reprinted in Looney and Professor Nelson. Oxford's poems can also be seen on the web at *Elizabethan Authors*: www.elizabethanauthors.com/oxfordpoems.htm.

Also, catch the sense of regret in the lines spoken by the Princess in *Love's Labour's Lost,* Act IV, at the conclusion of a long speech on the pursuit of fame:

But come, the bow: now mercy goes to kill,
And shooting well is then accounted ill.
Thus will I save my credit in the shoot:
Not wounding, pity would not let me do't;
If wounding, then it was to show my skill,
That more for praise than purpose meant to kill.
And out of question so it is sometimes,
Glory grows guilty of detested crimes,
When, for fame's sake, for praise, an outward part,
We bend to that the working of the heart;
As I for praise alone now seek to spill
The poor deer's blood, that my heart means no ill.

The comments Digby makes about different kinds of hawks reflect what Elizabethan hunters talked about while they rode across the fields or crouched in blinds waiting for geese to fly in.

---

137 Looney, John Thomas. *"Shakespeare" Identified*, (Ruth Lloyd Miller, ed.) Jennings, La.: Minos Pub. Co. (1919), #19; *Miscellanies of the Fuller Worthies' Library*, Vol. IV (1872), #19. *This Star of England*, p. 54, and *Elizabethan Authors*, www.elizabethanauthors.com/oxfordpoems.htm. Music was printed for this by William Byrd in 1587.

Some thought a haggard captured in the wild had more power and dash than an eyas raised by hand. For all the quotes about haggards and hawking, see *The Mysterious William Shakespeare – The Myth & The Reality,* Ogburn, Charlton, EPM Publications, Inc., 1984, p. 266 , *et seq.;* Sams, 167-168; *Ogburns*, p. 54.

The poem Elspeth recites that begins "*If women could be fair and yet not fond*," and which concludes:

> *Unsettled still like haggards wild they range,*
> *These gentle birds that fly from man to man:*
> *Who would not scorn and shake them from the fist,*
> *And let them fly, fair fools, which way they list?*

is Oxford's.[138] Compare the following lines from *Othello*, Act III, Scene 3:

> *If I do prove her haggard,*
> *Though that her jesses were my dear heartstrings,*
> *I'd whistle her off and let her down the wind,*
> *To pray at fortune.*

Compare also the following from *The Taming of the Shrew,* Act IV, Scene 1, the wedding night of Petruchio and Kate. Petruchio is declaiming what havoc he is going to wreak the rest of the night to tame his Kate:

> *Thus have I politicly begun my reign,*
> *And 'tis my hope to end successfully.*
> *My falcon now is sharp and passing empty;*
> *And till she stoop she must not be full-gorged,*
> *For then she never looks upon her lure.*
> *Another way I have to man my haggard,*
> *To make her come and know her keeper's call,*
> *That is, to watch her, as we watch these kites*
> *That bate and beat and will not be obedient.*
> *She eat no meat to-day, nor none shall eat;*
> *Last night she slept not, nor to-night she shall not;*

---

[138] Looney, #19; *Miscellanies of the Fuller Worthies' Library*, #19.

As with the meat, some undeserved fault
I'll find about the making of the bed;
And here I'll fling the pillow, there the bolster,
This way the coverlet, another way the sheets:
Ay, and amid this hurly I intend
That all is done in reverend care of her;
And in conclusion she shall watch all night:
And if she chance to nod I'll rail and brawl
And with the clamour keep her still awake.
This is a way to kill a wife with kindness;
And thus I'll curb her mad and headstrong humour.
He that knows better how to tame a shrew,
Now let him speak: 'tis charity to show.

To support his claim that words can be words of beauty and more than simple information, Oxford recites two lines from Christopher Marlowe's *The Tragical History of Faust,* which Digby dismisses as Old Pete dragging his leg across the deck of the *Bonaventure.* This is unfair to Marlowe because the two lines are taken out of context. They are standard iambic pentameter with little relief from their plodding meter. The third line, not recited in *The Death of Shakespeare*, shows why Marlowe moved blank verse far beyond *Gorbuduc* and other early plays:

Was this the face that launched a thousand ships,
And toppled the topless towers of Ilium?
Sweet Helen, make me immortal with a kiss.

The third line has the same number of feet as the first two lines (ten) but the rhythm is broken by "*Sweet Helen.*" What follows, "*make me immortal,*" is like a little boy running over thin ice before the reader gets to the *terra firma* of the final three syllables, "*with a kiss.*" Marlowe could make the tongue trip, and he made everyone who came after him try to write with the same fluidity. These lines, abandoned by Oxford in his sparring with Digby, will become one of the discussions Oxford has with Marlowe after they become acquainted with each other.

As Digby guesses, "*the labouring man*," is by Oxford, as is "*a crowne of bays*."[139]

The Queen visited Hedingham in 1558 where *King Johan* was performed. To borrow a phrase beloved by the biographers of Shakespeare, it is "doubtless" that young Edward watched the play. (Oxford's grandfather, the Fifteenth Earl, commissioned John Bale to write *King Johan.* The Queen returned in 1561 when Oxford was eleven. *An Elizabethan Puritan*, p. 32, 271. Earl John, the Sixteenth Earl, accompanied the Queen from Hatfield when she made her way into London to become Queen Elizabeth and succeed her sister, Mary. P. 31.

The *Bonaventure* actually existed.[140] Its true name, interestingly enough, was the *Edward Bonaventure*. Its name appears in various

---

[139] As to "*The labouring man*," Looney, #11, Fuller, #21, part of the Preface to *Cardanus Comfort* (1576); as to "A *crowne of bays*," Looney, #2, Fuller, #6; first printed in *Paradyse of Dainty Devices* (1576). Notice the similarities between "*A crowne of bays*" and Sonnets 133 (*Beshrew that heart that makes my heart to groan*) and 89 (*Say that thou didst forsake me for some fault*). Dorothy Ogburn believes that "*A crowne of bays*" may have been written as a reaction to George Gascoigne publishing poems of Oxford's, and Gascoigne being accepted by the Queen as poet laureate in 1576 while Oxford was in Italy. P. 57. But the entire poem seems to be about the loss of a woman's love to a rival. However, she may be right; the acceptance of Gascoigne as poet laureate may have been a sign of the Queen pushing back at Oxford. She was famous for working those who worshipped her. Once, while stroking Leicester's neck who had bowed in front of her, the Queen asked another courtier about Darnley, who was a player in Scotland with Mary Queen of Scots at the time. The courtier gave a courtier's reply and Elizabeth said she preferred Darnley to Leicester.

[140] See Hakluyt, Richard, *The Second Volume of the Principal Navigations* (1599), and Ogburn, Charlton, *The Mysterious William Shakespeare*, 1984; and http://www.oxford-shakespeare.com/Newsletters/Voyages

_Explor-02.pdf. More than one ship was named the *Bonaaventure.* In 1556, Richard Chancellor, returning from Russia on the *Edward Bonaventure,* "was cast away on the coast of Aberdeenshire." The greater part of the crew perished, including Chancellor who died while launching the boat that saved the Muscovite envoy. This act created a great amount of goodwill between Russia and England and led to the founding of the Muscovy Company. Clark, p. 136. (Lord Willoughby's visits to Elsinore in the 1580s were to secure freer records from 1581 through 1602 when it was wrecked off the coast of Hispaniola. In 1578, Oxford invested £3,000 in Frobisher's third voyage to find the Northwest Passage, and a lesser amount in Captain John Davis' voyage to Baffin Island in 1585. ("*I am but mad north-north-west: when the wind is southerly I know a hawk from a handsaw,*" Hamlet tells Guildenstern in *Hamlet*, Act II, Scene 2.)

In 1581, Oxford invested a further £500 in a voyage to the Moluccas, in which the *Edward Bonaventure* participated. The *Edward Bonaventure* also engaged in trade in the Mediterranean and the first voyage to the East Indies. It participated in the actions to repulse the Spanish Armada in 1588. Interestingly, it worked almost exclusively for the Turkey Company, formally known as the Company of Merchants of the Levant, which had been granted a patent by the Queen in 1581 (when Oxford was 31.)[141]

Of further interest are the locations where the *Edward Bonaventure* ran into trouble in its voyages across the northern hemisphere. On her return trip from the 1585 voyage to the eastern Mediterranean, the *Edward Bonaventure* and two other

---

passage for English ships trading with Russia.) There is no indication that the *Edward Bonaventure*, wrecked in 1556 on the coast of Aberdeenshire, was salvaged, although this is possible. And multiple ships named 'Edward' is not surprising when Edward VI reigned from 1547 to 1553.

141 Is this why the Queen called Oxford her Turk? Scholars have puzzled over this nickname (one of many she gave the men and women around her), and wondered whether Oxford went to Greece on his trip to Italy in the mid-1570s, and then on to Istanbul, although there is no evidence to support this idea. *Othello* takes place in Venice and Cyprus, and *Midsummer Night's Dream, Pericles* and *Timon of Athens* take place in Greece (except that Richard Roe has shown pretty conclusively that *Midsummer* was based on the Italian town of Sabbionetta, *The Shakespeare Guide to Italy*), but none of these put Oxford in Istanbul. There is no evidence that Mozart visited the seraglio in Istanbul either. In *The Death of Shakespeare*, Oxford acquires the nickname by impersonating the Turkish ambassador. See *An Heir for his Lordship*, Chapter 76.

ships were attacked by galleys of Spain and Malta near the island of Pantelleria, which lies between Tunis and Sicily. They successfully resisted the attack and returned to England safely. This location is one of the more logical guesses for the location of *The Tempest.* (However, Richard Roe has established that *The Tempest* was based on the island of Vulcano off the north coast of Sicily. See, *The Shakespeare Guide to Italy: Retracing the Bard's Unknown Travels*, discussed below.

The *Edward Bonaventure* participated in the defeat of the Spanish Armada, and was apparently under the command of a James Lancaster, who may have been in command when the ship was later lost off the Dominican Republic in 1593. Matus, p. 159. Ogburn says that the indexes of ships in the National Maritime Museum of London disclose the following references to the *Edward Bonaventure*: a merchant vessel sailing with the Turkey Company; engaging the Spanish in November, 1585, and the Armada in 1588; and participating in the first successful British voyage to India and back in 1591-93. At p. 741, fn. 2.

The relationship between the Earl of Oxford and the *Edward Bonaventure* is a long one. Although the Ogburns claim in *This Star of England* at page 229 that Oxford bought the ship in 1581, the written record only shows that he made an offer to purchase it. There is no documentation of a sale. Nelson, p. 188-189. Matus flatly states that the ship was purchased by others. The belief that the *Edward Bonaventure* was involved in a shipwreck on Bermuda appears to be untrue; it was lost off the coast of the Dominican Republic after it had been hijacked by some of its crewmembers while the rest of the crew were ashore obtaining supplies. One of the sailors left behind was a man by the name of Henry May, who *was* shipwrecked on Bermuda after he had gotten passage on a French ship in an attempt to get back to England. Nelson, p. 158-160, citing Julian S. Corbett, *Papers Relating to the Navy During the Spanish War, 1585-1587,* ([London]: Navy Records Society, 1898), xx; and Kenneth R. Andrews, *English Privateering: English Privateering During the Spanish War, 1585-1603* (Cambridge: University Press, 1964), 210, 214-215. His tale may have contributed to *The Tempest.*

The *Tempest* mentions the "still-vexed Bermoothes." The reference is probably the most misrepresented line in all of Shakespeare. First, the action in the play takes place on an island where Prospero has been shipwrecked on a voyage from somewhere near Milan, where he had been Duke. This is far from Bermuda.

Second, the reference to the "Bermoothes" is made by Ariel in answering Prospero's questions about the location of a ship he had *earlier* sent Ariel to batter with a "tempest." Ariel replies (Act I, Scene 2) that:

> *Safely in harbour*
> *Is the king's ship; in the deep nook, where once*
> *Thou call'dst me up at midnight to fetch dew*
> *From the still-vex'd Bermoothes, there she's hid:*

Ariel is telling Prospero the ship is "safely" hidden "in the [same] deep nook" Ariel was in when Prospero last called his servant "to fetch dew from the still-vex'd Bermoothes."[142] The ship is not in the Bermudas; nor is the island where the action takes place in the Bermudas. Ariel was sent to the "Bermoothes" when *he* was last "in the deep nook."

Third, Richard Roe in *The Shakespeare Guide to Italy* shows conclusively that the action in *The Tempest* takes place on Vulcano, an island off the north coast of Sicily.

Records do not show where Oxford was when the Spanish Armada arrived in the English Channel (or when his wife died on June 5, 1588), but he may have been on board when the *Edward Bonaventure* battled the Spanish that summer.[143] A poem

---

142 Some have suggested that the reference was to a district of London famous for its distilleries, a logical place to seek 'dew.' Whalen, pp. 120-121;. Anderson, p. 402, Farina, p. 23).

143 Anderson says (p. 222) that the English fleet left Plymouth on May 30. Anne died six days later on June 5. The fleet returned the next day, June 6. On June 19, they ventured out again, only to be driven back to port on June 21. On June 24, the fleet sailed again. Anne's funeral was the next day, June 25. The fleet returned July 12. On July 12, the Spanish Armada arrived off

celebrating the victory by John Lyly (Oxford's secretary for an extensive period of time) mentions him prominently (but see Professor Nelson's evidence discussed below that the poem was Burghley propaganda and not true).

De Vere, whose fame and the loyalty hath pearst
The Tuscan clime, and through the Belgike lands
By winged fame for valour is rehearst,
Like warlike Mars upon the hatches stands,
His tusked Boar 'gan foam for inward ire,
When Pallas filled his breast with warlike fire.

A letter from Leicester to Walsingham from Tilbury on August 1, 1588, has Oxford at Tilbury refusing to take command of Harwich, a seaport on the English Channel that was in Essex, Oxford's part of England. Whether he was on board any of the ships is unclear. The list of nobles who resisted the Spanish includes Oxford, but a draft of this list has been found in Burghley's papers, and it seems that he doctored the list to add his son-in-law (as well as other nobles) to those who defended England. (Nelson, p. 315.) His purpose? To let the Spanish know that none of the supposed "Catholic" earls were disloyal to Elizabeth. If Oxford was added to the list, as Burghley's draft suggests, he may not have been there. However, this piece of propaganda from the sly fox himself validates a lot of the complaints Oxford (and others) voiced about Burghley's duplicity, and casts a different light on Burghley's claims about

---

Cornwall and the English fleet left port immediately. The pivotal battle in which the fire ships were sent down into the Spanish fleet took place on July 28. Leicester wrote on the same day to Walsingham that Oxford "seemed only [that] his voyage was to have gone to my Lord Admiral [Howard] – and at his return seemed also to return again hither to me this day from London, whither he went yesterday for his armor and furniture." P. 225. Leicester was at Tilbury which was on the north shore of the Thames east of London. Leicester's letter is unclear but Oxford seems to have gone to Howard, who was commanding the sea forces, and then went to Leicester who was in command of the land forces at Tilbury. See discussion of Leicester's letter of that date discussed above.

Oxford's behavior. Also, there is no proof Oxford was *not* part of the English fleet that repulsed the Spanish ships.

The whistle Digby uses to call the eyas is based on one found on the Isle of Wight during an outing of a metal-detecting club. It was two and one half inches long and carried a Tudor rose and a pomegranate, the person insignia of Catherine of Aragon, Henry VIII's first wife. It may have been lost when Catherine visited the island in 1538.

The potato was introduced into England by Raleigh (*Sir Walter Ralegh in Ireland,* Sir John Pope-Hennessy, 1883), and was thought to be everything from an aphrodisiac to a poison.

Goose livers are so tasty that it is impossible to believe that Digby would not have relished them. Whether he would have been able to take sufficient equipment with him to provide Oxford with a bit of foie gras in the field is unsubstantiated (but a pleasant possibility nevertheless).

Oxford knew of the booming voice a falconer needed. Juliet, on her famous balcony, refers to it as she tries to get Romeo to come back to her (Act II, Scene 2):

> *Hist! Romeo, hist! O, for a falconer's voice,*
> *To lure this tassel-gentle back again!*
> *Bondage is hoarse, and may not speak aloud;*
> *Else would I tear the cave where Echo lies,*[144]
> *And make her airy tongue more hoarse than mine,*
> *With repetition of my Romeo's name.*

Chapter 63
That Night

Elspeth Trentham's 'frowardness' is fiction. That the Elizabethans thought an orgasm was necessary in order to conceive was a false belief that let many scurrilous men to defame a woman they had gotten pregnant by claiming that the

---

[144] "Echo" poems were not uncommon in Elizabethan times.

woman, even if she had been raped, must have enjoyed the act. See, *The Reader's Companion*, Chapter 24 and what happened to Mary Fitton when the Third Earl of Pembroke got her pregnant.

Chapter 64
Oxford Court - *Henry VI – Part 3*

Chapter 65
A Wedding at Whitehall

Baynard's Castle dates from long before William the Conqueror arrived. It was located inside the Roman walls where they came down to the Thames alongside the Fleet River, which was the second-largest river in London after the Thames. The Castle was the site of many significant events over the years. It came into the first Earl of Pembroke's hands in 1551 and the Pembrokes owned it until the civil war began in the 1640s. It was destroyed in the great fire of 1666. There is no evidence that it had been abandoned when Oxford gets in the wherry to be rowed upriver to his wedding.

John Taylor was known as the water poet. He was born in 1578. He would have been thirteen in 1591 so it is doubtful he commanded the eight-man wherry that takes Oxford to his wedding. John Taylor was a waterman who wrote poetry and other works. He was the first poet to mention the deaths of William Shakespeare in print in his 1620 poem, "*The Praise of Hemp-seed*".

In paper, many a poet now survives
Or else their lines had perish'd with their lives.
Old Chaucer, Gower, and Sir Thomas More,
Sir Philip Sidney, who the laurel wore,
Spenser, and Shakespeare did in art excell,
Sir Edward Dyer, Greene, Nash, Daniel.
Sylvester, Beaumont, Sir John Harrington,
Forgetfulness their works would over run
But that in paper they immortally
Do live in spite of death, and cannot die.

The composer of "London Bridge Is Falling Down" is unknown.

Shakespeare's plays and sonnets are full of sexual puns. Some are readily visible; others are more hidden. See Pauline Kiernan, *Filthy Shakespeare.* 'Worm' is used as a synonym for penis in Thomas Nashe's *The Choice of Valentines* when he describes how he went to a whorehouse and couldn't get it up: *Perhaps the sillie worme is labour'd sore, / And wearied that it can doe no more.* Nashe, with the help of the lady involved, successfully revives his 'worm' and he and the woman both reach orgasm, something that surprised the Victorian world when the poem was published at the end of the 19th century. Apparently, many Victorians thought women could not have orgasms. To their astonishment, Nashe's poem showed them that the Elizabethans had been way ahead of them. Such is progress.

Oxford married Elizabeth Trentham on December 27, 1591, if the notation in the court records of a gilt bowel given by Elizabeth to them as a wedding gift indicates the date. There is no evidence as to where the ceremony took place or who attended the wedding. Oxford apparently made peace with his daughters (or they with him) at some point as there is mention of his involvement in trying to arrange Lisbeth's marriage to the Second Earl of Pembroke and Susan writing a letter from Hackney.

William Byrd set a number of Oxford's poems to music. *The Earl of Oxford's March* is known from four different versions and was apparently quite popular. It still is. The best is by the Synergy Brass Quintet: *www.youtube.com/watch?v=Y3EhkLYfSw4.*

There are many tuckets in the plays (*Lear; Henry V, Henry VIII*). Iago recognizes that Othello is arriving by the sound of Othello's tucket. *The Earl of Oxford's March* may be a composer's take on Oxford's tucket.

Love's Labour's Won is listed by Francis Meres in 1598 as a play of Shakespeare's but there is no other mention or record of this play. Some scholars think Meres was referring to *All's Well*

That Ends Well, which may have been performed as *The Rape of the Second Helen* in the 1580s.

The poem Oxford recites to his new bride, *Loves Queene, long wayting for her true-Love*, is from *England's Helicon*, p. 112-113, printed in 1600. The poem is signed *Ignoto*, who, many scholars think, was a pen name for Oxford. It is obviously written from an older man to a younger woman. Oxford was 41 when he married Elizabeth Trentham. Did he have gray hair? Notice that the woman in the poem had given up waiting for a young man who had been slain by a boar he was hunting. This appears to be a precursor to *Venus and Adonis*, which Oxford will write and publish in 1593. Maybe Oxford was working on *Venus* when he wrote this poem, although it is far less accomplished than *Venus*.

Is the reference to a younger man slain by a boar evidence of an earlier love Elspeth may have pursued that was frustrated by the younger man's death?

John Farmer was an organist in Dublin who dedicated a book of music to Oxford in 1590: "Divers and Sundry Waies of 2 parts in 1, to the number of 40, upon a playn song." Oxford was 40 in 1590. Ward, p. 307; Ogburn, p. 720.

Castle Hedingham was put in trust for Oxford's three daughters on December 2, 1591 with Lord Burghley as one of the trustees. Relatives of Elizabeth Trentham were also listed as trustees. Nelson, p. 335. Elizabeth bought back the castle in 1604 and left it to her son, Henry, the 18th Earl of Oxford. Nelson, p. 435. Whose idea it was to put the castle in trust and allow Elizabeth to buy it back is unknown.

Scholars disagree over whether Oxford damaged the castle at the time it was put in trust. Professor Nelson states that "it is unlikely that Oxford ever spent much time at Hedingham." At p. 478, footnote 8. But this is based on Professor Nelson's conclusion that the castle and its appendages "were stripped at Oxford's direction and on his warrant." At p. 335. For support, Professor Nelson cites Thomas Watson's report of 1600, quoted at p. 379-380. But Wilson seems to be saying that Oxford "prodigally spent and consumed all even to the selling of the stones, timber, and lead of his castles and houses ..." but the time period is "within 2 following [1575, or 1577]." This is long before Oxford's marriage in 1591. Wilson was listing the profligate spending of earls, including Oxford, and may have erred. If so, his confusion may have been caused by the fact that the Queen gave Oxford's lands during his minority (1562-1571 and beyond) to the Earl of Leicester, who was penniless. Leicester may have stripped Oxford's lands, or, the warrants may have issued because no one had lived at the castle from Earl John's death in 1562. See Ward, p. 306, and Ogburn, p. 934. See, Majendie, L, *An Account of Castle Hedingham*, 1796, discussed in Gwynneth Bowen article at http://www.sourcetext.com/sourcebook/library/bowen/11exonerated.htm.

Pearson has a copy of a sketch map of Castle Hedingham which is noted as "c1606" by the Essex Record Office. But it may have been part of a report Burghley ordered when Elizabeth Trentham and others took title to the Castle in trust for Oxford's daughters.

That John Dudley, Earl of Leicester, may have plundered Oxford's landholdings during Oxford's minority finds support in the following assessment of wardship in England at this time:

> "[A] ward's lands were leased out in return for annual rents paid by the lessees to the Court, and the wardship of their bodies and the right to determine their marriages were sold to guardians who might or might not be the lessees of the lands ... [O]ften they passed into the hands of influential courtiers or officials whose interest in their young charges was all too often confined to making as large a profit out of them as possible. Such profits could be made not only by ruthless exploitation of a ward's lands, but also by selling the ward in marriage to the highest bidder." Hickes, p. 112.

As to Burghley himself: "During the last two and a half years of Burghley's life he received at least £3,000 from suitors for wardships at a time when his official salary as Master was only £133 a year." Hickes, p. 67. Burghley received eight wardships during his life. Edward de Vere, Earl of Oxford; Edward Manners, Third Earl of Rutland; Edward, Lord Zouche; Philip, Lord Wharton; Philip Howard, Earl of Surrey; Robert Devereux, Second Earl of Essex; Henry Wriothesley, Third Earl of Southampton; and Roger Manners, Fifth Earl of Rutland. Hickes, p. 34. These were not Burghley's only source of income.

The history of the Court of Wards can be read in Hickes.

The remark that it is easier to teach a woman to talk than it is to teach her to hold her tongue was made by the Queen to the French ambassador when he complimented her on her ability to speak six languages: "[T]hat it was no marvel to teach a woman to talk; it were far harder to teach her to hold her tongue." Chute, p. 145.

The Queen's belief that a play cannot be written that shows true love is based on her comments after seeing *Palamon and Arcite* in 1566. This will inspire Oxford to write *Romeo and Juliet.*

1592

Chapters 66-79

Chapter 66
Oxford and Lady Elspeth Return to Oxford Court

Bona Fortuna is fiction. Epping Forest is a large forest northeast of London about halfway to Castle Hedingham in Essex.

Chapter 67
Henry VI – Part 3

The Queen's suggestion that Sir Robert Cecil wear the medallion of his sister on the top of his shoe is a twisted version of an account in which the Queen reportedly saw Oxford's daughter, Elizabeth, wearing a miniature of Robert Cecil around her neck. The Queen asked to see it, and "snatched it away and tied it to her shoe." She later pinned it to her elbow. William Bowen in a letter to the Earl of Shrewsbury, 1602, quoted in *A Companion to British Art: 1600 to the Present,* Arnold, Dana, *et al.,* ed., John Wiley & Sons, 2013, and in *Patrons and Musicians of the English Renaissance,* David C. Price. Price makes "Bowen" read "Brown" and adds that the incident aroused the queen's jealousy and that she made Cecil write lyrics to a song to appease her. Robert Hayes, royal lutenist, wrote the music. What was going on here is impossible to figure out. Cecil was crook-backed and slight. Elizabeth nicknamed him her 'frog,' so it is difficult to understand her jealousy. In any event, the medallion in *The Death of Shakespeare* is of Cecil's sister and the Queen suggesting that Cecil wear it on his shoe is fiction.

Ditchley House is in Oxfordshire to the west of London and has a famous history. It dates from Roman ruins circa 70 AD. It was used by Winston Churchill in World War II to avoid German bombers. When Queen Elizabeth visited Ditchley in 1592, Sir Henry Lee was living there with Anne Vavasor and her twelve-year-old illegitimate son, Edward. At the time, Sir Henry Lee and Anne were each married to others, and their spouses were still alive. Thus, the visit was unusual because it honored Sir Henry and Anne.

Sir Henry was armourer to the Queen and keeper of the Tower of London. He met Anne when she was imprisoned there (along with her new baby, Edward) with Edward's father, the Earl of Oxford. Sir Henry became so enamored of Anne that he had a set of armor made for him with Anne's initials inscribed all over it. Sometime later, he convinced her to move to Ditchley and live with him, even though she had married another man in the interim. The relationship was long-lasting. At the visit made by Elizabeth to Ditchley in 1592, Sir Henry presented the Queen with a full-length larger-than-life portrait of her by Marcus Gheerhaerts, which became known as "the Forgiveness Portrait." It now hangs in the British Portrait Gallery in London. See, *The Reader's Companion*, Chapter 73 - Ditchley.

In *The Death of Shakespeare – Part Two*, Oxford will hire Gheeraerts to paint what is known as the "Pregnancy Portrait," now in the Royal Gallery of Hampton Court. In his *Royal Gallery of Hampton Court Illustrated*, George Bell & Sons, 1898, Edwin Law identified the portrait as "Queen Elizabeth in Fancy Dress" and attributed it, although doubtfully, to Zucchero. Plate 349, p. 138. Law's description is extensive, although he makes no mention that the subject might be pregnant. He gives the full sonnet on the painting.

When Elizabeth II came to the throne in 1952, the name of the painting was changed to "Woman in Fanciful Dress." The 20th century Elizabeth may not have liked having her namesake predecessor presented as being pregnant. Beauclerk has the best reproduction of this immense painting, 7' high by 4' 6" wide, which must be seen in person to be appreciated. The painting was recovered at a flea market after the restoration and was accepted by all at the time as of Elizabeth I. Beauclerk says that the painting has had numerous names, including "Shakespeare's Dark Lady." It is now listed as "Portrait of an Unknown Lady." See, discussion in *The Reader's Companion*, Chapter 12 above.

Oxford will commission the "Pregnancy Portrait" in *Part Two* and present it to the Queen in imitation of Sir Henry's Lee's gift of the Forgiveness Portrait.

Chapter 68
Oxford Court – Shackspear and *Love's Labour's Won*

Love's Labour's Won was mentioned in Meres but no record of it has been found. Most scholars think Meres got the name wrong and he intended to list another play.

Chapter 69
Much Ado About Nothing

The plot for Hero and Claudia comes from Bandello's 22nd story. Some believe the source for Hero and Claudia was based on Ariosto's *Orlando Furioso*, which was translated into English by Sir John Harrington in 1591. However, Oxford most likely read the original in Italian. See, the *Globe Shakespeare*, p. 693. The best discussion of the play is in Tanner, beginning at p. 180. As to 'nothing' implying a woman's vagina, see Tanner, pp. 182-186, who is one among many scholars noting the connection. See, Garber, pp. 377-380. Curiously, Pauline Kiernan makes no mention of *Much Ado About Nothing* in her book, *Filthy Shakespeare.*

Oxford would have been attracted to a plot where Hero is unjustly accused of infidelity, given the trouble Oxford had in dealing with allegations that impugned his wife's honor when he returned from Italy.

As with so many of the plays, Oxford is Benedict.[145] While the play could have been about Anne Cecil and Oxford, it seems more likely that he was Benedict and Anne Vavasor was Beatrice. Notice that Beatrice says

---

145 to links between contemporaries of Oxford and the characters in the play, see *The Reader's Companion* to Chapter 93.

He set up his bills here in Messina and challenged
Cupid at the flight; and my uncle's fool, reading
the challenge, subscribed for Cupid, and challenged
him at the bird-bolt.

Oxford's affair with Anne Vavasor's caused him trouble later on with her uncle, Sir Thomas Knyvet, who challenged Oxford for having ruined his niece's reputation. Oxford and Knyvet fought at least once. Both were injured, Oxford more seriously.[146] These fights appear in *Romeo and Juliet* but the above quote by Beatrice seems to be aimed at Knyvet. Anderson, p. 178-182; Ogburns, pp. 481, *et seq.*

Notice that what Ursula says of Benedict in Act III, Scene 1, is literally true: "*Signior Benedict, / For shape, for bearing, argument and valour, / Goes foremost in report through Italy*" to which Hero responds: "*Indeed, he hath an excellent good name.*"

Even more interesting is Beatrice's reference to an earlier relationship. In reply to a question by Don Pedro, Beatrice says:

Indeed, my lord, he lent it [his heart] me awhile; and I gave
Him use for it, a double heart for his single one:
Marry, once before he won it of me with false dice,
Therefore your grace may well say I have lost it.

---

146 Oxford's injury may be the source of his claim in some of his letters that he was lame, as well as the reference to being 'lame' in Sonnet 37:

As a decrepit father takes delight / To see his active child do deeds of youth, / So I, made lame by Fortune's dearest spite, / Take all my comfort of thy worth and truth[.]

(Of course, 'made lame by Fortune's dearest spite' may refer to Oxford being denied the fame that came from his plays." See Ogburns, p. 481 *et seq.* The nature of the wound inflicted by Knyvet or Oxford's lameness is unknown. In *The Death of Shakespeare*, Knyvet will stab Oxford in the thigh, and the similarity between this wound and the manner in which Thomas Brincknell died (see Chapter 81) will cause Oxford to think Thomas Brincknell has returned from the grave to revenge himself on Oxford.

Act II, Scene 1. See *The Reader's Companion* to Chapter 12 for more information about this connection between Oxford and Anne Vavasor.

Oxford's knowledge of Messina, and particularly of the time period in which the play takes place, shows Oxford must have visited Sicily. Richard Roe's *The Shakespeare Guide to Italy* settles the question about the personal knowledge of the author in writing the Italian plays, including *Much Ado About Nothing*, which takes place in Messina, Sicily.

Roe's book also discusses the relationship of Don John with the English, pointing out that Don John, the victor of Lepanto in 1570, was sent to the Netherlands to head up the Spanish forces there. His brother, King Don Pedro, probably did this to get him out of the way, but it did not endear Don John to the English. Even more interesting is that Oxford was in northern Italy in 1575 when Don John was leading an army in one of the many wars among the Italian cities. Oxford may have met him then. Furthermore, the contact may have triggered off Oxford's encounter with Duke Casimere on his way back from Italy. See, *The Reader's* , Chapter 37 – John Shackspear. Hamlet's review of Fortinbras' army may have come from these events. The contacts between Oxford and Don John, therefore, were many. See Anderson, pp. 91-92.

Comparing what Dogberry speaks in *Much Ado* with what the Earl of Arundel wrote about Oxford in 1580 shows that Oxford intentionally imitated Arundel's doggerel when he wrote Dogberry's lines in *Much Ado*. Professor Nelson has posted the libels on his website:

http://socrates.berkeley.edu/~ahnelson/LIBELS/libelndx.html.

Anderson discusses the similarities between the two at p. 168-169. Ward has the best discussion of the allegations that swirled around Oxford after he told Elizabeth about Arundel and Howard in December, 1580. See p. 206, *et seq.*

'Dogberry' and his bumbling confederates are Oxford's take on information in a letter Lord Burghley wrote to Sir Francis

Walsingham on August 10, 1586, in which Burghley complained about the ineffectiveness of the constables he saw on his way from London to Theobalds. The constables had been ordered to search for the Babington conspirators. Burghley referred to the watchmen as the "dogberries of Enfield," a town he passed through on his way to Theobalds. "Shakespeare Society's Papers," Vol. 1, London, 1844, beginning at p. 1. The complete text can be read at

https://books.google.com/books?id=mBhLAQAAMAAJ&pg=PA3&lpg=PA3&dq=constable+dogberry+burghley&source=bl&ots=8eaf4dYnBp&sig=ZGT0mXO10VSP9UPQ3jYQf_z8omc&hl=en&sa=X&ei=f5iaVfC-BcKLuASxppXwDA&ved=0CEEQ6AEwBQ#v=onepage&q=constable%20dogberry%20burghley&f=false.

The connection seems solid but excitement over connecting Dogberry of *Much Ado About Nothing* with the "dogberries of Enfield" may be tempered by the signature at the end of the short article – J. Payne Collier. Collier was a notorious forger of Shakespearean documents in the 19th century. He even fabricated a complete play. The letter from Burghley to Walsingham was supposedly given to Collier by a "Mr. Lemon of the State Papers Office." According to Collier, Lemon sent it to Collier too late to be included in Collier's biography of Shakespeare. Since Mr. Lemon appears to have been alive at the time of Collier's publication of the letter in 1844, and his readers were supposedly astute members of the Shakespeare Society, it may be unfair to accuse Mr. Collier of forging the letter when so many people could have called him out.

The word 'nothing' appears 352 times in *Much Ado*. The word 'ever' appears 23 times (for whatever value these counts are worth), while 'never' appears 30 times, not counting 'evermore,' 'everyone,' and other compound words with 'ever' in them.

Benedict's statement to Claudio in Act I that "*I can be secret as a dumb man*" may merit further inquiry. The Ogburns suspect that this is a reference to an agreement with the Queen, but even more interesting is that Oxford's widow, Lady Elizabeth Trentham, left a small sum in her will to "my dumb man." Oxford's countess died in 1609. Was this a bequest to Shakespeare, who was still alive?

Chapter 70
Henry VI – Part 3 at the Rose

Hunter reports that Henslowe's revenues in 1592 included £3 16 shillings and 8 pence for "*Henery VI*" for a performance on March 3, 1592. P. 119. But no one knows which part of *Henry VI* it was. Judging from Robert Greene's references in his September 1592 *Groatsworth of Witte*, to "a Tyger's heart wrapped in a Player's hyde," the successful performance must have been of *Henry IV – Part 3*. To put the amount of the proceeds into perspective, Chambers puts the average take at the Rose as 30 shillings a day from 1592-1597. Vol. I, p. 368. Riggs says that *Henry VI* was performed fourteen times between March 3, 1592 and June 23, so the "£3 16 shillings and 8 pence for "*Henery VI*" may have been a total take rather than a single performance. Nashe reported that 10,000 people or more witnessed Talbot's death.

Trying to figure out what Robert Greene intended in his *Groatsworth of Witte* published after his death on September 3, 1592, is a major industry in Shakespearean studies. Sams has a good copy of the document itself while Charlton Ogburn has, probably, the best analysis, beginning at p. 56. The Stratfordians interpret the document to be the first notice of Shakespeare in London. Connecting the comments made by Greene with Shakespeare is not certain. The Stratfordians believe that the references are to Shakespeare as playwright.

However, a close reading of the document shows that the diatribe written by Greene (or by Henry Chettle, another layer to this puzzle) was directed at players: "[T]hose puppets … <u>that spake from our mouths</u>, those anticks garnisht in our colors … trust them not: for there is an upstart Crow, unified with our feathers, that with his tyger's heart <u>wrapt in a player's hide</u>, supposes he is as well able to <u>bombast out</u> a blank verse as the best of you: and being an absolute *Johannes factotum*, is in his own conceit the only Shake-scene in a country." (Emphasis added.) If the reference was indeed to Shakespeare, it was to Shakespeare as a player, not as a playwright.

Robin's comment that "the ground rises to kiss his feet as he passes by," will appear in *Love's Labour's Lost*, Act V, Scene 2, as "the stairs, as he treads on them, kiss his feet."

The Tabard is famous as the place owned by Harry Bailey, the host in Geoffrey Chaucer's *The Canterbury Tales*. It is doubtful that there was a porch on the front of the Tabard for people to sit on. It appears that it was a typical inn, with an interior courtyard. It had a rebirth as an inn when stage coaches came into fashion but was ultimately done in by the railroads. It was torn down in the 1800s.

Chapter 71
The Tabard Inn

In 1592, Marlowe was arrested in Flushing for counterfeiting coins. He was sent back to England to be dealt with by Lord Burghley, who had taken over Walsingham's spy network upon Walsingham's death two years earlier. There is no record of any punitive action taken against Marlowe. See Riggs, beginning at p. 274.

King Edward II was entered in the Stationers' Register on July 6, 1593, five weeks after Marlowe's death, and published in 1594. It was apparently still being staged in 1622.

Chapter 72
The Heat of a Luxurious Bed

The title from this chapter comes from *Much Ado About Nothing*, Act IV, Scene 1, where Claudio, tricked by Don John into believing Hero, his betrothed, has been intimate with another man, tells Hero's father that he will not marry Hero:

There, Leonato, take her back again:
Give not this rotten orange to your friend;
...
She knows the heat of a luxurious bed;
Her blush is guiltiness, not modesty.

Clark believes that *Much Ado About Nothing* was Oxford writing about Philip Sydney as Claudio and Hero as the daughter of Sir Francis Walsingham. She reaches this conclusion because she believes the play was based upon an earlier version, *A historie of Ariodante and Genuora,* which was performed before the queen on February 12, 1583. At p 534, *et seq*. She also believes that Oxford was the basis for Benedict[147] and that Beatrice was based on Ann Cecil.

Anderson and the Ogburns believe Beatrice was based on Anne Vavasor. Anderson, p. 162; Ogburn, p. 481. See, *The Reader's Companion*, Chapters 2 – Greenwich Palace and 76 – Oxford Court - *Much Ado About Nothing.*

Meres did not mention *Much Ado About Nothing* in 1598 but did list *Love's Labour's Won* as one of Shakespeare's plays. Some think Meres was referring to *Much Ado.* See "Shakespeare's Many Much Ado's: *Alcestis*, Hercules, and *Love's Labour's Wonne*," by Earl Showerman in Brief Chronicles Vol. I (2009), at p. 109. Other scholars believe Meres was referring to *The Taming of the Shrew.* Gilvary summarizes some of the scholarly argument beginning at p. 94.

---

[147] The First Folio spells the character's name 'Benedick,' and this is how he is known. However, the Ogburns point out on p. 480 that Beatrice says "Benedictus! Why Benedictus?" and that there was an early 1600 play called *Benedicte and Betteris.* The Ogburns argue that Benedict was intended, i.e., 'well-spoken,' not Benedick, meaning 'well-wished.' Knowing Oxford's pride and his love of hidden meanings, it is almost impossible to believe that he would have written a play about Anne Vavasor and referred to himself as 'well-blessed' (obviously by her, if that was the name intended) instead of 'well-spoken.' This may be an example of where ignorance of the true author has prevented scholars from correcting an error that is as important as the name of one of the leading characters in one of the author's better plays.

Chapter 73
Ditchley House

Queen Elizabeth's visit to Ditchley and Sir Henry Lee began on September 3, 1592. John Greene had died the day before. Because Greene's death spawned *A Groatsworth of Wit* in October, the Ditchley visit has been moved back to May in *The Death of Shakespeare.* There is no evidence that any play was performed for the Queen during her visit to Ditchley in September.

Sir Henry Lee's reference to Don John being the cause of the loss of Sir Philip Sidney is incorrect. Don John died on October 1, 1578, eight years before Sidney was killed at the Battle of Zutphen. Sir Henry is confusing Don John with the Duke of Alva.

As to the Forgiveness Portrait, see, *The Reader's Companion*, Chapters 2 and 69.

The 1600 quarto of *Much Ado* has the name 'Kemp' appear instead of 'Dogberry' in the speech headings of Act IV, Scene 4. Gilvary, p. 94. Kemp obviously played the part. See Garber, p. 389.

Much Ado About Nothing is first mentioned with three other plays on a spare page in the Stationers' Register that Chambers dates to 1600. The play was formally registered on August 23, 1600. Gilvary, p. 91. Although the author of the article on *Much Ado* in Gilvary states that the plays in the informal listing were "to be staied," the prohibition, if displayed correctly, only applies to *As You Like It.* The three other plays, including *Much Ado*, were not stayed when formally registered on August 23, 1600. A quarto of *Much Ado* was printed the same year but the play was not reprinted until the 1623 First Folio. The first recorded performance was May 20, 1613, so *Much Ado* may have been called in. If it was, the reason is unknown (unless Anne asked it to be taken out of circulation—see Chapter 82— An Heir for his Lordship.)

As to too many jokes about cuckoldry, see Tanner, p. 186.

As to Anne Vavasor being impregnated twice by Oxford, see Nelson, p. 232. Oxford, Anne, and their baby was sent to the Tower on March 23, 1581, three months after Oxford had accused Howard, Arundel, and Southwell of conspiring to unseat the Queen. See Ward, p. 206, *et seq.*

"What is the definition of love in *Much Ado About Nothing*? The prime answer is there in the title: Love is much ado about nothing." Bloom, p. 200.

The description of Queen Elizabeth being able to look at one person, listen to another, all the while talking to a third person, is based on the following description:

> *Now, if any persone had eyther the gift or the stile to winne the hears of people, it was this Queene; and if ever shee did expresse the same, it was at that present, in coupling mildness with majesty as shee did, and in stately stouping to the meanest sort [or people]. All her facultyes were in motione, and every motione seemed a well guided action; her eye was set upon one, her eare listened to another, her judgment ranne upon a third, to a fourth shee addressed her speech; her spirit seemed to be every-where, and yet so intyre in her selfe, as it seemed to bee noe where else … distributing her smiles, looks, and graces, soe artividially, that thereupon the people … filled the eares of all men with immoderate extolling their Prince.*

Annals of the First Four Years of the Reign of Queen Elizabeth, Sir John Hawyard, London, 1840, p. 6.

Anne Vavasor's reference to Seneca is the basis for Hamlet's 'readiness is all' speech in Act 5, Scene 2. Seneca advised avoiding things one could not change, which includes what is past and what is to come. His philosophy embraced living each day and being 'ready' when the end comes. See Detobel, Robert, An Accident of Note: Chapman's Hamlet and the Earl of Oxford, "Brief Chronicles," Vol. II, p. 79, p. 88 et seq.

Oxford's son by Anne Vavasor was named Edward Vere (not 'de' Vere, as to which see *The Reader's Companion* to the Prologue, fn 16). He grew up in Sir Henry Lee's house at Ditchley. Oxford may have paid for his education at the

University of Leyden. He was knighted for bravery in battle in the Netherlands by his uncle, Sir Thomas Vere. He was a Member of Parliament for Newcastle-under-Lyme in Staffordshire in 1623 and was the first to translate into English the Greek histories of Polybius. It was said of him that he was 'all summer in the field, all winter in his study.' He died on active duty in 1629. For more information, see:

www.sourcetext.com/sourcebook/library/bowen/17vavasor.htm.

Ferdinando Stanley's mother, Lady Margaret Clifford, was next in line to the throne by virtue of her descent from Mary Tudor. Ferdinando would have become heir to Elizabeth had he survived his mother and Elizabeth. He predeceased both when he died on April 16, 1594. He was believed to have been poisoned by a massive dose of arsenic. He had turned in a step-brother who had tried to get him to take part in a plot by the Catholics to put him on the throne as a Catholic king. His act of loyalty to Elizabeth, however, made him suspect to both Protestants and Catholics. He may have been poisoned by Burghley (to get him out of the way), by the Catholic plotters to bring forward his brother, William, who may have been thought to be a better candidate, or by the relatives of the man he turned in. Essex may have been involved because Ferdinando had objected to Essex taking in some of the relatives who had tried to involve him in a plot against the Queen. It was known that Ferdinando feared for his life. Stanley raided the house of a relative of the man he turned in on April 2, 1594. He was dead two weeks later.

Burghley moved rapidly to marry Elizabeth Vere to Ferdinando's brother, William, who succeeded him as the Sixth Earl of Derby, but the wedding had to be delayed. Alice Spenser, Ferdinando's widow, claimed she was pregnant. William and Elizabeth had to wait to find out the gender of Alice's child. A son would have become the Sixth Earl of Derby instead of William. Instead, Alice gave birth to a daughter in December, 1594, and William thereby became the Sixth Earl of Derby. He and Elizabeth were married in January, 1595. Some scholars believe a *Midsummer Night's Dream* was written for their wedding.

The stricken deer hath help to heal his wound based on part of a poem by Oxford about a "stricken deer in Paradyse of Dainty Devices, 1576.[148]

> *The labouring man that tills the fertile soil,*
> *And reaps the harvest fruit, hath not indeed*
> *The gain, but pain; and if for all his toil*
> *He gets the straw, the lord will have the seed.*

The Earl of Oxford to the Reader in Bedingfield's Cardanus's Comfort (1576). *Fuller's* #21; *JTL* #11.

The inscription that Lettice Knollys reads is a modified version of the inscription on the floor of Holy Trinity Church that supposedly shelters Shakespeare's bones. (The original was replaced in the mid-18th century because it had sunk below the floor. Schoenbaum, p. 307.)

> *Good friend, for Jesus sake forbeare,*
> *To digg the dust encloaséd heare,*
> *Bleste be the man that spares these stones,*
> *And curst is he that moves my bones.*

Lettice Knollys was an extraordinary woman. (See, *The Reader's Companion*, Chapter 79.) Born in 1543 to one of Mary Boleyn's daughters, she lived to 97, dying in 1634.[149] She was Queen Elizabeth's first cousin once removed. In 1560, she married the first of her three husbands, Walter Devereux, who became the First Earl of Essex in 1570. She gave birth to a number of children, including Robert Devereux, who became the Second Earl of Essex (who was beheaded in 1601), and Penelope Devereux, who was the Stella in Sir Philip Sidney's

---

[148] Looney, John Thomas. *"Shackspear" Identified*, (Ruth Lloyd Miller, ed.) Jennings, La.: Minos Pub. Co. (1919), #17; *Miscellanies of the Fuller Worthies' Library*, Vol. IV (1872), #19. *This Star of England*, p. 54, and *Elizabethan Authors*, www.elizabethanauthors.com/oxfordpoems.htm. Music was printed for this by William Byrd in 1587.

[149] At 90, she was walking a mile a day, and died Christmas Day while sitting in her rocking chair.

Astrophel and Stella. Penelope married Lord Rich, becoming Lady Penelope Rich. The First Earl of Essex died in Ireland four years after his marriage to Lettice, but she may have already been involved in an affair with Robert Dudley, Earl of Leicester, who was the Queen's favorite. When Leicester secretly married Lettice in 1578, the Queen banished Lettice from court for life. In a later outburst to a Scottish diplomat, Elizabeth called Lettice a 'she-wolf.'

Lettice apparently had a good relationship with Dudley, and gave him a son who, unfortunately, died at the age of three. (The birth of this son was what caused Leicester's nephew, Sir Philip Sidney, to despair that his hope of inheriting Leicester's estate had been dashed.) Leicester died ten years later. Lettice was with him when he died. Because Leicester was accused of having poisoned his first wife, Amy Robstart, in 1560 (as well as others), the story went around that he unwittingly drank poison he had prepared for Lettice, having found out about her affair with Sir Christopher Blount. The mistake, if true, must have brought ironic smiles to Elizabethan courtiers, but the claim has not been substantiated.

Blount was a younger man (by twelve years), who Lettice married unexpectedly a year later. Again, she apparently had a good marriage with him. Unfortunately, he was beheaded along with her son, the Second Earl of Essex in 1601 for their part in the Essex uprising.

Lettice's first two marriages left her immensely wealthy but, being banned from the court, she stayed mostly in the countryside and played no role at court. Her efforts to save her husband and son in 1601 fell on deaf ears. King James forgave the debts owed by her second husband to the crown (upwards of £50,000)[150] and litigation over whether John Dudley[151] was

---

150 And scholars accuse Oxford of being a spendthrift?

151 Not Arthur Dudley, another possible illegitimate son of Leicester and Elizabeth, who disappeared in Spain where he had run when he was told he the Queen's son.

Leicester's rightful heir was finally resolved in her favor by the Star Chamber in 1603. A contrary decision would have divested Lettice of what she had inherited in 1588.[152]

The early historian John Aubrey wrote: "[Sir Henry Lee] erected a noble altar monument of marble, whereon his effigies in armour lay. At the feet was [that] of his mistress, Anne Vavasour, which occasioned these verses:

> *Here lies the good old knight Sir Harry,*
> *Who loved well but would not marry;*
> *While he lived and had his feeling,*
> *She did lie and he was kneeling.*
> *Now he's dead and cannot feel,*
> *He doth lie and she doth kneel.*

History of Parliament, a biographical dictionary of Members of the House of Commons.

The author of the effigy is not identified. Could it have been Oxford? He had the wit as well as the motivation to write it.

Conyers Reed mentions the "ribald epigram" but would not repeat it because "other versions have been preserved." (Read, Sir Henry Lee, p. 237.) He was obviously referring to the above-quoted verses. He did report, however, that "John Aubrey also tells us that at the feet of the effigies of Sir Henry lay that of Anne, and adds that 'some bishop did threaten to have this monument defaced (at least to remove Mrs. A Vavasour's effigies.)'" The bishop must have been objecting to the verses that Sir Henry put on what appears to have been a common tomb for him and for Anne:

> *Under this Stone intombed lies a faire and worthy Dame*
> *Daughter to Henry Vavsor Anne Vavasour [sic] her name*

---

[152] John Dudley, who was illegitimate, was trying to be declared legitimate to divest Lettice, his step-mother, of what she had inherited from his father, her second husband. This was the reverse of what Mary Vere, Oxford's sister, tried to do by having the marriage of Oxford's parents declared void. See *The Reader's Companion* to Chapter 92

She living with Sr. Henry Lee for love long tyme did dwell
Death could not part them but that here they rest within one cell.

Anne Vavasor appears to have been a remarkable woman. Although she and Sir Henry were never able to marry, they remained a 'married couple' until Sir Henry died in 1611. Letters show that Sir Henry included her in social engagements with Queen Elizabeth and with King James and Queen Anne (Read, *Sir Henry Lee*, p. 211). In 1608, Queen Anne had "long and large discourse" with Anne Vavasor on a visit to Sir Henry's home. And, as late as 1622, Anne Vavasor was the subject of a bigamy suit (possibly brought by Sir Henry's nephew to disinherit the still-living Anne) for "having two husbands now alive." She lost and was fined £2,000. Read, p. 243.

Elspeth Trentham's eagerness to spend the night in the parson's bed in Neat Enstone is fed by her cousin's hint that the bed is well-known for providing male heirs to those who spend the night in it. This is fiction.

Chapter 74
Edward II

Edward II was performed in 1594 but is believed to have been written earlier. Like *Dido*, it flouts the prevailing rules of the time. Even read today, it seems more outrageous than it needed to be. Whether Marlowe preferred boys to women is unknown. The same is true of Lord Hunsdon, who may, indeed, have been the father of Aemilia Bassano's son. Everyone seems to believe he was.

Ben Jonson's original name was Ben Johnson. Ben eliminated the 'h' when he became a playwright. He thought it made him look more sophisticated. He had not made the change by 1593. To avoid confusion, he already has his new name when he meets Marlowe and Oxford in front of the Steelyard.

The Steelyard was almost as old as the Boar's Head. It was located farther to the west and closer to the river. The Hanseatic traders from the Baltic founded it centuries earlier. It became the hangout for Ben Jonson and the other poets and playwrights who followed Oxford. Anderson says it was famous for a number of specialties, including smoked ox-tongue and pickled herring. Anderson, p. 256.

Chapter 75
Rosencrantz and Guildenstern

Peregrine Bertie, Lord Willoughby, was married to Mary Vere and, thus, was Oxford's brother-in-law. The Queen posted Willoughby to Denmark in 1582 to award the Order of the Garter to Frederik II, King of Denmark. Willoughby returned a few years later to negotiate lower taxes on English ships passing Elsinore on their way to and from the Baltic. While Willoughby was in Denmark, he visited Tycho Brahe's castle, Uraniborg, on the nearby island of Hven.

Tycho Brahe had made his mark by proving that the heavens were not eternally unchangeable, as had been believed since Ptolemy, who believed that the stars and planets revolved around the earth. Copernicus, a near-contemporary of Brahe's in Poland, suggested that the earth revolved around the sun (the heliocentric theory as opposed to the Ptolemaic system where everything revolved around the earth). Brahe proposed a compromise in 1577 in which the sun and moon orbited the earth while the other planets orbited the sun (the geo-heliocentric system). Brahe's theory was short-lived as Copernicus' theory became more and more accepted as the telescope allowed for more accurate measurements of the heaven. For a time, however, Brahe was the man of the hour.

Brahe was from one of four families in Denmark that dominated Denmark's political and cultural scene. The other three were the Balle, the Rosencrantzes, and the Guildensterns. Tycho Brahe was even descended from Rosencrantzes and Guildensterns himself. Willoughby reported that three of the twenty-four diners at a state dinner while he was there were Rosencrantzes and Guildensterns.

Brahe wrote a letter to Thomas Savile in December 1590 in which he wished to be remembered to Dr. John Dee and

Thomas Digges and included four copies of his portrait. His *Introduction to the New Astronomy,* published in 1588, included his geo-heliocentric system.

Thomas Digges (grandfather of the Thomas Digges who wrote a prefatory poem to the 1623 First Folio) was a noted mathematician and astronomer in England who advocated the Copernican theory. Digges may have been the first to propose an infinite universe filled with stars. As to his relationship with Dee, Raleigh, Giovanni Bruno, Marlowe, John Donne, the Earl of Northumberland, Thomas Harriott, George Chapman, Sidney, and Nicholas Hill (who may have been the first to champion Copernicus, and who may have worked as secretary for the Earl of Oxford), see *William Empson: Essays on Renaissance Literature: Volume 1, Donne and the New Philosophy* (2002), and Hugh Trevor-Roper, *Catholics, Anglicans, and Puritans - Seventeenth-Century Essays* (1987).

Sir John Dee (1527-1609) was a mathematician, astronomer, astrologer, occultist, navigator, and consultant to Queen Elizabeth I. He chose the date for her coronation. He straddled science and magic and, although a brilliant man, gradually fell into believing in the occult and is not considered a true scientist.

Sir Walter Raleigh (1554-1618) became one of Elizabeth's most famous courtiers. He obtained a patent to settle Virginia, although he never went on any of the voyages to the New World. He was sent to the Tower by Elizabeth for marrying without her permission, and by James for being involved in the Bye Plot. James let him out of prison to captain a fleet to the Orinoco that failed, which was what James wanted. He had given the information about the fleet to the Spanish to ensure Raleigh's death. The Spanish didn't believe the English would send them such information but the directions were found in the citadel Raleigh's troops sacked. James had Raleigh executed upon his return.

The mathematician Thomas Harriot anticipated Galileo in seeing sunspots and making a lunar map. He and Christopher Marlowe were friends of Raleigh. Harriot helped Raleigh design some of the great fighting ships of the navy, which was one of the reasons the English were successful against the Spanish in 1588.

Henry Percy, the 9th Earl of Northumberland, was given the "Wizard Earl" sobriquet for his scientific and alchemical experiments, his passion for cartography, and his large library. He was mildly deaf and had a slight speech impediment. Two known portraits of him show him leaning on his left arm. He used a telescope to map the moon several months before Galileo did the same. Some think the "school of night" reference in *Love's Labour's Lost* is to the 9th Earl and his coterie, but this has been discounted by more sober minds.

Sic transit fortuna is a twist of the Latin proverb, *sic transit gloria mundi.*

The most interesting connection between the play *Hamlet* and the names of two characters in the play—Rosencrantz and Guildenstern—is the fact that two young men named Rosencrantz and Guildenstern actually visited England in 1592. Frederik Rosencrantz was twenty-one years of age at the time; his traveling companion, Knud Guildenstern, was seventeen. They were on their way back to Denmark after making the Grand Tour of Europe and Italy. Both had studied at Wittenberg.[153] Their activities in England are unknown but it is likely they would have stopped in to see Lord Willoughby. See "In Search of Rosencrantz and Guildenstern" in *Shakespeare Matters,* Vol. 3: no. 3, Spring 2004, p. 1 and appendices on p. 17. The author, C. V. Berney, cites the proposal by Peter Usher in 2001 that *Hamlet* contains a hidden layer in which the debate between Ptolemaic cosmology is represented by Claudius, the Copernican system is represented by Hamlet and the University of Wittenberg, with Rosencrantz and Guildenstern representing Tycho Brahe's theory.

---

[153] Lord Burghley attended Wittenberg.

Lady Mary Vere, Oxford's full sister (as opposed to his older half-sister, Katherine), was known as a difficult person. Peregrine Bertie's mother, the Countess of Suffolk, wrote Burghley in 1577, when she realized Peregrine and Mary were intending to marry for love, that she was not in favor of the match and gave her reasons: "[i]f she should prove like her brother [Edward de Vere], if an empire follows her [i.e., her dowry were great], I should be sorry to match so. She said she could not rule her brother's tongue nor help the rest of her faults." Anderson, p. 126; Professor Nelson quotes the same language at p. 172 but adds that the Countess also said that she was "in fear of this marriage and quarrels."

Thomas Cecil, Burghley's oldest son, wrote in 1578 that "because of an unkindness, the Lady Mary 'will be beaten with that rod which heretofore she prepared for others.'" Nelson, p. 180. Anderson says this letter was written by Thomas "of the connubial pyrotechnics he had witnessed during a recent visit." Thomas apparently related that Peregrine's mother had visited the couple "to appease certain unkindness grown between her son and his wife." Anderson, p. 131. The complete letter appears in Ogburn at p. 592.

Clark thinks *The Taming of the Shrew* "caricatured the marriage of [Oxford's} sister … to Peregrine Bertie." P. 102. Anderson thinks the language in Sir Thomas Cecil's letter that Lady Mary 'will be beaten with that rod which heretofore she prepared for others' is a "succinct plot summary for *The Taming of the Shrew*." Anderson, p. 131. The Ogburns, both parents and son, agree. *This Star of England*, p. 158; Ogburn, p. 594. Anderson says that "[t]he numerous parallels between de Vere's sister and brother-in-law and *The Taming of the Shrew's* infamous couple leave little room for doubt as to the play's original biographical source." P. 130.

As with many other Shakespeare plays, there was *another* shrew play: *The Taming of a Shrew*. A quarto exists from 1594, when it was performed at the Rose (along with *Titus Andronicus* and *Hamlet!*). See, Sams, beginning at p. 136. *A Shrew* is half the length of *The Shrew*. Which one preceded the other, and whether they were both written by Shakespeare, or one by him and the other by another playwright, is a subject too complicated and distant to merit mention in *The Death of Shakespeare*. While Henslowe reports the playing of *The Taming of A Shrew* in 1594, in *The Death of Shakespeare*, it will be The *Shrew*. *A Shrew* will go unmentioned.

After Shackspear is given *The Shrew* by Oxford, he decides to add local color to the final version in order to include evidence in the text that the plays are by him. Thus, he makes Christopher Sly a native of Burton on Heath, a village near Stratford, and Marian Hacket, the fat ale-wife, a resident of Wincot, which is four miles from Stratford. Akrigg, p. 221, for the geographical distances only. Schoenbaum says Barton on Heath is fifteen miles from Stratford where Shakespeare's uncle, Edmund Lambert, who had married one of Mary Shakespeare's seven sisters, lived. Schoenbaum, p. 95

Schmidt defines "alewife" [not ale-wife, as the word appears in *The Taming* and in *Henry IV, Part 2*, Act 2, Scene 2] as "a woman who keeps an alehouse." Of course, an ale-wife is also an oily fish used almost exclusively in making fertilizer.

Lord Willoughby's comment that '*one must be brave, but in marriage, discretion is the better part of valor*' will reappear in *Henry IV Part 1*, Act 5, Scene 4, when Falstaff dusts himself off after faking his death and says:

Falstaff:

> *[Rising up] Embowelled! if thou embowel me to-day,*
> *I'll give you leave to powder me and eat me too*
> *to-morrow. 'Sblood,'twas time to counterfeit, or*
> *that hot termagant Scot had paid me scot and lot too.*
> *Counterfeit? I lie, I am no counterfeit: to die,*
> *is to be a counterfeit; for he is but the*
> *counterfeit of a man who hath not the life of a man:*
> *but to counterfeit dying, when a man thereby*
> *liveth, is to be no counterfeit, but the true and*
> *perfect image of life indeed. The better part of*

valour is discretion; in the which better part I have saved my life.

Chapter 76
An Heir for his Lordship

Osso bucco may be a late 19th century creation but it is obviously based on a peasant dish using veal shanks and gremolata, which is the dish served to Oxford in this chapter. As to Virginia Padoana, see Chapter 76.

There have been many attempts to decipher just where the Queen's nickname for Oxford—the Turk—came from. Some believe it was because he went to Turkey when he was in Italy. Feldman thinks it could be related to the Gaelic word "torc," as to which see pp. 41-42. Oxford's masquerade as the Turkish ambassador, as related by Elspeth in this chapter, is fiction.

Degree being vizarded,
The unworthiest shows as fairly in the mask.

Troilus and Cressida, Act I, Scene 3

Oxford's impromptu outburst at the end of this chapter is a based on Sonnet 2:

When forty winters shall besiege thy brow,
And dig deep trenches in thy beauty's field,
Thy youth's proud livery so gazed on now,
Will be a totter'd weed of small worth held:
Then being asked, where all thy beauty lies,
Where all the treasure of thy lusty days;
To say, within thine own deep sunken eyes,
Were an all-eating shame, and thriftless praise.
How much more praise deserv'd thy beauty's use,
If thou couldst answer 'This fair child of mine
Shall sum my count, and make my old excuse,
Proving his beauty by succession thine!
This were to be new made when thou art old,
And see thy blood warm when thou feel'st it cold.

Falstaff's remark that he would now be able to claim that he was "the cause of gardening in others!" is based on his comment in *Henry IV – Part Two,* Act I, Scene 2:

> *Men of all sorts take a pride to gird at me: the brain of this foolish-compounded clay, man, is not able to invent anything that tends to laughter, more than I invent or is invented on me: I am not only witty in myself, but the cause that wit is in other men.*

"Wit" meant more in the 16th century than it does today. It meant something closer to 'genius' but has degraded to the point where it means being facile in verbal repartee. See, *Studies in Words* by C. S. Lewis, Cambridge Univ. Press, second edition 1994, beginning at p. 84. "I take it that *wit* in the sense now current means that sort of mental agility or gymnastic which uses language as the principal equipment of its gymnasium." At p. 97. Lewis classifies this form of 'wit' as *the dangerous sense of wit.* Falstaff's comment that he is 'witty' does not mean he is clever, if even that, but that he is a genius and the cause of genius in others, as is borne out by Dryden's comment in *Dramatic Poesy* that Jonson was 'the more correct poet, but Shakespeare the greater wit.' At pp. 95-96. Dryden did not mean that Shakespeare was funny or clever, although Sir John's comment that other men are unable "to invent anything that tends to laughter ... more than I invent or is invented on me," can be taken as the beginning of the slide from the use of 'wit' to describe Shakespeare as genius to the evolution of 'wit' as causing 'laughter.' Oxford, however, always writing on many levels, was so in love with Falstaff that it is very difficult to limit Falstaff's remark to describing him merely as the cause of 'laughter' in others.

Oxford's question as to when Falstaff last saw his knee is based on Prince Hal's question in Act II, Scene 4, *Henry IV – Part One*:

Prince Hal: *How long is't ago, Jack, since thou sawest thine own knee?*

Falstaff: *My own knee! when I was about thy years, Hal, I was not an eagle's talon in the waist;*

Oxford is about to write *The Taming of the Shrew* where his request for a kiss from Lady Elspeth will reappear in Act V, Scene 1, as:

Petruchio: *First kiss me, Kate, and we will.*

Katharina: *What, in the midst of the street?*

Petruchio: *What, art thou ashamed of me?*

Katharina: *No, sir, God forbid; but ashamed to kiss*
[in the middle of the street].

Robin's disclosure to Lady Elspeth that he has been making copies of the plays and keeping them in his sleeping place under the stairs is fiction. No one knows who had possession of the plays that were used in the printing of the First Folio in 1623. The few plays published in 1609 contain a cryptic reference to the printer's copy having been in the hands of "the Grand Possessors." The reference was removed in the second edition. Some have thought the reference was to the two earls, "the learned brethren" to whom the First Folio was dedicated. Robin will continue to make a copy of each play and Falstaff in 1604 will spirit them out of King's Place in Hackney as Oxford lies dying to keep them out of the hands of Cecil who wants to destroy them. Falstaff will turn them over to Ben Jonson in the summer of 1623 when King James meets with Sir Horace Vere, Sir Robert Cecil, and Ben Jonson on the *Jupiter* downstream of Greenwich Palace to decide that the plays written by the Earl of Oxford will be published under Shakespeare's name.

'It is an abomination that scenes invented merely to be spoken should be published to be read,' is based on John Marston's *Preface to the Malcontent*, 1604, in which he says: "One only thing affects me; to think, that scenes, invented merely to be spoken, should be enforcively published to be read, and that the least hurt I can receive is to do myself the wrong. But since others otherwise would do me more, the least inconvenience is to be accepted; I have therefore myself set forth this comedie." Globe, p. xvii

Chapter 77
The Taming of the Shrew

"[There is] delicious irony that is Kate's undersong, centered on the great line 'I am asham'd that women are so simple.' It requires a very good actress to deliver this set piece properly, and a better director than we tend to have now, if the actress is given her full chance, *for she is advising women how to rule absolutely while feigning obedience*." Bloom, page 33, quoting lines from Act V, Scene 2. (Emphasis added.)

The father of Katharina (or Kate) in *The Taming of the Shrew* is *Baptista Minola*. Oxford borrowed money from a money-lender in Padua named *Baptista Nigrone* and in Venice from *Pasquino Spinola*. It appears, then, that the name of Kate's father in *The Taming of the Shrew* is a conflation of the names of these money-lenders. Ogburns, p. 88, 159; Ward, pp. 108, 109. Professor Nelson mentions their names but misses the connection. P. 123, 129. The Ogburns spot it and think Kate's father represented Burghley.

A further connection between the name of Kate's father in *The Taming of the Shrew* and another Spinola is found in a lawsuit in London in November, 1609. The suit was over ten acres of land and a garden in London that had been deeded by the Queen to Benedict Spinola on January 29, 1575. Spinola transferred it to Oxford at an unknown date. On July 4, 1591, Oxford transferred the property to trustees for the benefit of [his then wife? his wife to be?] Elizabeth Trentham. Nelson, p. 335.

This transaction raises a number of interesting questions. January 29, 1575, was shortly before Oxford's departure for the continent. His license to "pass beyond the seas" was issued on January 24. Nelson, p. 119. On January 30, 1575, he set up a trust for his wife and children and for the payment of his debts should he not return. Nelson, p. 120. Professor Nelson thinks Oxford "probably left London during the first week of February," because Burghley reckoned Oxford's accounts from "February when my Lord went.'" The transfer of the ten acres and garden to Benedict Spinola, therefore, looks like a security transaction to provide Oxford with money for his trip.

Was this Benedict Spinola related to the Venetian moneylender Pasquino Spinola? Did the two Spinolas and the ten acres of land have anything to do with the money that was sent out to Oxford while he was in Italy? Burghley refers to a "Mr. Spinola here in London" who was instrumental "from tyme to tyme for the whole tyme my Lord of Oxford was absent [in Italy]" in procuring "all of the money that was sent over to hym." Nelson, p. 153. It may be that the idea for the name of Kate's father in *The Taming of the Shrew* was "Mr. Spinola here in London" rather than Benedict Spinola in Venice. However, there is no evidence that Oxford ever dealt with "Mr. Spinola here in London," who worked with Lord Burghley, so the best guess is that that the moneylender in Venice was the source of the name of Kate's father (as well as the money Oxford spent on the continent).

The record does not show how long Spinola held the ten acres and garden before Oxford transferred the property to trustees for the benefit of Elizabeth Trentham on July 4, 1591. This date is a bright line as to when the Earl and his future wife began their relationship. They must have begun courting some time before July, 1591, unless Oxford backed into the marriage to keep Heneage, Burghley, and others from seizing his property to pay Oxford's creditors. Marriage was different back then. In Oxford's case, he needed the Queen's permission to marry. It is not out of the range of possibilities that the Queen may have directed her lady in waiting to marry Oxford to settle him down, to give Elizabeth Trentham a husband (and Oxford an heir), and to block his creditors. The triple play would have intrigued her.

A further question is whether the lawsuit in 1609 (the surviving document is dated November 26, 1609) is somehow related to the sale of King's Place in Hackney by Oxford's widow, which occurred on April 1, 1609. Nelson, p.432. The 1609 lawsuit over ten acres and garden was clearly not about King's Place:

> "[W] reference to a tenement and 10 acres of land in the city of London, belonging to be said that university [the plaintiff], which was first transferred to Benedict Spinola in 1575 by the Queen, and then to Oxford, and then in trust for Elizabeth Trentham.

The lawsuit was also not about Oxford Court since the property is described as "the Garden of Christes Church in the parish of St. Buttolph London." Nelson, p. 335.

Chapter 78
The Death of Robert Greene

Robert Greene died September 2, 1592.[154] A month or so later, Greene's autobiographical *Groats-worth of Witte, bought with a million of Repentance* was published. In it were passages that Stratfordians have long treasured because they believe Greene was referring to Shakespeare as a playwright. Unfortunately, they are wrong.

A modernized version of the relevant portion of *A Groatsworth* follows:

> To those Gentlemen his Quondam acquaintance, that spend their wits in making Plays, R. G. wisheth a better exercise, and wisdom to prevent his extremities.
>
> If woeful experience may move you (Gentlemen) to beware, or unheard of wretchedness entreat you to take heed, [here follows how Greene came to religion.] Defer

---

154 Thomas Nashe related how he, Greene, and "Will Monox" dined on Rhenish wine and pickled herring a month before Greene's death. See *The Reader's Companion* to Chapter 30. A site that claims Christopher Marlowe wrote the plays believes that Greene was poisoned at this meal. *http://themarlowestudies.org/z-ule/ch9-128-143.pdf.*

not (with me) till this last point of extremity; for little knowst thou how in the end thou shalt be visited.

Wonder not (for with thee Will I first begin), thou famous gracer of Tragedians, that *Greene*, who hath said with thee (like the fool in his heart) There is no God, should now give glory unto his greatness: for penetrating is his power, his hand lies heavy upon me, he hath spoken unto me with a voice of thunder, and I have felt he is a God that can punish enemies.

With thee I join young *Juvenal* [identified as Thomas Nashe], that biting Satirist, that lastly with me together writ a Comedy. Sweet boy, might I advise thee, be advised, and get not many enemies by bitter words: inveigh against vain men, for thou canst do it, no man better, no man so well: thou hast a liberty to reprove all, and none more; for one being spoken to, all are offended, none being blamed no man is injured. Stop shallow water still running, it will rage, or tread on a worm and it will turn: then blame not Scholars vexed with sharp lines, if they reprove thy too much liberty of reproof.

And thou no less deserving than the other two, in some things rarer, in nothing inferior; driven (as myself) to extreme shifts, a little have I to say to thee: and were it not an idolatrous oath, I would swear by sweet *S. George,* thou art unworthy better hap, sith thou dependest on so mean a stay. Base minded men all three of you, if by my misery ye be not warned: for unto none of you (like me) sought those burrs to cleave: those Puppets (I mean) that speak from our mouths, those Antics garnished in our colours. Is it not strange that I, to whom they all have been beholding: is it not like that you, to whom they all have been beholding, shall (were ye in that case that I am now) be both at once of them forsaken? Yes, trust them not [the Puppets]: for there is an upstart Crow [one of the Puppets], beautified with

> our feathers, that with his *Tiger's heart wrapped in a Players hide*, supposes he is as well able to bombast out a blank verse as the best of you: and being an absolute *Iohannes fac totum*, is in his own conceit the only Shake-scene in a country. O that I might entreat your rare wits to be employed in more profitable courses: & let those Apes [Puppets] imitate your past excellence, and never more acquaint them with your admired inventions. I know the best husband of you all will never prove an Usurer, and the kindest of them all will never seek you a kind nurse: yet whilst you may, seek you better Masters; for it is pity men of such rare wits [the three playwrights], should be subject to the pleasure of such rude grooms [the Puppets].

The writing is terrible, even for 1592, but it is clear that Greene is referring to three playwrights (whom he dare not name because of England's strict libel laws) when he writes: "To those Gentlemen … that spend their wits in making plaies." He begins with a plea to a playwright most people identify as Marlowe: "Wonder not (for thee will I first begin) thou famous gracer of Tragedians, that Greene, who hath said with thee …There is no God, shoulde now give glorie unto his greatness …"

Greene goes on to the second playwright: "With thee [Marlowe] I joyne young Juveall [Thomas Nashe], that byting Satyrist …"

The third target is more difficult to identify, although it seems to be George Peele, whom Greene calls "no lesse deserving than the other two, in some things rarer, in nothing inferiour …"

Having described the three playwrights, "[b]ase-minded men all three of you, if by my miserie you be not warned," Greene turns to "those Puppets [i.e., players] …that spake from our mouths, those Antics garnisht in our colours. … Yes trust them not: for there is an upstart Crow, beautified with our feathers that with his *Tygers hart wrapt in a Players hyde,*[155] supposes he is as well able to bombast[156] out a blanke verse as the best of you: and being an absolute *Johannes factotum*, is in his owne conceit that onely Shake-scene in a countrey. … [F]or it is pittie men of such rare wits, should be subject to the pleasure of such rude grooms."[157] Greene goes on to say "I might insert two more [players – he does not identify them, of course] and then returns to the three playwrights: "But now returne I againe to you three…"

Notice that the person with a "Tygers hart" has a "*Players*" hide. How much more specific can Greene get? The "upstart Crowe" is a "*player*," not a "*playwright*!" In other words, Shake-scene may be Shakes-peare, but he is a player, not a playwright.

The above analysis shows that the *tyger's hart* and Shake-scene comments provide no support for an argument that Shakespeare was such a successful playwright by the summer of 1592 that Greene would take time to warn his fellow playwrights about Shakespeare *as a playwright*. Greene is deriding Shakespeare as a player who "supposes he is well able to bombast out a blanke verse as the best of you."

The sober Shakespearean biographer, Samuel Schoenbaum, agreed (at least at first): "The thrust of the passage as a whole is against the actors … who batten on the [playwrights]." P. 152. Despite this admission, he too succumbs to the need to add to evidence favoring William Shakespeare as a playwright by quietly sliding to a position on the very next page that "[m]ost of the more reliable authorities now think that Greene was complaining because Shakespeare, a mere uneducated player, had the effrontery to compete as a dramatist with his betters." P. 153.

---

155 Henry VI – Part 3, Act II, Scene 4.

156 "Bombast," "cotton used to stuff out garments; metaphorically as 'fustian', defined as 'course cotton stuff; high-sounding nonsense' and, as, 'high-sounding and at the same time nonsensical.'" Schmidt. Similar in *Shakespeare's Words*.

157 See comment in First Folio – horse parker?

The playwrights who are the objects of warning on page 151 are quickly forgotten and Shakespeare is added to the list: "Greene's notorious letter castigated not only Shake-scene [sic] but also two old comrades." P. 153. The two 'old comrades' were Marlowe and Nashe. What happened to the third playwright Schoenbaum had identified as George Peele on page 151? Schoenbaum had to make room for William, newly anointed as the third playwright. Maybe Samuel said that William came before George. Slide a player in; slide a playwright out.[158]

Henry Chettle in *Kind-Hart's Dream* is no support for the argument that Greene was directing his criticism at Shakespeare as the third playwright. He describes Greene's *Groatsworth* (which some suspect Chettle wrote – he admits he "writ it over') as "a letter written to divers play-makers [which was] offensively by one or two of them taken." Chettle, therefore, confirms that *Groatsworth* was aimed at three playwrights, not actors. Chettle continues to describe, in very vague terms, the reactions of two of the three playwrights to Greene's last work. Efforts to apply Chettle's praise of the honesty and uprightness of one of them as directed at Shakespeare are unsuccessful—Greene was talking about playwrights and not an "upstart Crow, beautified with our feathers."

An interesting confirmation of this conclusion is found at the end of *Groatsworth* where Greene bids farewell "with this conceited Fable of that old Comedian *Aesope*" and relates the story of the ant and the grasshopper. Unable to stop, Greene launches into "Roberto's lament," which is clearly about him. He describes Roberto sighing sadly as he laid his head on his hand and his elbow on the earth. "On the other side of the hedge sat one that heard his sorrow …" Roberto asks the man his profession. "Truly sir, said he, I am a player."

---

158 The Globe substitutes Lodge for Nashe: "[T]here can be little doubt that [*Groatsworth*] was intended for Marlowe, Lodge, and Peele." P. 2356, fn 33. So much for clarity as to who were the objects subjects of Greene's bile, but all the scholars agree they were playwrights and any reference to Shakespeare in *Groatsworth* is as a player.

Roberto wonders at the player's elegant dress and says he took the player as a gentleman. The player tells Roberto he used to carry his "playing Fardle a foote-backe' but now his "share in playing apparel will not be sold for two hundred pounds." Roberto is surprised because he thinks the player's "voice is nothing gratious." The player doesn't like this comment and goes on to say how famous he has become for playing various roles. Greene goes on to have the player describe himself as "a country Author, passing at a Morrall, for twas I that pende the Morrall of man's witte, the Dialogue of Dives, and for seven years space was absolute interpreter to the puppets."

The player now sounds like a playwright (he "penned the Moral of man's wit, the Dialogue of Dives") but when Roberto asks him "how meane you to use me?" the player says, "why sir, in making Playes." Stratfordians have found comfort in this account because it seems to refer to Shakespeare and may explain where William Shakespeare was before 1592. However, the person on the other side of the hedge is a player and not a playwright; he wants to use Greene "in making Playes."

It looks like Greene is relating a meeting with Shakespeare who had acquired a "share in the playing apparel." Shakespeare had not yet become a sharer in the Lord Chamberlain's Men (that occurred in 1594) but he may have acquired an interest in another company. Or, he may have acquired money in other pursuits and invested the money in "playing apparel," which was the most valuable asset of any playing company. The comparison between the player and Shakespeare also fails because Greene was older than Shakespeare, and "the Morrall of man's witte, [and] the Dialogue of Dives" were written long before Shakespeare could have "penned" them. Finally, "absolute interpreter to the puppets" sounds like a player/director.

The man being skewered in *Groatsworth* is a player, therefore, not a playwright, and thus provides no support for the claim that Shakespeare wrote the plays. Despite these facts, Stratfordians cling to the life-ring they think Greene threw to them that Shakespeare was a playwright 'bombasting' out blank verse. Warton, at p. 398: "Dekker, in his satire against Jonson cited above, accuses Jonson of having stolen some jokes from the Christmas plays of the lawyers. 'You shall swear not to bombast [sic] out a new play with an old lining of jests stolen from the Temple-revels."' But Dekker's use of the word 'bombast,' as a verb to indicate quick-writing a new play by borrowing lines stolen from older plays, is no proof that his use is the same as Greene's.

Chapter 79
Whitehall Palace and *The Taming of the Shrew*

Lettice Knollys was a cousin of Elizabeth. (See also *The Reader's Companion* to Chapter 73.) She first married the Earl of Essex by whom she had Robert Devereux, who became the Earl of Essex and the last favorite of Queen Elizabeth. Lettice subsequently married Leicester, thereby incurring Elizabeth's wrath. The Queen banned her from court for many years and, when allowed to come back, upset Elizabeth again and was never allowed back. Lettice next married Sir Christopher Blount who died with her son by Essex in the abortive attempt in 1600 to pry Elizabeth away from Sir Robert Cecil. Lettice lived quietly in the countryside thereafter, dying at the age of 94 in 1626.

As to the staging of *The Shrew* (and a play called *The Taming of A Shrew*), see *The Reader's Companion* to Chapter 75 – Rosencrantz and Guildenstern.

1593

Chapters 80-91

Chapter 80
Henry Is Christened (in the Boar's Head)

Henry de Vere, 18th Earl of Oxford, was born on February 24, 1593, while his parents were living in Stoke Newington, which is just to the north of the district where the Curtain and the Theater were located. Nelson, p. 343. The location of his baptism is unknown. In *The Death of Shakespeare,* Oxford and his family stay at Oxford Court until they move to Hackney in 1597.

As to "Roscius" and "Soul of our Age," see *The Reader's Companion* to the Prologue.

"Women are made to bear," is spoken by Petruchio to Katharina in *The Taming of the Shrew*, Act I, Scene 1.

"*In nomine patri et fili sancti*" is a corruption of "*In nomine Patris et Filii Spiritus Sancti*," part of the Latin Trinitarian formula. Falstaff drops the 'spiritu' part, probably as a dig at Oxford, and makes the phrase "in the name of the father and the holy son," meaning, in bad Latin, Oxford's holy son.

The incantation the men speak over the baby will return in what the witches speak in *Macbeth*, Act IV, Scene 1:

First Witch

> *Round about the cauldron go;*
> *In the poison'd entrails throw.*
> *Toad, that under cold stone*
> *Days and nights has thirty-one*
> *Swelter'd venom sleeping got,*
> *Boil thou first i' the charmed pot.*

All

> *Double, double toil and trouble;*
> *Fire burn, and cauldron bubble.*

Second Witch

Fillet of a fenny snake,
In the cauldron boil and bake;
Eye of newt and toe of frog,
Wool of bat and tongue of dog,
Adder's fork and blind-worm's sting,
Lizard's leg and owlet's wing,
For a charm of powerful trouble,
Like a hell-broth boil and bubble.

All

Double, double toil and trouble;
Fire burn and cauldron bubble.

Third Witch

Scale of dragon, tooth of wolf,
Witches' mummy, maw and gulf
Of the ravin'd salt-sea shark,
Root of hemlock digg'd i' the dark,
Liver of blaspheming Jew,
Gall of goat, and slips of yew
Silver'd in the moon's eclipse,
Nose of Turk and Tartar's lips,
Finger of birth-strangled babe
Ditch-deliver'd by a drab,
Make the gruel thick and slab:
Add thereto a tiger's chaudron,
For the ingredients of our cauldron.

All

Double, double toil and trouble;
Fire burn and cauldron bubble.

Second Witch

Cool it with a baboon's blood,
Then the charm is firm and good.

Falstaff with horns is from *The Merry Wives of Windsor*, Act 4, Scene 4. Mistress Ford says:

> *Marry, this is our device:*
> *That Falstaff at that oak shall meet with us,*
> *Disguised like Herne [the hunter], with huge horns on his head.*

Elspeth's fright that her son would go to Limbo and not to Heaven if he died before he was baptized was real. She was a member of the Church of England, but the doctrine of the Catholic Church on this question may have been the reason she was so upset when she found Oxford had taken their baby out into a snowstorm. "Infants who die unbaptised cannot be saved because (1) they have not received the sacrament, and (2) they cannot make a personal act of faith that would supply for the sacrament." *The Hope Of Salvation For Infants Who Die Without Being Baptised*, published with the approval of the Holy Father in 2007, § 21. *The Hope* states the following:

> It is clear that the traditional teaching on this topic has concentrated on the theory of *limbo*, understood as a state which includes the souls of infants who die subject to original sin and without baptism, and who, therefore, neither merit the beatific vision, nor yet are subjected to any punishment, because they are not guilty of any personal sin. This theory, elaborated by theologians beginning in the Middle Ages, never entered into the dogmatic definitions of the Magisterium, even if that same Magisterium did at times mention the theory in its ordinary teaching up until the Second Vatican Council. It remains therefore a possible theological hypothesis. However, in the *Catechism of the Catholic Church* (1992), the theory of limbo is not mentioned. Rather, the Catechism teaches that infants who die without baptism are entrusted by the Church to the mercy of God, as is shown in the specific funeral rite for such children.

The above document can be read online at:

http://www.vatican.va/roman_curia/congregations/cfaith/cti_documents/rc_con_cfaith_doc_20070419_un-baptised-infants_en.html.

The eastern Catholic Church did not have the problem faced by the western church (and Elspeth Trentham) because the eastern church thought sin was not original but came about through acts of the adult. Presumably, babies that died before they were baptized in the east went to Heaven.

Chapter 81
If Thy Body Had Been As Deformed As Thy Mind

Dr. Stephen W. May [Studies in Philology, 1980] [R.E.S. 36, 104 (1975)] attributes *My Mind To Me A Kingdom Is* to Oxford but the poem has also appeared in collections attributed to Sir Edward Dyer. William Byrd published *Psalms, Sonnets, and Songs of Sadness and Piety* in 1588 which included *My Mind To Me A Kingdom Is*. The song can be heard at

http://www.youtube.com/watch?v=cXNI49_FJBU&feature=player_embedded

My mind to me a kingdom is;
Such perfect joy therein I find
That it excels all other bliss
That world affords or grows by kind.
Though much I want which most men have,
Yet still my mind forbids to crave.

No princely pomp, no wealthy store,
No force to win the victory,
No wily wit to salve a sore,
No shape to feed each gazing eye;
To none of these I yield as thrall.
For why my mind doth serve for all.

I see how plenty suffers oft,
How hasty climbers soon do fall;
I see that those that are aloft
Mishap doth threaten most of all;

They get with toil, they keep with fear.
Such cares my mind could never bear.

Content I live, this is my stay;
I seek no more than may suffice;
I press to bear no haughty sway;
Look what I lack my mind supplies;
Lo, thus I triumph like a king,
Content with that my mind doth bring.
I little have, and seek no more.
They are but poor, though much they have,
And I am rich with little store.
They poor, I rich; they beg, I give;
They lack, I leave, they pine, I live.

I laugh not at another's loss;
I grudge not at another's gain:
No worldly waves my mind can toss;
My state at one doth still remain.
I fear no foe, nor fawning friend;
I loathe not life, nor dread my end.

Some weigh their pleasure by their lust,
Their wisdom by their rage of will,
Their treasure is their only trust;
And cloaked craft their store of skill.
But all the pleasure that I find
Is to maintain a quiet mind.

My wealth is health and perfect ease;
My conscience clear my chief defense;
I neither seek by bribes to please,
Nor by deceit to breed offense.
Thus do I live; thus will I die.
Would all did so as well as I!

Oxford's affair with Anne Vavasor caused a number of incidents over the 1980s. He and Thomas Knyvet fought and wounded each other, Oxford more seriously than Knyvet, who was an officer of the court for many years and related to Anne.

Their men went at it a number of times, and some of them died. As to these 'brabbles and frays' (Burghley's phrase in a letter he wrote to Christopher Hatton about the Oxford-Knyvet street altercations), see Gwenneth Bowen, *Touching the Affray at the Blackfriars*, and *More Brabbles and Frays*, which can be viewed at:

http://www.sourcetext.com/sourcebook/ library/bowen/

Also, Ogburns, pp. 373-374, Ward, pp. 227-232, and Nelson, P. 280, *et seq.* Oxfordians believe the fights in the early 1580s between Oxford and Knyvet, and between their men, were "ces nouveaux Montagues et Capulets." Albert Feuillerat: *John Lyly*, 1910.[159]

Retainers of important noblemen were known to brawl and even kill each other. Carolly Erickson, in *The First Elizabeth*, p. 257, describes how Leicester and Sussex went at each other:

"Abandoned by the queen, the earl was easy prey, and his enemies crowded in. Sussex took to stalking him with a large armed body-guard, so that Leicester had to surround himself with an even larger one to protect himself. There might have been bloodshed had the queen not intervened to prevent it. During the holiday season of 1565, the factions declared themselves sartorially. The followers of Norfolk — and his allies, Sussex, Heneage and others — were all conspicuous in yellow laces, while Leicester's men wore blue ones. At a court where no detail of dress went unnoticed, the massing of matched laces was tantamount to a

---

[159] Of course, an argument can be made that the Montagues and Capulets in *Romeo and Juliet* were also formed out of the 'brabbles and broils' between the Second Earl of Southampton and his wife's family, the Montagues, after the Second Earl's marriage fell apart. The register of the Privy Council records that, on February 23, 1580, "Edmund Prety, servaunt to the Erle of Southampton was, for certain misdemeanours by him used against Mr. Anthony Brown, the eldest sonne of the Lord Montacute [Montague] … committed to the Marshalsea." Akrigg, p. 13. Was Oxford channeling the Montagues and Wriothesleys, when he wrote *Romeo and Juliet*, as well as his own difficulties with Anne Vavasor's relatives?

declaration of war." P. 257. (The yellow laces will be further addressed in regard to *Twelfth Night.*)

Thomas Vavasor wrote the following challenge on Jan 19, 1585 to Oxford:

> "If thy body had been a deformed as thy mind is dishonorable, my house had been yet unspotted, and thyself remained with thy cowardice unknown. … [I]f there be any spark of honour left in thee, … use not thy birth for an excuse, for I am a gentleman, but meet me thyself alone and thy lackey hold thy horse. For the weapons I leave them to thy choice … Thyself shall send me word by this bearer, by whom I expect an answer." Ward p. 229.

The outcome of this challenge is unknown. Thomas was probably related to Anne, possibly a younger brother who was not old enough to challenge Oxford and rectify the blot on his family's name brought on by Oxford's seduction of Anne in 1580. Oxford was wounded by Knyvet in March 1582, and it is Knyvet who stabs Oxford in this chapter, not Thomas Vavasor.

Rocco Bonnetti was a Venetian officer who appeared in England in 1569 and began teaching the foil method of fighting,[160] i.e., by using a light, pointed weapon that was sometimes bladed sides and designed to injure an opponent by thrusting instead of cutting with a blade. The English traditionally used weapons that injured by cutting. The Italians brought in techniques much like those used in modern contests

---

160 "Foil" is used here to distinguish the sword from the broad sword, and the method of fighting, thrusting from swinging a bladed weapon. A rapier was a bit of both. Shakespeare uses rapier and sword interchangeably. The word 'sword' appears 396 times in the plays; the word 'rapier' only 29. In *Romeo & Juliet*, two times. Tybalt calls for his 'rapier' in Act I; Romeo asks Mercutio to put his 'rapier' down in Act III. "Sword" appears once in the text and twice in stage directions. There do not seem to be any differences intended. Mercutio is killed by Tybalt thrusting him in the body.

using foils. See, *The London Masters of Defense;* http://iceweasel.org/lmod.html

The Italians sought out clients from the upper classes while those versed in the English way of fighting taught citizens from the middle and lower classes. Each laughed at the others. Thus, Mercutio's sarcastic description of Tybalt in Act II, Scene 4, of *Romeo and Juliet*:

> *More than prince of cats, I can tell you. O, he is the courageous captain of compliments. He fights as you sing prick-song, keeps time, distance, and proportion; rests me his minim rest, one, two, and the third in your bosom: the very butcher of a silk button, a duellist, a duellist; a gentleman of the very first house, of the first and second cause: ah, the immortal passado! the punto reverso! the hai!*

Knyvet has obviously been studying under an Italian master. Oxford, tucked under Falstaff's arm, listens to Knyvet railing at Falstaff and incorporates their banter into *Romeo and Juliet.* See Ward, p. 269, Ogburn, p. 686, for more on the fencing terms.

Chapter 82
Lopez and the Ghost of Thomas Brincknell

The use of honey and other ingredients to dress wounds dates from a Sumerian clay tablet, circa 2000 B.C. The Health Section of the Washington Post, Tuesday, August 7, 2011.

"Merrie-go-down" is from Ovid's *Metamorphosis*, Book VI, 556.

López will fall in 1594, caught between a scheming Essex and the surprising failure on the part of Burghley to protect the doctor from the paranoia caused by the Catholic threat to eliminate Elizabeth. Oxford will try to save him but without success. See Chapter 96.

The theaters were closed from February 2, 1593 to June, 1594. 10,775 people died of the plague between December 29, 1592 and December 20, 1593. *A Compact Documentary Life.*

Shakespeare's son-in-law, John Hall, attended Cambridge, receiving his BA in 1594 and his MA in 1597. He settled in Stratford-upon-Avon in 1600. He was never licensed to practice medicine, which was not unusual for the time, and he appears to have been a good physician. Schoenbaum, p. 297. Hall was a devout Puritan. He left casebooks behind him that were published after he was dead that showed he had treated many prominent people. Curiously, there is no mention of William Shakespeare in Hall's casebooks, despite the fact that they both lived in Stratford for sixteen years after John's arrival, much of the time in the same house. Perhaps William was never ill, although many scholars think he was in poor shape as he lay dying in the early months of 1616. If he was, there is no record his son-in-law treated him. The absence of a record, of course, does not mean that John did not treat William.

Chapter 83
Abandon'd & Despised

The title is taken from *Henry VI – Part Three,* Act 1, Scene 1, where Henry VI has told Richard he can have the throne after Henry's death, and Clifford, in disgust, says:

> *In dreadful war mayst thou be overcome,*
> *Or live in peace abandon'd and despised!*

Falstaff's rejection of Oxford is based on a letter Falstaff wrote that Poins reads in *Henry IV, Part 1*, Act II, Scene 2:

> Poins:
>
> *[Reads] 'John Falstaff, knight,'--every man must know that, as oft as he has occasion to name himself: even like those that are kin to the king; for they never prick their finger but they say, 'There's some of the king's blood spilt.' 'How comes that?' says he, that takes upon him not to*

conceive. The answer is as ready as a borrower's cap, 'I am the king's poor cousin, sir.'

Prince Henry:

Nay, they will be kin to us, or they will fetch it from Japhet. But to the letter.

Poins:

[Reads] 'Sir John Falstaff, knight, to the son of the king, nearest his father, Harry Prince of Wales, greeting.' Why, this is a certificate.

Prince Henry:

Peace!

Poins:

[Reads] 'I will imitate the honourable Romans in brevity:' he sure means brevity in breath, short-winded. 'I commend me to thee, I commend thee, and I leave thee. Be not too familiar with Poins; for he misuses thy favours so much, that he swears thou art to marry his sister Nell. Repent at idle times as thou mayest; and so, farewell. Thine, by yea and no, which is as much as to say, as thou usest him, Jack Falstaff with my familiars, John with my brothers and sisters, and Sir John with all Europe.'

My lord, I'll steep this letter in sack and make him eat it.

Chapter 84
The Death of Christopher Marlowe

The events leading up to Marlowe's death are neatly summarized by Nicholl at p. 266. Thomas Kyd was interrogated about papers found in his room, which Kyd said were Marlowe's. A letter hand-written by Kyd detailing "Marlowe's monstruous opinions" can be read at p. 98 in Brooke.

"*Cut is the branch that might have grown full straight, / and burnéd is Apollo's laurel-bough!*" is from *Faust.*

Oxford's impromptu poem written on the churchyard wall is adapted from a poem written near Donne's grave:

Reader! I am to let Thee know
Donne's Body only lies below;
For, could the Earth his Soul comprise,
Earth would be Richer than the Skies!

Globe, p. 744, comment to Act V, Scene1. Supposedly written by an admirer with a piece of coal on the wall over John Donne's grave the day after his burial.

Chapter 85
Matrimonium Clandestinum

Edward, Lord Windsor, Lady Katherine's husband, was a Catholic noble who lived most of his life on the continent. He died in Venice in January, 1574. He lies buried in a marvelous sarcophagus in the Basilica of San Giovanni & San Paolo. No one knows who paid for Lord Windsor's burial. Oxford arrived in Venice a year later. Did Oxford pay the expenses of his brother-in-law's tomb? Probably not.

The description of the courtroom is taken from the drawing of the room used by the Court of Wards, *Elizabethan London*, figure 10. Also at

https://en.wikipedia.org/wiki/Court_of_Wards_and_Liveries

As to the history of the efforts of Oxford's half-sister, Katherine, to strip Oxford of his titles and patrimony, see, *The Reader's Companion*, Chapter 9 and to Chapter 85, Nelson, p. 14, *et seq*., and Streitz, p. 90, *et seq.*

Earl John's relations with women were the cause of at least three separate court proceedings after his death. All claimed that he had not legally married Margery Golding, and that his title did not descend through Edward de Vere, his son.

The first attempt was made in 1563 when Katherine, Oxford's half-sister by his father's first marriage, and Katherine's husband, Edward, Lord Windsor, made demand of the Archbishop of Canterbury that "lord Earl of Oxford and Lady

Mary his sister be summoned to produce witnesses ... about certain articles touching and concerning the said Earl and his sister ..." Oxford was thirteen at the time.[161] Arthur Golding, Oxford's uncle and tutor (and translator of Ovid's *Metamorphoses* while Oxford and Arthur were both living at Burghley House) submitted a response that said the petition "to contain grave prejudice to the lady the Queen" because Oxford, and his sister, Mary, are both wards of the Queen. Golding recites that "no plea ... may be moved ... or proposed before any ecclesiastical or secular judge ... during [the Earl's] minority in the Court of Wards and Liveries ..." Nelson, p.p. 40-41.[162] Golding's response was found in Lord Burghley's papers. Nothing further is known about this proceeding. Professor Nelson quotes T. L. Golding as saying that searches at Lambeth Palace and Canterbury failed to turn up any additional documents. P. 449, fn 25.

Katherine did not file her claim in the Court of Wards because Lord Burghley was chief judge at the time and would not have allowed Katherine to divest him of a royal ward.

However, information about Katherine's 1563 petition was the subject of interest in the second attempt to invalidate Oxford's titles, which began in 1584 when Richard Masterson filed a complaint against Hugh Key concerning a parcel of land in Ashton. The Sixteenth Earl had leased the property to Hugh Key and Key's mother, Margaret Key, for their lives, or for eighty years. The Earl died owning the property and title descended to Edward, subject to the lease, of course. The reversion of the property was sold by the Earl of Leicester

---

161 Golding erroneously describes Oxford and Mary as being fourteen in his response. Mary was at most ten. Beauclerk seizes onto the age Golding gives for Oxford and claims that Oxford would have been fourteen at the time if, as Beauclerk asserts, Elizabeth was Oxford's mother. P. 59.

162 Oxford's comment to Lord Ellesmere that the proceedings "touch the legitimacy of my blood and the right to my hereditary possessions" is based on Golding's demurrer filed in the 1563 proceeding: "to touch the legitimacy of the blood and right of hereditary possessions." Nelson, p. 4.

during Oxford's minority, or by Oxford himself, after he came of age, to Sir Christopher Hatton. Hatton gave a lease to Masterson who entered the property while Key still occupied it.

Why Masterson thought he could oust Key is unclear from the documents. However, Key, in his defense in the action, claimed not only that he had a valid lease from the Sixteenth Earl, but that Masterson's title from Hatton was invalid because the Earl's marriage to Margery Golding was defective, which, if true, would divest Oxford's title and invalidate any transfer to Hatton.[163]

The question of the validity of Earl John's marriage to Margery Golding was handed over to a special commission headed by Sir John Popham, Attorney General, and Sir Thomas Egerton, Solicitor General. "This high-level involvement of the Queen's legal staff in what was a routine legal matter over a piece of property of John de Vere's indicates the Queen had a direct interest in the outcome of the events." Streitz, p. 91. Professor Nelson, like Streitz, has an in-depth analysis of the answers given in 1585 by the five witnesses who were found who had some knowledge of Earl John's marriage to Oxford's mother. Streitz, pp. 90, *et seq.*, and Nelson, p. 14, *et seq.* The interrogatories (twenty in all, with some having many subparts) and the answers given by the witnesses can be read at

http://socrates.berkeley.edu/~ahnelson/DOCS/depos16.html.

http://www.oxford-shakespeare.com/HuntingtonLibrary/EL_5870.pdf

---

163 There was bad blood between Oxford and Hatton. Is it possible that Hatton gave a lease to Masterson because he knew that Key could be encouraged to claim that Masterson's lease was invalid because the marriage of Oxford's parents was invalid? In other words, could Hatton have obtained the reversion to the Ashton property with the intention of creating a situation that would result in Oxford being "unearled"? It would have been sweet revenge for Oxford's treatment of Hatton. However, in *The Death of Shakespeare,* the Machiavellian will be Sir Robert Cecil, intent on carrying out his vendetta against Oxford.

The witnesses knew nothing of the real estate transactions between the Sixteenth Earl and Hugh Key and Key's mother, but they knew something about the relationships Oxford's father had with the women he married and/or entertained. An analysis of their answers, given over two days beginning January 19, 1585, is given at the end of *The Reader's Companion.*

There was evidence that Earl John had taken a woman named Joan Jockey into his house and lived with her as man and wife, this while his first wife, Dorothy (neeé Neville) was still alive. Also, there was evidence of a contract to marry Dorothy Fosser, the woman Earl John left standing at the altar to marry Margery Golding, Oxford's mother. Did this contract invalidate John's marriage to Margery Golding? An argument can be made that the marriage with Joan Jockey was bigamous and without effect because Dorothy Neville was alive when that marriage took place. The continuation of the Joan Jockey marriage after the death of Dorothy Neville, however, might have brought it 'out into the sun' and turned it into a legitimate marriage, had not the Earl's relatives and friends brutally attacked her (see below). But if the attack was carried out after Dorothy's death, Joan would have left Earl's Colne, scarred and battered, but still married to Earl John. His pre-contract with Dorothy Fosser did not constitute a marriage, and Dorothy Fosser later married John Anson, the second of five deponents, which served as some evidence that Earl John and Dorothy Fosser were never married. (But Anson would not want to present testimony that might invalidate his marriage.)

The dispute between Masterson and Key over who had the right to use the Ashton property would have been a "routine legal matter" had it not involved the Earl of Oxford and Sir Christopher Hatton. The timing of the transaction between the Earl and Hatton is crucial; if it occurred while Oxford was a minor, it was done by Robert Dudley, Earl of Leicester, the man Queen Elizabeth appointed to administer Oxford's estates during Oxford's minority. Lord Burghley had the wardship of Oxford's person and the money his estates earned, while Leicester was in control of Oxford's property during Oxford's minority. This control may have extended for some time after Oxford came of age in 1571, given Oxford's inability to understand money and the reluctance on the part of trustees to give up property they were managing (and, in most cases, probably milking).

But there was another reason for the Queen to involve herself in this "routine legal matter." A decision that Earl John had not legally married Margery Golding would have invalidated every real estate transaction Oxford or Leicester, as guardian of Oxford's property, had entered into since the Earl John's death in 1562. Appendix B in Ward, p. 853, lists 56 separate sales of land from 1572 to 1592. Properties sold during Oxford's minority are not listed but there are indications some occurred. A decision invalidating Earl John's marriage to Margery Golding would have wreaked havoc on English land ownership and diverted millions of pounds into the pockets of less-than-scrupulous attorneys who would represent people with claims that they were the lawful owners of the lands Oxford and Leicester had sold.

Finally, and most importantly, an adverse decision would have stripped Oxford of his titles, as well as any noble lineage Burghley had hoped his daughter and granddaughters would acquire when his daughter, Anne, married Oxford.

Oxford was 'undoubtedly' affected by this attempt to transform him into a common man. The recurring theme of bastardy in the plays (*King John* and *Lear*, to mention just two) may have come from his half-sister Katherine's attempts to dislodge him from his title. The Queen even called Oxford a bastard once. Although it was playful to her, it was probably not to him, and shows that the court knew his legitimacy had been challenged. This may also have contributed to his difficulty in accepting his daughter, Elizabeth, as his child.

There appears to be no record of what happened as a result of the 1585 inquest. Given the strong interest of the Queen, Lord Burghley, Sir Christopher Hatton, and the Seventeenth Earl of Oxford in having Masterson's claim upheld, it is more than probable that a generous settlement was offered to Key and he quietly abandoned Ashton to Masterson.

A third attempt was made in 1660 to invalidate Earl John's marriage to Margery Golding. This came about in a suit in which collateral heirs fighting over the Office of Lord Great Chamberlain. A fourth attempt occurred as late as 1902: "[The sad story about Earl John's relationships with women] persisted in later contests for the office [of Lord Great Chamberlain] and have been heard, possibly finally, as recently as 1902, when, in a sort of general struggle for the office, it seems to have been held that the office ceased to be hereditary in the Vere family after the death of the fifteenth Earl, ..." *An Elizabethan Puritan*, p. 46. Emphasis added. No citation for this statement is given. The author concludes: "[S]o there was no need to have so often dragged out this sixteenth century romance."

The suit in *The Death of Shakespeare* is based on the records of the attempts to divest Oxford of his titles when the depositions were taken in 1585. A summary follows:

<u>Deposition Testimony of Witnesses 1585</u>

The witnesses were Rooke Greene,[164] John Anson,[165] Richard Enowes,[166] Thomas Knollis,[167] and William Walforthe[168].

With regard to the first eight interrogatories, they all agreed that:

Earl John married Dorothy Neville, sister to Henry late Earl of Westmoreland.

---

164 Age 70. Recusant, in prison from 1578 to 1593.

165 Age 60. Married Dorothy Fosser, the jilted bride. He was clerk, parson of Weston Turville. She had been Dorothy Neville's maid.

166 Age 92. Participated in the disfigurement of Joan Jockey.

167 Age ? Earl John paid the Vicar of Clare £10 annually to marry him to Margery Golding.

168 Age 60. Keeper at Castle Hedingham when Earl John married Margery Golding. Served Earl John 20 years. Possibly 'Walforthe.'

They had one child – Katherine, now Lady Katherine.

Earl John and Dorothy Neville never divorced.

Earl John and Dorothy Neville separated before she died.

Dorothy Neville died in January 1558 near Salisbury.

9. Did Earl John marry Joan Jockey while Dorothy Neville was alive? (All 5 say yes.)

Rooke Greene said yes (by report) but did not know when.

Anson said yes, two years before Dorothy Neville died; he knew from Dorothy Fosser, whom he married.

Enowes said Earl John married Joan Jockey at Corpus Christi tide [time?] at White Colne Church in the lifetime of the said Lady Dorothy, the which the said Lady Dorothy took very grievously, and it was about half a year after the Lady Dorothy departed from the said Earl.

Knollis said yes.

Walforthe said yes.

10. Did Joan Jockey know that Dorothy Neville was still living when she married Earl John?

Rooke Greene had no knowledge.

Anson said yes.

Enowes said that Joan Jockey did know that the said Dorothy was living at the time of her marriage with the Earl, for she dwelled in Earl's Colne,[169] and after that marriage the Lady Dorothy wrote to Mr. Tyrrell, then the same Earl's comptroller, to know if it were true that the said Joan were married to the same Earl.

---

[169] Was Dorothy dwelling in Earl's Colne at the time, or does 'she' refer to Joan? Enowes says, in answer to interrogatory 13, that he and the men who disfigured Joan Jockey broke down the door of the house where Joan Jockey was living in Earl's Colne.

Knollis said yes because Dorothy's father lived in Earl's Colne.

Walforthe said yes because Dorothy's father lived in Earl's Colne.

11. Did Earl John marry a woman named Anne, and did she know that Dorothy Neville was still living when she married Earl John?

Rooke Greene forty years past [=1545] testified that he saw a woman near Tilbury Hall of whom it was then reported to this examinant that the said John, Earl of Oxford, kept her, but more or otherwise he cannot depose.

Anson said yes – one Phillips married one that the same Earl of Oxford had before kept, but whether the same Earl ever married the same woman or what her name was he knoweth not.

Enowes the woman that the same Earl kept at Tilbury Hall was never married to the same Earl of Oxford, but that woman's name this examinant remembereth not.

Knollis knew one other woman which the same Earl of Oxford kept at Tilbury Hall who was called Anne, sometime servant to one Mr. Cracherode, and that she was never married to the said Earl.

Walforthe knew the woman called Anne which the Earl kept at Tilbury Hall, which Anne had before served Master Cracherode, but the Earl was never married to that woman.

12. Did Earl John marry any other woman? All say no.

13. How long did Earl John live with Joan Jockey, Anne, or any other woman?

Rooke Greene had no knowledge.

Anson said Earl John got rid of all of the women after Dorothy Neville died.

Enowes same – he was with the Lord Darcy and Lord Sheffield came to Earl's Colne, and this examinant & two more with him brake open the door where the same Joan was and spoiled her, and this examinant's fellow, John Smith, cut her nose, and thereupon after she was put away.

Knollis – same as Enowes.

Walforthe – same as Enowes.

14. When did Earl John marry Margery Golding?

Rooke Greene saith the marriage between the said Margery and John, late Earl of Oxford, was, as this examinant hath heard, at Pauls Belchamp about the third year of King Edward the Sixth [=1549-50], and sure he is it was after the death of the said Dorothy, his first wife, & in the summertime, which Margery was the sister of Sir Thomas Golding, but what her father's name was this examinant knoweth not.

Anson - about St. James tide next after the death of the said Lady Dorothy, and the said Dorothy Fosser [his wife] told him that the Earl was married to Margery on a Tuesday in the morning at Belchamp Hall in the house late Sir Thomas Golding, and that the same Earl had appointed with the same Dorothy Fosser to have married with her the next day, being the Wednesday following, at Haverhill, and saith he hath heard that the vicar of Clare, being chaplain & almoner to the same Earl of Oxford, did marry the same Earl & Margery as aforesaid.[170]

Enowes said the Earl did marry the said Margery Golding after the death of the said Lady Dorothy at Pauls Belchamp, Mr. Golding's house in the summertime about St. James tide, and this examinant was one of them that with the rest of the Earl's men did fet the same Margery after the marriage to Hedingham Castle.

Knollis said that marriage was wrought by the vicar of Clare who had £10 yearly of the same Earl for his labour, and this marriage was at Mr. Golding's her brother's house

---

170 Nelson says Wednesday and Thursday. P. 18. The witness was testifying from memory.

Walforthe said this marriage was at Pauls Belchamp, and this he knoweth & remembereth for that this examinant killed a buck at Hedingham great park, where this examinant was then keeper, for the same marriage, and saith this marriage was brought to pass by the vicar of Clare.

15. Did Earl John marry Margery Golding during Dorothy Neville's life?

Rooke Greene had no knowledge.

Anson no as to Dorothy Neville but he cannot answer for others.

Enowes no.

Knollis no.

Walforthe no.

16. Did Earl John make a contract of marriage with Dorothy Fosser? (3 say yes; 2 no.)

Rooke Greene – no. He was supposed to marry Dorothy Fosser but where seeing the same Margery [Golding] he grew into such a present liking of her as he presently married her which greatly grieved Dorothy Fosser who complained and was awarded £10 a year.

She married John Anson within a year. Dorothy did never affirm that she was married or contracted to the same Earl[171] but that he had deceived her in not marrying with her as he had promised whereupon she had had her banns once asked in the church.[172]

Anson said that Dorothy Fosser was contracted unto the said Earl of Oxford at Sir Edward Greene's at Sampford Hall,

---

171 Would a contract have invalidated John Anson's marriage to Dorothy Fosser as well as Earl John's to Marjory? Or would Dorothy only have a breach of marriage action?

172 Did Dorothy have the banns asked *after* she was left at the altar to strengthen her claim that the Earl had contracted with her?

but saith that there followed no marriage upon that contract for that after the banns asked and a licence for the marriage obtained, the day before the marriage should have been accomplished the Earl married Margery Golding, and he heard this from Dorothy herself, whom he after married. Dorothy Fosser died at Felsted in Essex about the fourth year of the late Queen Mary [=1556-7]

Enowes Earl should have married the same Dorothy, before which time by the means of the vicar of Clare the Earl was drawn to Mr. Golding's where he married Margery Golding, and he never heard that he was pre-contracted with any other woman.[173]

Knollis heard there was a contract between the said Dorothy Fosser & the said Earl, but he married her not, for the day before the same Earl should have married with the same Dorothy he married with the said Margery, whereupon afterwards the same Dorothy Fosser in the life of the same Earl of Oxford married with John Anson, now parson of Weston Turville in the county of Buckingham

Walforthe heard it reported that the same Earl of Oxford was contracted to the said Dorothy Fosser and a time appointed for her marriage, but he saith that before the day in which that marriage should have been the said Earl married the said Margery Golding as is aforesaid by him, and that thereupon afterwards the said Dorothy married with John Anson, now parson of Weston Turville, in the life of the same Earl.

17. Did Dorothy Neville outlive Joan Jockey or Anne?

Rooke Greene had no knowledge.

Anson - no

Enowes - no

Knollis - no

---

173 Enowes doesn't say Earl John *did not* contract with Dorothy Fosser.

Walforthe – no, and he thinks she is still living.

18. What was the suit brought by Lady Katherine against the Seventeenth Earl?

Rooke Greene says Lord Windsor wrote him but didn't respond when Greene wrote

Lord Windsor he had no knowledge or a pre-contract or marriage.

Anson said he never knew of any such suit by Lord Windsor.

Enowes – cannot depose.

Knollis– cannot depose.

Walforthe– cannot depose.

19. Who were of counsel in the suit by Lady Katherine?

Rooke Greene – Lord Windsor said he was going to sue but he heard no more.

Anson said he remembers a consultation with Doctor Dale, Doctor Jones, Doctor Aubrey, Mr. Vaughan, & Proctor Biggs about the contract pretended to have been between the same Earl of Oxford and Dorothy Fosser, who gave advice to sue a commission to prove that contract, affirming if it were proved that then the marriage of the Earl with the said Margery was matrimonium clandestinum.[174]

Enowes – cannot depose.

Knollis– cannot depose.

---

174 'Clandestinum' is 'secret, clandestine' in Latin. 'Matrimonium clandestinum' does not seem to have been a legal term for a particular marriage in English law. The witness may have been flashing his knowledge of Latin, and he may have been referring to Earl John's failure to have the banns announced in church. Black's Law Dictionary defines it as (1) a marriage that rests merely on the agreement of the parties, and (2) a marriage entered into a secret way, as one solemnized by an unauthorized person, or without required formalities.

Walforthe– cannot depose.

20. Anything else? All 5 say nothing else.

<u>Summary</u>

1. While Dorothy Neville was living, Earl John married Joan Jockey.

2. He married her at Corpus Christi time at White Colne Church.

3. He married her about a half a year after Dorothy Neville moved out.

4. Joan Jockey knew Dorothy Neville was still alive because Dorothy's father lived in Earl's Colne (Knollis and Walforthe).

5. Earl John kept a woman named Anne near Tilbury Hall but he never married her, although Anson says that "one Phillips married one that the same Earl of Oxford had before kept, but whether the same Earl ever married the same woman or what her name was he knoweth not."

6. Earl John did not marry any women other than Dorothy Neville & Margery Golding.

7. Three witnesses say Earl John *contracted* with Dorothy Fosser to marry her.

8. Anson recalls a conference among advisors and gives the names.

9. The advisors recommended to "sue a commission to prove the contract."

10. The advisors said that, if the contract were proved, the marriage of the Earl with the said Margery was matrimonium clandestinum.

11. Anson reported that he accompanied Lord Darcy and Lord Sheffield, his fellow servant, John Smith, and another servant, to Earl's Colne, where they broke open the door where Joan was and spoiled her. John Smith cut her nose, after which she was 'put away.' Knollis and Walforthe confirm this.

12. Earl John married Margery Golding on a Tuesday in the morning at Belchamp Hall in the house late Sir Thomas Golding. He was to have married Dorothy Fosser the next day at Haverhill.

13. The marriage was officiated by the vicar of Clare.

14. Dorothy Neville wrote to "Mr. Tyrrell," the Earl's comptroller, to know if her husband had married Joan Jockey. This may have been the same man Margery Golding married shortly after Earl John's death.

15. Walforthe thinks Joan Jockey was still alive in 1585.

16. Nelson, p. 19. Earl John and Margery "had observed ceremony," but two impediments were implied: "first, as the Earl had married Joan Jockey, his marriage to Margery Golding was bigamous; second, as the Earl was pre-contracted to Dorothy Fosser, his marriage to Margery Golding, which in any case lacked banns, was clandestine."

Chapter 86
Yorick

Joan Jockey disappeared from history after she was disfigured. Her appearance in *The Death of Shakespeare* is fiction, as is Rowland Yorke's appearance as Yorick. She is a votary of the Order of St. Clare, the same order that Isabella will be about to enter when she becomes ensnared with Angelo in *Measure for Measure*. Unlike Francisca, however, Joan Jockey speaks with men. *Much Ado About Nothing,* Act 1, Scene 4.

While Joan Jockey's appearance in *The Death of Shakespeare* is fiction, the witnesses to her disfigurement were real. See the previous chapter. There was no trial, apparently. The trial in *The Death of Shakespeare*, therefore, is fiction.

Yorick's reference to his destiny—*There's a divinity that shapes our ends, / Rough-hew them how we will*—will appear in *Hamlet*, Act V, Scene 2, as part of Hamlet's explanation to Horatio as to how he found out that Rosencrantz and Guildenstern had been given secret orders to murder him.

Yorick is based on Hamlet's description of the jester in Act V, Scene 1:

> *Alas, poor Yorick! I knew him, Horatio: a fellow of infinite jest, of most excellent fancy: he hath borne me on his back a thousand times; and now, how abhorred in my imagination it is! my gorge rims at it. Here hung those lips that I have kissed I know not how oft. Where be your gibes now? your gambols? your songs? your flashes of merriment, that were wont to set the table on a roar? Not one now, to mock your own grinning? quite chap-fallen? Now get you to my lady's chamber, and tell her, let her paint an inch thick, to this favour she must come; make her laugh at that.*

In *The Death of Shakespeare*, Rowland Yorke is the man Oxford knew as "Yorick" when he was a boy. No one knows, of course, who Oxford was referring to when he wrote the famous lines about Yorick quote above. But there was a man named Rowland Yorke who played a significant role in Oxford's life. The Rowland Yorke who testifies in this chapter is the imaginary father of the younger Rowland Yorke, who is known to history for turning traitor and helping the Spanish take the sconce of Zutphen. He died in 1588. The Spanish may have poisoned him because they didn't trust him. Nelson, p. 105, et seq. and 345.[175]

Before he turned traitor, the real Rowland Yorke was known as a 'cutter' who worked for Oxford, and is credited with introducing the stabbing method of sword-fighting into England as opposed to the more traditional method of fighting with a

---

175 Nelson quotes a letter making reference to the Earl of Derby's death (poison by Burghley was one hypothesis in the letter so that Burghley could marry Lisbeth to the surviving brother) which seems to quote Yorke, but Rowland Yorke died in 1588, so the comment must have been made by another Yorke. (Or, Yorke didn't die and was still alive in 1594.) Nelson, p.345, for the letter, and p.106 for Yorke's death in 1588.

buckler and broad sword. Nelson, p 48. Yorke met Oxford on the continent while Oxford was on his way home and is thought to have been the man who told Oxford that Oxford's wife had cuckolded him while he was gone. Oxford refused to meet theose people waiting for him at various ports in England and went directly up the Thames to London where he secreted himself in Sir Edward Yorke's house, Rowland's brother. Some think Sir Edward was in the employ of Leicester and that Rowland was used to poison Oxford's mind. Yorke may be the source for Iago in *Othello*. Clark p. 146-147.

Thus, Yorick has to regretfully admit to Sir Anthony Bacon that he was, indeed, the father of the traitor who died in 1588.

Falstaff's reference to keeping his plans secret from Oxford so that Oxford cannot utter what he does not know will be put in the mouth of Hotspur in *Henry IV – Part 1*, Act II, Scene 3, when Hotspur resists the efforts of his wife to find out what he is up to:

> *constant you are,*
> *But yet a woman: and for secrecy,*
> *No lady closer; for I well believe*
> *Thou wilt not utter what thou dost not know;*
> *And so far will I trust thee, gentle Kate.*

Chapter 87
Graze On My Lips; Feed Where Thou Wilt

Titian lived in a magnificent villa that looked out on the island of Murano. Anderson, p. 95. His painting of *Venus and Adonis* seems to be the source for the poem of the same name. (See Beauclerk for a reproduction of the painting.) Oxford would have seen the painting in Venice. The King of Spain got the original, but Titian had copies made. The one he kept shows Adonis wearing a small bonnet on his head. The original does not have the bonnet. The poem mentions this detail:

> *He sees her coming, and begins to glow,*
> *Even as a dying coal revives with wind,*
> *And with his bonnet hides his angry brow;*

Looks on the dull earth with disturbed mind,
Taking no notice that she is so nigh,
For all askance he holds her in his eye.[176]

Interestingly, Titian's original was brought to England by Phillip, son at the time to Charles V. Philip had come to England to marry Queen Mary in July, 1554. Mary died four years later. Philip is credited with convincing English peers to allow Elizabeth to succeed Mary, despite the fact that Elizabeth was not Catholic. Philip then made a half-hearted effort to marry Elizabeth, but she declined his offer. In any event, Philip's father had already engaged him to marry a French princess. Philip returned to Spain where he became Philip II, apparently taking the *Venus and Adonis* with him. He ruled Spain during the 1588 Armada attack and died at the age of 71 in 1598. Since Oxford was only eight or nine when Philip returned to Spain, it is unlikely that he saw Philip's *Venus and Adonis* while the painting was in England.

The paintings Robin refers to are in the royal collection, although the second one is attributed to a 'follower' of Titian. See Law at plate 149 and 164.

Most scholars think *Venus and Adonis* was written by Shakespeare while the theaters were closed from February 1593 to June 1594. However, the fact that the public theaters were closed does not mean performances stopped at court, so this belief may be mere speculation. It would seem to be relatively easy to determine whether performances for the court continued during this time, if they did.

---

176 Adonis has a funny little cap on his head in Titian's copy of the painting but the word "bonnet" appears two other times in the poem, quite clearly referring to something more like a war helmet. Venus, in lamenting Adonis' death near the end of the poem, says "*bonnet nor veil henceforth no creature wear!*" and, in the next stanza, "*And therefore would he put his bonnet on, / Under whose brim the gaudy sun would peep,*" eroding, perhaps, Oxfordian delight in learning about Titian's painting showing Adonis wearing a 'cap' which the poem refers to as a "*bonnet [hiding] his angry brow.*"

The poem *Venus and Adonis* went through sixteen editions before 1640. "Readers thumbed it until it fell to pieces." Schoenbaum, p. 176. Kermode says there were nine editions during Shakespeare's lifetime. Kermode, p. 44.

The Queen was well aware that she was Venus. William Reynolds, who bought a copy of the very first edition, wrote the Privy Council in September, 1593, that "there is another book made of Venus and Adonis wherein the queen represents the person of Venus, which queen is in great love (forsooth) with Adonis, and greatly desires to kiss him, and she woos him most entirely, telling him although she be old, yet she is lusty, fresh and moist, full of love and life … and she can trip it as lightly as a fairy nymph upon the sands and her footsteps not seen, and much ado with red and white." Beauclerk, p. 178. Her reaction to the publication of the poem is unknown.

Oxfordians take quiet pleasure in the fact that Adonis is killed by a boar at the end of the poem.

Oxford may have been thinking of the subject when he told lords Howard and Arundel (if they are to be believed) about his liberties with the Queen. In July, 1587, a prisoner in Newgate Prison told an informer that "the Earle of Oxford he said the Quene did woo him but he would not fall in at that tyme." Nelson, p. 306. This piece of gossip predates *Venus* by six years.

The reason Oxford wrote the poem has been the subject of almost as much scholarly discussion as what it was all about. Stratfordians should be discussing where Shakespeare got the immense classical learning displayed in the poem *and* the ability to carry out his project in a difficult poetic form. No simple limerick this. Like Athena bursting forth from the head of Zeus, Shakespeare bursts onto the London literary scene fully formed, a master who never, as far as we know, wrote any earlier poem that might have taught him how to pull off *Venus and Adonis*. Listen to C. S. Lewis:

> The characters are in action by line 3. This is promising. We get, too, but not so soon nor so often as we might wish, lines of the deliciousness which was expected in

> this type of poem; 'leading him prisoner in a red-rose chain', 'a lily prisoned in a gaol of snow'. But in that direction Shakespeare does not rival Marlowe. We get, with surprised pleasure, glimpses of real work-day nature, in the spirited courtship of Adonis's [sic] horse or the famous stanza about the hare. The account of Venus's [sic] growing uneasiness during the hunt and her meeting with the wounded hounds gives us a fairly strong hint that the poet has powers quite beyond the range which the epyllion requires. At p. 498.

But here Lewis begins to wonder, "how the work ought to be taken." He casts about for an explanation in trying to understand how the characters act and concludes that Venus "is a very ill-conceived temptress. She is made so much larger than her victim that she can throw his horse's reins over one arm and tuck him under the other, and knows her own art so badly that she threatens … to 'smother' him with kisses. Certain horrible interviews with voluminous female relatives in one's early childhood recur to the mind." He is distinctly uncomfortable with words he thinks the author should have avoided: "'satiety', 'sweating', 'leaden appetite', 'gorge', stuff'd', glutton', 'gluttonlike'." He concludes: "And this flushed, panting, perspiring, suffocating, loquacious creature is supposed to be the goddess of love herself? … It will not do."

Lewis concludes that *Venus and Adonis,* failed "because he [the author] was embarrassed by his powers, essential for drama, which he could not suspend while writing an epyllion." Really?

Schoenbaum makes no reference to the content of the poem, thereby sliding by a difficult subject. So does Marchette Chute.[177] After all, what could sensible scholars make of language such as:

---

[177] Chute acknowledged that "young Elizabethans" (does this include women?) read *Venus and Adonis* "for the detailed description of an attempted seduction [without mentioning that it was the woman who was doing the seducing] and for the lush, rather over-wrought Renaissance imagery."

'Fondling,' she saith, 'since I have hemm'd thee here
Within the circuit of this ivory pale,
I'll be a park, and thou shalt be my deer;
Feed where thou wilt, on mountain or in dale:
Graze on my lips; and if those hills be dry,
Stray lower, where the pleasant fountains lie.

Within this limit is relief enough,
Sweet bottom-grass and high delightful plain,
Round rising hillocks, brakes obscure and rough,
To shelter thee from tempest and from rain
Then be my deer, since I am such a park;
No dog shall rouse thee, though a thousand bark.'

Readers who "thumbed it until it fell to pieces" knew the author was talking about sex. But it was sex driven by the female, which was novel in itself. And, if it was about the Queen, who was Adonis? And how did William Shakespeare (whose name appeared for the first time in print on the dedication) get his poem past Whitgift and the Bishop of London, who had to approve everything that was printed? And, finally, how did William get away with publishing this poem without losing a thumb, a hand, or some other part of his body?[178] Nothing was

---

Without identifying any of the images that were 'lush, [and] rather overwrought," Ms. Chute went on to point out that there was "a risk in this kind of writing, unless the reader himself is also young and very much in earnest, that the flood of words may give an occasionally comic effect that was not intended." At p. 115-116. Ah, but the words that were not 'occasionally comic?' Ms. Chute does not say.

178 "From 1586 onwards, every title proposed for publication had to be licensed by the Archbishop of Canterbury [John Whitgift—who died in the same year as Elizabeth] or the Bishop of London—a censorship distinct from that applying to plays, which had to be approved by the Master of the Revels in the office of the Lord Chamberlain and certified as 'allowed' before they were performed." Kermode, p. 45. [This is an interesting congruence with the Queen granting Oxford his £1,000 pension in the same year, which supports a claim that the money was to help Oxford write the history plays.] The Archbishop and the Bishop banned Marlowe's translation of Ovid's *Elegies,* which were burned in 1599. *This Star of England*, p. 847, fn. 3. Anyone who thought about publishing a book in these times would have known of the

done to him or the printer, Richard Field, yet, as the above letter from William Reynolds to the Privy Council shows, the Queen had to know people were thinking she was Venus.

All these questions go unanswered. A more important one may be why William (or whoever the author was) made only one more attempt at writing a classical poem—*The Rape of Lucrece*—before turning his energies to writing plays exclusively. Chute touches on this when she talks about the theaters being closed and Shakespeare having found a rich patron in the Earl of Southampton:

> There was nothing in this [Shakespeare's fame from having been identified as the author of *Venus and Adonis* and, in the following year, *The Rape of Lucrece*] to prevent Shakespeare continuing his profession as an actor, but it gave him no special incentive to go on writing plays. The average play did not bring its author more than six pounds, and the approval of Harrison [the printer of *The Rape of Lucrece*] and Southampton would have guaranteed him much more for a new narrative poem. A play would bring nothing but applause, with the revenue from any printings going to the acting company owning the play.

So why does Ms. Chute think Shakespeare went back to writing plays when he could have raked in the higher profits from writing high-end poetry? If he had continued to write poetry, she says, "his genius for characterization would have

---

man whose name was, unfortunately, John Stubbe. Stubbe wrote a book against the Queen's marriage to a Frenchman. His punishment was to have his hand cut off. 'I can remember,' wrote Stow the chronicler, who was present at Stubbe's punishment, 'standing by John Stubbe [and] so soon as his right hand was off, [he] put off his hat with his left, and cryed aloud "God save the queen." The people round about stood mute, whether stricken with fear at the first sight of this kind of punishment, or for commiseration of the man whom they reputed honest.' Stow, *Annales*, 1605, p. 1168. Page, who published the book, exclaimed, when his bleeding stump was being seared with hot iron, 'There lies the hand of a true Englishman.' Dictionary of National Biography, 1885-1900, Volume 55, Stubbs, John, by Sidney Lee, pp. 118-119.

been permanently blocked." Having the "instinct for avoiding a pitfall that [would have destroyed] him," Shakespeare returned to the "only audience that could give him … [the] liberty" to express his "genius for characterization," "the penny public of the London theater … who did not judge by Italian rules of the unities or French rules of diction or English rules of decorum but only by what they enjoyed." Pp. 119-120. Shakespeare turned his talents to writing nothing but plays for his acting company: "Such complete devotion to the theater was not merely unusual in an Elizabethan writer; it was unheard of, especially when a writer had, like Shakespeare, achieved so lofty a literary eminence in so short a time. Pp. 120-121. Calls for elegies for famous people who died thereafter, including the Queen in 1603, went unanswered. "He was the one writer of the period who wrote for the stage and for the stage only." P. 121.

True, but her explanation of *why* the author of *Venus and Adonis* turned back to the theater seems inadequate. Even recognizing that Edward de Vere was the author of *Venus and Adonis*, and even recognizing that the poem was intended by him to be a jab at Elizabeth, *vide* C. S. Lewis' comments set out above, why did Oxford write it, how did it get past Whitgift, why wasn't someone, even the printer, punished, and why was it dedicated to the Earl of Southampton? Chute does not argue that Shakespeare used his genius to provide plays to the Lord Chamberlain's men to generate funds for him to invest around Stratford, but she could have. However, if Shakespeare did not write the plays, the question becomes why the Earl of Oxford wrote them. He certainly didn't do it for the money and, being the unknown author, he certainly didn't do it for posthumous fame. The answer to this question is at the core of the authorship question, not whether Shakespeare was a front man for Oxford's.

The best Oxfordian explanation of *Venus and Adonis* is Roger Stritmatter's *"A Law Case In Verse: Venus and Adonis and the Authorship Question*, Tennessee Law Review, Vol. 27, 307.

Chapter 88
Richard Field and the Printing of *Venus and Adonis*

See, *The Reader's Companion*, Chapter 20. Richard Field, who was three years older than William Shakespeare, was also from Stratford-upon-Avon. That the two families knew each other is confirmed by the fact that John Shakespeare sued Henry Field, Richard's father, for 18 quarters of barley at one point, but they had apparently made up by the time Henry died in 1592 because John is listed as one of the appraisers of Henry's goods. Richard went up to London when he was fifteen and was apprenticed to a Huguenot printer named Thomas Vautrollier. Thomas was married to a French woman named Jacqueline (Professor Nelson says 'Jaklin' – p. 315) who, when Thomas died, married her dead husband's young apprentice. Charlotte Stopes thought Jacqueline might be the Dark Lady and mused that, "she was a Frenchwoman, therefore likely to have dark eyes, a sallow complexion, and that indefinable *charm* so much alluded to." Schoenbaum, who quotes this passage at page 175, thinks Mrs. Stope's "reasoning is not impeccable."

All of that is really known about Jacqueline Vautrollier is that she was savy enough to be partners with both her husbands. Marchette Chute guessed that "Shakespeare got about two pounds from Field for the manuscript [to *Venus and Adonis*] since, from the publishing point of view, he was an unknown writer." P. 112. She may be right. Her acceptance of the idea that Shackspear be paid a percentage of gross sales has no basis in fact and, as Ms. Chute suggests, payment for the manuscript may have been only a few free copies, as this was common practice with unknown authors.

Richard Field did not print *The Rape of Lucrece*, published the following year in 1594. John Harrison, who had handled the distribution of *Venus and Adonis* through his outlet—The White Greyhound in Paul's Churchyard—picked up *Lucrece* as well as the right to subsequent editions of *Venus*. This was a canny decision on the part of Harrison since, "[n]o other work by Shakespeare achieved so many printings …" Schoenbaum, p.

176. Field printed other fine works, including an elegant edition of Ovid's *Metamorphoses* shortly before he published the first edition of *Venus*. The association between William Shakespeare and Richard Field is something that Oxfordians will have to explain in order to get public consensus to shift from William Shakespeare to the Earl of Oxford as the author of the plays.

Venus and Adonis has been the subject of a number of special printings over the centuries attempting to do homage to the beauty of the poem. See, *Picturing Venus and Adonis – Shakespeare and the Artists*, by Georgianna Ziegler, *Venus and Adonis – Critical Essays*, Garland Publishing, Inc., New York and London, 1997, beginning at p. 389.

Robin's thought that Shackspear was Moron is based on Oxford's description of a character in *Menaphon* that was cut from Chapter 21 in *The Death of Shakespeare.*

Chapter 89
The Sign of the Ship

The Sign of the Ship is fiction, as is the Queen ordering Oxford to appear before her for having written *Venus and Adonis.*

Chapter 90
Conference with Venus

One of Charles Arundel's accusations against Oxford was that Oxford said "that the Ingelishe men were doltes and idiots for ther was better sporte in *passa pecora*—which they knewe not—then in all ther occupiynge." Nelson, p. 214.

Professor Nelson has the following to say about this phrase: "The *passa pecora* that surpasses all sexual habits practised by the English is an unorthodox position, recorded by Aretino and translatable as the 'grazing sheep.'" His footnote to this comment says that Aretino used the word "pascipecora." "Pecora" is "sheep" in Italian.

But Professor Nelson does not tell the reader that Aretino (Pietro Aretino) was a prominent Italian poet of the early 1500s who wrote the text to a series of explicitly pornographic drawings published under the title *I Modi*. The artist who created the drawings was none other than Julio Romano, the man alluded to in *The Winter's Tale*. A character identified as the Third Gentleman explains in Act V, Scene 2, how the statue of Hermione appeared life-like:

> *No: the princess hearing of her mother's statue, which is in the keeping of Paulina,--a piece many years in doing and now newly performed by that rare Italian master, Julio Romano, who, had he himself eternity and could put breath into his work, would beguile Nature of her custom, so perfectly he is her ape: he so near to Hermione hath done Hermione that they say one would speak to her and stand in hope of answer.*

The reference to Julio Romano caused amusement among early Shakespeare scholars because they only knew Romano as a painter and concluded that Shakespeare's tavern sources had inaccurately told the Bard that Romano was a sculptor. (The same scholars chuckled over characters sailing from one inland Italian city to another in *Two Gentlemen of Verona*, and to the reference to a Bohemian seacoast in *The Winter's Tale*. Their amusement was ill-founded in both cases.) Romano was indeed a sculptor. He sculpted the tomb of Baldassare Castiglione, the author of *Il Cortegiano*, the foremost book in Italy about how the medieval courtier should act. Oxford had it translated into Latin and wrote an excellent introduction to it in the same language.[179] In Chapter 2 of *The Death of Shakespeare*, the Queen waves *The Courtier* in front of Oxford and reads him selections from the introduction he wrote.

---

[179] Oxford's letters, quoted in Nelson and other biographies and scholarly works, do not do him justice. His introduction to *The Courtier* is as polished as anything written during the 400 years since his death. Gabriel Harvey said it was a 'courtly epistle more polished than the writings of Castiglione himself.' For once, Harvey was not exaggerating.

In light of this information, Professor Nelson's reference to Aretino appears to fall a little short. But the connection between Aretino and Oxford goes farther than simply the poems that accompanied *I Modi*. In *Venus and Adonis*, Venus implores Adonis to take advantage of her:

'Fondling,' she saith, 'since I have hemm'd thee here
Within the circuit of this ivory pale,
I'll be a park, and thou shalt be my deer;
Feed where thou wilt, on mountain or in dale:
Graze on my lips; and if those hills be dry,
Stray lower, where the pleasant fountains lie.

Within this limit is relief enough,
Sweet bottom-grass and high delightful plain,
Round rising hillocks, brakes obscure and rough,
To shelter thee from tempest and from rain
Then be my deer, since I am such a park;
No dog shall rouse thee, though a thousand bark.'

The image of 'grazing' is consistent with the analogy being worked here, that Adonis should act like a 'deer' and have his way with Venus, but he is given permission to move from 'grazing' on her lips to grazing 'lower, where … pleasant fountains lie.' As with many subtle allusions in the Shakespeare canon, the reference to 'grazing' is first made to Venus' lips before asking the reader to imagine what it would be like to 'stray lower, [in order to graze] where the pleasant fountains lie.' Was the author making a reference to *passa pecora*? Was he making a sly reference that some of his readers would know was to *I Modi*?

The first edition of *I Modi* contained only drawings and was destroyed by the church. No copy survives. The second edition was printed in 1527 and added Aretino's poems. No copy of the second edition survives, with the exception of a few fragments in the British Museum. However, a 1550 pirated copy (owned by Toscanini at one time, among others) was discovered in 1920. *I Modi* is known today from a set of engravings produced in 1798 in Paris known as the Carracci prints. They can be viewed at *https://en.wikipedia.org/wiki/I_Modi.* The prints have French titles. The use of the phrase *passa pecora* is only found in an Aretino poem that accompanies the drawings, none of which shows couples engaging in oral sex.

The loyal subject who wrote the Privy Council was William Reynolds, who wrote either Burghley (Anderson) or the Privy Council (Beauclerk) in September, 1593, that "there is another book made of Venus and Adonis wherein the queen represents the person of Venus, which queen is in great love (forsooth) with Adonis, and greatly desires to kiss him, and she woos him most entirely, telling him although she be old, yet she is lusty, fresh and moist, full of love and life ... and she can trip it as lightly as a fairy nymph upon the sands and her footsteps not seen, and much ado with red and white." Anderson, p. 269; Beauclerk, p. 178.

The Queen's reaction to the publication of *Venus and Adonis* is unknown.

Chapter 91
Sir Robert Cecil Gibed at Christmas

In the play, Buckingham suggests that Richard can surpass his elder brother Edward's two young sons by claiming that their father was previously betrothed before he married their mother, thus making them illegitimate. In real life, claims were made by Richard and others that Edward's two sons, who disappeared when Richard had them committed to the Tower for their protection, were illegitimate, thus justifying Richard's assuming the crown. This is similar to the claims by Oxford's sister that he was illegitimate for the same reason. Her first attempt to 'unearl' Oxford came when Oxford was a teenager, and thus Oxford's knowledge of her claims, as well as the historical record, have led some to think that Oxford thought it worthwhile to put the claims that Edward's sons were illegitimate into *Richard III*. See Ogburns, p. 978.

Cecil was misshapen (see *The Reader's Companion* to the Prologue and Chapter 5) and Oxford may have been thinking of him when he wrote *Richard III.*

C.S. Lewis described *Richard III* as "Tamburlaine rewritten from the perspective of the Jew of Malta." P. 185. Many think the play is a portrait of Robert Cecil. Anderson, p. 24; the Ogburns, p. 322;

The recent discovery of Richard's remains confirms much of Shakespeare's description of Richard's infirmities.

And all the clouds that lour'd upon our house / In the deep bosom of the ocean buried may be the first use of 'lour,' an obsolete word now.

1594

Chapters 92-97

Chapter 92
A Play for Lady Mary

The Countess of Southampton, born Mary Browne, daughter of Viscount Montague (do we hear Romeo and Juliet?), was apparently a formidable woman. She first married the Second Earl of Wriothesely, by whom she (reportedly) had a son named Henry, who became the Third Earl of Wriothesley (the dedicatee of *Venus and Adonis* and *The Rape of Lucrece*). Her relationship with the Second Earl was stormy. Her husband's relationship with the Queen was even stormier. He became embroiled in the Ridolfi Plot and was imprisoned in the tower for 18 months. His son, Henry, the Third Earl, was born a few months after his release from the Tower. The father was "tetchy, ill-tempered and proud, both weak and obstinate," while his wife, Lady Mary, was "no longer the demure young thing of her wedding portrait" but "on her way to becoming the self-willed, self-pitying, sensuous woman of her middle years." Akrigg, p. 13. The Ogburns characterize her as an "audacious lady, a type of high-handed dowager still extant today." P. 139.

The Second Earl died on October 4, 1581, widowing Lady Mary and sending her eight-year-old son to Burghley's House to become one of Lord Burghley's royal wards.

Lady Mary did not remarry until 1594, almost 13 years after her husband's death. Her new husband, Thomas Heneage, would die a few months later.[180] Lady Mary would marry Sir

---

180 Leaving his widow, Lady Mary, with an enormous problem. In 1596, the Queen's auditors submitted a statement that she still owed £7,800 of the more than £12,000 Sir Thomas had owed the Queen at his death. In reconstructing the accounts to show where money had been spent, Lady Mary created the first written mention of William Shakespeare by claiming that he

William Harvey in 1598 over the objection of her son, then languishing in the Tower for having secretly married Elizabeth Vernon, one of the Queen's ladies-in-waiting. There was a great deal of negotiation between and among Lady Mary, her son, the Third Earl of Southampton, and the Earl of Essex over Lady Mary's marriage to Heneage. "The serpentine Lord Henry Howard,[181] who enjoyed a reputation as a smooth negotiator, was brought in to reconcile mother and son." Akrigg, pp. 73-74.

The Countess of Southampton died in 1607. The inventory of her estate listed a 'double necklace of pearls' and a "jewell of gold set with dyamondes called a Jesus [a religious medal].' Akrigg, p. 151.

The description in *The Death of Shakespeare* of Lady Mary using a boy to attach a fish to her hook because she was irritated that Lady Lettice was catching more fish than she was is fiction. Mark Antony supposedly did the same thing when he became irritated at Cleopatra catching more fish from the Nile than he was. Cleopatra figured out what he was doing and had a boy attach a salt fish to Antony's hook, which made everyone laugh. A haberdine is an old name for salt cod.

"She bears a Duke's revenues on her back" is from *Henry VI, Part 2*, Act I, Scene 3, and describes Duke Humphrey's wife: "*She sweeps it through the court with troops of ladies / more like an empress than Duke Humphrey's wife.*" The connection between the character in *Henry VI, Part 2* who 'bears a Duke's revenues on her back' and Lettice Knollys is clear. The Queen banned Lettice from court for appearing in dresses more magnificent than Elizabeth's, who boxed her ears for it (as Queen Margaret boxes the ears of Duke Humphrey's wife for the same reason).

---

and other actors had been paid for a play performed before the Queen. However, records show that Shakespeare's company was performing somewhere else that date and the entry may be padding by Lady Mary to reduce her husband's debt to the Queen.

181 The same man who, along with the Earl of Arundel and Francis Southwell, libeled Oxford in 1581.

Elizabeth decreed that "as but one sun lighted the earth, so there should be but one [sun] at the Court, which henceforward would be closed to the Countess of Leicester." *Hidden Allusions*, p. 318, quoting Wilson, "Queen Elizabeth's Maids of Honour," p. 121.

The Cambridge History of English and American Literature in 18 Volumes (1907–21). Volume V. The Drama to 1642, Part One, states the following about *The Rape of Lucrece*:

> It has been usual to recognise a certain advance in *Lucrece;* which was thus entitled at its publication, though it had been licensed as *The Ravishment of Lucrece* and has, later, been generally called *The Rape of Lucrece*. The reasons for this estimate are clear enough. There is the natural presumption that, in the case of so great a genius, there will be an advance; and there is the character, and, to some extent, the treatment, of the subject. This latter still busies itself with things "inconvenient," but in the purely grave and tragic manner, the opportunities for voluptuous expatiation being very slightly taken, if not deliberately refused. The theme, as before, is a stock theme; but it is treated at greater length, and yet with much less merely added embroidery of description and narrative, which, at best, are accidentally connected with the subject.
>
> On the whole, however, while allowing to it an ample success of esteem, it is difficult to put it, as evidence of genius and as a source of delight, even on a level with *Venus and Adonis,* much more to set it above that poem. It is a better school exercise, but it is much more of a school exercise, much more like the poems which were being produced by dozens in the hotbed of late Elizabethan poetic culture. ... In short, the whole thing has rather the character of a verse theme, carefully and almost consummately worked out according to rule and specification by a very clever scholar, than that of the spontaneous essay of a genius as yet unformed.
> From *Venus and Adonis* alone, a cautious but well instructed critic might have expected either its actual

later sequel of immensely improved work or, perhaps, though less probably, nothing more worth having. From *Lucrece,* the legitimate critical expectation would be, at best, a poet something like Drayton, but, perhaps, a little better, a poet whose work would be marked by power sometimes reaching almost full adequacy and competence, but rarely transcending, a poet somewhat deficient in personal intensity himself and still more in the power of communicating it to his characters and compositions.

Lucrece does seem to be more "carefully and almost consummately worked out according to rule and specification by a very clever scholar, than that of the spontaneous essay of a genius." The genius obviously banked his fires when he wrote *Lucrece* and, thus, merits little attention in *The Death of Shakespeare.*

In *Love's Labour's Lost*, there is a masque called *The Nine Worthies.* James Greenstreet, who favors the Earl of Derby as the author of the plays attributed to William Shakespeare (the Earl married Oxford's oldest daughter, Elizabeth, in 1595), argues that the masque is derived from two sources: *The Nine Worthies* performed at Chester, and *The Nine Worthies* written by Richard Lloyd. In 1584, Richard Lloyd accompanied William Stanley to France. Two years later, Richard Lloyd published a play entitled *A brief discourse of the most renowned actes and right valiant conquests of these puisant Princes, called the Nine Worthies.* Lloyd's play contains material that is very similar to the masque in *Love's Labour's Lost.* For example, in Lloyd's *Nine Worthies*, there is the following description of Alexander the Great:

This puissant prince and conqueror bare in his shield a Lyon or,
Which sitting in a chaire bent a battel axe in his paw argent.
In the masque in Love's Labour's Lost, we find the following repartee from Costard to Sir Nathaniel interrupting the declarations of Alexander:

O, Sir, you have overthrown Alisander
the conqueror! You will be scrap'd out of the painted cloth for this. Your lion, that holds his poleaxe sitting on a close-stool,

will be given to Ajax. He will be the ninth Worthy. A conqueror and afeard to speak! Run away for shame, Alisander.

A poleaxe is a battle axe but, instead of a chair, Shake-speare substitutes a close-stool, that is a stool containing a chamber pot, the forerunner of the water closet or flush toilet.

Richard Lloyd was William Stanley's tutor, and his chaperone on the initial stages of his journey abroad, leaving England for France with William in 1582. In *Love's Labour's Lost*, the *Nine Worthies* is produced by Holofernes, a name taken from Rabelais' *Gargantua and Pantagruel*, where Holofernes is Gargantua's tutor. The young earl may have produced his play while in Navarre.

In 1594, William became the Sixth Earl of Derby upon the death of his brother, Ferdinando, and married Elizabeth Vere in January 1595. See Lineage – the Earls of Derby. If *Love's Labour's Lost* was written in the 1580s and updated in the 1590s, Oxford may well have included Holofernes and *The Nine Worthies* in the play to give his future son-in-law a laugh. Or William may have had a hand in it.

The Nine Worthies were performed at Chester near the Derby estate. The seasons of the year are mentioned at the end of both *The Nine Worthies* and *Love's Labour's Lost.* In *The Nine Worthies,* they are *Ver, OEstas, Autum,* and *Hiems.* In *Love's Labour's Lost,* they are only two: "Hiems, Winter; Ver, Spring." "Ver" is "Spring" in French, and very close to "Vere."

Some Stratfordians believe Holofernes is based on the Italian scholar John Florio. "I. Holofernes" is a near anagram of "Iohnes Floreo " Florio was a translator and grammarian of Italian, and Holofernes used Italian expressions. But so did Derby.

The author of The Cambridge History of English and American Literature in 18 Volumes (1907–21). Volume V. The Drama to 1642, Part One; VI. The Plays of the University Wits; § 6, in speaking of the songs in Lyly's plays, has this to say about *Love's Labour's Lost* (*http://www.bartleby.com/215/0606.html*):

"Whoever knows his Shakespeare and his Lyly well can hardly miss the many evidences that Shakespeare had read Lyly's plays almost as closely as Lyly had read Pliny's *Natural History.* It is not merely that certain words of the song of the birds' notes in *Campaspe* gave Shakespeare, subconsciously, probably, his hint for "Hark, hark, the lark"; or that, in the talk of Viola and the duke [footnote omitted] he was thinking of Phillida and Galathea; [footnote omitted] but that we could hardly imagine *Love's Labour's Lost* as existent in the period from 1590 to 1600, had not Lyly's work just preceded it. Setting aside the element of interesting story skilfully developed, which Shakespeare, after years of careful observation of his audiences, knew was his surest appeal, do we not find *Much Ado About Nothing* and *As You Like It,* in their essentials, only developments, through the intermediate experiments in *Love's Labour's Lost* and *Two Gentlemen of Verona,* from Lyly's comedies?"

The Third Earl of Southampton, Henry Wriothesley, came of age on October 6, 1594. Agrigg, p. 11.

See *The Reader's Companion*, Chapter 7 and 21.

Chapter 93
A Double Maske

Hidden Allusions reports that *A Maske of Amazones and A Maske of Knights* was presented at court on January 11, 1578-9, with the French Ambassador being present. It is described in the court records as "an entertainment in imitation of a tournament between six ladies and a like number of gentlemen who surrendered to them." At p. 136.

A Double Maske will become *Love's Labour's Lost* when it is reworked and published in 1598. It has connections to Henry of Navarre and events that took place in France in the 1570s.[182]

---

[182] Notice the title, which may be evidence of Oxford's love of puns and difficult words. It isn't *Love's Labours Lost*; it is *Love's Labour's Lost*, a much more difficult grammatical structure to follow.

France was ruled by Charles IX, son of Catherine de Medici. The heir apparent was the Duc d'Anjou, who would become Henri III upon his father's death. Anjou's younger brother was the Duc d'Alençon, who was engaged in lengthy marriage negotiations with Elizabeth I of England in the 1570s.

Charles was a weak king ruled by his mother, Catherine (who had brought haute cuisine, among other things, with her from Italy when she married Charles' father). She was the daughter of a Florentine merchant but cousin to Pope Clement VII. King Francis I of France accepted her as the wife for his second son, Henri, but the French court dismissed her as a low-born daughter of an Italian shopkeeper. However, her husband succeeded his father as Henri IV and Catherine became queen of France. She had no influence over her husband but became the power behind the throne when her nine-year old son became Charles IX, King of France, in 1560.[183]

France, in the 1560s and 1570s, was divided by religious wars between the Catholics and the Protestants, or Huguenots. In what everyone took as an attempt to end these wars, Catherine arranged for her daughter, Marguerite, Charles' sister, to marry Henry of Navarre, king of a small principality in the southwest of France. Henry was a Protestant. The offer to have Marguerite marry Henry was viewed as proof that the Catholic rulers of France wanted to end the division between Catholics and Huguenots. The wedding was performed August 18, 1572.

A few days after Marguerite's marriage to Henry of Navarre, the Massacre of Paris began in which Catholics killed every Huguenot they could find. It may have been planned by Catherine de Medici, or it may have been the outcome of Catholic fears of Huguenot plans. In any event, hope that

---

183 Charles IX's older brother, Francis II, married Mary Stuart, Queen of Scots. When Francis died shortly after he became king, Mary went back to Scotland where she ruled as Queen until she fled to England where she was imprisoned and eventually beheaded by her cousin, Elizabeth, to stop Catholic plots trying to put Mary on the English throne.

Catholics and Huguenots could live together came to an end. Henry of Navarre was only saved from being murdered by his wife's pleas to her brother, Charles IX, who offered life to Henry if he turned Catholic. Henry agreed and was spared. See Durant, p. 348, *et seq.*, for an overview of the massacre. Henry was held a virtual captive in Paris until he escaped in 1576, along with the king's brother, the Duc d'Alençon, and the Prince de Condé. Two years after that, in 1578, Marguerite, who had remained a captive in Paris, served as an intermediary between her brother and her husband to bring about peace. She was finally released to join her husband, Henry of Navarre.[184]

It is at this point that *Love's Labour's Lost* crosses path with Marguerite of Navarre. Marguerite and her mother, Catherine de Medici, accompanied by a group of maids-of-honor, *l'escadron volant* [the 'flying squadron'], set out from Paris to meet with Henry in Navarre in 1578. The negotiations over Marguerite's dowry were carried out with pageantry, gallantry, and continual entertainment. The connections with *Love's Labour's Lost* are clear. See *Hidden Allusions*, p. 130, *et seq.* Connections with Tom Nashe and other contemporaries are shown in Anderson, p. 259, *et seq.*, Ogburns, p. 200, *et seq.*, Sams, p. 72, Wilson, p. 161, *et seq.*, Akrigg, p. 211, *et seq.*

Oxford went through France on his way back from Italy in 1576. Although his route is unknown (see, *The Reader's Companion* to Chapter 23 in which there is a reference to a letter stating that Oxford intended to return home via Lyon, which is very close to the Castle of Tournon in the Rhone Valley), Oxford may have met Marguerite. The story of *All's Well That Ends Well*, is about Bertram, Count of Roussillon, which *Hidden Allusions* (quoting

---

184 The Earl of Oxford visited Paris in 1575 and probably met both Henry and Marguerite. Henry wrote a letter to him in 1595, twenty years later, when he was king of France, thanking Oxford for "the good offices [Oxford] has performed on [his] behalf in [Queen Elizabeth's] presence, which I beg you to continue …" *Hidden Allusions*, p. 132. See *The Reader's Companion* to Chapter 23.

George Lambin's *Voyages de Shakespeare en France et en Italie*) puts in Tournon, France, not far from Lyon. The death of Helene de Tournon in 1577 closely parallels Hamlet finding out upon his return to Elsinore that Ophelia has died. Helene was the daughter of one of the ladies-in-waiting to Marguerite of Navarre. Oxford may have met one or both on his way home. See, *Hidden Allusions*, p. 120, *et seq.*

Eva Turner Clark makes a persuasive argument in *Hidden Allusions*, beginning at p. 128, that the events in *Love's Labour's Lost* was the convergence of the trip Catherine de Medici and her daughter, Marguerite, made to Navarre in 1578, and the progress of Elizabeth through the northeastern counties of England in the same year. See pp. 157-161 for a table listing the characters in the play alongside real personages, including Don John of Austria as Don Adriano de Armado, and Jaquenetta as Mary Queen of Scots. She thinks Boyet was Biron, but that conflicts with Biron in the play being Marechal de Biron, who accompanied the King of Navarre. Others think Boyet is a representation of Sidney, who was not dead in 1578. Moth appears to be, as she suggests, De La Motte, but others see traces of Thomas Nashe. Anderson, pp. 259-261; Sams, p. 72. Clark thinks Holofernes was first intended to represent the Duc d'Alençon and then Gabriel Harvey. At p. 158.

Bloom has a perceptive analysis of the many wonders that make up this play.

Gilvary, beginning at p. 101, has, as usual, a great deal of useful information about *Love's Labour's Lost.*

Chute, beginning at P. 102, marvels at *Love's Labour's Lost*: [Here he] "gave final proof that he was capable of doing almost any kind of writing and doing it well." Although Ms. Chute thinks the author got the names of the characters from pamphlets put out by Richard Field and others, she recognized that it was "a Londoner's play, written for people who knew all the latest jokes with words." At p. 103. Yes, those in the court, which the supposed author would have had difficulty knowing.

Elizabeth was accompanied on her 1978 progress by the whole court, including Oxford, Burghley, the Earl of Leicester, Sir Christopher Hatton, and Sir Philip Sidney. At Audley End, Gabriel Harvey addressed each one of them in a separate speech in Latin. Plays followed at Cambridge. *The Progresses and Public Processions of Queen Elizabeth*, John Nichols, London and New York (1823), Vol II, p.111, *et seq.*

The original conceit of having nothing to do with women may be a reference to Elizabeth's order in 1561 that women were not to be allowed in the universities as well as her violation of that rule seventeen years in 1578 when she visited Cambridge. Anderson, p. 29; *Hidden Allusions*, p. 167, *et seq.* The Princess makes the following curious comment in Act V, Scene 2:

> *as much love in rhyme*
> *As would be cramm'd up in a sheet of paper,*
> *Writ o' both sides the leaf, margent and all,*
> *That he was fain to seal on Cupid's name.*

which can be understood as a link to Oxford when it is remembered that he wrote his charges against Howard down the page, up the side, and across the top. Nelson, p. 258. This unusual way of writing was probably a habit and remarked on by those who saw Oxford write this way, or saw books or documents he had annotated.

Finally, all the fluff that has been written about the School of Night, based on a few comments about a wizard earl (not Oxford), may be based on text in *Love's Labour's Lost.* Biron and Ferdinand are talking about Rosaline. Biron is head-over-heels in love with her.

> Ber. *Is ebony like her? O wood divine!*
> *A wife of such wood were felicity.*
>
> *O, who can give an oath? where is a book?*
> *That I may swear beauty doth beauty lack,*
> *If that she learn not of her eye to look:*
> *No face is fair that is not full so black.*

Fer. *O paradox! Black is the badge of hell,*
The hue of dungeons and the school of night;

But some scholars believe that the type setter made a mistake and should have printed "scowl" of night. Some texts print it this way; other scholars think it should read "suit" of night. From such slender threads entire novels are constructed. (Louis Bayard's *The School of Night,* in which Raleigh, Marlowe, and others meet their deaths as Shakespeare turns them in to the authorities because Marlowe jilted him.)

The word 'light,' and other words containing it, such as 'delight,' appear forty-one times in *Love's Labour's Lost.*

Another connection between Oxford and the play is that a woman named Mary Hastings was originally betrothed to Oxford when both were young, but the contract was later abrogated. She married another man *at the same wedding in which Oxford married Nan Cecil.* Mary was soon widowed and became infamous later on when he spurned an offer of marriage from Ivan the Terrible, leading the court gossips to nickname her the "Empress of Moscovia." She may be the inspiration for having the men masquerade as Russians in the play. *Hidden Allusions*, p. 137.

That Oxford helped Henry and the two French dukes escape from the Louvre is fiction. Oxford didn't leave Siena in Italy until March; Henry had escaped from the Louvre the previous month. Henry and the two dukes used a rope to escape (as did Sir John Oldcastle when he escaped from the Tower of London much earlier).

Oxford's use of the Countess of Mirandola is based on Arundel's claim that Oxford told him "that the cownetesse of Mirondola came fiftie miles to lie w*i*th him for loves." Libels 4.2/2.5, available at

http://socrates.berkeley.edu/~ahnelson/LIBELS/libelndx.html.

This claim was confirmed, of a sorts, by Henry Howard (made First Earl of Northampton by James VI), "that the Countesse of Mirandala came fifty myle to lie with him as [A] the quene of Amazones did to lye with Alexander." Howard, in the Arundel Libels 3.3. Footnote 30 to Libels 4.2/2.5, states that "Mirandola [lies] approximately 60 miles S.W. of Venice."

Chapter 94
A Nidicock for Lady Lisbeth

On April 16, 1594, the Fifth Earl of Derby, Ferdinando Stanley, died. His widow, Alice, wrote to Sir Robert Cecil the following month that she had heard that Ferdinando's younger brother, William, who was now the Sixth Earl of Derby, was planning on marrying Oxford's daughter, Lisbeth. Alice said she did not know whether the news was true or not but that "I [only] wish her a better husband." Ward, p. 317. She obviously didn't like her brother-in-law, but this may have been because a male heir would deprive her of the Derby inheritance.

Lady Alice's news about the proposed marriage was correct. She soon thereafter announced that she was pregnant.[185] This forced the couple to put off their marriage until Alice gave birth to her child. A male child would deprive William of the title.[186] Instead, Alice reportedly gave birth to a daughter in December and William and Lisbeth were married in January, 1595 (which some scholars think was the occasion for the writing of *A Midsummer Night's Dream.*)

---

185 Nelson opines that this may have been "merely fictional" – at p. 349 – but Ogburn states, without citation, that Alice had a girl. At p. 731. Father Garnet reported that she was pregnant – Nelson, p. 346 – but by September 13, William was acting like the pregnancy was over and he would remain the Sixth Earl of Derby (and not be 'unearled' – Father Garnet - by a male child) and able to marry Lisbeth. Nelson, p. 347. Since no male child surfaced, it may be that historians have assumed Alice had a girl when, as Nelson suggests, she may have made up her pregnancy to gain leverage to bargain with her brother-in-law over her husband's will, which had left everything to her.

186 The Jesuit priest Father Garnet wrote: "The marriage of the Lady Vere to the new Earl of Derby is deferred, by reason that he stand this in hazard to be unearled again, his brother's wife being with child, I know it is seen whether it be a boy or no." Nelson, p. 346.

Most people at the time concluded that the Fifth Earl, Ferdinando, had been poisoned.[187] There were various reasons put forward for this conclusion (the Catholics as retribution for having exposed an attempt to draft him into a plot to depose the Queen, relatives that he had abused, Leister, to whom the relatives had retreated, and even Lord Burghley, nominated by Rowland Yorke who thought Oxford's former father-in-law did it to marry Lisbeth to William to create an heir who might succeed Elizabeth.) Nelson, p 345.

Sir George Carey, who would become Second Baron Hunsdon when his father died in July 1596, and later Lord Chamberlain when Sir William Brooke, 10th Baron Cobham, died the following year, wrote to his wife in May, 1594, that Ferdinando had given the bulk of his estate to his sisters (one of whom was Carey's wife) to keep them from "the nidicock his brother." Nelson, p. 345. Sir George obviously approved of Ferdinando transferring property away from William, particularly where Carey's wife was to benefit, but the remark gives posterity a peek into what Sir George, at least, thought of William. (Professor Nelson thinks Carey was in effect calling William a "ninny.") Carey's assessment of William is supported somewhat by William's behavior a few years later when he issued a challenge to all and sundry to combat with him if they believed his wife, Lisbeth, had been unfaithful to him. (He may have had some basis for the challenge since it was widely believed that Lisbeth had an affair with the Earl of Essex as well as Sir Walter Raleigh in the 1590s.) No one accepted William's challenge.

History sometimes lies silent for long periods and then suddenly comes awake. The months of April through June of 1594 were particularly busy when it comes to events that relate to Shakespeare, Oxford, his daughter, Lisbeth, the death and succession of the earls of Derby, and the formation of the Lord Chamberlain's Men.

---

187 Wilson, pp. 171-175; Daugherty, Leo, *Brief Chronicles*, Vol. III (2011), p. 253; Riggs, pp. 341-342; *Marlowe*, p. 226; *Cambridge Companion to Christopher Marlowe*, p. 207;

April 16, 1594	Ferdinando Stanley, the Fifth Earl of Derby, dies. He leaves three daughters but no male heir. He was the eldest son of Lady Margaret Clifford, who was next in line to the throne by virtue of her descent from Mary Tudor. Ferdinando would have become heir to Elizabeth had he survived his mother *and* Queen Elizabeth. He predeceased both when he died on April 16, 1594. Any claim by his brother, William, who became the Sixth Earl of Derby, evaporated when Lady Margret, his mother, predeceased Queen Elizabeth, when she died in 1596. Had Elizabeth died before Lady Margret, and William had a son by Lady Elspeth, Lord Burghley's attempt to get a great-grandchild into the royal succession might have succeeded.
May 2, 1594	Lady Southampton, widow of the Second Earl of Southampton and mother of the Third Earl of Southampton, marries Sir Thomas Heneage.
May 9, 1594	*The Rape of Lucrece* is published.
May, 1594	Formation of the Lord Chamberlain's Men.
June 7, 1594	Lopez is executed.
June, 1594	The theaters reopen.

In *The Death of Shakespeare*, the marriage of the Countess of Southampton to Sir Thomas Heneage—May 2, 1594—will come after Lopez is executed and the Lord Chamberlain's Men are formed.

Peregrine Willoughy and Oxfod were brothers-in-law Peregrine having married Oxford's full sister, Mary. The two men were close. For example, it was reported that Willoughby and Oxford were found walking in Willoughby's garden at the time Oxford was thought to be involved in the Knyvet broils in the streets of London. Professor Nelson, pp. 281-828. And: "In September 1596 we find that lord Oxford staying with his son-in-law at Cannon Row." Ward, p. 319.

In December, 1577, over a year after Oxford had returned to England and rejected Nan as unfaithful, Peregrine Bertie's mother, Lady Suffolk, proposed the following stratagem to get Oxford to take Nan back in a letter to Burghley:

> [W]e will have some sport with him. I will see if I can get the child [Lisbeth] hither to me, when you [Mary Bertie, Lord Willoughby's wife] shall come hither; and whilst my Lord your brother is with you I will bring the child in as though it were some other child of my friend's, and we will see how nature works in him to like it, and tell him it is his own after.
>
> *Star of England*, p. 139; Anderson, p. 129 has a shorter version of this, Ward a longer version. P. 155-6.

There is no evidence that Lady Suffolk got the opportunity to place Lisbeth before Oxford and see if he would recognize his child. However, it is an interesting coincidence that Paulina in *The Winter's Tale* presents Leontes' daughter to him in a similar way. Leontes, in a rage, refuses to believe the baby is his and orders it to be abandoned:

> *Carry*
> *This female bastard hence and that thou bear it*
> *To some remote and desert place quite out*
> *Of our dominions, and that there thou leave it,*
> *Without more mercy, to its own protection*
> *And favour of the climate.*

Act II, Scene 3.

No one knows what the relationship was between Lisbeth and William, Sixth Earl of Derby, before they married. The first mention of marriage is made in the letter from the widow of William's older brother mentioned above, which was dated May 9, 1594, only three weeks after the brother's death. Ward, p. 317. Ward imagines that Lisbeth and William had fallen in love while Lisbeth was a maid of honor at court, but there are a number of factors that seem to go against that conclusion. First, William only returned to England from a three-year sojourn abroad after his older brother died. Second, Lisbeth rejected earlier suitors, including, among others, the Earl of Southampton and Lord Northumberland.[188] Third, there is no indication that the relationship with William began before his older brother died. Fourth, there were rumors that Lisbeth had affairs with both Essex and Raleigh after she married William. Daugherty, Leo, *Stanley, William, sixth earl of Derby*, Oxford Dictionary of National Biography (2004; online ed. Jan 2014). See also a review of Daughtery's book *The Assassination of Shakespeare's Patron: Investigating the Death of the Fifth Earl of Derby*, Cambria Press (2011) in *Brief Chronicles*, Vol. III (2011), p. 253, *et seq.* Finally, she was the daughter of the Earl of Oxford and obviously no blushing violet like her mother was. In fact, her husband William turned over to her the Isle of Mann to govern later in their marriage and she apparently did an excellent job. Consequently, in *The Death of Shakespeare*, Lisbeth goes after William because she expects him to become the Sixth Earl of Derby and, if his mother outlives Elizabeth, king of England. (Her belief, however, is in error.)

Ward says that the Stanleys were the richest family man in England. *Star of England*, p. 981, citing Ward, p. 319.

In 1599, George Fanner wrote that "[t]he Earl of Derby is busied only in penning comedies for the common stage." *Star of England*, p.439. Some think he is the true author. See his wikipedia page and visit *http://www.rahul.net/raithel/Derby/*. The Sixth Earl of Derby married Oxford's eldest daughter and Derby

---

[188] "Lord Burghley has tried to marry Elizabeth Vere to Lord Northumberland [but] she cannot fancy him." Mary Harding to the Countess of Rutland in 1592, quoted in *Star of England*, p. 980, citing Ward, p. 314.

and Oxford spent time together on numerous occasions. *Star of England*, p.539, 981, Anderson, p. 287.

Stow says that the Earl of Derby married Oxford's daughter "at Greenwich, which marriage feast was there most royally kept." Anderson, page 287. Anderson, however, in a footnote to p. 287, says that the actual ceremony took place four days later on January 30. See Anderson's sources, p. 533. And, he thinks the ceremony took place at Cecil House at Stamford, far north of London. However, if there is evidence that the ceremony took place four days later at Cecil House, it probably took place at Lord Burghley's house on the Strand. Stamford is too far away to have hosted the wedding after only four days to travel there.

Ward has references from letters showing Oxford with Derby or Derby visiting him at Hackney where Oxford and his wife went to live in September 1597 as well as interesting connections between Oxford and Derby after Oxford moved to Hackney. Ward, p. 321.

Chapter 95
The Lord Chamberlain's Men

The record is silent as to how Shakespeare became a shareholder in the Lord Chamberlain's Men. The history of the acting companies during Elizabeth's reign is far from clear. Players came and went as patrons died or ran out of money. To make matters worse, patrons changed names. For example, Ferdinando Stanley, Lord Strange, became the Fifth Earl of Derby when his father died. Ferdinando's company was sometimes known as Lord Strange's Men, but they became Derby's men when he became the Fifth Earl. The Lord Chamberlain's Men acquired their name from Henry Carey, Lord Hunsdon, who was Lord Chamberlain at the time of their formation in 1594. When Carey died in 1596, his son, George Carey, became Lord Hunsdon but the Queen did not make George Lord Chamberlain. The acting troupe he inherited was known as Lord Hunsdon's Men until George became Lord Chamberlain a year later when the company went back to being known as the Lord Chamberlain's Men. When King James took the throne, they became the King's Men, a name they kept until the theaters were closed.

Their chief competition was the Admiral's Men, whose patron was Charles Howard, Lord Effingham, Elizabeth's Admiral of the fleet. Howard had a company of players from the 1570s. Edward Alleyn joined them in the 1590s. They were based at the Rose while the Lord Chamberlain's Men performed at the Theater and the Curtain north of London. In December, 1597, the Burbages tore down the Theater and dragged the timbers across the Thames to build the Globe. *Historical Dictionary*, Howard, p. 158; Globe Theater, p. 123. *Star*, p. 982. Nicholl, p. 225. Riggs, pp. 254, 262-263. *A Documentary Life In Large Format*, p. 113; *A Compact Documentary Life*, pp. 126, 146. *Age*, p. 105.

This leaves out many other companies, such as the Queen's Men (Ward, p. 279), Pembroke's Men (*A Compact Documentary Life*, pp. 126), and others, including Oxford's Men who appear and disappear over the years. An overview can be read at p. 83 of the *The Oxford Companion to Shakespeare*. For a detailed discussion of the Elizabethan theater in three volumes, see Chambers. Volume II is devoted to the companies.

Chapter 96
The Execution of Dr. Lopez

Lopez will be executed on June 7, 1594. See Chapter 82 – Lopez and the Ghost of Thomas Brincknell. The circumstances surrounding Lopez's fall from Queen's physician to Spanish spy are lost in the mists of time. He may have been a spy for Spain but the Queen didn't seem to believe the charge and held back on the warrant for his execution. Also, it is reported that Lopez affirmed before he was executed that he was a loyal Christian. He may have been destroyed in the clash between the Burghley/Cecil faction and the Essex/Southampton faction at court. Leo Daugherty reports that Essex launched a smear campaign against Lopez in Essex's bitter correspondence with the Fifth Earl of Derby in the months before the Earl was poisoned. (Both Essex and Burghley, as well as the Catholics, are suspects in the poisoning of the Earl in April of 1594.) *The Assassination of Shakespeare's Patron: Investigating the Death of the Fifth Earl of Derby*, Cambria Press (2011), reviewed in *Brief Chronicles*, Vol. III (2011), p. 253, *et seq.* At first, Lopez may have languished in the tower like so many other prisoners but the order for his execution may have come because he knew something about spy networks of either Essex or Burghley, or both.

Michael Lok may have been related to Henry Lok who was a servant of Oxford's for many years. Michael Lok was one of the primary participants in the Frobisher voyages that took place in 1576 and 1577. Oxford invested £3,000, the amount Antonio invested in *The Merchant of Venice*, but Oxford had put up bonds, not cash, and the money was owed to Michael Lok who, apparently, was never repaid. Ward, p. 239.

There is no evidence either that Oxford or Michael Lok witnessed Lopez's execution. The £3,000 debt Oxford owed Lok, and the fact that the character in *The Merchant of Venice* is named Shylock, have spawned much speculation that Michael Lok was the source for the character's name. There are parts of *The Merchant* that show Shylock as a human being but others that do not reflect well on Jewish people. Oxford's intention to show a Jew on stage as a human being may have been blunted by changes to the text made by Shackspear. See *Part Two.*

Chapter 97
The Wedding of Sir Thomas Heneage and the Countess of Southampton

Although *The Reader's Companion* to Chapter 24—Lord Willoughby's—places Southampton House next to Willoughby House outside Cripplegate, the Southampton House in this chapter has been shoe-horned in between Arundel House and Somerset House along the Thames. The image of the arrival of the Queen at Lady Mary's wedding to Sir Thomas Heneage by royal barge outweighed a historically correct arrival by carriage at the location of the real Southampton House.

The Ogburns believe that the character Amorphus in Jonson's Cynthia's Revels is Oxford and that, if Amorphus "walks most commonly with a clove or pick-tooth in his mouth," Oxford must have used a toothpick. P. 422. They go on to cite *Every Man Out of His Humor*, *The Winter's Tale*, and *All's Well* for evidence that the use of a toothpick was considered a sign of elegance. (The Ogburns cannot resist putting in here Bertram's comment: "By my troth, I take my young lord to be a very melancholy man.... Why, he will look upon his boot and sing; *pick his teeth and sing. I know a man that had this trick of melancholy [who] sold a goodly manor for a song.*" (Italics in original.) P. 422. Oxford sold many of his manors. He sold one to John Lyly. Was it for a song?

That the toothpick is gold and the stand is in the shape of the horns of a bull Oxford purchased in Palermo is fiction.

Finley is fiction. His comments about *Love's Labour's Lost* are based on Bloom.

The formation of the Lord Chamberlain's Men may have been the result of market forces brought about by the closure of the theaters and the desire on the part of the better players to migrate to a new acting troupe. The idea that the Queen was so pleased with *A Double Maske* (believed by some to be an early version of *Love's Labour's Lost*) that she realized the closure of the theaters was draining her of players and playwrights is fiction. Therefore, her suggestion that the theaters be reopened and Lord Hunsdon, as Lord Chamberlain, form the Lord Chamberlain's men is also fiction.

Lisbeth's understanding of the succession law at the time is flawed. Lady Margaret Clifford would have been succeeded as heir presumptive by her eldest son, Ferdinando Stanley, Lord Strange, Fourth Earl of Derby, had he outlived her. Since he predeceased her, the crown would have gone to his eldest daughter, Alice, not to Ferdinando's younger brother, William. Alice survived Elizabeth, but she and her two younger sisters were pushed aside to put James on the throne.

Was Southampton Oxford's son by Elizabeth? The Ogburns and Charles Beauclerk, among others, think so. This is known as the Prince Tudor Theory. Oxford did have a fling with Elizabeth in 1573. Oxford ran to the Continent in June, after he and the Queen made two visits together to the Archbishop of Canterbury. The only information as to why he ran away is contained in a letter written by Gilbert Talbot in which he explains that Oxford had "a cause of suit" before the Queen, "which she did not answer so favourably as was expected, checking him, *it seems*, for his unthriftiness." Talnot goes on to say that Lord Burghley was troubled and said that he was sorry the Queen had made such haste, "and had answered him so, . . ." The answer the Queen gave him is not explained.

In any event, the Queen sent messengers after Oxford. Walsingham reported to Burghley that, while Oxford was still on the Continent, the Queen "conceivath great hope of his return *upon some secret message* sent to him." The content of the secret message has not been discovered. Whatever it was, Oxford soon returned and, to everyone's surprise, was immediately accepted back into the court, which was traveling toward Bristol, which is to the west. Nelson, pp. 110-113.

It is very interesting (and also unexplained) that the father of the Third Earl of Southampton fled to Spain at the same time that Oxford fled to the continent. Did they both run because Elizabeth gave birth to a son? They might not have known what the other one was doing. A case can be made (good enough for a novel) that the Second Earl ran because Elizabeth's son was being foisted on him and his wife. Oxford apparently believed at the time that the son did not survive.

Anti-Oxfordians likely conclude that he fled England because he was rebuked by the Queen, but it appears more likely that something had happened between Oxford and the Queen of a more serious nature. There is no question that the Queen and Oxford were involved in a close relationship. If the evidence does not support a conclusion that they engaged in a sexual relationship, as Conyers Read believes, the letter Oxford sent from Paris, that he looks forward to a "son of [his] own, and

Sonnet 33, seem to support that they did. This conclusion is buttressed by numerous references in the plays to the exchange of rings and the bedding of women. Furthermore, it was openly bruited about, even by Mary, Queen of Scots, in a letter to Queen Elizabeth, that Oxford claimed he had not slept with Anne after they were married "for fear of losing the favor which he hoped to receive by becoming [the Queen's] lover," and the opportunity to seek an annulment from Anne in order to marry Elizabeth. Anderson, p. 73. The full text of Mary's letter to Elizabeth is reprinted in Ogburn, p. 1249-51.

Sonnet 33 may be support that the Queen and Oxford were intimate and that the Queen gave birth to a son (modern spelling):

Full many a glorious morning have I seen,
Flatter the mountain tops with sovereign eye,
Kissing with golden face the meadows green;
Gilding pale streams with heavenly alchemy:

Anon permit the base clouds to ride,
With ugly rack on his celestial face,
And from the forlorn world his visage hide
Stealing unseen to west with this disgrace:

Even so my Sunne [son?] one early morn did shine,
With all triumphant splendor on my brow,
But out alack, he was but one hour mine,
The region cloud hath mask'd him from me now.

Yet him for this, my love no whit disdaineth,
Suns of the world may staine, when heavens sun staineth.

In the first quatrain, the author describes the sun gilding streams and spreading golden light as it rises. In the second quatrain, however, "base clouds" come in, "an ugly rack on his celestial face," as he steals west unseen. In the third quatrain, "my Sunne one early morn did shine" like the sun described in the first quatrain, but "he was but one hour mine." The cloud that masked the sun in the second quatrain now masks the "Sunne" in the third. The "Sunne" is the disgrace that steals unseen to the west. The concluding couplet expresses the thought that the author loves the "Sunne" nevertheless, and the further thought that "suns of the world" (including the "Sunne" of the sonnet) may stain "when heavens sun staineth."

The "sovereign eye" in the second line is undoubtedly the Queen, despite the use of masculine pronouns in lines 6 and 7.[189] This is confirmed by the last line, in which the author says "heavens sun staineth." The Queen would have been taken as the Heaven's sun.

The third quatrain is puzzling at first: "Even so my Sunne one early morn did shine / With all triumphant splendor on my brow."[190] In line 11, "he ["my Sunne"] was but one hour mine." It is possible, in a poetic sense, for the sun to be described by the author as "mine," and only shine "but one hour." But this is unlikely since the sun shines on the entire world. However, if "Sunne" means "son," the meaning becomes clearer. The author is saying he had a "son" that was "but one hour" his. His "Sunne" was then "masked" from the author by the "region cloud," which fled west with "this disgrace."

This interpretation is reinforced by a letter Oxford wrote to Burghley from Paris after hearing news that his wife, Anne, was pregnant with their first child. In this letter he tells his father-in-law, and grandfather to be, that, "for now it hath pleased God to give me *a sune* [sic] *of my own* (as I hope it is) …" Nelson, p. 123. This statement is extraordinary for three reasons. First, Oxford refers to "a sunne of my own." The Earl was a man of exact words, as his plays and poetry show. The implication is clearly that he already had a son, but, for some reason, it was not his to keep. Anne would give him a son, who would live only a short

---

189 The masculine pronouns in lines 6 and 7 were put in to not only to distance the author from a claim that he was referring to the Queen, but also to separate the "celestial face" in line 6, the sun in the sky and the Queen, from the "Sunne" that was but one hour the author's.

190 Notice that "Sunne" is capitalized even though it is not at the beginning of the line in which it appears.

while, but that pregnancy would be later. The son he would father by Anne Vavasor would also be born later, so this is not a reference to Edward Vere. Whoever Oxford is referring to in his letter to Burghley has not been identified.

Second, he spells the word son in his letter to Burghley as "sune." This further reinforces the conclusion that the word "Sunne" in Sonnet 33 is intended to be read as "son."

Third, he makes the parenthetical comment "(as I hope it is)" that indicates he has some doubt that the child his wife is carrying is his. This would be borne out on his return from England some 15 months later, and has nothing to with whether the "Sunne" in Sonnet 33 was an earlier child that was taken away from Oxford, but adds to the oddness of this letter, ostensibly written by a man to his father-in-law upon learning that he is to become a father. Burghley's reaction is not recorded.

If the "Sunne" referred to in Sonnett 33 was Oxford's, the "Sunne" was Elizabeth's disgrace. He would have been born sometime in 1574, after their affair, which had been going on for quite some time by then. In *Part Two* of *The Death of Shakespeare,* Oxford will grapple with Lady Mary's implication that he is the father of the Third Earl of Southampton.

Lineage Tables

The Earls of Oxford

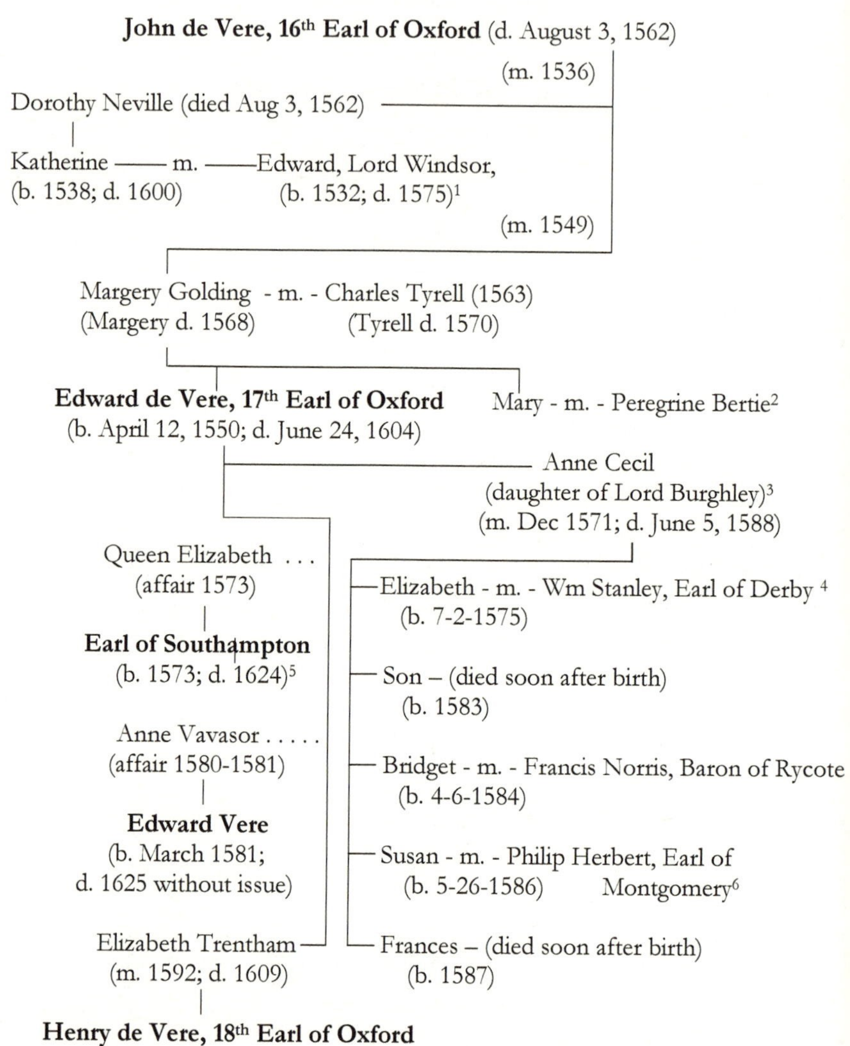

---

[1] Edward, Lord Windsor, died, January 24, 1574 in Venice. Oxford's half-sister, Katherine, wife of Edward, Lord Windsor, sued Oxford in 1563 to have their father's marriage to Oxford's mother declared void, which would have 'unearled' Oxford.

[2] *See,* Peregrine Bertie

[3] *See,* The Family of William Cecil, Lord Burghley

[4] *See,* The Earls of Derby

[5] *See,* The Earls of Southampton

[6] *See,* The Earls of Pembroke

[7] Only the earls of Oxford used "de" before their last name. All others used "Vere."

William Cecil, Baron Burghley

Mary Cheke - m.- **William Cecil, Baron Burghley** - m.- Mildred Cooke[8]

Sir Thomas Cecil

Edward de Vere — m. — Anne Cecil

Sir Robert Cecil — m. — Elizabeth Brooke

Elizabeth	Son	**Bridget**	**Susan**	Frances
(7-2-1575)	(1583)	(4-6-1584)	(5-26-1586)	(1587)
m.		m.	m.	
Wm Stanley, Earl of Derby [9]		**Francis Norris Baron of Rycote**	**Philip Herbert Earl of Montgomery**[10]	

[8] Mildred Cooke's sister Anne was the mother of Francis Bacon, later Sir Francis Bacon. Thus, Sir Francis was nephew to Lord Burghley and cousin to Robert Cecil. Sir Francis played a significant role in the trial of Essex and Southampton in 1601. Bacon's interrogation of the two men brought out answers that forced Cecil to come out from where he was hiding to confront Essex as to who had heard him (Cecil) claim that only the Infanta of Spain had the right to succeed Elizabeth on the throne of England.

[9] *See,* The Earls of Derby

[10] *See,* The Earls of Pembroke

The Earls of Southampton

Thomas Wriothesley - m.—— Jane Cheney
(created 1st Earl in 1547; died 1550)

Henry Wriothesley – 2nd Earl - m. - Mary Brown[11]
(born 1545;[12] died 1581[13]) (daughter of Viscount Montague)

Henry Wriothesley – 3rd Earl— m. — Elizabeth Vernon (1598)[14]
(born Oct 6, 1573)[15]

---

11 Mary Browne was thirteen when she married the 2nd Earl of Southampton. They separated in 1580 because of her alleged adulterous relationship with another man. In an attempt at reconciliation, the Countess sent her young son, the future 3rd Earl of Southampton, to her husband with a letter but the 2nd Earl rejected her offer to reconcile and kept their son away from her. The 2nd Earl died in 1581 but Mary was unable to get back her son because he went to Lord Burghley as a royal ward. In 1594, Mary Brown married Sir Thomas Heneage, who was Treasurer of the Royal Chamber. He died 15 months later in October, 1595, owing an accounting of what he had spent as Treasurer on entertainments for the Queen. The Queen demanded an accounting and the Countess submitted records that mention Wm Shakespeare as being one of the players paid by Heneage in 1594, which is the earliest known reference to William Shakespeare as a member of the Lord Chamberlain's Men. However, the play they supposedly performed before the Queen on the date specified was a play performed by the Admiral's Men; the Lord Chamberlain's Men were performing elsewhere. Since the accounting was made some time after the actual performance, there is a suspicion that the Countess, trying to avoid a massive judgment against her for money her dead husband had spent, was being creative in adding Shakespeare. Ogburn: pp. 65-66, citing Stopes. In January, 1599, almost immediately after her son's marriage to Elizabeth Vernon, she married again, to Sir Wm Harvey, with whom she had been living. Because the 2nd Earl was no longer living, Southampton had to approve the match as the senior male member of the Wriothesley family and apparently balked at her mother's choice.

12 5 years of age at his father's death; the Master of Royal Wards sold his wardship to Sir Wm Herbert, who sold it back to Henry's mother, Jane.

13 The 3rd Earl of Southampton was 2 days short of 8 years old at his father's death. He became a ward of Lord Burghley and lived at Burghley House. Oxford, also a ward of Burghley, had left Burghley House ten years earlier when he came of age in 1571. Thus, the Earl of Oxford and Southampton never lived at Burghley House at the same time.

14 Lord Burghley (*See* William Cecil, Lord Burghley), as Southampton's guardian, tried to get Southampton to marry his granddaughter, Elizabeth de Vere (Burghley Family; Oxford Family) in 1590, but Southampton refused and reportedly paid a £5,000 fine to Burghley.

15 There is no documentation for this date except for a letter from his supposed father announcing the news of the birth of a son. There is no record of a baptism. The 2nd Earl was in the Tower in 1571 for his involvement in the Ridolfi Plot; released May 1, 1573 to Sir Wm Moore; July 1573 to his father-in-law, Viscount Montague. Henry was born less than 9 months after his father's release from the Tower. The Queen may have allowed conjugal visits, but the evidence tends to indicate he was only allowed to see his wife in July.

The Earls of Derby

Henry Stanley, 4th Earl of Derby[16] - m. - Lady Margaret Clifford
(died 1593)

Ferdinando Stanley, Lord Strange, 5th Earl of Derby[17]
(1559 – 1594) - m. - Alice Spenser[18]

William Stanley, 6th Earl of Derby - m. - Elizabeth Vere[19]
(1561 – 1642)

James Stanley, 7th Earl of Derby
(1607-1651)

---

16 Established Lord Strange's Men, which continued in existence under his two sons, and which performed many of Shakespeare's plays.

17 Ferdinando Stanley's mother, Lady Margaret Clifford, was next in line to the throne by virtue of her descent from Mary Tudor. Ferdinando would have become heir to Elizabeth had he survived his mother *and* Queen Elizabeth. However, he predeceased both when he died on April 16, 1594. The succession would have gone to his daughters, who survived Lady Margaret, and not his brother, William, as Oxford's eldest daughter, Elizabeth, is portrayed as believing in *The Death of Shakespeare*. Ferdinando was believed to have been poisoned by a massive dose of arsenic. He had turned in a step-brother who had tried to enlist him in a plot by the Catholics in exile to put him on the throne as a Catholic king. His act of loyalty, however, made him suspect to both Protestants and Catholics. The relatives ran to the Earl of Essex who took them into his service, which made Ferdinando fearful for his life. Ferdinando raided the main relative's house on April 2. He was dead two weeks later. He may have been poisoned by Burghley (to get him out of the way – Rowland York thought so – see Nelson p. 345), by the Catholic plotters to bring forward his brother, William, who may have been considered a better candidate, or by the relatives of the man he turned in. Burghley moved rapidly to marry Elizabeth Vere to Ferdinando's brother, William, but the wedding had to be delayed. See following footnote. Some of Lord Strange's Men formed the Lord Chamberlain's Men under Lord Hunsdon, which may have been intended to bring the players under control of the Queen. Edward Alleyn joined the Admiral's Men.

18 When Henry Stanley died in 1593, his son Ferdinando Stanley succeeded him as 5th Earl of Derby. When Ferdinando died less than a year later, his younger brother, William, should have immediately succeeded Ferdinando as the 6th Earl of Derby. However, Alice Spenser, Ferdinando's widow, claimed she was pregnant. William was engaged to marry Elizabeth Vere. William and Elizabeth had to wait to find out whether Alice gave birth to a son, who would have become the 6th Earl of Derby and 'unearled' William. However, in December 1594, Alice gave birth to a daughter and William became the 6th Earl of Derby. He and Elizabeth Vere married in January, 1594. Some scholars believe *Midsummer Night's Dream* was written for their wedding.

19 The eldest daughter of Edward de Vere, the 17th Earl of Oxford. Only the earls used the 'de' after their first names. Thus, Edward Vere, Oxford's illegitimate son, and the fighting Veres, Sir Francis and Sir Horatio, but Henry de Vere, who succeeded his father as the 18th Earl of Oxford.

Peregrine Bertie

(Lord Willoughby de Eresby – 1555-1601)

Richard Bertie (horse master) – m. 1553 - Katherine Willoughby[20] (died 1580)
(Duchess of Suffolk &
Baroness Willoughby de Eresby)
(Widow of the Duke of Suffolk)

Susan Bertie[21] — m. 1570 — Reginald Grey of Wrest,
(b. 1554) later restored as the fifth Earl of Kent (died 1573)

— m. 1581 — Sir John Wingfield

Peregrine Bertie - m.- **Mary (Vere) Oxford** (died 1624)
Lord Willoughby de Eresby (m. 1577/8)
(b. 1555; d. June 25, 1601))

Robert Bertie

[20] In 1577, Lady Katherine wrote to Lord Burghley that she would place Oxford's daughter Elizabeth (2 years old at the time) in front of Oxford the next time he came to see her to see if Oxford took to the child in the hope that this would reunite him with the mother, Anne, Burghley's daughter. Nelson: p. 76. Compare *The Winter's Tale*, Act II, Scenes 2 and 3, in which Leontes' baby daughter, which he thinks is not his, is placed in front of him in the belief that he will recognize her as his own. The attempt fails in the play. Whether Lady Katherine put Oxford's daughter in front of him is unknown. If so, it didn't work because Oxford continued to stay away from his wife for quite some time. Lady Katherine is well-known for many things, including talking Henry VIII into letting women read the Bible.

[21] Susan Bertie became Countess of Suffolk upon her mother's death in 1580. Aemilia Bassano was born January 27, 1569 in Bishopsgate, London, into a family of Italian (possibly Jewish) court musicians. At age seven (1576), she went to live with the Willoughby family at Grimsthorpe Castle in Lincolnshire under the tutelage of Susan Bertie. Aemilia arrived four years before Susan's mother, Lady Katherine, died, and may have known something about the letter Lady Katherine wrote in 1577 that is referenced in footnote 1. Upon her mother's death in 1587, Aemilia became Lord Hunsdon's mistress, by whom she had a son, Henry, in 1592. Hunsdon was 45 years older than she was. *See,* the Lords Hunsdons. Bassano was then married to her cousin, Alfonso Lanier, who died in 1613. A daughter named Odillya lived only ten months. In 1611, Bassano published *Salve Deus Rex Judaeorum*, the first book of poetry published by an English woman. Bassano memorialized Susan in her book as the "daughter of the Duchess of Suffolk." Her son by Hunsdon lived to 1633.

The Earls of Pembroke

William Herbert, 1ST Earl of Pembroke[22]— m. — Anne Parr
(died 1562)

Henry Herbert, 2nd Earl of Pembroke — m. — Mary Sidney[23]
(died January 19, 1601)

William Herbert, 3rd Earl of Pembroke[24] — m. — Mary Talbot[25]
(1580 - 1630)

Philip Herbert[26], Earl of Montgomery[27] — m. — Susan Vere[28]
(1584 - 1649) (became the 4th Earl of Pembroke upon his brother's death in 1630)

---

22 Established Pembroke's Men, , which continued in existence under his two sons, and which performed many of Shakespeare's plays.

23 *See,* The Sidney Family. Mary Sidney, Countess of Pembroke, was Robert Dudley's niece and Sir Philip Sidney's sister. Mary Sidney was Henry's third wife. His first marriage to Catherine Gray was probably annulled when Queen Mary came to the throne. His second wife was Catherine Talbot, who died in 1576. When Henry died in May, 1601, she did not remarry, but remained at Wilton House and became a noted literary figure in Elizabethan and Jacobean England.

24 William founded Pembroke College, Oxford, and continued his patronage of Pembroke's Men. He became Lord Chamberlain in 1615. He refused to give up the position until he could secure his brother, Philip, as his successor in 1626. William, therefore, was Lord Chamberlain in 1623 when the First Folio was printed. A relative, Henry Herbert, became Master of the Revels in June of that year. Ben Jonson, one of William's patrons, was supposed to get the office but did not. See, *The Incomparable Pair and "The Works of William Shakespeare"* by Gwynneth Bowen at http://www.sourcetext.com/sourcebook/library/bowen/12pair.htm. William and Philip are described in the dedication to the First Folio as "the incomparable pair of brethren." (Notice that the two brothers were the sons of Sir Philip Sidney's sister, Mary.)

25 The dwarfish and deformed daughter of the Earl of Shrewsbury, by whom William had no children. He had an affair with Mary Fitton in 1600 when she was twenty years of age and impregnated her. When he refused to marry her, he was sent to the Fleet Prison. When Mary gave birth to a boy who died, he was released. He wrote a poem about the affair. See Ancilla to Chapter 24 - Lord Willoughby's. He had two children by Lady Mary Wroth, daughter of his uncle, Robert Sidney, after the death of Lady Mary's husband, Richard Wroth.

26 Philip had a quarrel with Henry Wriothesley, 3rd Earl of Southampton, in 1610 over tennis. Compare the Earl of Oxford's famous quarrel with Sir Philip Sidney, also over tennis, in 1579.

27 The Earl of Pembroke began paying Jonson a stipend of 100 marks per annum in 1616, increased temporarily to £200 a year in 1621. *This Star of England*, p. 1208. Philip became the 4th Earl of Pembroke upon his older brother's death in 1630.

28 *See,* Oxford Family. Susan was the Earl of Oxford's third daughter. There is a drawing by Inigo Jones of Susan Vere dancing in one of Jonson's masques. *This Star of England*, p. 1208.

The Lords Hunsdon

Sir William Carey[29] - m. - Mary Boleyn[30]

Henry Carey, 1st Lord Hunsdon[31] - m. - Anne Morgan (1545)

Mary Hyde - m. - **George Carey, 2nd Lord Hunsdon**[32]

. . . . **Aemelia Bassano**[33] - m. - Henry Lanier[34]

Henry (b. 1593)

[29] Gentleman of the Privy Chamber to Henry VIII. Died suddenly from the sweating sickness June 23, 1528. Henry Carey, his son, was two and became a ward of his aunt, Anne Boleyn. When Anne was beheaded in 1536, Henry was ten. His mother, Mary, died in 1543, and he was returned to his family.

[30] Sister to Anne Boleyn, who was mistress to Henry VIII before Anne. Many believed that Henry Carey's father was Henry VIII, not Sir William.

[31] Born 1526; died July 23, 1596. Appointed Lord Chamberlain in July 1585. Patron of the Lord Hunsdon's Men, and, from 1594, patron of the Lord Chamberlain's Men.

[32] Born 1547; died September 9, 1603. Became 2nd Lord Hunsdon when his father, Henry, died in 1596. However, George Carey did not become Lord Chamberlain on the death of his father. The Queen instead appointed William Brooke, 10th Lord Cobham, to be Lord Chamberlain. Cobham lived in the Blackfriars district and, despite being the patron of the Lord Chamberlain's Men, opposed the attempt in 1597 by James Burbage to have a theater built there for adult companies. This caused Burbage financial difficulty because the lease had run out on the Theatre. Burbage had bought the playing space in the Blackfriars for the Lord Chamberlain's Men to perform plays. Cobham also apparently objected to the name Sir John Oldcastle, one of his ancestors, for the character that became Falstaff. When Cobham died in March, 1597, the Queen appointed George Carey Lord Chamberlain, which post he held until his death in 1603. Cobham's daughter, Elizabeth Brooke, married Sir Robert Cecil on August 31, 1589.

[33] Mistress to Henry Carey; raised in the Willoughby family from age 7. *See*, Peregrine Bertie, footnote 2.

[34] Born in 1593. Assumed to be the son of Lord Hunsdon., by whom she became pregnant in 1592. Aemilia married Alfonso Lanier on October 18, 1592. Lanier died in 1613; Aemilia lived to 1645. In 1611, she published the first book of poetry by an English woman, *Salve Deus Rex Judaeorum.*

The Sidney Family

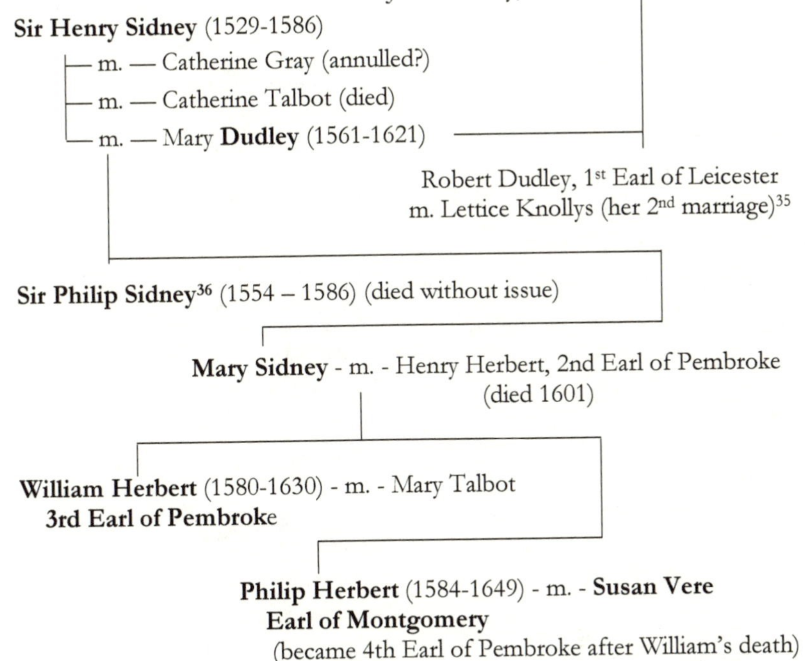

35 Lettice Knollys was a grand-niece of Ann Boleyn. At age 17, she married Walter Devereux, 1st Earl of Essex, by whom she had Penelope Rich and Walter Devereux, 2nd Earl of Essex, as well as other children. Her first husband died in 1576. She then married Robert Dudley, 1st Earl of Leicester, in 1578. Elizabeth was outraged when she found out about the marriage and banished Lettice Knollys from court for life. It was rumored that she had been carrying on an affair with Leicester while her first husband was still alive. Some even claimed Leicester poisoned her first husband, who died of dysentery in Ireland. She had no children by Leicester. After Dudley died in 1588, she married Sir Christopher Blount, a much younger man, a year later. He was beheaded in 1601, along with her son by her first marriage, the 2nd Earl of Essex, for their participation in the Essex revolt. She lived to 1634, dying at the age of 91.

36 Philip Sidney was knighted in 1583 when he was designated by Prince John Casimir of Poland to represent him by proxy at a ceremony inducting Casimir into the Order of the Garter. Since a representative could not be of a rank lower than a knight, Queen Elizabeth knighted Sidney so he could fulfill the honor. (This parallels William Cecil being made Baron Burghley so that his daughter's marriage to the Earl of Oxford would not be morganatic.) Sidney was wounded at the Battle of Zutphen and died October 17, 1586. His body was brought back to London in a ship with black sails. Pamphlets, poems, and sermons turned him into a national hero. He was not interred until February 16, 1588, eight days after the execution of Mary, Queen of Scots. It is unknown whether this delay was caused by lack of funds to bury him or a conscious decision on the part of Burghley, Walsingham, and the Queen to use Sidney's burial to distract a populace that might have reacted unfavorably to Mary's execution. Thousands of nobles and commoners followed Sidney's hearse to his grave and nothing was heard about Mary's death. *Hidden Allusions*, fn 19a, pp. 247-248.

~ Glossary ~

acrostic: a poem in which the first letter of each line spells a name.

alewife: woman who keeps an alehouse; an oily fish.

an: if.

angel: a gold coin worth 10 shillings; called so after the Archangel Michael on one side.

apparitor: process server.

arras: a tapestry, wall hanging, or curtain.

arsenic: poison, referred to as 'inheritance powder.'

Bedlam: Bethlehem Hospital, where the insane were dumped.

bed trick: where a man sleeps with his wife but thinks she's someone else.

bergamot: pear-shaped orange the rind of which yields an oil used in the making of perfumes.

besmutched: to besmirch.

bewray: betray; disclose.

bill of exchange: a written document evidencing an obligation to repay a loan.

calliver: a smooth-bore forerunner of the rifle.

cheat: whole meal bread, coarser than manchet bread.

chirurgeon: surgeon; doctor.

Court of Wards (and Liveries): established by Henry VIII to regulate feudal dues, wards, and questions of livery.

eyas: a sparrow hawk.

eyrar: a brood of swans.

felo de se: to commit a felony on oneself, such as suicide.

foul papers: the original drafts of a manuscript of playscript.

froward: forward; brazen.

furniture: baggage.

Gad's Hill: an area on the road from London to Canterbury.

glister: to glisten, to glitter.

gremolata: chopped herb condiment classically made of lemon zest, garlic and parsley.

haberdine: salt cod.

haggard: a mature hawk caught in the wild and trained to hunt.

I Modi: erotic drawings by Giulio Romano.

Ipocras wine: a spiced wine. When strained through a woolen cloth, the cloth resembled Hippocrates' sleeve.

invention: creation, but also a fictitious statement or story; a fabrication.

groat; an English silver coin worth four pence

kickshaw: appetizer, hors d'oeuvres, from quelquechose.

limbo: between Heaven and Hell; where babies went who died before they were baptized.

livery: clothing worn by servants that identified them as servants of a particular nobleman.

manchet: fine white bread.

marriage *in futuro*: a promise to marry in the future, which is not a marriage, although suit can be brought on the contract.

marriage *per verba de praesenti*: a marriage validated by words, even if performed in secret, if followed by consummation.

matrimonium clandestinum: a marriage that rests merely on the agreement of the parties, or a marriage entered into a secret way, as one solemnized by an unauthorized person, or without required formalities.

medlar: apple-like fruit that tasted best as it began to rot.

mon choux: my cabbage; my dear.

moniment: archaic spelling of monument; but also a record without a monument. 'Thou art a moniment without a tomb.'

morganatic; a marriage in which, because one of the parties is not of sufficient birth, the children cannot inherit the parent's title.

motley: jester, a fool; multi-colored cloth.

ne: neither; nor.

Neapolitan Malady: syphilis.

nidicock: a ninny; a fool.

Orpharian: a flat-backed stringed instrument, member of the cittern family.

petits cadeaux: little gifts.

pomander: a mixture of aromatic substances contained in a pierced metal sphere.

quincunx: an arrangement with four points and a fifth point in the middle

Roscius: a Roman slave who became a famous actor.

samphire: samphire, rock samphire, or sea fennel grew on rocky cliffs near the sea and was used as a condiment when pickled and in salads when fresh.

Seneca: a first century Roman philosopher ('readiness is all') and tragedian.

sprezzatura: a certain nonchalance, so as to conceal all art and make whatever one does or says appear to be without effort and almost without any thought about it.

Tycho Brahe: Danish astronomer who argued that the sun and moon orbited the earth.

virginal: keyboard instrument.

ward: a minor under the jurisdiction of a court; a minor whose father, a vassal-in-chief to the king, has died.

weed: clothes.

whiffler: a servant who precedes a noble to make way and announce his presence.

whittawer: a person who converts animal skins into white leather.

wittol: a man who knows he has been cuckolded by his wife and tolerates it.

Readers interested in further information about

The Death of Shakespeare–Part One

&

The Reader's Companion to The Death of Shaksepeare

can visit

www.doshakespeare.com

The Death of Shakespeare–Part Two

will be forthcoming.